DESCENT INTO DARKNESS

Book 2--The Chronicles of Deneb

Zanne Raby

www.ridgecrestbooks.com

DESCENT INTO DARKNESS

eISBN-13: 978-1-7775565-2-5
ISBN-13: 978-1-7775565-3-2

Cover design by: S.M. Raby

Library of Congress Control Number: 2021914973

DEDICATION

I would like to dedicate *Descent into Darkness* to my good friends Michel, Debbie, and Gary whose encouragement guided me on this trek across the dimensions of space and time. Long may we soar together.

Per ardua ad astra

TABLE OF CONTENTS

Zanne Raby

DENEB-7

Zanne Raby

CEPHEUS-9

ADITI

PROLOGUE

Year 2085 CE – Wesselan, Deneb7, Denebian Solar System - Cygnus Constellation

Colonel Pallav Kóbor, newly promoted Inspector of the Wessel Defence Force, coughed. The stench of the smouldering remains of the Great Plains Wesselan Army Base lingered in his nostrils, its taste still acrid rising like bile in his throat. Blinking, he tried to banish the horror from his mind's eye – the tendrils of thick black smoke snaking from twisted funeral pyres upon which vehicles and equipment had burned with such fierce intensity that they were rendered unrecognizable. And on top of it all – the tell-tale aroma of roasting humanoid flesh, so reminiscent of the grilled steaks that he used to throw on the barbecue for his wife Tara and their two teens in the time he thought of as "the Before".

That was when days lasted twenty-four hours, and he could sit out on the back deck with a cold beer listening to old country tunes while the sun sank behind the moss-covered oaks. Five years ago and how his life had changed. In the Before, he was NASA's Chief of Security in the United States of North America. That was until his wife decided to partner up with Dr. Daniel Radu and kidnap him and his colleagues from the Space Ark Project and before they were unwillingly transported thousands of light years from Earth to arrive three years later on alien shores. Except there were very few shores on the desert planet of Deneb7 and most of them were located in his new homeland, the powerful and war-like nation of Wesselan.

Power, recognition, prestige: they were all his here in this new world. Yet for everything there is a cost, and Pallav struggled to banish the memories of the terror that he had unwittingly released, to fight the ghosts of yesterday and to be the man they thought he was. And so he coughed again seeking relief, while Tara handed him a handkerchief and their little Wesselan foster child Jolanta stared up at him with her great luminous opalescent eyes.

"You gonna be okay?" his wife asked, narrowing her eyes knowingly.

Pallav shrugged. He could never trick her. Tara: the beautiful dark haired, doe-eyed love of his life. The Nobel-prize winning astrophysicist who married her high school sweetheart and carried him along on her astronomical rise to fame. All the way to NASA where her research discovered those very special Earth-like planets nestled in the Goldilocks zone of their stars: rocky orbs where water flowed all wrapped up under a nice cozy atmospheric blanket so that humans could set up shop in comfort.

And humanity needed that. It wasn't long after Tara's discovery that Earth shuddered in Her death throes. Entire countries had fallen to the relentless assault of the oceans, the scaled denizens of Neptune's realm now sole inheritors of the once-prosperous cities where human feet had trod what had been terra firma. As the waves lapped against the vacant buildings, slowly caressing them with their watery embrace, millions upon millions of people streamed into the heartland of the continents where they sought refuge against the unyielding onslaught of the oceans.

A reprieve. A temporary victory. For Earth had not finished punishing Her children for the transgressions humanity had unleashed upon Her. The years marched forward, a mere blink of an eye for the rocky planet third from the sun, while deep within the continents new cities erupted from the heat-scorched land like a pox on Her skin. In Her feverish state, the fiery breath of the wounded Earth rushed over the globe, searing and desiccating crops in the field before they could sprout to life. So once again, humanity set off in search of land in which life could be sustained.

Across the Atlantic, a continent of promise beckoned to the displaced masses: the mighty United States of North America. For time immemorial, its vast northern reaches had remained pristine and unsullied by human development. The blistering heat that had seared other nations into ashes and cinders created a blossoming of bounty for the Great White North. Unfettered from its carpet of snow and ice, development in the north boomed and the country of Canada eagerly welcomed its southern neighbours in the millions. Enjoying prosperity and peace, the two great nations of North America merged to become the world powerhouse of the mid 21st century, and there was no way that they were going to surrender their privileged lifestyle. What had been a land of opportunity morphed into Fortress America: firmly shuttered, locked and hostile. Migrants go home.

The world's overpopulated? Let nature take Her course – isn't that what Malthus wrote?

Fear turned to desperation; desperation turned to rage. It didn't take long before terrorist groups grabbed the reins to take control, and suddenly a life or death battle erupted against a deadly bioengineered Chimera bactovirus that blazed across the globe. All the while, the leaders of the world plotted to abandon humanity in the very Space Arks that the three most powerful alliances were building to shuttle tens of thousands of citizens to a newly constructed colony on Mars.

That was when shit hit the fan, when Pallav's brainy little angel of a wife had teamed up with that asshole, Dr. Daniel Radu - the project manager for the United States of North America's Space Ark programme - to basically abduct the entire team of the USNA Space Ark *Mayflower* and pirate the massive intergalactic craft to safety on a journey of over two thousand light years. Oh, and to warm Radu's bed all the while Pallav lay wide awake in their cabin, feigning sleep until she finally slipped back under the covers reeking of that bastard, sending him into a spiral of hatred and revenge.

Somehow, he'd managed to keep his fury under wraps during the interstellar journey until the mammoth Space Ark *Mayflower* was pulled from the skies to its final resting place on the parched desert floor of Deneb7. There it collapsed, a battle-scarred Godzilla fighting in the arena for survival in a torrent of dust and stone in the Cauldron: the most wretched corner of that blistering hot planet, where not even Tagarian snakes or sleek Denebian lizards chose to dwell. His wife's choice for an innocuous place to make a landing unseen didn't quite turn out the way they expected. Not at all. Instead the *Mayflower* found itself helpless when out of the blue, a gossamer-fine gravity web engulfed the Ark, its crew compelled to watching impotently as the full force of the Denebian war machine lined up in welcome.

And what a welcome wagon they were – the combination of the armed might of the three great Denebian nations! Pallav watched half in horror and half in appreciation as Wesselan's vicious Stryker Skykillers plummeted down from the clouds, shrieking like blood thirsty demons, while Fyjerlan's armed drones, accompanied by Geitenia's mechanized infantry, swarmed like army ants over the lip of the Cauldron to form a defensive perimeter about the beached leviathan.

Yet he had not been alone in his appreciation. The Denebian Commanders were wide-eyed in awe at the alien craft's refusal to surrender. It had been a futile fight they knew, for gravity knows no master, but the determination of the *Mayflower*'s crew had earned them the Denebians' respect and obtained a choice position on Wesselan's Armed Force for both Pallav and Major Fynn Vogel, the *Mayflower*'s senior helmsman. That and a friendship with Gomalan, the Wesselan Armed Forces' High Commander, who took Pallav under his wing and unknowingly provided the very canvas upon which Pallav could paint his revenge.

For knowledge is power, and that is exactly what Gomalan had handed to the angry human giant who had once been NASA's Chief of Security: the Styrian Treaty with its arcane clauses and decrees. And buried deep within the ancient document was the very dagger that could be cruelly wielded to finally sever his wife from the clutches of that vile adulterer, Radu. For the ancient Denebians had crafted the Treaty with the threat of alien colonization in mind, limiting space migrants to the Denebian nation in which they first landed. That is, unless they possessed special skills that were hotly in demand, like those of Pallav and Fynn.

But adultery wasn't on the Wessel's special skills list, as Pallav so indelicately put it to the Wesselan High Commander, a hint of a vindictive sneer snaking across on his broad-boned face. That would leave Radu and his two brats on the wrong side of the border – in Geitenia, backwards Geitenia where lives are lived in darkness, and superstition is perceived as a valued tradition. It was all very legal and above board – the best kind of revenge – and so while Pallav and Fynn and their families had settled in luxury in Wesselan, the rest of the crew were forced to remain in Geitenia, bringing with them the seeds of change while they eked out a living among the tribespeople of Urkyn.

And that wasn't all that they brought. No, the humans had another house warming gift for their kind Denebian hosts. There was a little stowaway that had crept aboard the *Mayflower* before launch. Silently and deadly, it had taken the life of Daniel's wife Poppy before the Space Ark's science team cracked the genetic code of the Chimera bactovirus.

Although the Nolan-Fong serum had saved the lives of the *Mayflower*'s crew, the humans would never be rid of the vestiges of that bioengineered disease that coursed throughout their veins. Dormant, the bactovirus sat idle, waiting for a chance to rise up again in a murderous rampage.

Even so, it was a gamble that Pallav was willing to take to save his marriage and wreak his revenge – that the Denebians would be immune to human diseases. So Pallav had committed the unthinkable, destroying all mention of the deadly disease from the *Mayflower*'s medical databanks so that the crew could find refuge on that little rocky orb that circled seventh in orbit from the star Deneb. And with that little act, that swipe of the screen, the hulking man from Custer, South Dakota condemned the planet of Deneb7 to years of darkness, fighting an alien designer disease that silently slipped in and out of society, leaving in its wake a trail of death and destruction.

Pallav had seen firsthand the fruits of his deception and the sights still haunted him, the guilt ate at his soul. For the Denebians had not been immune to human diseases. The very young and the elderly had the resilience to overcome the ravages of the Chimera bactovirus while the workers fell like flies. Pallav shuddered when Gomalan told him how he'd been bedridden with a nasty strain of the Denebian flu. At first just a little headache, the aged warrior related. Then his whole body was aflame while he coughed until his ribs ached and blood began to pool under his skin. The High Commander and his wife Magdar spent some time in bed while his ageing mother nursed them with home-made kyttel soup and cloudberry tonic. A couple of days later, as if nothing happened, Gomalan returned to his office in the Wesselan Defence Headquarters a few kilos lighter while the flower of the nation lay suffocating in pools of their own blood and secretions.

"It's the Geiten," the High Commander had snarled and seeing the questioning look on Pallav's face, Gomalan sighed and clasped a meaty hand on the big human's shoulder.

"I keep forgetting you're not one of us. You see, the Geiten living in Wesselan are a danger to our way of life. Just take a detour on your way home tonight and fly past Little Geitenia – you'll see what I mean. They live like rats, sharing filthy hovels with their mangy animals. A bloody health hazard! I don't know why the Surgeon General doesn't deal with them. But mark my words Pallav, these creatures bring disease to Wesselan. They're the cause of this virulent strain of the Denebian flu. And between you and me, I know that the Chief of Police's working on a solution."

It took all his power for Pallav to hide the horror from his cold green eyes while Gomalan railed about the Geiten of Wesselan. Rounded up in the middle of the night, torn from their slumber, the Geiten were thrown into a riot of confusion that reigned in the streets. Shoved into awaiting transports, their screams could be heard as the vehicles lifted off, taking their charges to Collection Centres where they would be kept under protective police custody.

Indignation rocked the planet. Their kin in Geitenia rose up and formed an alliance with the Fyjers who had their own grievances to air with the Wessels. Fyjer Starhunters swooped from the skies to enact a fiery vengeance. Burned out hangars and cratered runways were a testament to a bevy of unprovoked air strikes on Wesselan Aerospace Wings. Even the River Panni dam had been attacked, that source of dissent in a world where drought held the planet in its grip for most of the year.

But the worst damage, the sights and smells that stole into Pallav's dreams at night, had been to Grand Plains Wessel Army Base when high explosive and plasma incendiary rounds had torn into the Firehall and the Base Hospital where thousands of soldiers lay hooked up to ventilators and fighting for their lives. Because of him – all because of a few stupid little swipes on the touchscreen that he had made back on the *Mayflower* to get even with Radu.

Pallav had opened Pandora 's Box and now it was up to him to solve the mystery of how the Wessel Armed Forces bases with their unassailable protective measures had been destroyed by an army of ignorant shepherds and their small fry ally. And he was itching to get started.

CHAPTER 1 - A JOURNEY BEGINS

People cry, not because they are weak. It's because they've been strong for too long.

–JOHNNY DEP

"Pallav? You alright?" Tara's voice broke him from his reverie, and he pasted on a phony smile.

"Sorry darling, I was a million light years away. I'll be fine," he promised. Sweat trickled down his back in the unrelenting heat of the Denebian day, his disruptive pattern shirt already sticking to his body as he shrugged into his rucksack.

"Daddy, I'm gonna miss you." The chirpy sing-song voice of little Jolanta gave him cause to smile at the child as she held out her arms to him. Swooping her up, Pallav dropped a kiss on the little girl's rosy brown cheek, her eyes glistening with tears.

"And I'm going to miss you too, little one." Hugging the orphaned girl to his chest, he burrowed his face into the cloud of dark hair that was as soft as a feather before pinching her cheek and gently setting her down. Guilt pierced his heart at the sad resigned look on the child's face. Had it not been for him, Jolanta would be snug as a bug with her biological parents and not in lockdown high above the capital city living with a pair of humans.

Poor little thing... she's known so much loss in her short life, he thought. Surrounded by death as the human Chimera bactovirus raged across Deneb, Jolanta had been cruelly abandoned by her mother after Tara retrieved the fallen child from the cobblestoned marketplace in the centre of the capital city. He could still picture his wife walking through the door with the tiny tot in tow. Shocked, surprised, but then captivated, Pallav let the child into his heart. It wasn't like his two teenagers wanted him around anymore. No,

Luke and Isabella were busy chartering their own course in the Wessel world with Gomalan insisting that they attend the best boarding school in the nation.

Taking advantage of his position, Pallav had initiated a thorough search for Jolanta's parents only to get confirmation that they were amongst the thousands in Styria who had succumbed to the pandemic. Since her arrival, the young orphan had been his little shadow, never leaving his side, following the big man's movements with her luminous opalescent eyes. He smiled inwardly at the thought of Jolanta climbing into her little cot and begging her new daddy for a bedtime story. Guilt-ridden he realized that he'd miss her more than his own children who were so immersed in their new lives that even their weekly holotalks were rushed and awkward. Laughing at himself, Pallav knew he was totally under the child's spell.

"I promise to be back in time for market day, so no tears, okay?" Taking the little urchin's chin in his hands, Pallav stared into her eyes. "And you have a promise to make to me too young lady, don't you?" The little brown head nodded up and down, serious eyes acknowledging the responsibility her adopted father had assigned to her.

Tara laughed at the two conspirators before being encased in a giant bear hug from her hulk of a husband. "You be careful Pallav. If what you think's actually going on, you're putting yourself in a world of danger."

Shrugging, Pallav pulled her closer. "Don't you worry about me, I can take care of myself." A well-muscled hand smacked his father's Glock 19 9 mm that lay sheathed in his thigh holster. Then absentmindedly, Pallav confirmed that the small but lethal Wessel-issued Adyms Mk II blaster sat snug against his waist while Tara stood before him, her brow furrowed.

"But sabotage? Pallav, we've only arrived on Deneb, and there's a wealth of knowledge that you and I are missing. Sometimes I wonder if Gomalan gave you this assignment because we're both dispensable – humans, undesirables." Pulling away from her husband, Tara glanced out the crystallite windows to stare vacantly at the alien landscape. The morning rays of the star Deneb dazzled and danced in bursts of brilliance on the glass-walled buildings while off in the distance, the sluggish waters of the River Panni snaked slowly through the capital city. And far below their aerie perch, she could see Wessels zip along the perfectly straight autowalks on their way to work. It seemed like any other morning, but today a new danger had wormed its way into the lives of the Kóbor family.

"Now why would you think that?" Pallav's brows furrowed in confusion. "This is a golden opportunity. Gomalan trusts me, and I get results. It's as simple as that. And Tara? It's like I told you - the only people who despise us humans are the Geiten. Just think of that bastard Redlan and how he treated the others."

Tara lowered her head in shame, remembering how her crew mates were eking out an existence in Geitenia while she and her family were housed in luxury in Styria. How the Geiten of Aessen had abused her and Fynn's wife Erica, and how the young pilot had been brutally attacked – it filled her with revulsion.

"The whole thing's still so raw," she started. "My time in Urkyn…you know, it was horrific." Tara shivered as she thought of Daniel and the love she had left behind before looking once more at the bustling capital city that sprawled as far as the eye could see. "Thank God Wesselan's a world apart."

Pallav shook his head. "But it's not. The Geiten have been living here for centuries - intermarrying, working, studying. But always maintaining their distinct identity and trying to impose their ways here. If my hunch is right, then the attacks on Wesselan are being coordinated by an underground Geiten faction that somehow managed to infiltrate our military installations. Maybe even the government. I don't know how deep this goes. We all need to be cautious Tara."

Glancing at the archaic wrist watch that Pallav still insisted on wearing, he clasped a hand on Tara's shoulder. "I've got to get going. But everything you need to know's on the list inside the medicine cabinet."

On tiptoes, Tara stretched up to throw her arms around Pallav's neck, and as their lips touched, worry thread its way into her thoughts, unable as she was to close her mind to the dangerous storm through which her husband must travel.

***

Village of Urkyn, Geitenia – Deneb7

Golden sand shimmered as the midday sun beat down on the little girl who stood quietly beside her parents, impatiently shifting her weight from one tiny foot to the other. Her lively green eyes stared in anticipation at her father and she pulled on his sleeve, demanding attention. Nagib's face was pale, more from distress than the raging pandemic fever that had left him weak and wobbly but lucky to be alive. For many of the men had succumbed to that strangest of strains of the Denebian flu, men who were in the prime of their lives, while he and his family had been spared the ultimate fate.

Ignoring his young daughter, Nagib surveyed his surroundings, his gaze taking in the rows of scaffolds upon which the flower of Urkyn lay in eternal repose. But still there was no sign of Logi or her son. Shrugging his skeletal shoulders, the gaunt man looked down on his little daughter and his lips parted in a sympathetic smile. *After all*, he thought, *it's the bride who's supposed to be late on the day of her promising.*

"Daddy, he's not coming," Brynn insisted, her little bronze face as radiant as the starflowers whose blossoms carpeted the scrubby hills that surrounded the village of Urkyn.

The clicking of Charra's tongue was followed by a pinch to the girl's ear and Brynn swallowed a gulp of pain as her mother knelt down to face her.

"You better hope that Alonz shows up. His father agreed to this match before he walked the star trail to take his place amongst the ancestors." Releasing Brynn's ear, Charra wiped a tear from her daughter's cheek and patted her shoulder.

"He's the best match we could make for you, my daughter. Alonz comes from a good family whose geiten are renowned for their black hides. One day you'll understand that the geiten are the key to our survival. They give us meat, milk and hides. And the black hides are the most coveted of all my child, so by being contracted to Alonz, riches will flow to you and your offspring. Your future will be secure. Now, no more tears; it's bad luck to cry on the day of your promising ceremony."

Nagib looked overhead at the sun and shook his head. "I'm starting to think that Brynn's right, Charra. Maybe they're not coming after all." His wife threw her hands to her hips and swivelled to face her husband.

"We wait, husband. And you'd do better to wipe that dirt smudge from your tunic."

With her chin pointing at him defiantly, Nagib knew he was beaten and lowered his head timidly. "She's only nine Charra, and she's so full of life. Can't this wait a few more years?"

"What are you, stupid or something?" his wife fumed. "It's for this very reason, wasn't it, that we made the match in the first place. This daughter of yours has too much spirit, and I blame you for encouraging her. If we wait any longer, her behaviour will shame us and then no family will want this girl who doesn't know her place in the world."

Frowning partly in frustration and mostly in impotent anger at his wife, Nagib turned his back on Charra. *My fault? As if this wife of mine knows her place*, he fumed, tucking his hands into the sleeves of his billowing tunic. But still, he knew that Charra was a good woman, one who bore him strong children and had nursed him through the illness with no complaints. And she looked the other way when he stayed high in the hills with his flocks, long past the hot days of summer after the other shepherds had driven their animals back to the valleys and winter villages where the Geiten congregated during the short months of the Cooling. Truth be told, he knew Charra did not love him, nor did he care much for her. But theirs was a partnership built for survival and in that they had succeeded in their match. Only he held hope in his heart for more than this for his daughter, the sprite who touched his heart with her dear ways.

Around them, the circle of villagers started to rustle impatiently like the tall grasses in the wind, everyone wondering if sickness had carried away the young bridegroom and his mother, or if they had fallen prey to the bloodwolves that had recently learned to appreciate the taste of Geiten flesh. And mingling amongst the Geiten of Urkyn was a cluster of beings who from a distance could pass for foreigners from any one of the planets that made up the Interstellar Collective for Peace and Security.

Earlier that year, when Ru the God of Fire was washed away from the land by the Tears of Ur, the Geiten of Urkyn led their flocks on the long trek from the rich alpine pastures to their wintering quarters, as their ancestors had since the beginning of time. There they would congregate, contracting marriages and transacting commerce. But this year, a surprise lay in store for the good tribespeople, for waiting in their winter village was the Clan Mayflower – the human refugees who had been granted asylum in Geitenia. And there they were – bringing with them their foreign ideas and disruptive ways.

Lestos Marag, his weathered face bearing the stamp of the harsh life of a shepherd, stood silently next to the leader of the Clan Mayflower, Dr. Daniel Radu. The erstwhile project manager for the Space Ark program watched the old man's grandson Shalo hard at play with his own two lads. Lewis, a carbon copy of his father at eight years old right down to the blonde flat top and piercing blue eyes, squatted in the dust playing marbles with his

11

younger brother Max. All about the circle, the laughter of the Geiten men resounded as they relived the day of their promising ceremony, while the women of the tribe chatted around the young bride to be.

Daniel surveyed his little group as the villagers awaited the arrival of the potential groom. Ebony skin glowing like obsidian, Reeta Nuako rested her head on her husband Abeiku's shoulder. Their young daughter Lark slept soundly in her arms while her mother-in-law Dashawna tried to keep track of her ever-rambunctious grandson Teuvo. Her husband Dodzi shielded his eyes, stared out at the horizon and shook his head then whispered to Daniel, "We've been waiting for over an hour. Perhaps you should make a recommendation to let the children wait in the shade."

Flame-haired Barb Nolan, widow of the famed microbiologist Dr. Vance Nolan, prodded her son Pat in the ribs as the young man and his friend Renzo debated over the lack of opportunities in their new homeland.

"You got good eyes," she said, pointing to a ridge that skirted the village. "Tell me what you over see there?" Pat squinted in the sunlight, but the shimmering sands gave up no secrets.

It was Renzo, the twenty-one year old son of the *Mayflower*'s nurse Dom Calvo, who first spotted the small caravan slowly making its way down the sandy ridge and through the stunted shrubs. A tall woman led a boy by the hand, followed by a large dog who skipped nimbly amongst the rocks accompanied by a helmeted and robed man. The woman waved to the villagers and Charra waved back. "See I told you," she said sharply to her husband, "they've come after all."

And slowly the three members of the Geiten of Thalia approached the little congregation. Bowing to Nagib, the tall dark man peeled off into the village hall where the priestly Taklich began his preparations for the ceremony. Dirt-caked and sweat-stained, Logi and her son Alonz stepped into the circle of villagers while their dog danced about and the boys gathered around to rough its mangy hide with dusty hands.

Taller by a head than Charra, Logi was as dark as the ebony charrstone that littered the scree slopes of the Tagar Mountains. Eyes that twinkled like the night sky crinkled and smiled as she hugged her friend in a tight embrace, her voice cracking with emotion.

"It's so good to see you healthy," she started, "after all the death that's run through our nation. But did you fall ill Charra? Or your family? Oh I have a hundred questions for you! But now we're here… and there're things that we have to discuss."

Nagib pulled his wife from the tall woman's embrace. "Indeed there are Logi, but not with Charra." His eyes were hard as he looked over the boy Alonz who was to be matched with his daughter. For the young teen was smaller than he had expected, puny in fact, and with a look of misery that hung about him.

"I thought… I meant… women things with your wife…" Confusion gave way to sadness as Logi continued. "Nagib, before my husband died, he told me that everything had already been arranged for the promising ceremony. He authorized me to bring our son to your village so that he could be raised by men and learn the ways of our people."

Nagib's emerald eyes bore into her as he pointed to the boy Alonz. "How old is he?"

Logi blinked in surprise. "Alonz has lived through thirteen seasons of the Cooling. I have told my son that he is to dwell in your peha and to be obedient to the rules of your clan. He has learned his role well and is ready to be promised."

Taking Charra's hand, he pulled his wife away from prying ears. "This boy is sickly, ill-featured - look at him! And that isn't the deal I made with his father. If he lives with us, their black-hided geiten stay with Logi. So unless her older brother Geneen is generous, Brynn and this Alonz will get nothing when I tread my way on the path to the ancestors."

Charra's nostrils flared and she grabbed her husband rudely by the bicep. "Do you want to shame us?" she railed. "This woman is a widow. And she is my friend. How can you even suggest to repudiate the contract that was made? No Nagib, this will take place. But leave me to deal with Logi, for I agree with you for once. We will not take Alonz in."

Husband and wife nodded their heads in unison and Charra smiled at Logi in triumph. Taking young Alonz by the hand, she rewarded him with a cold smile. "You may tell your Taklich that we are ready. Now go while I speak with your mother."

Thick black eyebrows knit together as Charra spoke quietly with Logi. "My friend, we will not take your son into our peha, for this was not agreed upon by our men. You understand, I hope, that what they agreed to beforehand must be honoured. My husband insists that Alonz return to your village until our children are old enough to be joined in the eternal union, whereupon she will become your daughter. That is, if you wish this match to proceed after all."

Curling her lip with frustration, Logi clicked her tongue at Charra. "How is Alonz to learn the ways of the men if he dwells with me and the old mothers? Really Charra, do you not see?"

The smaller woman stood her ground as she squared her shoulders and planted hands on her hips in a sign of stubbornness.

"It is decided Logi."

Charra smiled at the sight of Alonz and Brynn and softening took her friend's hand in hers.

"They are both very young and have many years before the eternal union takes place. Years will pass, and your son will learn the ways from the old men of your tribe. And my Brynn - she is as beautiful as a summer sunset. She will give your Alonz strong sons and comely daughters. You will find no better match."

Logi slowly nodded her head in agreement as the Taklich strode into the circle. The two youths stood side by side, while the parents took up their places behind them.

Roasting within the kyttel gown that her mother had painstakingly sewn for her, Brynn squirmed in discomfort, her face questioning as her father's eyes bulged in their sockets.

"What now?" he whispered, embarrassment evident in his face.

But Charra would have none of it and smacked her daughter squarely on the head while pushing her forward towards the Taklich who ignored the young girl.

As the religious man droned on about how the gods created females to serve mankind, to be obedient and bear the sufferings inflicted upon womanhood with steadfastness, Brynn watched a pybar soaring high in the sky on its red and green silken wings. Floating on the currents, it glided upwards through the clouds, circling on the winds as it surveyed the blistering lands below where fleet footed lizards ran between the rocks, seeking shelter from its steely gaze in cool crevices. Erupting like a flash of lightning from the heavens, it dove earthwards, talons sharp in outstretched claws, ready to pounce on a sleek lizard basking happily in the midday sun, unaware of its fate. And then, suddenly, a shriek tore through the still air as the life was snuffed from the little creature that lay broken in the predator's bloody claws.

***

Wesselan Armed Forces Headquarters, Styria

The silver chip lay on his desk, taunting him. *Look at me! Access me! See the secrets that I bear within my silicon circuits.*

Gomalan threw the Surgeon General a look of desperation and mopped his face with his sleeve as the horror of the situation loomed over him.

"You sure about this? I mean, there can't be any room for error."

A flutter of the eyes, a slow nod. "Absolutely 100% certain, High Commander."

Taking the little wafer in his fingers, Gomalan played with it as he calculated his next move. "And who else knows? That is, besides you and me."

"Well that's just it. Automation generates the results from the samples which are then reviewed individually by the Chief Flight Surgeon. Any anomalies are usually brought to the attention of the member and a decision is made on flight status which is then transmitted to the Squadron Commander. But of course, not in this case. Col Eng, our Chief Flight Surgeon, actually brought these results to me immediately, wondering what to do. And now I'm here. Because this is something that can change the course of history."

Gomalan closed his eyes and begged the gods for a flash of insight. But none came. Narrowing his eyes, he made a decision that he hoped he'd not have reason to regret. "Tell no one of this. And order the Chief Flight Surgeon to absolute silence. If this gets out I'll have her head and yours. Understood?"

"Yes Sir, understood. Now what are we going to do about this?"

Pocketing the little chip, Gomalan stood up from his desk and pulled himself to his full height and loomed menacingly over the smaller man. "I'll let the president decide and get back to you. In the meantime," he said, making a slashing motion with his hand, "absolute secrecy."

Watching as the Surgeon General disappeared down the polished halls, Gomalan tapped his wristcuff and was surprised at how calm his voice sounded as he spoke to his Aide-de-Camp. "Two things. I need a meeting with the president in about an hour. Urgent. Don't take no for an answer. And second thing. I want Reyhart in my office ASAP."

Gomalan fingered the chip and wondered if it would be easier to destroy it and to erase all knowledge of the horror it carried. But that would be cowardice and he knew that before he met with Wesselan's aged President Meryx, he had to be absolutely sure, beyond a shadow of a doubt, that the results were conclusive.

With a push of a button, the magnetic steel doors to his office began to snap shut while the windows smoked over, shutting out the sunlight and any prying eyes. As the holoscreen raised from the floor, Gomalan prayed that there had been some mistake, that there would be something he could find in the details to deny the allegations that the Surgeon General had been lobbed like mortars and had exploded in his mind with deadly destruction.

But there it was, floating in front of him like the wreckage from a ship in space.

Vogel, F.A. Service Number R71 541 390
Lt Col, Wessel Aerospace Force
Squadron Commander, 19 Fighter Squadron Styria
Routine Physical Assessment Results. NORMAL
Anomalies Present.
DNA not consistent with Denebian life forms
Antibodies present to current Denebian Pandemic
DNA of current Denebian Pandemic microorganism tailored to match genetic diversity of patient – suspected designer disease of human origins
Flying Status: UNFIT
Notes: Suspected Patient Zero of current Denebian Pandemic – alien infectious disease. Recommendation: Collection Centre for Treatment or Disposal

CHAPTER 2 - TAKING CARE OF BUSINESS

A lie may take care of the present, but it has no future.

– ANONYMOUS

Lt Col Fynn Vogel scratched his head as he handed Gomalan's message over to his wife. "I don't get it babe, I was given command of the biggest bad-assiest fighter squadron I've ever laid eyes on, and whammo! I'm suddenly grounded. And I don't even know why. But at least I gotta coupla days off before I'm slated to report in."

Erica Rosendahl, veteran combat pilot and helmsmen to the now defunct Space Ark *Mayflower*, grabbed the message from her husband's hands and began scanning it rapidly. Fynn broke into a smile at his wife's habit of moving her lips while reading and he pulled her in for hug. "Leave it babe. I don't care if it means I get to spend more time with you." Wrapping his arms around her, he cuddled the growing girth about Erica's waist and cradled his head against her shoulder.

"Hey, go easy there Freckles. Between your octopus arms and our little fly-girl's kung fu kicking, seems I can't get any peace around here no more." Untangling herself from Fynn, Erica arched her back and groaned. "I can't believe I talked myself into nine months of this. Next time, it'll be your turn."

Fynn screwed up his face and grabbed a big pink aamfruit. "Don't think they do that here babe," he retorted, munching away while Erica re-read the message.

"Says here something about your medical," she replied as juice ran down her husband's chin. Erica chuckled, handing Fynn a cloth. "Probably they don't want you slobbering all over the controls of your warbird. Just ask Gomalan what's the issue instead of moping around here pestering me."

Throwing the core into the compost, Fynn took the message from Erica's hands. "You just want the house all to yourself so you can watch those crazy Wessel reality shows after your long hard day in the office. Desk jockey!"

Proudly patting her baby bump, Erica laughed. "Can you see me flying with this? Y'know, I've never piloted a desk before, but Flight Ops & Plans's a lot more action than I thought it'd be. I'm cool with it."

Ops and Plans, Fynn thought with a look of surprise on his face, wondering how sitting behind a desk for an eight-hour shift could be all that interesting. *After all the schmoozing I did with Meryx to get her on the Meganeur Squadron, and now she prefers sitting behind a desk. Still... I'm glad she's happy. I sure don't want her lobbying any time soon to fly fighters in this war.*

"It won't be long now till our little girl greets the world." Throwing a quick grin at her husband, Erica continued, "And I can't wait to be able to sleep again without someone jabbing me in the ribs."

Everything was ready now for the new member of the Vogel-Rosendahl family. Meryx had seen to that: the best medical treatment, the finest furniture for the nursery, luxurious soft blankets and tiny rompers in delicate shades. Erica had never mentioned to her husband how the busy President of Wesselan had taken the time away from running the country during a war to bring her hot cooked meals while Fynn had been away on duty.

"But you know what, Fynn? I miss flying. I mean, I like my job – don't get me wrong. It's busy and it's challenging, but it's not what I was trained for. So I've been talking to Meryx..."

Oh oh!

"And he said that after the baby's born, he'll find us a good nanny..."

Oh no! A nanny'll make 'em learn Denebian before English... brainwash our kid into being just like a Wessel!

"...And that means I'll get right back up in the saddle again. I didn't like Meryx at first, but I'm telling you, he's been a real sweetheart to both of us."

Fynn pasted a smile on his face, thoughts of a stranger raising their daughter while his wife zipped across the Collective in a super gigantic Meganeur. "Yeah, a real sweetheart," he muttered unhappily under his breath.

***

The tall thin man knocked politely on Gomalan's door, his pale hair impeccably parted and slicked back. He waited patiently, hearing the argument raging on the other side while military personnel marched through the halls of Wesselan's Department of Defence, their footsteps echoing throughout the corridor. He allowed himself a languorous smile as a shapely sergeant strode by, her hips swinging and her lips curling at the sight of the sophisticated well-dressed civilian. As the shouting reached a crescendo, the door swung open and Caydnn stormed out. His face bright red, the Air Marshal of the Wessel Aerospace Force turned to the visitor and wheezed. "He's all yours. May the gods go with you."

Reyhart tugged on his custom-made tunic and brushed off a non-existent speck. His polished shoes were silent as he entered the office of the High Commander. Stopping two feet in front of the console, Reyhart bowed his head silently in greeting. Without a word, Gomalan motioned for the tall man to sit and Reyhart did so gracefully, elegantly crossing his legs at the ankles, his hands politely folded in his lap.

Pouring out two fingers of Vulpeculan brandy, Gomalan handed a crystallite glass to Reyhart who shook his head, waving it away. His pale eyes bore into Gomalan and the High Commander inwardly shuddered.

"I was told this was most urgent Sir," Reyhart began, noticing the uneasiness of his host. Uncrossing and recrossing his long legs, the man watched Gomalan with impassiveness.

Taking a sip of the caramel liquid, the fiery burn of the brandy released Gomalan from the man's spell. "It is indeed. I have a mission for you. One which if you fail…"

"Ah," Reyhart interrupted, his eyes unfriendly, "but we both know that will not occur. So please continue."

Swallowing his revulsion, Gomalan reflected on the evil in this creature and sneered. "If you fail, you will be put to death as a traitor."

"Well now, those are rather high stakes. But I like to gamble, especially when the prize is, shall we say, extravagant. So tell me, what is this mission that's so important and what's in it for me."

"I need two people dead. I need you to make it look like an accident or something."

"Now where's the challenge in that?" Reyhart replied, a faint smile not quite reaching his cold eyes.

"I need it done by the setting of the sun."

The man blinked and stared outside where the sun sat high in the sky. "That gives me about seven hours," he said appraisingly. "So tell me, who are these two people. And again, I ask, what's in it for me."

Pressing a button on his console, a holoscreen rose from the floor and an image of a middle-aged man and woman flashed before the two conspirators. Gomalan scrolled down to retrieve their personal data, all while Reyhart's pale eyes darted from side to side, tucking away the details.

"Ah, the Surgeon General. But who is that lovely lady?" he asked, his voice without a hint of emotion.

"She's our Chief Flight Surgeon. Just make it quick - painless if you can," Gomalan whispered in disgust.

"It can be done." Reyhart analyzed the holograms of his two victims and a thought spun in his head. *A handsome man, a lovely woman. Meeting at a seedy motel. An affair that's ran its course. A murder and a suicide*, he thought before swinging his cold gaze back on Gomalan. "At a price of course."

"Name it."

Reyhart got up from the low chair and brushed off his trousers. "Two million gold Crowns," he uttered listlessly, while his hand swept in a graceful gesture. "And that bottle of Vulpeculan brandy."

***

Meryx drummed his fingers angrily against his console while he fought to control the famous temper that he knew if left unbridled would lead to a pounding headache. Bursting up from his chair, the president grabbed the tiny silicon wafer from the holodisplay and threw it to the ground, crushing it beneath his heel. "See to it that this doesn't get out," he growled while Gomalan exhaled deeply and mopped his brow in relief.

"Already taken care of, Sir." The big man inwardly shuddered at the thought of Reyhart and wondered if the deed had been already completed. "There'll be a draw of two million gold Crowns once I verify that my agent has succeeded."

"Good, good." Meryx paced in agitation about his office while a battle raged inside him. "I can't believe it! Fynn... patient zero! By the gods! I've welcomed him into our nation, brought him into my home, and for Ru's sake, I even gave him command of the best fighter squadron in Wesselan. All this war, all this death, all this shit! I nearly died! Our nation's been decimated by this blasted disease! And it's all because of Fynn! Damn him!"

But the High Commander had trod down that very same road earlier and having taken the time to reflect, arrived a very different conclusion.

"It's quite likely Sir that this human disease has been around for centuries on their planet and the humans have acquired a natural immunity to it. Fynn probably has no idea that he's a carrier – back on his planet, it could be a very common illness."

The pacing, the drumming of the fingers – it was all driving Gomalan mad as he tried to no avail to shut out thoughts of the two innocent people who he'd condemned to death. And all for naught if Meryx wasn't going to act to their advantage.

"No matter," Meryx replied. "I need the Foreign Minister here at once – we've got to put a stop to the war – we Denebians are fighting amongst ourselves all because of these humans, whether they know it or not – they're to blame."

At this the High Commander grabbed the elderly president brusquely by the arm, putting an end to his irritating and incessant pacing. "Think this through Sir," he said, his eyes narrowing to slits as a cunning smile curled across his face. "We have human blood – full of nice juicy antibodies. Powerful human antibodies. Very useful to us. They can be decoded and replicated - vaccinations can be developed conferring immunity on our troops."

Pulling free of Gomalan, the president raised his eyebrows. "I'm listening. Go on."

"Well, let's just say that this afternoon the Surgeon General briefed me on finding a specimen with antibodies from amongst survivors."

Waving his arms about in agitation, Meryx snapped. "Preposterous! We both know that no Denebian immunity has developed. Denebians have not been able to build long term immunity to this alien disease."

Gomalan shook his head. "Of course that's true, but hear me out. Let's just say that sadly, the survivor has perished in the war but what remains is a vial of blood. Full of antibodies and ready for decoding to be used to create a vaccine."

His patience at an end, Meryx let loose his temper. "So our soldiers are immune – so what! The war continues on for no reason! Denebians killing Denebians to no purpose and with no benefit."

Even more enraged he became as the High Commander dared to hold his arm out to stop him in his tracks. Knowing Gomalan well, the president wondered what the old warrior had up his sleeve, and with curiosity trumping anger, Meryx waited with bated breath.

"Please Sir, if I may continue. Immunity accords Wesselan a strategic advantage. Our troops, strengthened and hale once again, will easily sweep away the sick and weakened armies of the so-called Coalition. We capture the fertile Wessla Valley south of the Empty Quarter, the beating heart of Fyjerlan, and push the Fyjers back to the inhospitable northern regions where they will languish. Destroying their base of power will ensure our nation's safety so that they will never again be capable of mounting an attack against us."

Retaking his seat, Meryx cradled his pounding head in his hands. "And what of the Geiten? We've incarcerated them, destroyed their homes, blamed them for something out of their control…we can never make it up to them, you know."

"Pffft, Geiten! They've always been a scab on our backsides. It's time to get rid of them once and for all. That's one thing this war's shown us – Wesselan's crawling with Geiten traitors who've infiltrated our bases – by the gods Sir, they targeted a hospital! We should show them no mercy, wipe them from the face of Deneb if you ask me."

Resigned, the president sighed. Agony and bitterness mingled in his voice as he looked up at Gomalan. "And the humans?"

"We'll need to keep a few of them in case more blood specimens are required – the ones in Wesselan, for instance, should prove adequate I would say."

Staring emotionless at the framed holograms of Fynn and Erica on his desk, Meryx nodded. "Yes, that would do. But the rest, the humans in Geitenia, they're superfluous to our needs. Expendable."

Pulling himself up with difficulty, Meryx suddenly felt very old and tired. His head pounded, his stomach churned and he wanted nothing more than to crawl under the covers and find relief in blessed sleep. Clasping the High Commander on the shoulder, Meryx's rasped in despair. "Take care of it, old friend. Make this go away."

Nodding in assent, the High Commander bowed to his president before marching smartly away. Alone again, Meryx picked up the holographic frame of the young human couple that adorned his console. *There's not a devious bone in that boy's body*, he reflected. *Gomalan's right… Probably he has no idea that he brought the shadow of death to Deneb.* The old man stared hard at the image of Fynn – the cheeky grin, the tiny brown flecks that blossomed over his cheeks, the honest hazel eyes that stared back at him; Erica beside her husband, an arm thrown about her husband's waist with her blue eyes twinkling with mirth. *No*, he thought, pushing the doubt from his mind, *my Fynn; my Erica – they're innocent.*

And putting down the images of the two aliens who he loved as if they were molded from his own flesh and blood, the president's thoughts jumped neatly to the future, where his little goddaughter would soon be squirming in his arms while her parents smiled down on him.

***

Tracked bulldozers plowed through the wreckage of Wesselan's Great Plains Army Base, their blades indiscriminately ripping out the pale green shoots that had sprung up between charred remnants of equipment that littered the grounds. Docking the drab beige hovercraft, Colonel Pallav Kóbor quickly scanned his surroundings and looked appreciatively at the hectic activity that had already begun to transform destruction into order. Contractors swarmed across the grounds, equipment trucked building supplies into orderly piles while soldiers marched sharply in platoons, arms shoulder high. *Some things never change*, he thought as a young captain sprinted over to greet him.

Halting in front of the alien colonel, the captain shot Pallav a sharp salute, her middle finger bearing an oversized bauble with a blood-red rock the size of an egg.

"Welcome to Great Plains Army Base, Sir."

Catching her breath, the young woman remembered to hold out her hand in human greeting.

"Captain Bafa Villutomi, 2IC Security Company. I'll be your escort for your stay here."

Pressing her comms device resulted in Pallav's visit schedule floating in the air before them. Eyes wide, he stole a glance at Villutomi, hoping hard that surprise was not visible on his face.

Rooting through the hovercraft's back seat, Captain Villutomi grunted as she hauled out Pallav's duffle bag before hitching it on her shoulder.

"I'll take you to your quarters Sir and then you have a quick meeting with the Base Commander before we head over to my Company." Pallav's furrowed forehead confused Villutomi and she gulped at the imposing alien who regarded her with eyes as pale as a spring-time leaf.

It's always the same, he thought as they went through pass control. Pallav was pleasantly surprised with the extra layer of security put in place and willingly he submitted to a quick blood draw, DNA and body scan. *Defensive perimeters, security cameras, lights, a visit to the Commander… all standard no matter what planet you're visiting.*

The sound of the big alien's laughter surprised Villutomi.

So he's not a monster after all, she thought before the composed look returned to Pallav's features. *Maybe just half a monster,* she decided quickly before depositing him in the Command Suite.

Breezing through the standard welcome and vanilla-flavoured interview with the Base Commander, Pallav strode off through the HQ's corridors in search of his escort who enthusiastically skidded out of a nearby office. Through the labyrinthine HQ, Villutomi shepherded Pallav along the autowalks, speeding past compounds and equipment yards until they reached a suspended netting that enclosed what seemed like an Old English barrow. Long and narrow, its sides were sheathed with what looked to Pallav like the Denebian version of Hesco bastion. Rising upwards towards the sky, the mound would have seemed incongruous with the flat plains of the Base except for the crop of weeds crowning its heights and securing it from overhead surveillance. Well concealed within the walls, the entrance bore the two officers deep within the bowels of the edifice where the constant hum of artificial lights and ventilation systems dampened the normal office din.

Ducking his head, Pallav followed Villutomi into a cavernous room where a senior officer sat bent over his desk, scrutinizing a voluminous file. *So this is the officer responsible for the failure,* Pallav reflected unkindly as the man stood to acknowledge the alien whose inspection would tear apart his operating procedures. With difficulty Pallav concealed his distaste for the sloppiness that confronted him. Before him stood a middle-aged greying Wessel male whose crumpled uniform and hunched shoulders bore no indication of command other than the rank slashes on the collar of his tunic. Papers were strewn about his desk and piles of documents lay in untidy stacks about the office.

"Major Sterton," the man said in a nasal tone as he bowed in greeting. Smiling obsequiously, he motioned for Villutomi to close the door and for Pallav to take a seat. His eyes like ice, Pallav imitated a shallow bow and waited for his escort to leave the two men alone.

"You understand my task Sterton?" Pallav asked, anxious to start digging into the details.

Sterton raised an eyebrow in reply. "Of course. We've sequestered a fully equipped workstation for your stay. And Captain Villutomi will be available to assist you with anything you may need."

Pallav said nothing, knowing that silence often brings out hidden information. People, like nature, abhor a vacuum. Sterton scratched the back of his head nervously and picked up a document, brandishing it in front of Pallav.

"Since the attack, my staff and I have reviewed everything over and over again and we've come up with nothing. We can't figure out why the incoming missiles weren't picked up and destroyed. I don't want to colour your investigation – but I can assure you that our defensive systems were fully functional that day. Training's up to date; we exercise our defensive posture as per directives. The only thing that is out of normal parameters is the company's strength – so many of my troops have died or are out of commission from the pandemic. But from my preliminary investigation, that had nothing to do with it."

As Sterton's shoulders sagged in exhaustion, Pallav felt sympathy replacing his initial aversion and he clasped the major on the shoulder. "Listen, this base wasn't the only one targeted." He was surprised as tears filled the Sterton's amber eyes.

"No, I know that. But it doesn't stop me from feeling responsible, you understand. Both my daughters died in the shelling. As a parent you think you can protect your kids, and I had an added responsibility to secure the base from threats. I failed on both accounts - as a father and as an officer. Thirty years in and now this, right at the end of my career."

Pallav grimaced and searched his memory for a standard reply to the grief-stricken and wondered how an earth condolence would sound to Denebian ears.

"My sympathies Sterton," he tried awkwardly as the major stared at his hands. "I got kids myself and yes, you're right, you'd do anything to keep them safe. I'll get to the bottom of this so that other parents can be spared the same. Now I'm going to need to tour your installations before I wade through the preliminary reports and analysis."

Like clockwork, the ever efficient Villutomi appeared at the door. "Sir, I'll take it from here."

With a nod from Sterton and a smile for the tall alien colonel, the young captain ushered Pallav out of the building and back into the light where an idling hovercraft ferried them about the Base Defence Company's installations.

CHAPTER 3 - JUST FOLLOWING ORDERS

It is so hard to believe because it is so hard to obey.

– SØREN KIRKEGAARD

There was a hush in the room as the significance of the orders sank in. Looking from Caydnn to Ravenna, Gomalan waited impatiently for either of them to break the silence.

Another meeting loomed on his agenda, and he remembered with nostalgia his earlier years when the only concerns he had were to have a clean weapon and shiny boots. His empty stomach churned with stress and then he remembered that Magdar had scheduled a dinner party that night.

It'll have to be a light lunch today, that is, if I even have the time, he thought to himself as he surveyed his commanders impatiently. Shuffling in his seat, his brow furrowed as Air Marshal Caydnn's mouth opened and closed, reminding the High Commander of a River Panni bottom feeder. His thoughts swept between the office and home. *I'm keeping my fingers crossed that Magdar's organized something other than fish for tonight,* he reflected, his thoughts quickly shifting back to his two generals.

"I'll ask again. Any questions?"

Pressing her hands to her temples, Ravenna's dark eyes questioned her superior officer. "We'll need some time to coordinate the joint land-air strikes." Leaning towards Gomalan, her voice dropped almost into a whisper. "But I'm not clear on one thing – why Urkyn? It has zero strategic value. We've already begun executing the mission in line with our Operational Plan. This is a major shift from the original focus that, in my opinion, is leading us away from victory."

Caydnn nodded in agreement. "I concur with General Ravenna, Sir. By destroying Urkyn, we accomplish absolutely nothing. My recommendation is that we stay the course… concentrating on striking the Fyjer aerospace wings, then their strategic assets thereby removing their ability to continue to wage the war. With the Fyjers neutralized, Geitenia would fall within a few weeks."

"The time for your opinions and recommendations is past," Gomalan said patiently. "You have a clear objective in front of you, one that should be very easy. Your duty now is to prosecute it. And before the shepherds lead their herds up to the alpine pastures of the Tagar Mountains. That gives you less than a week. Now… we're all very busy people, aren't we? So frag the Op Order and just get on with it. Unless there are any burning impediments?"

The commanders of the Aerospace and Army looked to each other for support, then silently shook their heads in resignation while Gomalan surreptitiously checked the time. Shortly Kóbor would be reporting in, so with a wave of his hand, he quickly dismissed his generals.

That was easy enough, he thought as he poured himself a glass of the bitter drink his doctor prescribed for stomach issues. "To be consumed before meals," he read aloud with a groan before reaching for the little snack that Magdar had so thoughtfully prepared for him. And as the acrid liquid flowed down his throat, Gomalan relaxed, wondering what news the alien colonel would bring him.

***

Deep in the valley, nestled beneath the rolling hills that bracketed Urkyn, the villagers clustered around the sides of a recess that had painstakingly been carved out of the rocky ground. Renzo nudged Pat in the ribs and pointed to a series of narrow channels that they had carved into the hard stone from the heights above and the two young men almost leapt with excitement. "It's coming," Jian yelled, his deep voice resounding across the valley.

Loose pebbles tumbled over the rocky sides of the hilltop as Daniel, Dodzi and Marco scrambled downwards under the shadow of the tall structure that they had so painstakingly built over the long months of the Cooling. Slapping Daniel on the back, Dodzi smiled broadly, "We did it! It's working!"

The blades of the wind turbine spun in the breeze, their steely surfaces reflecting in the noon day sun, the first product of the bloomery furnace that Daniel and Angelo had laboriously constructed with Dodzi's assistance. The long sleek blades spun rhythmically and while the villagers stared in awe, the narrow channels began to glisten as water flowed, crystal-clear and cool, into the deep cistern chiseled into the base of the hill.

Pulling his son-in-law in close, the wizened patriarch of the Marag clan whispered secretively, "This human invention will disrupt our way of life." But Nagib was wonderstruck by the precious water cascading from the hilltop into the growing pool below and understood its magic.

"But father, no longer will the village need to disperse when the Breath of Ru envelopes us in its scorching cloak. Our people can make a life here, regardless of the time of year. No longer will the elderly, women and children have to make the long and dangerous trek to the lush foothills of the Altai Mountains, while we men bring the flocks to the high alpine pastures. This is a true gift that the humans have brought to the people of Urkyn."

Shaking his head in disagreement, Lestos narrowed his eyes and glanced at the sun overhead. "It will not be long now before the days grow hot again my son. Soon the geiten will be dropping their young, and their journey must be made early enough so that mothers can be nourished by the spring shoots before the birthing." His eyes challenged his son-in-law. "This device… this…wind turbine… it stands to destroy our way of life. Whether it be a gift or a curse… the Council of Elders must convene to discuss the way ahead for our people."

Hanna clucked her disapproval and crossed her arms stubbornly. "Husband, there are times when tradition must give way to progress. Think about the suffering our people face – the hunger swelling the bellies of our children, our flocks emaciated and bleating pitifully when the scorching kiss of the hot months arrives too early. This," she said arching her arm towards the spinning blades, "this can give us a new and better way of living."

Blinking in disbelief, Lestos walked away from his wife to talk with the village elders. *The young, yes, I would expect this from them, for they do not yet comprehend the power of tradition, of holding fast to a belief that has been passed down through the generations… a rich connection to our past. But Hanna! Never would I have believed she'd gainsay me. And in front of our son-in-law! No, certainly this device is a great disruptive factor that should not be allowed to destroy our way of life – freely, off the land, just like our flocks of geiten."*

While many of the villagers looked on dumbstruck, young Brynn and her twin brother Shalo cupped their hands and dipping them into the little channel, drank of the cool water while their mother looked on in awe. Breaking from her reverie, Charra grabbed the twins by the ear. "This is not for your amusement," she screeched, pulling them away from the hillside while scanning for her errant elder son Geneen.

Releasing the chastened youngsters, Charra curled her lip in derision. "These humans," she spat, "they always seem to find a way to change things."

Nagib nodded his head in agreement, "But this is a good change Charra. Don't you see what it means? You won't have to leave the village anymore."

Biting her lip, the young woman watched as Shalo and Brynn raced off with their elder brother Geneen, kicking a leather ball between them. "I'm not so sure Nagib," she offered questioningly. "I don't think that the elders will find this wind turbine acceptable. But I can see how useful the water source will be. No more having to truck water back and forth when the wells run dry. More free time on our hands." Charra smiled at her husband, a thick eyebrow raised playfully, her wide mouth inviting. Laughing, Nagib took his wife by the hand and together they trekked down the hill and back to the village, passing the human Calvo siblings.

Shading her eyes from the brilliant sun, young Lucia called her brother Renzo over to her side. "Hey, you tell me what you see up there?"

"It's not Superman – that's for sure," he laughed while his sister pursed her lips in displeasure.

"You idiot. Whatever it is, it's hovering between the clouds, too high for a bird. Go get Dad," Lucia ordered.

Disbelief stamped on his face, Renzo took his sister by the elbow. "You've been reading too many thriller books. It's just some sort of weird flying thingy. Now c'mon, I heard one of the women talking about a feast." Patting his stomach, Renzo yelled for Pat and the two friends strolled off anticipating a smorgasbord of Geiten culinary delights, leaving Lucia behind with her thoughts.

Not to be put off, she searched for her father who was chatting with Barb. Jealousy surged through the teen, who was certain that her father had an unhealthy romantic interest in the red-headed widow. Rolling her eyes,

Lucia stuck herself between the adults and with hands on hips, demanded attention.

"Dad, there's something very peculiar up there. It's as if it's spying on us." Pointing into the clouds, Lucia glowered at Barb who pointedly crossed her arms and raised an eyebrow.

"It's some sort of plane," Barb interjected. "And you're right my dear, it can tell we're pointing at it. Just look! It's trying to avoid detection by slipping into the cloud cover now."

Almost invisible against the backdrop of the clouds, the airborne vessel resembled a twentieth century dirigible on steroids. It ascended vertically as the villagers craned their necks to peer into the sky. High above the clouds it soared, hidden from view and dampening the excitement over the wind turbine. The Geiten shrugged, deciding it now was time to celebrate and they began straggling back to the village.

Daniel knitted his brows together as he scanned the skies and pulled Angelo aside. "I'm not comfortable with this. Not at all. We've heard about the Geiten and Fyjers attacking Wesselan and very little retaliation's taken place other than rounding up people, closing their borders, invoking the Collective and enacting sanctions. But I'm not aware of any full-scale armed response. Does that make sense to you?"

Angelo scratched his head. "I can't figure these Denebians out. Have you noticed how half the young men suddenly slipped away? You know Renzo's been seeing a local girl, and her brother asked him to join this rebel group in the fight against Wessel domination."

Raising an eyebrow, Daniel stared at his one-time mentor. "No, I wasn't aware of that. A rebel group, eh?"

A high pitched squeal caused both men to look skyward. "Look, it's back!" Pulling his comms device out of his pocket, Daniel concealed himself under a rocky outcrop in the hillside. "I'm gonna get in touch with Fynn. He might be able to shed some light on this."

As Daniel punched in the codes for Fynn's HomeLink System, the speck of a saucer shot to a great height. But instead of Fynn, Erica's holoform coalesced before him into the dusty air. Daniel gasped at the sight of the Space Ark's former navigator, whose bulging belly doubled the size of the woman's normal slender frame. But his eyes almost popped out of their sockets when Tara appeared by her side, a mug of steaming boricha in her hands. Trying to conceal his surprise, Daniel raked a hand through his hair and graced the two ladies with a brilliant smile.

"Well, I never," he started, tongue-tied. "That is – Erica – congratulations – it must be any day now."

Her bubbly laughter confirmed the obvious and her blue eyes lit up with happiness. "Yup, Fynn and I are ready to welcome our little daughter into the world and the sooner the better."

Arching her back, the young woman groaned theatrically. Throwing an arm casually around the diminutive brunette by her side, Erica chirped, "Tara here's been giving me some advice, since I have to do this with a Wessel midwife. Who, by the way, tells me females here give birth drugged to the hilt and they induce amnesia afterwards. So I guess the whole experience won't be too bad."

Glancing over at Tara, Erica's eyes searched for confirmation. Tara, mother of two, raised both eyebrows in disagreement her eyes widening, before winking to Daniel. "Hey stranger, what are you calling for? You're interrupting two women on a mission."

"Well, I was actually looking for Fynn. He around?"

Disappointment crossed Erica's flushed cheeks. Once again, side-lined in favour of her big shot husband. "He's not," she snapped. "But you're in luck… I am." With that the two women laughed companionably.

"Okay," he responded, and Daniel pointed his comms device skyward and focused in on the strange airborne device. "Can you tell me what the hell this thing here is?"

The smile was frozen on Erica's face as she scrutinized the image. Tilting her head, she watched as Tara zoomed in, magnifying the image until its form became recognizable.

"Ummm… yeah. That's a Theia Observation Aerial Platform. Zoom in a bit more on the tail, okay Tara."

Her slender eyebrows knit together as she read off the call sign. "This makes no sense. This here TOAP's outta Farb AeroSpace Wing and its mission is either mission control or air recce. You know, intel gathering. But Urkyn's not been identified as a strategic target. And what's even odder is that I reviewed all the flight plans for today and not one TOAP was scheduled to leave the stables." A look of disbelief crossed her face and Erica grimaced. "I need to check into this. No orders were sent out, I'm sure. You sit tight; I'll get back to you."

As Daniel thanked them and delinked, Erica's mind was racing. *Something or somebody screwed up. And it wasn't me.*

***

"Definite tampering Sir," Pallav confirmed, his voice a reflection of calm while his mind tried to make sense of everything that he had uncovered. "It was no true professional job either, the perp left a trail of bread crumbs so wide and long that a blind man could've followed it on a dark and stormy night."

"Well, this sheds light on the incident at Great Plains."

Hidden on Gomalan's lap was a plate of savoury tarts that he'd been trying to eat for the past hour. Now cold and congealed, their appeal was lost to him. Hunger pangs growled and his empty stomach leapt in frustration. The old warrior sighed. *War always means hunger. At first, no time to eat; and later, nothing to eat*, he thought miserably before trying to understand the scope of the breach.

"Tell me again – what exactly are we talking about here? A singular occurrence, or is this widespread throughout the defence system?"

Gomalan could see the hologram of the big human clench his jaw. "Very serious, Sir. My findings should be discussed one-on-one and not via any other means – the Defence Holocom System may've been breached. At the moment I'm in Rolynda and it'll take me a few days to get back to headquarters. Until then, my interim recommendation to ensure the protection of our military installations has been given in person to the Security Company Commanders."

Gomalan's amber eyes glowed with anger at the impertinence of the alien's actions, but the grey-haired High Commander acknowledged the wisdom behind Pallav's words. Rolynda was indeed normally a two day trip, but this information was vital. Meryx was demanding results and any delay would be unacceptable.

"No later than tomorrow evening Kóbor. Find a way; you're resourceful."

A faint smile flickered across Pallav's broad face as he admired the vista of the broad River Panni Valley from a bunker on the outskirts of Bâcha. "Will do, Sir," he responded before his hologram faded into the ether.

Turning the tablet over in his hand, he frowned as he reflected on the depth of the intrigue that he'd uncovered. For the rebel infiltration was only the tip of the iceberg. This new revelation was buried so deep that no one would have ever found it lurking within the defence network. No one except a human hailing from a country where intrigue was as common as leaves on the trees. *Giving me über-access was probably the wrong thing my friend,* Pallav thought as he opened the tablet again, *when you need to conceal something like this.*

Fingerprint, iris scan, code and he was in once again. *How very careless can they be,* he thought at the extreme laxity of the Wessel security protocols. *My mother always told me to keep my nose out of things that didn't concern me. Well now, wasn't she wrong!* Tapping his finger against the screen, red letters danced menacingly before him.

TOP SECRET - SPECIAL OPERATIONAL INFORMATION WESSEL AEROSPACE FORCE

FRAGO 001 TO HIGH COMMANDER OP ORDER
REF: OP ORDER GOLDEN THUNDER

SITUATION: Information linking village of URKYN/ GEITENIA with creation of deadly bacterial-viral organisms responsible for recent outbreaks within our borders has surfaced. Further mass dissemination of contagion via imbedded Geiten agents expected within WESSELAN between 48 to 72 hrs from 7th day of month of Lenz, with the Geiten goal of complete eradication of Wesselan populace. To eliminate possibility of panic, reprisals and demonstrations within our borders, knowledge restricted to Commanders of 98 Bomber Sqn and 107 Fighter Sqn.
MISSION: 98 Bomber Sqn, supported by 107 Fighter Sqn, Wessel Aerospace Force, to attack the village of URKYN grid reference 162165 - 2330L 5th day of month of Lenz.

EXECUTION:
Concept of Ops: 98 Bomber Sqn will accomplish the complete destruction of URKYN with 12 x Stormfury Bombers attacking from the east across the River Panni Valley. The destruction of the entire village including its population is critical to this operation.

Tasks to Subordinate Units: 107 Fighter Squadron will employ 36 x Stryker Skykiller Fighters to accompany bombing raid and thereafter eliminate any pockets of resistance.

COORDINATING INSTRUCTIONS. No Change to Op Order.
SERVICE SUPPORT: No Change to Op Order
COMMAND AND SIGNALS: No Change to Op Order
ACKNOWLEDGE

HIGH COMMANDER WESSEL ARMED FORCES GOMALAN

CHAPTER 4 – GIVE ME BACK MY HOMETOWN

"Life is the art of drawing sufficient conclusions from insufficient premises."

– SAMUEL BUTLER

Jolanta's ears picked up at the sound of the door opening. Skidding across the floor, the child launched herself at Pallav and like a limpet, clung to his legs. "Hey there, little one," he said with a smile, picking the waif up in his arms and kissing her on a plump dusky cheek, so soft it reminded him of velvet. "Where's your mommy?"

Depositing his rucksack on the floor, he twirled the little alien girl in his arms and grinned as she squealed in delight before gently lowering her to the ground. With Jolanta jumping up and down in protest and begging for more attention, Tara appeared and looked in confusion at her husband.

"You weren't supposed to be home for a few more days," she said, pushing stray strands of hair behind her ears before being enveloped in his arms.

"You and me, we need to talk," he started ominously. Before his wife could argue, Pallav interrupted. "Right now. You think the neighbours would look after Jolanta for a few hours?"

Tara's world went cold. *Oh my God, he's found out about Daniel and me back in Urkyn. Shit! He's not about to overlook it this time, but what can I say? I'm an idiot!*

Wondering why his wife suddenly turned as white as a sheet and her breathing rate was over the roof, Pallav led Tara to the plush sofa. "You don't look so good," he said as he HomeLinked the couple next door, who conspiratorially winked at each other thinking that husband and wife wanted some quality time together after his absence.

Taking Pallav by the hands, Tara sighed in disappointment over her recent tryst. *How am I going to bring myself to admit it all to him. Once again.* But before she could confess to her transgressions, Pallav bolted to his feet and began searching the rooms, pulling up cushions, overturning tables and chairs, peering behind the artwork she'd just purchased, examining the light bulbs and lifting the carpets until he nodded in satisfaction and returned to his wife's questioning look.

"No surveillance devices. Good. I just had to make sure." Sitting beside her, Pallav exhaled long and hard. "Tara, there's something I need to tell you. You know what I've been up to, right? Well, it took me all of a day to find the breach."

As the colour came back to Tara's cheeks, Pallav scratched his head in confusion. "I would've been able to identify the issue right off the bat if it wasn't for that captain assigned to me as an escort officer. She really got in my way, steering me down rabbit holes and wasting time. Anyhow. After that, I mean it was so obvious I was surprised the Company Commanders hadn't found it, so I started to dive in. You know, if the Force Protection of the Wessel Defence Force is that inept, the High Commander needs to know about it, right?"

Tara stared with relief at her husband. *Thank God it's not what I thought. Just something he needs to get off his chest.* Nodding in agreement, a shade of a smile encouraged him to continue.

"Well, this is it. You know me, I always dig too deep. I also found something that I wasn't supposed to. A top-secret document that gives orders for Urkyn to be wiped off the face of the planet by the Wessel Aerospace Force. And for every living thing to be liquidated within the next few days. Oh, and the orders were signed by Gomalan."

Pallav shook his head in disbelief. "Tara, do you realize what this means?" he said softly. "Gomalan is going to make sure that our crew mates from the *Mayflower* are exterminated."

Without waiting for him to finish, Tara reached for the HomeLink System controls and watched as Erica's form materialized. Already in her pyjamas and with her long blonde braids swinging about her swollen bump, Erica looked ready to burst. "Hey there partners, what's up?"

Tara scrunched up her face. "Darling, we're going to come over for a little visit."

Pallav chimed in, "Is Fynn there? I need to see him ASAP."

As Erica looked in horror about her disheveled home, he added quickly, "Don't worry, we know you're no Suzy Homemaker. Just get your husband out of bed, I've got a mission for him."

Before Erica could argue, Pallav cut transmission and grabbed the keys to their Hover-V. The night was clear with the Moon of Haldane hanging overhead and while the couple trekked across the skies, domestic scenes played out beneath them in Wessel habitation units. People sitting down to dinner after a hard day at work, children being ferried to dance class. The pandemic seemed to have run its course in Wesselan, but at a cost. Many of the high-rise buildings were darkened, their occupants now only ghosts and memories.

Tara marvelled at the beauty of the evening, the unfamiliar stars glistening in the black velvet heavens, her husband's hand resting lightly on her thigh as they sped across the city. She thought about Daniel, of Lewis and Max and the times they had spent together as a pseudo-family, sleeping under soft furs and eating by campfire in the evenings with their Geiten neighbours of Urkyn. She could image his strong tanned hands caressing her, his hungry lips trailing kisses down her neck and she recoiled in horror and anguish at the thought of death screaming down from the skies, extinguishing his spark of vitality. Tipping her head back, Tara closed her eyes, willing the little Hover-V to surge faster along the skylanes. For so many lives depended on them – friends who had followed her across the galaxy and now sat companionably around smoky fires while the night cast a growing shadow over their lives.

The thrum of the engines reverberated throughout the vehicle as Pallav swooped down, the Hover-V weightlessly darting under the pilings of a bridge before swinging neatly around the corner of a magnificent tall cream-coloured building. Its veranda beckoned to them, bejewelled with brilliant flowers that glowed under the flickering porch light. Reversing gears, he forced the Hover-V down onto the docking pad, the abrupt jolt startling Tara from her reverie. As the little craft's doors swung up and open, Erica appeared and waved to the couple from the long window that ran the length of the stately home's front.

Pallav frowned and concern lined. his face. "I don't see Fynn." Erica's voice called out to them. "That's 'cause he's not here." Giving her new friend a hug, Erica could sense Tara's anxiety.

"So," Erica continued, her eyes narrowing in consternation as she cut to the chase. "What's going on? And what's this about Fynn? Why'd you guys need him anyway?" The strain on Tara transferred itself to the young woman, who searched their eyes with a mix of fear and hope.

"I was hoping he could help me out," Pallav replied as his glance stole about the room. The luxurious caramel-coloured leather sofa and oversized armchair complemented by a sleek marble coffee table seemed out of place amongst the bare walls and stone floor bereft of any carpeting.

"You wanna explain exactly what this help is then?" Erica asked, taking a seat and gesturing for the couple to join her. Instead, Pallav ran a finger over his lips, his look swearing them to silence. Tara placed a restraining hand on the young pilot as her husband then rampaged throughout the dwelling, hot on the hunt for any surveillance devices. Nodding in satisfaction, Pallav swallowed nervously.

"I need Fynn to carry out a rescue mission, and it's got to happen tonight. Time's running out. Where is he?"

Whipping her head about angrily, Erica breathed out through clenched teeth. "Why is it that everyone thinks only of Fynn in a crisis?" Rolling her eyes, Erica snorted. "He's stuck in medical quarantine; his test results came back positive for contact with the pandemic, and he won't be home for a few days."

The blood drained from Tara's face as the thought of her colleagues from the Space Ark *Mayflower* perishing in the bombing became a cruel reality and she turned in anguish to her husband. "Is there nothing we can do?"

Before her husband could respond Erica erupted, fatigue wearing away at her patience. "Will someone tell me what's going on here? You were mentioning a rescue mission for tonight." Her brows knit in suspicion. "And earlier today, Daniel linked in to beam me a hologram of a TOAP flying over their village. That I know wasn't supposed to be airborne." Erica glanced from Pallav to Tara in confusion. "Something's fishy going on here. Why do you need Fynn? If there's a rescue mission, normally a SAR bird out of Bâcha would be dispatched."

Reaching into his pocket, Pallav pulled out his comms device. Strictly forbidden by all rules to take into the secure zones, he knew, but then again, he never thought those orders were absolute when one's job was to keep the nation safe. Opening the screen, he thrust the device into Erica's hands and watched as her mouth flew open.

"Just give me one sec," she said, flying into the bedroom to pull her flight suit from the laundry basket only to reappear moments later with a look of determination on her face.

Her bright braids bound up in a crown atop her head, silver bars gleaming on the collar of her flight suit, a wide grin spread across her face and she nodded. "I'm ready. Let's go save the world."

***

Fires burned brightly as Daniel stepped into the ceremonial circle formed by a ring of flames and took his place next to Lestos. Packed to overflowing, it seemed that the entire village had turned out, some reclining on their haunches as if about to watch a movie in the local cinema. Children sat cross-legged at the feet of the young mothers and fathers who were casually gossiping by the dim light of the guttering torches. The entire atmosphere was nonchalant, almost one of merriment. That is, until the Council of Elders arrived, their grizzled white beards flowing regally down their chests, faces lined and weather-beaten. At that, the onlookers straightened up and the murmur of small talk that had floated across the evening breeze suddenly ceased. It was as if the winds themselves had been quieted.

The Elders shuffled to their places within the circle of fire to sit comfortably on plush ottomans. Shadows played across their stern features as they tucked withered arms into the sleeves of their tunics and appraised the two men within the circle – one, an old familiar friend with whom many of them had hunted and tended their flocks; the other – an outsider who brought with him many strange and alien ways. But the two must be reconciled, the old with the new, and harmony must be maintained. And so the Presider stood, his joints creaking in the silence as he let his eyes travel about the circle of the people of Urkyn.

It was some time before the Presider struck the ground with his ceremonial staff and motioned for Daniel and Lestos to come forward. With a flourish, his voice cracked out over the assembly. "Geiten of Urkyn! This Assembly has been called to discuss the apparatus that the Clan Mayflower has recently erected. We have all seen the power of this new device and its promise to deliver life-giving water to our village, even during the months when the Breath of Ru is upon us. This…this wind turbine, as it is so called, brings with it the possibility of change that is as wide-reaching as the desert sands of the Empty Quarter. Tonight, this is what we must explore and resolve. And on the morrow, once the fires of the circle have cooled, and the words spoken tonight remain only as memories on the ever-blowing winds, we will continue on, as one people, with one rule, under one tribe."

Shuffling forward, Lestos took the baton from the Presider's gnarled hands and thrust it high into the darkness of the night. "I speak for the Clan Marag, and I am against this new device. Listen to me, people of Urkyn. For centuries, our traditions have guided us on our pathway through the difficulties of life. Our beliefs tie us together, bringing a sense of belonging… carving order in an otherwise chaotic world while all around us swirls a vortex of turmoil. The Geiten traditions, handed down from father to son, from mother to daughter, are a testament to an identity that has flourished over the centuries. We live our lives simply, as our forefathers did before us, following the movements of the seasons.

"In harmony with nature, we care for our families and the flocks upon which our lives depend. During the months when the Breath of Ru hold sway over our lands, we take refuge in the cool alpine pastures of the Tagar Mountains, fattening our herds on the lush grasses, making the alpine cheeses that we sell in the markets, and hunting for fragrant golden honey. Tiny jewel-like berries and pungent herbs that scramble over the rocky slopes are harvested, while our children collect the nutritious ripe nuts from the trees that grow in the valleys of the Altai Mountains. And when the days grow cooler and the nights grow longer, when the young herders and their families travel down the well-trodden paths into the valley of Urkyn, and when the village elders and the little ones return from the distant southern climes, we gather together again in unity, welcoming old friends, re-awakening acquaintances and making matches. It is our way.

"My fellow Geiten, we lead a privileged life, following in the footsteps of our parents, our grandparents, while teaching and leading the future of our people. What the newcomers bring to us may seem like a gift. A gift that would cause our people to remain in Urkyn, not only during the months of the Cooling, but also when the Breath of Ru descends upon us. What would this do to our people? It would disrupt our way of life. It would transform us into an unnatural tribe, one that would have more in common with the Wessels than our own brethren. Is this what we want? To live like the Wessels? To be confined in buildings, restricted by borders, to know limits in our lives? Do you never again want to drink from the crystal mountain springs that burst from the great goddess Deneb's body? Do you not want to touch the clouds as you ascend the rocky slopes? Or do you want to live where every day is the same, where you wake to see the sun rising from behind the ridge onto this dusty village?

"Make no mistake my fellow Geiten. This is about our way of life, which the introduction of the wind turbine can dramatically change if we allow it to be used year-round. It is for this reason that the Clan Marag stands against the wind turbine and that we continue to uphold the age-old Geiten traditions, by not allowing this new device to corrupt our lives."

Bowing ever so slightly towards the Council of Elders, Lestos wordlessly passed the baton to Daniel and stepped back into the shadows. A low murmur rose from the crowd of villagers who waited for the fair-haired alien to speak. Angelo shoved his way to the front and locking his eyes on the leader of the Clan Mayflower, nodded confidently for him to begin. Daniel slowly surveyed the gathering, concentrating lastly on the Presider whose milky-white eyes regarded him coolly. Lowering his head he smiled. *I never thought I'd be making a presentation by torchlight to a group of nomads.* Shaking his head, the smile still flirting on his lips, he threw out an arm, pointing in the darkness to the ridge upon which the blades of the turbine quietly turned in the wind.

"Up there, high on the ridge, is a device that is common on the planet from which the Clan Mayflower originated. Invented thousands of years ago, the people from Earth used primitive windmills not only to pump water but also to mill grain. And we can use this Earth-technology on Deneb to our advantage. Water pulled from deep within the planet is being stored at the base of the hillside to provide us with a guaranteed source, a reservoir, during the hot season you call the Breath of Ru.

"In my country, windmills were also responsible for opening up land for civilization to flourish. For wherever there is water, there can be life. Crops can be grown, herds can be watered, and people can build permanent villages that will flourish and grow over the years. No longer will you need to pack up your pehas at the end of the Cooling and make the long migration with your flocks to the Tagar Mountains. No longer will the elderly and the children need to leave their hearths and venture for weeks to the southern encampments, journeys during which they are subject to the ravages of hunger and marauding beasts. The wind turbine will empower the village of Urkyn, taking us to the forefront of the great Geiten civilization.

"Lestos talked at great length of tradition, and you see before you a man who is not of your people. One who you might say cannot understand and therefore does not respect the Geiten traditions. And this is partly true for my clan hails from a faraway planet, a planet that was destroyed by war and famine, a planet that was beset with disease and sickness. So you see, we humans too had to deal with drought and scorching heat.

"Some nations chose to stick their heads in the sand, while others adapted and engineered solutions to embrace the power of nature. The wind is one such power and we learned to harness it, to power our cities and to fight the encroachment of drought. And where there was water, life were able to thrive. Those nations that chose to allow nature to take its course suffered grievously. You can say that their people were living in harmony with their lands, just as their forefathers had before them, and yes, that would be true. But time changes everything and there is a time for change. And that time is now, the time to embrace the change that we have brought to Urkyn, to strengthen our village, to empower our people with choices. And so I put the choice before you – to accept the gift of the wind turbine to buttress Urkyn against the harshness of the Denebian seasons, or to turn your back on progress and walk in the footsteps of the ancestors into a future that is only but a mirror image of the past."

The Presider nodded as Daniel passed the baton to him and stood on wobbly legs. Throwing open his arms, he waited in silence as the villagers shuffled in the firelight. "We have heard two sides of this issue – to ignore the power of this device, or to adopt the new technology as our own. People of Urkyn, we are one cohesive tribe. Our strength lies in maintaining this unity. It has always been this way. Therefore, we must decide as one people on the path ahead – should our encampment become a permanent village, with fixed structures and services? For this is the essence of the question."

Without warning, an eerie sound echoed over the gathering, as down from the ridge plunged a colony of hog-nosed bregas, their leathery wings tucked tightly against their reptilian bodies. Screeching shrilly, they plummeted to the valley floor below, their dagger-like teeth barred as they zigzagged and wound their way about the flickering torches, devouring the nocturnal insects that milled about like sparks in the firelight. Children shrieked and hid within their mothers' arms while the Elders turned inwards, their ears deafened to the cacophony, their eyes blind to the panic amongst their people. Noiselessly their lips moved, the sound of their fierce debate drowned out by the cries of the swirling and swooping creatures. Then vaulting up as one body, the bregas suddenly receded into the inky darkness from which they came. The Elders shook their heads and wrung their hands as the discussion began to wind down. Babies bawled for their fur-lined nests, children closed their eyes in fear, and a feeling of shared uneasiness descended upon the assembly.

Grey heads finally nodded in agreement as a consensus was reached. The old men turned in unison to face the crowd and clutching the baton, the Presider broke the silence. "The Council has ruled in favour of the wind turbine. We shall accept the march of progress."

***

Sitting on the forks of the Sirga and Panni Rivers, its camouflaged hangars and orderly edifices stretching along the eastern shores, Air Marshal Farb Aerospace Wing was a hive of activity that sunny day. Row upon row of Stryker Skykillers with their dull desert colours nestled between the gigantic Meganeurs and Stormfury Bombers while Nyoerd Helocruisers sat dwarfed in their shadows. Crews sauntered along the flight line, servicing the predatory beasts that bristled with missiles and cannons, waiting for the moment when they would lock their prey in their sights. Bright yellow mules were pulling the powerful colossi into hardened shelters, out of harm's way from any marauding Fyjer attack that managed to breach Air Marshal Farb's advanced C-RAM system.

Deep in the bowels of one of the squat hangars, festooned with disruptive camo-netting, the 98th Bomber Squadron's commander bit his fingernails as he sat facing his counterpart from the 107th Fighter Squadron. "Just so we're clear on this... after the drop, the infantry are going in to mop up? I mean, they're not using the RAITs?"

Lt Col Scooter Ardelorn shook his head. "Negative. Your guys drop, my warbirds scream in and strafe any survivors. Then after a pause, real live infantry and not those robotic critters go in to clear whoever and whatever remain in the rubble."

The Commanding Officer of the 98th trembled unconsciously and looked away. "Seems like the big guy wants this place to be erased from the map entirely. Leave no survivors type mission. And we both know from Stumpy that this here stuff about the disease being designed and spread from Urkyn's just pure bullshit."

"Yeah...Stumpy's report from his TOAP mission indicated that Urkyn's a peaceful village. By the gods, this's nothing short of insanity! Before this," Lt Col Cookie Cooke grumbled, waving the message that began the madness, "we were taking out North Geitenian Army Base then crossing into Fyjer airspace to knock out the installations at Tagar Mountains. But cancelled so we can obliterate a civilian village?"

The commander of the 98th Bomber Squadron threw the message full of falsehoods to the floor.

"For the sake of the Ur! Cookie – y'think we should push back?"

The grey-haired Lt Col rubbed his forehead as he pondered the senselessness of this attack, unwarranted and futile in his view, before sighing in exasperation. "It's hopeless Scooter. The infantry've already moved out for their attack. The gears are in motion, my friend. Tomorrow, we go in with guns ablazing, and bombs ablasting, and trust that the gods forgive us for our sins."

CHAPTER 5 - WHOSE BOMB WAS IT ANYHOW?

Shall I tell you what the real evil is? To cringe to the things that are called evils, to surrender to them our freedom, in defiance of which we ought to face any suffering.

– LUCIUS SENECA

Pushing her sleeves up, Tara stood in front of her husband. "So how'd I look," she asked, swimming in Erica's spare flight suit.

Trying to hide a grin on his face, Pallav bent down to cuff the pant legs that promised to trip the diminutive astrophysicist. "You'll pass muster." Standing back, he surveyed his wife with a critical eye while Erica passed her a flight cap.

"Okay team, let's make tracks," he announced before vaulting into the family Hover-V and soaring through the early evening skies.

Hidden from sight and hunkered down behind the now empty gymnasium of Air Marshal Farb Aerospace Wing, Pallav pulled three orange lozenge-shaped wafers from an envelope and passed them around.

"Gramblers," he explained, holding one up before placing it on the roof of his mouth. "Touch it once with your tongue to activate it, it transmits thoughts between us. No breaking silence from now on."

"So handsome, you can hear me now?" Erica asked telepathically, incredulous of the device.

The big man blushed in embarrassment. "That's correct, so watch what you're thinking there. Okay, everyone got it all straight then? Let's synchronize watches."

"Darling, no one wears a watch anymore except you," Tara chuckled and brandishing her multi-function comms device wiggled it in front of her husband who raised his eyebrows and shrugged.

"Philistines!" he transmitted to a chorus of laughter. "Okay then. Recapping," he continued more seriously, "Tara, your pass'll take you into

Farb's nerve centre where you hack into the defence network. Once you're in and have sabotaged the satellite tracking systems, you let us know. In the meantime, I've already submitted a fabricated requisition to get MEG 86292 towed out from its shelter and prepped for a bogus mission. It's sitting pretty on the flight line, all ready and waiting for blast off."

Brandishing the cube with the fictitious details, Pallav handed it over to Erica who raised an eyebrow and turned to Tara.

"So, you're sure about Cepheus-9 then? I mean, how'd we know the team's not gonna give the locals a big blast of bacteria and it's like Death on Deneb all over again?"

Pallav swallowed and his mind went into overdrive, for he had completely forgotten about the humans' role as carriers. "They're two entirely different species," he replied weakly, and his guts churned until Tara hooked her arm through Erica's.

The diminutive professor patted her friend's hand reassuringly. "And I heard it through the grape vine that the Denebian Institute of Virology sent samples of the bactovirus to the Collective so they can develop immunity protocols. Nothing to fear, girlfriend."

"Got it. I'll make sure the team's aware. Just one more thing – the gang'll be okay on Cepheus-9, won't they?"

Tara smiled reassuringly. "When my great big hulk of a husband here got me this fantastic new job of housekeeper and cook, my astrophysicist brain started to atrophy. So Magdar suggested I look into booking us a girls' weekend away. As if that would solve everything. She was thinking Lacerta, but I mean, everyone goes there. It's like the Dominican Republic of the Collective."

"You're a braver woman than me, planning a trip with Magdar." Erica whistled in amazement. "That'd be like swimming with the sharks."

Pallav narrowed his eyes and groaned. "Chick talk," he thought disparagingly before screwing up his face in embarrassment, as he realized the others could hear what was going through his brain.

Ignoring her husband, Tara took Erica by the elbow. "That's when I began investigating the other planets in the Collective and voilà, I hit on Cepheus-9, another planet with Earth-like conditions. The Collective's full of them, who knew? Anyhow, what you've got to be careful of though is that it's densely settled. The coordinates I programmed in take you to one of the only islands that isn't, and that's because it's a wildlife refuge."

Erica grimaced. "Like dangerous fanged animals roaming around, waiting to get their first taste of human flesh?"

"No, nothing like that," Tara explained calmly. "The Cepheusians killed off all the big game years ago. Birds – lots of them too; amphibians, lizards, and lagoons filled with rainbow coloured fish, that's all."

"And remember Erica, you're not going to be putting down," Pallav reminded the space jockey. "You get into orbit, they take the shuttle down, and you get your pregnant belly back here in time for Fynn to help deliver your baby girl."

A quick thumbs up in confirmation, then Erica looked up questioningly at Pallav. "So you're sure now the explosion's gonna be big enough to burn the crap out of the hangars?"

"Yes Ma'am. Fire'll be hotter than hell. They'll never realize they're missing a plane. This Base's going to be lit up like a Roman candle." Pallav smiled at the thought, his itchy fingers ready to unleash chaos. "Once the balloon goes up, you'll have enough cover to high tail it out of Dodge. The Base'll go into lock down a few minutes after the big bang. So Tara, as soon as the systems are offline, get the hell out of there."

"Got it," she replied, anxious to get the job done. "I think that's everything Pallav. We're ready to go."

Erica's blue eyes shone with excitement and she hugged Tara before planting a quick kiss on Pallav's reddening cheek. "Well gang, wish me luck."

"You listen to me fly-girl," Tara admonished, taking Erica's hand. "Don't take any risks. If it looks like security's too hot, abort the mission. If anything goes wrong in Geitenia, put down at the landing coordinates and we'll come and get you."

"Fynn would never forgive us otherwise," Pallav added before putting on a serious face. "Okay, let's do this."

Tara pulled her cap down and shoved her hands in her pockets before casually sauntering off to the bunker, while Erica threw Pallav a quick salute and waddled off, her phony mission at the ready. Pallav felt his stomach churn with anxiety while he waited for word from his wife. Nerves on edge, he stared at his great-grandfather's ancient wristwatch as the seconds ticked off into minutes and he swallowed nervously, mentally reviewing the placement of the explosives to pass the time.

"I'm in the Meganeur and ramping up for take-off," Erica's thoughts portalled through the Gramblers. "Tara, how you doing?"

"The access codes got me into the system okay. I'm just taking it offline... right about... now."

"Okay, we're good to go. Tara, RV back at the Shop-A-Mart docking pad. Erica, you ready to roll?"

"Affirmative. Fans are turning, lift off can be achieved instantaneously."

"Alright gang, hang on to your hats. I'm about to bring the 4th of July to Farb."

***

He couldn't relax, try as he might. High atop Farb's Space Control Tower, Air Marshal Caydnn watched nervously as the pride of the Wessel Aerospace Force jockeyed into position, a long procession of Stormfury bombers taxiing down the runway, readying for launch. The orange glow of the Denebian sun lit up the sky in fiery glory as it slipped below the horizon and soon, Cadynn reflected, the days would be blanketed in the stifling summer heat once again.

But this year, there's no way we can slip away for a vacation in the mountains. Ah well, this war won't last long. Not now, anyhow, he thought sourly as the lead plane's engines roared to life.

Caydnn clenched his jaw in anger.

This is so fucked up, he sighed. *By the gods, Gomalan's gone mad. Imagine – the Geiten – capable of somehow designing a microbiological agent! Those pathetic ignorant geiten-herders – impossible! Goffa's propaganda and lies! But what can I do? An order's an order, after all.*

Off in the distance, the Moon of Haldane was riding amongst an armada of clouds.

It's such a beautiful evening, Caydnn thought as delicate pink wisps floated like ribbons through the dusky sky. The peace of the night was cut asunder as the deep pounding of the Stormfury bombers' engines resounded across the flight line, the sleek Stryker Skykillers joining their burly-winged brethren readying for the evening launch, eager to spread fire and fury from above.

Checking the time, Cadynn's lips tightened into a thin slash across his broad face. *Ten minutes to go... I'll be home in half an hour then. Right on time to take Delia on a walk before bed.* His thoughts meandered to his family's new hound and he chuckled absentmindedly at how it would be sitting loyally by the door awaiting for his arrival.

But something was disturbing him, something incongruous with the mission at hand.

By the gods! What's that Meganeur doing over there? Tail number MEG 86292.

Caydnn pulled the senior controller over by her sleeve and pointed off into the distance where the giant behemoth sat, fans spinning, ready for blast off.

Zooming in on the giant airship, Major Lincoln shook her head. "I don't recall seeing a Meganeur launch on the system Sir, but let me check." Bringing up the display arms, the two scanned the data that was visible in sparkling clarity, suspended in the air before them.

His brow furrowed, Caydnn turned angrily to Lincoln. "Contact that pilot ASAP, and scrub their mission," he barked, wondering why Gomalan himself would authorize a transport detail in the midst of an air attack.

The man's gone mad, he grumbled to himself furiously.

"Sir, the system seems to have gone off-line. I can't... I can't get through. I'm trying to override the maintenance function." Lincoln's fingers worked furiously as Caydnn fumed silently. "I don't understand," she continued, her voice raising in panic. "Nothing's responding. We're effectively mute."

Caydnn grimaced and walked over to Corporal Bayes who sat transfixed at his display, intimidated by the brass in the tower that night. "Sometimes," the Commander explained testily, "it's necessary to forego technology and use the old-fashioned methods. Bayes, is it? You run over and get the attention of that pilot and tell whoever it is to stand down. Got it?"

The young man nodded and raced off. Caydnn relaxed at the sight of the corporal lopping across the flight line, until a hulking giant figure poked out from around a hangar only to quickly pace away.

Why, that's Kóbor, isn't it? What the devil's he doing here? He's supposed to be down south, finishing the inspections of the military installations.

Snatching up the Meganeur requisition once again, Caydnn scanned it quickly and the errors jumped out at him as plain as the nose on his face. "Dammit! We've got to stop that Meganeur from lifting off! Lincoln, someone's trying to ..."

The sky was suddenly splashed with a brilliant blast of orange, followed by black billowing mushrooms of smoke that burst through the air. Caydnn watched as the hangars seemed to lift up and crumble, then collapsed before his eyes. The unfortunate Cpl Bayes raced in terror for his life only to be picked off his feet by the blast waves and flung into oblivion. Farb was a panorama of fire as great tongues of greedy flames leapt about amidst the deafening roars of the detonations. Caydnn and Lincoln vaulted down the stairs, racing to be free from the tottering structure, when a powerful explosion tore the footings from the tower, ripping apart the control room and flinging it in pieces through the air.

But why, Kóbor? Caydnn wondered as the life ebbed from his broken body.

For many years after, the citizens of Bâcha would remember the night that Farb burned, when the pride of the Wessel Aerospace Force's fleet had been obliterated – mangled and shredded – its pilots incinerated in the fiery pyre. But what remained secret was that on a distant launch pad, a giant beast of gleaming metal had soared into the air amidst the smoke and fire – a phoenix rising from the flames – as Erica rocketed through the carnage to save her one-time crewmates from death and destruction.

***

Chief of Police Tuya Pol sat braiding her daughter Hinodé's long dark hair while her two sons jumped back and forth like crickets trying to bag the hologram of an elusive Capacian Eyrox. Suddenly, her husband Galen rushed into the living room.

"Boys, switch that thing off," he shouted and depressing a button, the outer walls of the Pol habitation unit became at once transparent.

"What the...?" Tuya exclaimed at the evil orange glow that dominated the night sky. It was then that she noticed the flashing red light emanating from under her sons' discarded sweaters, and grabbing her comms device, the form of the Department Head of the Wessel Emergency Response Department coalesced before her.

The hawk-like man scanned the living room and nodded at Galen before addressing Tuya. "Chief Pol, Farb's engulfed in flames; there's been a massive explosion. Extra security is necessary to cordon off the area until the fires are under control and have been extinguished." Behind him Tuya could see the ERD cameras zoomed in on the Base, First Responders swarming in.

"I'm on my way. You can count on the full cooperation from the Bâcha Police Force. My officers will be on the scene ASAP," she replied, racing into the bedroom and vaulting into her uniform.

Twisting his head around as casualty reports started to roll in, the Department Head nodded grimly before abruptly cutting comms.

Her daughter stared up as Tuya reappeared, quickly knotting the hated tie about her neck before throwing on her uniform tunic. "Mommy, can you finish my hair first," Hinodé queried while her brothers, Paimen and Tailen, sat cross-legged in front of the holoscreen, transfixed by the catastrophe that had struck the nearby military airfield.

Striding over to his wife, Galen handed Tuya her cap and kissed her on the cheek. "I'll get the kids to bed, and honey – I don't think I'll be waiting up tonight."

"No need." Shaking her head at the eerie sight that filled the holoscreen, Tuya added darkly. "It looks like this'll be an all-nighter." Wrapping the kids in a quick hug, she raced to the door before calling over her shoulder on the way out, "Geiten sabotage again. They'll be paying for it before the night is over, the filthy scum."

As the sound of her Hover-V slowly receded, Galen contemplated Tuya's parting shot and shook his head disapprovingly. *She's so sure about the Geiten; it's all so black and white for her,* he reflected as he pulled out the braid and began to comb his daughter's long silky hair. *There's no comfort when the grey shades of doubt weave themselves through the thoughts colouring our minds.*

***

Urkyn: The Circle of Fire

Marco punched the air jubilantly and hugged Daniel within the Council circle.

"Thank God we won't have to make the trek to those mountains," Carmen whispered to her husband Angelo, relieved that there was no need to pack and cart their belongings up the torturous distant mountain trails.

"No, thank Daniel," he responded with a smile. "This is all his doing." The Mayflower Clan huddled together, grateful that some permanency might bring the familiar back into their lives. Thoughts of a small medical clinic materialized in Dom's mind where he could practice medicine and

Barb would offer her services as a dietician. Jian pondered on the martial arts studio he left behind when Alice had ordered his wife Hoshi and him to attend the meeting that fateful night back on Earth, taking from them everything that they had built over the years.

However, the jubilant mood did not extend to everyone. Lestos and Nagib grumbled in the shadows, the elderly man gathering allies against the ruling of the Elders. "This changes nothing," he groused to those milling about him. "The Elders have been corrupted; they do not speak for us."

Raising an eyebrow Nagib retorted, "But father, the ruling was a clear majority. If we are to follow the ways of our people, must we not also uphold the decision of our own Council?"

Murmurs and agitated voices reverberated about the circle as herders joined Lestos.

"Before the sunrise, we should leave with our flocks."

Nagib shrugged his shoulders in defeat and slunk into the shadows to find Charra and their children while the whispering began from dissenting tongues.

"I'm with you."

"We can break from the village of Urkyn, it's happened before."

"Silence!"

The Presider held the baton high and waited for calm to descend upon the assembly. "Our decision has been made. I call for the circle to be broken."

As the fires were extinguished and the villagers returned to their pehas to a sleepless night, troubled voices rose through the dark. The sounds of harnesses jingling and the bleating of the geiten mixed with the clip-clop of their tiny hooves on the rocky ground. Hushed voices rustled in the night air before a stillness once more descended on the village.

Having tucked Lewis and Max under their warm hide covers, Daniel sat outside staring into his dying fire. Mesmerized by the sparks arching heavenward, his mind was a thousand miles away as Pat, panting heavily and accompanied by Renzo, trotted up.

"Look," he gasped, pointing to a series of brilliant lights that seemed to grow ever larger. Catching his breath, hands on his knees, Pat and Renzo exchanged glances as Daniel squinted at the blinding points of light that veered behind the ridge.

"Those belong to a Meganeur," Pat stated, straightening up.

***

Wesselan Defence Headquarters

The giant alien stood ramrod straight before them, hands clasped behind his back and eyes staring unblinkingly ahead while Meryx and Gomalan digested the latest in a series of bloody attacks against Wesselan. Behind them, a wall of holoscreens glowed orange and red as 3D images of the explosions lit up the presidential office. Sweat flowed in rivulets down Pallav's back as he relived the moment when the blast waves from his explosions threw him violently to the pavement, stunning him with its ferocity until Tara appeared and pulled him away to safety.

Thank the Lord that my wife never obeys anything I ask of her, he thought, knowing that if she had returned to the docking pad, his life may have been ended in the fiery hell of his own making.

The image suddenly shifted from the blast site to an undisclosed location within Wesselan, mercifully tearing Pallav from his reverie. Masked and dressed from head to toe in black, hands on her hips in defiance, the spokesperson of the Black Hide sneered into the reporter's holocapture.

"Great Plains. Khulan. Dilem. And now Air Marshal Farb. Your mighty aerospace wings – attacked and destroyed by those who you deem inferior. You Wessels, sitting now in your cozy homes – you are no longer safe. Your aerospace force has lost its teeth; your army is impotent to stop us."

The black-clad woman paused to laugh maliciously, and Pallav's green eyes were a reflection of shock. *The Geiten are taking responsibility for Farb*, he thought incredulously, breathing a sigh of relief.

"Three generations ago," she continued, her voice rising in pitch, "our people were forcefully removed from the western banks of the River Panni from where the water once flowed freely to peaceful Geiten encampments. And little by little, our rights have been eroded. We have been exploited as scapegoats, vilified in our beliefs, forced to exist in a world of drought. And now our people within Wesselan are being rounded up and thrown in Collection Centres."

Something very familiar about the figure in black struck Pallav - the voice, the posture - he wracked his brains trying to place the black-clad woman.

"After three generations though..." the reporter interjected, "I mean, this is truly ancient history..."

"Ancient history? Ha! Our nation's knowledge is handed down from mother to daughter, father to son. The experiences and memories of the Elders define us, we live our past on a daily basis. And no more will we allow the Wessels to dictate our lives. The Black Hide will strike again, mark my words, rising up against Wessel tyranny to overthrow the stinking corruption of your nation. This is our beginning, but soon it will be your end."

The woman in black stood ramrod straight in triumphant, flinging her head back while thrusting her right hand up in a tight fist as the images on the holoscreen faded into the ether. That's it! She's given herself away, Pallav realized with a start. For on her middle finger was nestled that magnificent ring sporting a gigantic blood-red stone.

CHAPTER 6 - BY THE LIGHT OF THE MOON

You cannot escape the responsibility of tomorrow by evading it today.

– ABRAHAM LINCOLN

The sand sucked at his legs as he raced from the village, stumbling over rocks, vaulting over the thorny bushes that caught at his pant legs while behind him, the sounds of Pat and Renzo's frenzied breathing spurred him on. The darkness of the night was complete as the trio scrambled up the rock face, clinging onto scraggly branches and clawing for finger holds. The rhythmic whirr of the wind turbine grew louder as he crested the hill and Daniel stopped for breath, waiting for the others.

A platoon of clouds parading across the skies suddenly parted, and from their ranks the Moon of Haldane peaked ever so briefly, throwing its silvery light across the Denebian landscape. But even without its celestial illumination, Daniel knew exactly what sat at the base of the ridge. He had seen it before, its bloated carcass floating from the skies in an act that seemed so impossible he had to convince himself he was not in a dream where magic reigned. The creature dominated the Geitenian desert - like a whale out of the water the Meganeur lay, its fans still turning, its hull alive as static electricity jigged like blue imps across its surface. And from it, a figure emerged ever so gingerly, its gait awkward and constricted. Stretching momentarily, it began a cumbersome trek towards the ridge.

"That's Erica," Pat whispered and bounded down the sharp drop with great strides, careless of the litter of rocks and thorns underfoot. Raising an eyebrow, Daniel watched as Renzo ran behind Pat, and with the wisdom that comes with age, he cautiously picked his way down the steep path as the voices of his young counterparts joined happily with the pilot.

"There's no time to waste," she said and heedless of a greeting, grabbed Daniel by the forearm. A gleam of fear shone in her eyes, as she turned to Pat impatiently, "You go back and get the others together. Bring them here, and I'll get ready for lift off."

The young man gasped still catching his breath, while Daniel shook his head. "Erica, I don't know what's going on, but no one's going anywhere until I get some answers."

"Dr. Radu, we don't have much time," she declared in a plaintive tone. "We only have a few hours to get you out of here. The Wessels - they know!"

A thousand questions raced through Daniel's mind and he allowed them to course over him momentarily. *They know! They know…that we caused the pandemic…and now…we're in serious danger! But where's Fynn? Why would he ask Erica to come to us when any day their baby'll be born! And where are Tara and Kóbor? We can't leave them behind!*

Erica threw her hands up in the air in desperation. "Now," she said to Pat, pushing him in the darkness of the night. "You've got to go!"

Daniel looked at the spent youth and realizing that he would have more success in rounding up the troops, he grabbed Pat by the shoulders just as he was about to stumble off. "You and Renzo stay here. Help Erica get ready for launch. I'll be back as soon as I can with everyone."

But how? he wondered as he surged back up the steep ridge. *What made them suspect us? And what's going on that we have to clear out ASAP? I suppose they advised the other nations - it just hasn't trickled down to Urkyn yet. Then we're no longer safe – there's no haven for us anywhere on Deneb! I gotta keep it quiet then; not tip off the tribe. I can't even let a whisper get out.*

His feet had wings as he raced over the cool sands, skirted the treacherous stones and jumped across the little drainage canals that they had dug from the crest of the ridge and through the parched ground. The fires were banked, glowing red and orange, as he skid to a halt in front of the Morelli dwelling. *No time to waste*, he repeated to himself as he burst within, the darkness of the peha enveloping him.

"What the?" It was Carmen, sleepily rising to her feet and reaching for a stout staff to confront the unwanted intruder.

"It's Daniel, don't panic," he gasped as he took the staff from Carmen's raised hand. *What the hell am I saying, it is a panic*, he realized as the woman relaxed and rooted about, lighting an oil lamp.

Angelo pushed the hair out of his eyes and raised up on one elbow. "What're you doing here at this time of the night?"

A loud yawn broke the silence as Marco stretched and pulling a shirt over his bare torso, got to his feet.

Daniel threw the younger Morelli his pants. "No time to explain. Get dressed and quietly rouse all the others. We have to evacuate Urkyn immediately. I'll explain later."

The Morelli peha was a buzz of activity as the three quickly donned their clothing and set off in all directions to gather their companions while Daniel returned to his dwelling where inside his two boys slept soundly. Shaking Lewis awake, Daniel instructed him to dress before readying his younger brother for their night-time exodus. Max laughed gleefully as they met up with the others in the quadrangle between the Mayflower pehas, so excited was he at a nocturnal ramble while Lewis sidled over to his friend Teuvo who was eager to embark on this new adventure.

His voice lowered to a hush, Daniel signalled to the little group to follow in his footsteps as they made their way across the jagged ridge that rose from the desert, leaving the village of Urkyn behind them in the gloom. Confused and sleepy, the *Mayflower* crew huddled around Daniel at the base of the ridge and gaped in awe at the Meganeur, its fans kicking up the gritty sand, ready for launch.

Renzo rushed from the bowels of the metal colossus, ushering them inside while searching for his father and younger sister. As the crew climbed into the cargo hold, the young man pulled his father aside, a strained look on his face. "Dad, I'm staying put," he shouted to Dom over the roar of the engines. "Well," he continued, "actually I was going to tell you earlier, but with the wind turbine and the meeting tonight, I haven't found the time."

"What do you mean?" Dom asked. "We're actually all clueless as to why we we're even here – all I know is that Daniel said it was urgent."

Renzo screwed up his face in a grimace. "Yeah, well... the shit's hit the fan and we've got to evacuate this place. But listen Dad, I'm promised to Lila, you know - the Geiten girl from the Resul clan? She left with her family to the Glodati Mountains after the decision the Elders made tonight. I was just about to let you know...I'm going with her."

Dom reached out to his son. "First I lose your mother, and now you," Dom moaned. "Come with us, then find Lila later."

Renzo shook his head sadly, hugging his father and sister while Pat helped settle the crew into the cargo-net seats. "No Dad, I'm sorry but I've come all this way across the universe to find Lila and I'm not gonna lose her now. Not now, not ever."

Erica's voice crackled across the cargo hold. "Ready for lift. Everyone get strapped in and get ready to pull some G's."

As the ramp began to close, Renzo broke from his family and jumped down from the Meganeur to watch as the engines screamed to life. Sand and small pebbles whipped through the air and the young man covered his face with an upturned hand while he fought back the tears that threated to fall. As the airship lifted from the ground with a nimbleness that belied its immense size, Renzo turned and quickly made his way along the well-trod path that would lead him to the Glodati Mountains and to the alien girl who had captured the young human's heart.

***

Tax'n narrowed his eyes as Captain Bafa Villutomi rushed to him and with a squeal threw herself into his arms. He sniffed distastefully, disgusted with the charade he had to play and repulsed by the Wessel Officer who he'd promised to take as a wife.

Still, he thought, *it's a small price to pay if the Black Hide's to win the freedom of our people.*

His thoughts shifted to the stupid woman who imagined he cared for her when all they needed was fodder – someone expendable – someone who didn't matter - to be thrown in the firing line if the balloon went up.

And then there's tonight, he reflected as his body shivered involuntarily in response to her hungry lips on his mouth.

"I did it," she gushed enthusiastically. "And it was all too easy!"

Planting kisses on the reluctant Tax'n, Bafa gurgled in his arms. "You were spot on Tax'n. I didn't even care one jot, not one, when I came face to face with the burned out buildings and the torn up corpses of the Wessel soldiers when I was taking that big oaf of an alien colonel around on his inspections."

Tax'n looked shocked at his sham of a fiancée who so easily turned her coat for a little bit of Geiten honey. Shaking off the surprise, he watched her for any signs of duplicity. "That big alien, he's the Inspector of the Wesselan Defence Installations. He can't be as dumb as you think. But you say he never suspected anything then?"

"Nu-uh," she trilled, pulling him closer to her and Tax'n momentarily repressed a shudder of loathing at the thought of coupling with a Wessel.

"He's big and dumb. Never said more than two words to me. Looked at things, didn't take evidence, no holograms, no notes, no – he just shook his head from time to time like an aurox in harness. Seems like the High Commander wasted a promotion on that lump."

The others laughed raucously at the description of the newly promoted Inspector, who foolishly trusted their Wessel plant.

"But I wonder," Tax'n said breathlessly as her tongue caressed his neck in searing circles. "I wonder… who really did destroy the air base at Bâcha then?"

Suddenly, the delights of Bafa fell away. Pushing her away rudely, he sat up and faced her, his opal eyes serious and questioning.

Bafa raised an eyebrow and shrugged. "Does it really matter? I mean, we took ownership of that too."

A few of the others nodded nervously in agreement, uneasy with Tax'n's treatment of the young woman. Walking over to a decanter, she poured out two glasses of Vulpeculan brandy and handed one to Tax'n who sniffed at it delicately. Loathing the act of drinking the foul substance, he knew he must play the game and so he clinked glasses before throwing the burning liquid down his throat in one quick motion.

"It matters." But before he could expound on the subject, the Black Hide himself sauntered into the confines of the shelter and smiled at the little ruse that Tax'n was playing out so well.

"Bafa, you amaze me once again," the Black Hide said in an ingratiating manner. Sidling up to her, the leader took her chin in his rough hands and smiled into her beaming face. "We have you to thank, only you Bafa, for providing us with the bogus passes and the access codes. Without your help, we never could've succeeded in destroying the three enemy bases."

Quick as a snake, the Black Hide rounded on Tax'n, his deep voice sharpening as he leaned in and grabbing the young rebel by his unbuttoned tunic, he twisted the coarse material in his hands. "Now while your woman's been working, you've been idle. Look at you, you're a disgrace." Releasing Tax'n, he shoved him forcefully against the wall and looked at him with disgust.

Tax'n's eyes went wide with horror, for he could not determine with any degree of certainty if this were part of the ruse, or if the Black Hide were truly unsatisfied with the part he was playing. Swallowing in fear, he saw the reflection of a smile briefly play on the Black Hide's narrow lips.

Raising his face proudly to his leader he queried in a calm voice. "Then what do you need of me?"

The Black Hide snorted, then exhaled sharply as he stared at the rebel lackey. Tax'n withered under the scrutiny as the Black Hide seemed to be carefully weighing the abilities of his underling, his curled upper lip giving new concern for the Geiten rebel.

Abruptly, he turned his back on Tax'n, who breathed a sigh of relief as his attention focused once again on Bafa. "You've done well, my dear. I have another mission for you. One that will push the movement closer to achieving our ultimate goal." Reaching out, he caressed her cheek and smiled at her, his teeth brilliant under the mask, his eyes smouldering.

A wave of indignation shot through Tax'n as the woman who he had reluctantly taken to be his fiancée smiled back suggestively at the leader of the rebel faction.

True, he thought, analyzing the jealousy that surprised him, *she'll be more compliant if she believes He thinks she's special*. But he could not hide the anger that surged through him as Bafa melted at the touch of their leader.

Glancing about the room, the Black Hide released Bafa and began to pace. "Tonight, we draft an ultimatum to the Wessel government." He pointed at one of the rebels and signalled for him to capture the moment for broadcast. Turning his back to the group, the Black Hide repeated a well-rehearsed script as the holocam ran.

"Over the past few days, your bases have been targeted and destroyed, not only by Coalition action, but with assistance from the Black Hide rebels. City by city, you will be erased from the map until the only memory of Wessels will be in Geiten children's fables. Your mighty nation will crumble and you will cease to exist. But there is a chance for your survival. We have requested it before - for the Collection Centres to be closed, for our people to be allowed to return to their homes, to their jobs. For the water to flow once again to Geitenia. But by your intransigence you have brought death and destruction to your people. So we ask it again. If these conditions are not met, our vengeance will be swift and merciless. We will not back down, we will never give up in the struggle for justice. You have been warned. If these conditions are not actioned within 48 hrs, you will face our wrath."

Motioning for the holocam to be cut, the Black Hide spun around. "Bafa, I have one more thing to ask of you. Tonight, I want you to lead a planning team."

The young woman looked at Tax'n hesitantly. "Of course," she responded after her fiancé nodded at her.

The Black Hide's voice was caressing and sweet as he toyed with the young Wessel officer's emotions. "But then again, perhaps I ask too much of you, my dear. Perhaps it should be Tax'n's turn to prove himself loyal to the cause."

Tax'n's eyes widened at the threat and puffing his chest out, he raised his chin defiantly. "How can you doubt my loyalty, after everything I've done?" An eyebrow lifted and his eyes slipped towards Bafa who stared admiringly at the Black Hide.

"Walk with me," the leader commanded and the two men left the shelter to savour the fresh night air. The silvery light of the moon shone down upon them, casting the silhouette of the Black Hide against the stone wall. Pulling out a wad of jewelweed from his tunic, the Black Hide offered a pull to Tax'n. Accepting the offer, he waited for the effects to kick in – pure exhilaration coursed through his veins and Tax'n tilted back his head in ecstasy. The Black Hide rested his powerful torso against the wall beside the smaller man.

"Do you love her?"

Taken aback, Tax'n tried to hide his agitation. "Of course not. You gave me a mission to recruit a willing Wessel officer, one who would do anything for us. And that's what I did. Love never entered into the equation."

"Hmmm, that's a good thing. Still, she's proven to be very useful to us. It's a shame that very soon, I'll have no more need of Bafa. And you, well if you don't feel anything for her, then you can bring Capt. Villutomi's participation with us to an end." The Black Hide paused to see if his minion understood and he grinned cruelly as Tax'n shrugged.

"Makes no difference to me, one way or the other. I didn't exactly relish honouring my marriage proposal to a Wessel."

"But you're a Half-Breed yourself, aren't you Tax'n? And Bafa, well she's quite… interesting I would say… a woman who would betray her country for a man."

His sour laughter rang in Tax'n's ears, and he squirmed uncomfortably. "So, I need to know that you'll stand fast with us. She's to plan the assassination of President Meryx, and you're to lead the team to carry it out. Just make sure she dies in the crossfire."

Tax'n's dark head nodded in response, his eyes narrowed into mere slits, the jewelweed taking the edge off his fear. Throwing his arm around the Black Hide's shoulders, he felt his heart beat ever so quickly as the leader traced a rough finger along his young charge's lips. Then the two laughed in the moonlight, laughed at the gullible young woman who had fallen into their trap, unaware of the eyes that watched from behind the opened door.

CHAPTER 7 - NO LONGER SAFE

Oh, but you must travel through those woods again and again... said a shadow at the window... and you must be lucky to avoid the wolf every time...But the wolf... the wolf only needs enough luck to find you once.
— EMILY CARROLL

There was a commotion in the cockpit – the sound loud enough to pour out into the cargo hold rumbling about angrily, where the once Mayflower Clan of the Geiten of Urkyn huddled, strapped tightly into the net seating that ran the sides of the giant airship. The pounding thrum of the fans that powered the mammoth Meganeur through the night sky muffled the words, so that Daniel could only guess at what was transpiring between Erica and Pat. Barb cast a worried eye at Dom, who reached out to take her hand while both Olivia and Lucia stared silently ahead.

Unhooking his harness, Daniel shuffled over to the cargo door and watched as the village of Urkyn receded in the distance. He could still make out the white demarcation of his clan lines; the fire in front of his peha was now almost extinguished when suddenly he felt a pang of homesickness for Nasaton and the house that he had shared with Poppy. Looking back into the hold, he saw his two boys sound asleep, nestled together like pups in a litter – one dark like his mother, the other a tow-headed miniature image of his father. Growing up in the barren rocky sand and dust of a foreign land, they knew no stability – Max born amongst the stars – both boys nomads of the universe. Deneb had taken them in and the Geiten of Urkyn had been kind to them. *And what have we done?* he reflected. *Brought sickness to the planet. Instigated a war. Now we're off again…and I'm about to find out what's going on! But first one last look at Urkyn.*

It was then that Daniel saw the tiny dots bathed in pearly moonlight, carefully picking their way along the trail that led south to the Glodati Mountains. *Lestos and his family*, Daniel realized, recognizing the familiar crabbed walk of the elderly herder. Their little flock of geiten pranced delicately behind the mighty aurox that laboured as they drew the carts laden with their scant belongings. In vain, Daniel waved to the family that had adopted them into their tribe, a final silent salute to friends he'd never see again.

In the distance, the mighty River Panni shone like a silver ribbon, capturing his attention in its majesty. "The artery of life," he whispered, until a sight caught his eye that left him breathless. Racing down the aisle, Daniel vaulted up the steps that led to the cockpit of the Meganeur where Pat and Erica continued their pointless bickering. Both heads turned as Daniel erupted into their midst.

"You need to turn back Erica," he shouted, grabbing her by the shoulder. Gesturing to the line of armoured vehicles racing along the plains, Daniel barked. "I don't know what those are, but they're heading to Urkyn."

Erica calmly banked the Meganeur and turned north, away from the river and away from the threat. "They're ACOLEV's – light armoured tanks that use acoustic levitation. And behind them, those are air cushioned armoured troops carriers."

Pat growled in anger. "That's why she came. She knew this was about to happen. Urkyn's scheduled to be wiped off the map by Wessel forces. I've been asking her to go back, to tell the Geiten to evacuate the village. But she won't."

"Strap yourself in Dr. Radu," Erica replied as if it were another day on the job for her.

Before them, the horizon began to vanish and blur as the Meganeur climbed its way into the heights of the stratosphere. The planet of Deneb floated below them, a delicate orb shining like gold in the rays of its powerful star.

"You see," Erica said, concentrating as she steered the giant Meganeur into a geosynchronous orbit about the planet, "you're no longer safe on Deneb. That brigade you saw back there? Well, like Pat said, it was sent to wipe you all out. You've got Pallav to thank actually; he discovered the nasty little plot and orchestrated this rescue mission."

"Thank him for what?" Daniel asked in dismay as the Meganeur dropped in the shadows of the wings of a telecommunication satellite. "I'm still not a hundred percent sure what's going on," he added as Pat swung about in his seat to face him.

"She's taking us to another planet - Cepheus-9," he spouted angrily, his face splotched red and white.

Daniel scrunched up his face in confusion. "What? Okay, I get it about the rescue from the Wessel attack. And I'm thankful. Heck, we all are. But why not set us down somewhere else on Deneb? We've already travelled half way across the universe to live here. Well I mean, there." Pointing to the little brown planet, Daniel raised his shoulders in confusion. "You owe us some answers."

"Sit tight," Erica replied. "I'm about to zip us out of orbit and this baby has punch!"

Slipping from fly-by-sight into manual mode, Erica deftly pulled back on the stick, inching the Meganeur out from behind the telcomsat. A million pin pricks of Denebian sunshine reflected from its long slender wings as the giant airship slowly glided past. Then suddenly the beast seemed to roar to life, surging in a furious leap into the great abyss of inky darkness punctuated by beams of light streaming past at incredible speed. Daniel felt nailed to his seat as the Meganeur accelerated into space, his ribcage jumping with every heartbeat, his breath coming in great gasps. And then it was as if he were weightless, as if the Meganeur had come to a gentle stop. So he would have believed had it not been for the blur of asteroids that floated by.

They were careening through space once again and Daniel felt a rush of wonder overpowering him. Memories of days spent on the Space Ark flooded his consciousness, of him commanding the team he had built based on initial trickery, in a quest for the perfect world. And now it had begun once again, except this time he was the captive.

Erica turned to him and smiled. "It'll take less than a week to get to your new destination. The Meganeur's not comfy like the *Mayflower* – but we've got stretchers and rations to make it livable. And like I said, it's only for a few days."

Erica unhooked her harness and stretched her aching back, her bulging baby bump filling the cockpit. "This thing's on auto-pilot till we reach orbit around Cepheus-9, so I'm off to powder my nose, then kick back and get some rest before the little songbird's born."

Knowing well enough not to stand in the way between a pregnant woman and a toilet break, Daniel waited until Erica had left before tackling

Pat who had slumped down in his chair. Looking as if he were about to be ill, the young man covered his face with his hands.

"If I could've stopped her, trust me I would have Dr. Radu. She said we needed to abandon the Geiten, to sacrifice them so we could escape."

"We have the time to figure it out Pat," Daniel replied, his eyes drinking up the flight of the Meganeur. "But to be honest, it doesn't make any difference. We're hostages and stuck for the ride."

"You haven't heard the best of it," Pat grumbled. "Colonel Kóbor somehow procured us Geiten passports with a back story. Yup, we're all gonna masquerade as Geiten, stranded on Cepheus-9 when the Collective cut off all travel to Deneb."

Laughing sourly, Daniel ran his fingers through his sun-bleached hair. "Makes sense. Red heads and blondes. If we pass for Geiten, then we'll probably see flying pigs on Cepheus-9."

***

"So, let me get this straight…" Gomalan could see the vein throbbing at Meryx's temple and raising his eyebrows he tried to warn Pallav who stood like a statue in front of the president and his commanders. "A rebel group aligned with the Coalition has infiltrated our Department of Defence and these rebels somehow disarmed our security systems?"

Colonel Kóbor's green eyes bored into the president, at once threatening and intimidating. Meryx blinked at the unusual sensation and rose to his feet. "Well," he thundered menacingly, "did I miss something?"

"No Sir, that's correct. The Black Hide's agents had both the access passes and codes to enter into the Defence Network. It was the Geiten rebels who shut down the C-RAM systems, rendering our military establishments essentially defenceless. Based on my initial investigation, I've ensured that all security protocols were immediately modified to render the previous passes and codes ineffective. Any attempted use will trigger a series of events that will ultimately identify the originator and their location. In essence, the traitors will be uncovered without any awareness on their part. That is, until their arrest for sabotage and treason."

General Ravenna was uncertain, and she struggled with her uneasiness. Air Marshal Cadynn's missing presence was like a knife wound to her, for the Commander of the Aerospace Force had been an ally in the battle

67

against the power hungry Gomalan. Without him, the High Commander had already begun to bypass her, dismissing the issues she raised and leading her to fear that another sinister thread lay beneath today's discussion. Her thoughts drifted to the last time she'd spoken with Caydnn, when disbelief had bubbled to the surface in their conversation. For how, they wondered together, could the wintering grounds of one tribe of the junior member of the Coalition be a strategic target. And why, on the evening of the attack, when the Brigade Commander stormed in with the 17th Mech Infantry, had he reported that he found Urkyn half-empty – dwellings abandoned, corrals almost devoid of livestock. Ravenna was certain that someone had tipped the Geiten off, and watching Colonel Kóbor closely, a strange feeling came over her that he had something to do with it.

"Do you have suspects then," she asked, scanning the alien closely for any sign of hesitation, any clue that she was on the right track.

Pallav turned towards Ravenna, his green eyes inscrutable, and she felt that the alien was burrowing into her soul. "Not exactly ma'am. But I believe I have a lead and given authorization to continue with the investigation, I'm confident I can smoke out this band of rebels."

It was then that she noticed it, a slight furrowing of the alien's broad brow before the curtain fell again over that impenetrable face, and any doubt was cast aside. Now she was certain–Colonel Kóbor was hiding something and with a smile that never reached her eyes, she cast a line.

"I'll make sure he has whatever he needs," she said before obviously glancing at the time. Pasting a look of impatient busyness on her face she took the bull by the horns. "Why don't you and I go over your requirements in my office?"

Pallav shook his head. "No need, Ma'am. The High Commander's put a fast airship at my disposal and other than extending the temporary assignment of my escort officer for another week, I'm well positioned to wrap this up."

"No more surprises then, Kóbor?" Meryx asked, looking up from under his thick brows at Pallav.

"Negative Sir," he confirmed, his voice brimming with confidence. "Our security's tightened up so that the rebel faction's out of business. But I'm in a race against time to catch the traitors before the Black Hide can strike again."

"Good then. Carry on, Colonel."

Meryx took the stiff salute and waited until the heavy door closed behind Pallav.

"Ravenna my dear, I want you to afford every possible assistance to Colonel Kóbor. Make sure that escort officer he was talking about's available without any delay."

Ravenna nodded before adding, "Sir, it's about Kóbor…"

With a wave of his hand, Meryx cut the general off. "You're dismissed Ravenna. You," he said, pointing to Gomalan, "stay with me." He watched dispassionately as her mouth opened and closed like a fish before rudely turning his back to her and waiting for the sound of the closing door.

Gomalan canted his head and stared in wonder at the resident. "She doesn't know, does she?"

"Why we attacked Urkyn? No, she's got no inkling, I think it's more a personal dislike of Kóbor. Probably tried it on with him and got turned down."

The president guffawed at the ludicrous thought of the handsome alien in Ravenna's clutches and then his face became clouded.

"But then again, neither did that idiot Caydnn – then he went and got himself killed! And as for Ravenna – if she had an ounce of intelligence in that pretty head of hers, then her staff would've smoked out the poison from within the ranks. By the gods, what do I have for generals? Fools?" Meryx slapped his desk while Gomalan checked his shock at the president's description of Ravenna – for the scar-faced battle-seasoned general had never seemed anything short of terrifying to him.

"I'm an old man, my friend," Meryx continued. "I feel my age. It's a miracle this pandemic didn't set me on the trail of my ancestors." Throwing himself down into his chair, the president stretched his stocky legs in front of him. "What kind of world do we live in when aliens are our best defence against a war that they themselves caused?"

Oh, so the old man doesn't want to blame his precious Fynn for the outbreak, Gomalan realized in surprise.

"You mean Vogel and Kóbor… they're both good men. Solid officers. We can't forget they had no idea whatsoever that they were carriers of a disease that would decimate our planet. But listen Sir, this has been a blessing in disguise. Emigration's at an all-time low, the birth rate's exploding like fleas on a mangy cur, and our cities are bursting at the seams. This war gives us the excuse to grab the fertile Fyjerlan southern lands and make them our own. And at the same time, we get rid of the Geiten – those ignorant, filthy, villainous pestilence carriers."

Gomalan sighed before continuing. "Only you and I know the truth about the humans Sir. But think for a moment – if it weren't for the absolute slovenliness of the Geiten – I mean – have you ever seen how they live? Disgusting, worse than animals…if it weren't for them, then the disease would never've spread like wildfire. We should've purged Wesselan of these parasites long ago."

"Ah, I know you're right. But we never wanted this war in the first place. These Geiten rubes, these Fyjer simpletons – scum of the earth! Imagine… it was them who struck first without even declaring war! They might think they have the upper hand, but now the tables are turned. And we will carry death to them, until they are on their knees, ground into the dirt, begging and pleading. Then, we will set out the terms."

His mouth a stubborn line, Meryx commanded. "Begin Phase 2 of Operation Golden Thunder. And Gomalan? On your way out, ask my Executive Assistant to send me the new Surgeon General."

***

Waves of revulsion washed over her, like the pounding tidal surf, while the acrid taste of bile welled up into her throat. Choking it back, Bafa attempted a smile as Tax'n reached for her.

"It's been a long night," she said, struggling to keep her voice calm now that the plan to assassinate the president had been put to bed and her role in the play had come to an end. "And I just want to get some sleep before I report back to the base in the morning."

She flinched at the signs of relief that Tax'n could barely conceal. *How did I not see it before? He wants me about as much as a bout of stomach flu!* She caught his eyes drifting to where the Black Hide stood, watching from behind a mask of appreciation.

Throwing her his most winning smile, he wrapped her in his arms. "How about I pick you up after work then? We need to celebrate! Soon the Wesselan Government'll be on its knees. Overthrown! And then it'll be safe for you and me to be seen together, a real couple."

Kissing Bafa on the cheek, he released her from his grasp and looked deeply into her eyes, a penetrating milky-white glare that he knew had a predictable effect on the stupid young Wessel officer. "And I wonder what your parents will say when we tell them?"

Another crock of bullshit! Talking about marriage when he's itching to plan my death! Bafa concealed a shudder and took in Tax'n as he really was. The crooked nose that spread across his narrow face, the receding hairline, the jagged teeth that jutted from a jaw like some prehistoric riverine creature, and she narrowed her eyes. *To think that I actually loved him! That I was willing to betray the oath to my country for that revolting creature.*

Grabbing her jacket before her disgust became too apparent, she blew him an insincere kiss. "We'll cross that bridge when we get to it. See you tomorrow then." And waving to her one-time colleagues, Bafa fled from the rebel stronghold.

I have to stop this madness, she realized, jumping into her aerocar and engaging the fans. *But I'm not safe from those bastards. And Tax'n knows everything about me – even where my parents live. There's no place dark enough for me to hide.*

Her mind raced as Bafa found her way back to Great Plains Army Base. Sentries manned the gate, their pulsar weapons at the ready as they waved her through. High above, drones patrolled the perimeter and a momentary sense of security descended upon the tormented young woman.

He's got an access pass; they've got all the codes. Oh by the Fires of Ru, what have I done? I'll be court martialled; obliterated for treason. My family will shoulder the humiliation of raising a traitor.

Setting down at the docking port, Bafa crawled out of the aerocar and limped up the stairs to her room in the Officers' barracks.

I need to disappear, she realized, reaching into her locker for an olive drab duffle bag. *But where? They'll find me, there's no place for me to go.*

Sitting on her bed, Bafa collapsed in tears as the reality of the situation hit her. *It's hopeless. The plan's foolproof, I saw to that.* Reaching for a tissue, she blew her nose and sat up straight.

But we're wrong about the Geiten. All that shit about how they're the cesspool of Wesselan, vermin, parasites to be exterminated... I can't stomach it. They don't deserve to be rounded up and treated like livestock. And when I met Tax'n... and the Black Hide... I thought I could make a difference, to protect the people of the man I loved. The man I loved! Ha! He used me for my rank, for my connections. He never cared one jot about me. I could see it in his eyes tonight; how could I ever have been so blind? No... I don't agree with the way things are going in Wesselan, but joining the rebels was the stupidest thing I ever did in my entire life. I should've just left the army and emigrated to Cepheus-9 where I coulda found decent employment with the Collective.

Sitting up, she stared at the hologram on her bedside table – an image of Tax'n smiling a big grin and a hairy arm draped around her slender shoulders while she made puppy-dog eyes at him.

The day we went to Siddi Oasis, she remembered sadly, *when he professed his undying love to me. I bet the couple he introduced me to weren't even his parents.* Throwing the holoframe down in disgust, an idea began to formulate that might save her from being murdered by the Black Hide.

"Activate console," she commanded. Two sleek silver hands rose from the floor in front of her window and between them energy crackled and shivered in a sheet of sparkling light.

"Bring up form WAF-51: Request for Compassionate Leave. Death of Paternal Grandmother. Location: Capacia Province, Cygnus-Morea. Request for fourteen days. Stop. Transmit to Major Sterton."

Bafa slammed down on a button that deactivated the holoscreen and began rummaging through her locker, throwing odd bits of clothing into her duffle bag. *That should work and Tax'n'll find out for sure. Nothing escapes that guy. Then let the wild goose chase begin. But just one more thing to do.*

Time was now of the essence if Bafa's plan was to work. Jumping into her uniform, she threw her duffle into the aerocar then trekked down the autowalks until she reached the bunker. Scanning her access card, she skirted the suspended netting and strode into the bowels of the building that hummed with activity. Walking past the soldiers buried under the routine administration of reports and returns, she casually entered her office and flipping on the light, began in earnest to enact the trap that would seal the fate of her one-time lover and the Black Hide.

CHAPTER 8 - WE'RE HOME AGAIN

You don't have to let it linger within the palm of your hand. The tip's already in your finger: all beginning comes to an end.

– ANA CLAUDIA ANTUNES

"What the devil's that awful noise," Pallav grumbled as he bent down, waiting for the blink of light to complete his iris scan. As the door to his luxurious hilltop home swished open, he was jolted by a cacophony of screeches and the ear-jarring clashes of timbals and it suddenly all made sense as little Jolanta ran to him with her tiny hands covering her ears: Spring-break. His kids were home.

"For God's sake, turn that down!" he shouted from the relative safety of the foyer. Throwing his backpack to the ground, with one arm he scooped up the little girl and was rewarded with a sticky kiss. Peeking around the corner, he could see Isabella sprawled on her bed, legs in the air, the holoscreen lit up while his daughter giggled with a Wessel teenager who tossed her pigtails at the sight of him then pointed in fear at the huge alien looming in the door.

"Dad!" There was a look in those green eyes that tugged at Pallav's heart strings and he bent in to kiss his daughter on the forehead. But that momentary glimpse of pleasure evaporated as she wiped off the imprint of her father's lips with the back of her hand. "Dad, can't you see I'm busy?"

Turning her back on her father, Isabella grumbled to her friend, "Yeah, that's my father. I guess I'll have to stay home tonight." Pulling a gargantuan pout, the teen sighed. "Mom'll want us to all have dinner together. Yeah, what a harsh reality."

Shaking his head, Pallav moved off to identify and destroy the source of the earth-shattering noise. His hands clamped over his ears, he stormed into the family room to find his son Luke propped on his stomach as a hologram

73

of a tiny purple creature sporting a monstrous mane of green hair threw itself around the room while producing the god-awful noise that passed as Wessel music.

Without warning, the creature fizzled into the ether and Luke turned about with eyes blazing. "Hey, what's the big idea?" His eyes widened and the teen gulped, "Dad, you're home. We were wondering what was keeping you."

Blessed silence descended upon the Kóbor home and at the sound of her husband's voice, Tara appeared from the balcony on which she'd sequestered herself. With a blue smear of paint on her elfin face, and a stray strand of dark hair poking out from behind an ear, his wife simply raised an arched eyebrow.

"Working late again?"

Nodding in response, the growl of Pallav's empty stomach filled the room.

"Let me get you something to eat," Tara replied with a chuckle, and he followed her into the kitchen where she popped the heating ring on a gun-metal container that lay in its own tray.

"I really hate that stuff," Pallav grunted as the container warmed its greasy grey contents to the perfect temperature. "I know, I know, we have to adjust to living here, but just for once... could you actually cook something for my supper?"

Handing her husband the tray, she watched as he sniffed it gingerly before almost inhaling the braised aurox in onion gravy.

A gentle tug on his pant leg caught his attention. "Daddy, can you take me to the park?"

Looking down into Jolanta's golden brown eyes, the big man smiled. "Not tonight little one, I have to work."

Disappointment clouded the little girl's face, and he picked her up in his arms. *The only person who's really glad to see me*, he thought as he revelled in her smile while wondering how his kids changed from tiny angels into such aloof detached beings who regarded him as simply a nuisance.

"Tara, I might have to go away again."

He watched her face crumple and he steered her to the balcony while Jolanta clung to him like a limpet.

"Someone's gone missing. Someone I need to find. I got a few leads and I'm going to run them to ground tonight."

74

When he looked back into their home, Luke and Isabella were cheerfully chatting with friends from school and he shrugged his shoulders. Then he saw his wife's angry face.

"Now of all times, when the kids are home. How long's it been since you've seen them? Can't this wait?"

Putting Jolanta down, he shepherded the little girl back inside and returned to Tara.

"Can it wait?" Leaning over the balcony, he placed an arm about her shoulders. "Only if you want us to lose the war. The Black Hide's infiltrated the Army and I know who one of the saboteurs is. Trouble is, she's gone to ground. Tara… you haven't seen the carnage they've enacted. And this is just the start, I'm sure of it. No one's safe until they're caught and neutralized."

Tara bit her lip. "The kids really had their hearts set on going dune-surfing."

"I'll see what I can do. Sorry darling."

Taking her hand in his, Pallav planted a kiss on her open palm before padding off into his office to log in to the Wessel Defence Network. Layers of traffic raced across the system, and he reached for his hated wire-rimmed reading glasses as he scrolled through sparkling screen after screen.

She's not in Cygnus, that much is clear.

File after file authored by Capt. Villutomi crossed by his field of vision. Boring monotonous details that gave nothing away. His eyes burned and blurred. Screen after screen of visit requests, incident reports.

The voice that surprised him cracked as Luke peeked into Pallav's office. "What're you doing Dad?"

"I'm trying to find the location of a suspect, but I'm drawing blanks." Rubbing his eyes, Pallav saw the sprout of down gracing his boy's upper lip and it dawned on him that his son topped Tara now. Luke stood next to his father, tall and muscular and with dark hair and exotic piercing blue eyes, the young teen was the envy of all his new friends.

"Maybe I can help you; what's his name?"

"It's a she. Captain Bafa Villutomi resides in barracks at Great Plains Army Base. Engaged to be married to a cretin named Tax'n… Aha!"

Luke looked on transfixed. "What is it?"

"She slipped up," he explained with a grin, pointing to the military holo-mail floating in front of them.

"See here Luke? This here is a request for catering for a function to take place on the Base. And here, the caterer has asked for contact details. She gave them her personal holo-mail address. So now," he said with a grin, "we can crack into her account."

Excitement lit up his son's eyes. "Can I give it a try Dad? We're learning about crypto-security and how to defeat hackers. Maybe I can reverse engineer it?"

With pride bursting from his chest, Pallav ruffled his son's dark hair. "Let's work on it together, you and I."

***

"That's it, you've nailed it!" Erica beamed at Hoshi's successful landing of the little shuttle on her first attempt on the flight simulator and clapped her on the shoulder.

"Well, it's not all that difficult really," Hoshi replied as Daniel took his place in the simulator for a second attempt, a look of consternation on his face. One look at him and Erica could almost feel his nervous energy arcing across the cargo bay.

"It's okay Dr. Radu. Like I said before, the shuttle'll do all the work. You've just got to know what to do in case something goes haywire."

Daniel nodded stiffly and was ready to see if he had the right stuff, but his concentration was instantly destroyed when Erica bent over in pain. "Ohhh...," she groaned, grabbing the older woman in support.

Easing her to the deck, Hoshi held Erica's hand as the space jockey gasped. "Get Dom!" Leaping from the simulator, Daniel raced down the cargo hold looking for the burly nurse who was chatting with Barb.

"It's Erica," Daniel shouted. "I think she's going in to labour!"

The two men charged down the cavernous hold of the Meganeur only to arrive to see Erica standing calmly beside Hoshi who was on her second successful approach to the planet surface.

"Right on the nose again!" Erica laughed as she hauled Hoshi's arm up in the air in a sign of triumph. "I think we've got a winner here!"

Dom and Daniel stared at each other in confusion. Waddling up to them, Erica chuckled, "False labour. The Doc told me about that. I can't say I enjoyed it much. It'll be great to get back to Styria where there's loads of drugs to keep me nice and comfy while Fynn does all the work of delivering our baby girl."

Reaching over, Dom grabbed Erica's wrist and quickly made a mental note of her pulse. "You need rest," he admonished feeling the thready pulse beating a bit too quick for his liking. "You shouldn't be on your feet all day instructing these two on how to land the shuttle."

"Well *I'm* not landing it," Erica countered. "I'm staying in orbit, while Hoshi puts her ace piloting skills into action. The second you guys put down on the surface of Cepheus-9, I'm blasting off back to Deneb."

Daniel nodded in agreement. "She's right. Hoshi's a natural. Whereas me… well let's just say if it comes down to it, I can probably manage a crash landing… I think I'm hopeless."

"Practice makes perfect, Dr. Radu. And you've got two whole days ahead of you to do just that." Erica motioned for Daniel to resume his training and reluctantly, he took a seat in the shuttle simulator. "Two pilots are required, we've been through this before."

Furrowing his brow in frustration, Daniel resumed his training. He frowned in concentration while the shuttle simulator descended from the exosphere. As he nosed it further down into the simulated Cepheusian atmosphere, a hologram of a vivid turquoise ocean came into view.

"My God, it reminds me of the waters off the Seychelles," Dom whispered as sweat beaded on Daniel's brow.

"Keep the nose down for now," Erica instructed, placing a calming hand on Daniel's shoulder. Entering the mesosphere, the shuttle began to pitch violently as turbulence shook the tiny vessel.

"Hold her steady, scan between the altimeter and your speed indicator," Erica coached as the simulator rocked to and fro like a ship at sea. "It's always a bit rough at this altitude. Now gently lower the nose a little more… a little more…"

The shuttle glided down through the clouds and suddenly a band of golden sand appeared encircling a little isle.

"Tara programmed the coordinates for the landing site just offshore, so there's nothing to worry about. The shuttle'll fix on those; you just enjoy the ride. Unless, that is, a gremlin kicks up in the system. That's when you guys would need to jump into action – to get her down and land her safely. The raft'll deploy the minute you touch water."

Tara. Daniel's concentration was interrupted by the thought that he would never see her again and he sighed loudly before his anger bubbled to the surface once again. *Never again, Radu. Remind yourself!*

Erica's voice broke him from his dual melancholic-infuriated reverie. "You're doing fine Dr. Radu; you're on the home stretch." Peeking over Daniel's shoulder, Erica watched as the planet surface came rushing to them. Lush tropical trees and verdant meadows were surrounded by a cerulean sea that seemed to welcome the shuttle's arrival.

"Once you're within 1000 feet of the surface switch to visual and postural mode…so look up a bit and press back into the seat – keep an eye on your rate of descent – you don't want to go thundering in."

The simulator gently rolled with Daniel's movements until he hovered above the open meadow. "Bring both of your heels down now on the pads… gently…gently… and voilà! You're down!"

Wiping his sweaty hands on his trousers, Daniel vaulted from the simulator and was rewarded with an awkward hug from Erica.

"You're going to be on the switch on the other end though, right?" he asked as the very pregnant woman winced then nodded, her face shiny with perspiration.

"I'm still not comfortable with you going back to Deneb alone," Dom interjected as the young woman arched her back and screwed up her face, wondering how to get rid of the unwanted attention. "At the very least, let me check you over."

"The examination – okay. But as to anyone going back with me? You know we've been over this a hundred times before," Erica replied as he accompanied her to a pallet near the ramp. "No one can and that's that. First of all, I'm putting down in the badlands between the River Panni and the Sirga - there's a chance I may be spotted. If it's just me alone, well, I can bullshit my way out of it. Then there's the problem that you guys'll have nowhere to live back on Deneb. I mean, Pallav and Fynn'll be picking me up, and I get to go home after we hit the delete and destruct button on this here Meganeur. But where would you go? It's not like you look like the locals y'know."

A little crowd had gathered round, watching the interaction between the burly nurse and the pilot.

"But we do," Dashawna replied. "Dodzi and I were always mistaken for Geiten. And we could make our way back into Geitenia, there'd be no problem there."

So there goes the child-minder, Daniel thought selfishly before nodding his head at the older woman's wisdom. "She's right Erica. You can't go back by yourself. For the love of Pete, you're close to bursting. If anything happened on the way back, what'd you do?"

"This thing can fly itself once I'm out of orbit, but yeah, I do need to be in the cockpit to land it. Otherwise, I guess…"

"You guess wrong lady," Dodzi said. "We're going back with you, whether you like it or not."

***

Fynn had to admit himself, Denebian flowers were surprisingly beautiful. But it hadn't been easy finding them - it's not like a Wessel picks up a bouquet at a corner shop. With what was called the Denebian flu rampaging across the land, most businesses had closed down, their employees either resting in quarantine or shallow graves. So Fynn prided himself on a successful mission, having found a garden in the city that boasted blossoms the size of dinner plates and after a quick look-about, liberated a dozen of the beauties for the woman he loved ever since their eyes met over the salad bar in the Aerospace Academy.

Jumping over the hedge to their beautiful, white-washed house, Fynn self-consciously grimaced at the sight of his battered arms. *I look like a heroin addict,* he thought, row upon row of puncture marks dotting the bruised skin of his inner arms. *If I never see another hypodermic needle, it'll be too soon. The Doc sure had a hard time finding whatever he was looking for…I guess human blood's a mystery to them all.* Stopping in his tracks, he pulled down the sleeves to his jacket. *Still, no need to scare Erica out of her wits.*

Brandishing the combination of red and white flowers, Fynn opened the door and chuckled at the sight of the mess before him. "Babe, I'm home!" No response.

Funny, I left a message that I was getting out today, he thought, walking into the kitchen and fumbling through the cluttered cupboards for a vase. *Probably gone out for a walk… unless… maybe she's at the hospital? Oh God! I should check!*

Throwing the bouquet into the sink, Fynn reached for the HomeLink System intending to contact Tara, when an envelope floated down from the crowded end table with the word "FYNN" written in bold letters across its face. Tearing it open, Fynn stood motionless reading the note his wife had left him.

> Hey Fynn,
>
> I should be back before you get home, but just in case I'm not I had to step out for a little while. Pallav and Tara know everything, get in touch with them if I'm not home soon. And don't worry, I'm doing well and soon we'll both be holding our little girl in our arms. Love you to the stars and back, Erica xo

Not exactly the reception I was expecting, he thought. *And why would she tell me to call Pallav if she's not home soon? God, I hope he's not taken her to the hospital and her thinking she's gonna surprise me with our baby girl! Nah... she'd've said. Still, I can't let Erica coming home to see me looking like this.*

The smell of stale sweat rushed up as he peeled off the flight suit he'd been stuck in for the past two weeks and he curled his lip in disgust. The image staring back at him from the bathroom mirror was startling – dark smudges circled two bloodshot eyes in a face where even his freckles seemed to have lost their colour. *Hello old age,* he joked before stepping into the water stall. Stretching luxuriously, he sighed as jets of hot water followed by warm air streamed over his body.

Ah, to feel human again. Having been quarantined for the better part of two weeks, Fynn decided to wait outside in the sunshine for Erica. Wessels passed by on autowalks, Hover-V's zipped through the sky while the sound of birdsong gurgled through the air. A woman watched her sons from the riverbank as they played in the water, splashing and laughing and Fynn smiled. In a few years, their daughter would be learning to swim and he relaxed, letting the warmth of the day ease his thoughts.

But when the sun began to set with no sign of Erica, Fynn grew uneasy. Returning to the sanctuary of their home, he pulled out the note that his wife had left for him. *It's not dated* he realized suddenly, and wondering if she had gone into labour, his first instinct was to contact Meryx for the president had promised Fynn he'd look after her.

Connecting into the HomeLink System, his relief was short lived when the elderly man's hologram floated in front of him, his eyes filled with sadness. "Fynn! I didn't know you were going home today. You should've called me son, I'd have come to get you."

Surprised at the state of the president, Fynn felt his stomach churn. "It's Erica, isn't it?"

The old man looked defeated, his red-rimmed eyes sinking in his wrinkled face. "I'll be over as soon as I can, just hang tight." Sagging visibly, Meryx cut transmission and tried to steady himself, for he knew he had the most of all horrible messages to convey to his foster son.

CHAPTER 9 - THE MAYFLOWER CLAN

Our fate is to face the world as orphans, chasing through long years the shadows...

– KAZUO ISHIGURO

Having slipped past Space Guard into orbit around Cepheus-9, the Meganeur hung like a dragonfly ready to devour the satellites that whizzed by at break-neck speeds. Enrobed in the light of the twin Cepheusian suns, they sparkled as they revolved around the blue orb that floated like a sapphire in the black velvet of space. The massive Denebian transport ship hummed with activity as its passengers milled about the portholes, curiosity bubbling and frothing between them.

"It's so beautiful," Olivia gushed to her mother. Barb hugged her daughter tightly and smiled at Dom. "Kinda reminds you of Earth, doesn't it?"

Raising an eyebrow, Dom peered down to the planet surface, his silence a fortress which Barb had yet to breach. She knew how he despaired for Renzo who had chosen to stay behind on a planet caught in the grips of war. And he could not tear himself from the thoughts of his wife, Dr. Ariane, whose eternal resting place under the scorching Denebian sands was now forever lost to him.

The shared tragedies had brought the two close, but Barb knew he needed time to work through his grief, to move past the pain before he could feel once again. His raven-haired daughter Lucia beckoned to Olivia and the two slipped away to leave their elders to themselves, for the young dwelled in the future while their parents still resided in the realm of memories.

"So you're okay taking us down then," Daniel asked of Hoshi as the two sat in the cockpit, Erica having taken advantage of the lull to relax before her return journey to Deneb. Abeiku and Marco were prepping the shuttle for departure, loading as much of their possessions as would fit onboard the cramped vessel in an attempt to remind the refugees of their short-term home on Deneb while Dashawna and her daughter-in-law Reeta were engaged in an animated discussion that echoed throughout the hulking ship.

Trying to ignore the argument, Hoshi turned her attention back to the curtain of darkness that engulfed them and nodded.

"It seems I found a new talent late in life. Who'd have guessed I've got the makings of a space pilot? I spent my entire adult life working for the USNA Government, managing major procurement projects, busy but bored, while I could've been zipping around the clouds, free from the nine to five and the mind-numbing cubicle-life."

Staring out into the vast emptiness before her, Hoshi shrugged. "But it doesn't matter now. We all have to embrace the new identities Pallav created for us, don't we? And that doesn't mean I'm going to be rocketing off into space again any time soon."

"And with us masquerading as Denebians… all supposedly stranded on Cepheus-9 when the Collective locked down the borders. Well, at least Kóbor did a good job with the back stories, so we won't look suspicious."

Pulling out a small chip, Daniel allowed it to rotate in the palm of his hand. The little wafer disgorged a beam of light that coalesced into a three–dimensional map, pointing the way to their Cepheusian salvation. "My family's supposed to report to the Dopang Branch of the Immigration Refugee and Citizenship Bureau. But at least it's not too far for the boys."

"You're lucky. Jian and I have to wait a few days on the wildlife refuge, then Pallav's assigned us to go to Subting Precinct and request refugee status there."

Hoshi twisted the hem of her tunic between hands that had grown strong and callused with the hard work of life in Urkyn. "We're about to be split up, like dandelions seed heads, scattered in the winds to the four corners of the globe. How will we ever cope?" Concern darkened Hoshi's eyes and mingled with the fear of once again becoming outcasts, undesirables in a new land.

Daniel placed a consoling arm about the older woman. "You're resourceful and resilient, Hoshi. Look at everything you accomplished back in Urkyn… we started with nothing but in the end we built an entire community. Us humans – we became the strength of the village: treating the sick, taking care of the dead, and leaving Urkyn with a reliable source of water. We were the Clan Mayflower of the Geiten of Urkyn. And I'm proud of that."

"I still don't see why we can't just say we're human… it would make more sense to me. All this subterfuge, what's the use if it separates us?"

"That's Kóbor for you, all cloak and dagger." Daniel rolled his eyes. "But I agree with you, I don't want our gang to be torn apart."

Hoshi patted Daniel on the arm companionably. "We'll find a way, don't you worry. After everything we've come through, you can bet we're not going to let our friendship slip away now." Then peeking outside the cockpit, Hoshi grinned at the younger set playing a pickup game of baseball in the cavernous cargo hold while the shuttle was being loaded. With a twinkle in her eyes, she chuckled, "Why don't we join them? If I ever told the folks back home that I played baseball in a spaceship they'd never believe it."

"C'mon then, let's go." Jumping down the ladder, Daniel stopped to watch Marco wipe the sweat from his brow while Abeiku loped over to him.

"That's the last of it, Dr. Radu. We're ready to launch anytime now."

Crack! Smash!

"Someone's belted that into the outfield," Hoshi joked as Pat jumped in the air only to miss the homerun that his sister Olivia just landed. Sticking her tongue out at her hopeless brother, her red tresses flying behind her, Olivia trotted between the make-shift bases, dancing for victory at home plate. Retrieving the errant ball, Pat chided himself, completely oblivious to the broken glass that now littered the deck.

"That's the third time in a row she's done it," he exclaimed, throwing his arms up in the air in a gesture of frustration.

Impatient to feel the sand between his toes and the waves lapping against his skin, Abeiku grew impatient. "Well Dr. Radu? Do we wake Erica from her beauty sleep and get the show on the road?"

Daniel waved him away as little Lewis took to the plate, the bat far too big in his six year old hands. Angelo lobbed the ball gently for the little boy who swung too high. Lewis gritted his teeth and turned to Olivia in confusion, who ran out to help him practice his swing. Daniel stifled a smile as a look of determination came over his eldest son's face. Shuffling his feet, Lewis gave the bat a little swing and then nodded to Angelo who approached a little closer before throwing a gentle pitch. And crack! The bat connected solidly with the ball and sailed past the second base, with Lewis staying rooted to the spot in wonder at his accomplishment.

"Run!"

Everyone was shouting encouragement at the little tow-haired boy who carried the bat awkwardly as he raced to the makeshift first base.

"Throw down the bat! Throw it down!" Daniel could hear himself screaming with pride as Lewis made first base safely and then reality struck him. *I wonder what life'll be like for them on Cepheus-9 without their friends around.*

Watching the group at play suddenly made him depressed. All his life he'd relied on his family and friends for strength and guidance and now he'd be alone in a new world where everything would be foreign to him. And worst of all, he'd be forced to live a lie, pretending to be Denebian while turning his back on his human heritage.

The boys'll grow up without family traditions – no Santa Claus at Christmas, no Easter egg hunt, no picnics with BBQ and three-legged races. Their lives'll be nothing like mine, and after a few years, when they're both in school, I won't be able to relate to them. They'll be speaking the local language like the natives whereas me… I'll always be using the universal translator. But it's almost time to push off. Erica's gotta get back to Wesselan.

Striding to the centre of the playing field, Daniel took the baseball from Angelo and motioned for everyone to approach. A sea of eager faces greeted him, reminding him of the evening that he'd hijacked the *Mayflower* and fled into space. Except the sea had shrunk to a pond. *So many faces missing*, he reflected, his mind conjuring the ghosts of his wife Poppy, of the young biochemist Alice Fong and the brilliant but garrulous microbiologist Vance Nolan. He could picture the brave Dr. Ariane with her soft eyes smiling at him from above, while the image of his beautiful Tara, her children and loutish husband Pallav swam before his eyes.

It seemed Erica understood, for she waddled up beside him. "I wish Fynn were here," she mused, cradling her swollen belly.

"I'm gonna miss you, Dr. Radu, she whispered, tears glistening in her eyes. "It hasn't always been easy for me since we left Earth, but you always believed in me, no matter what. And that meant the world to me."

Facing the little crowd, her sapphire eyes glistening with emotion, Erica controlled her voice with difficulty. "This isn't goodbye you know. I'm not leaving you guys for long. As soon as this war's over, Fynn and I'll come for a visit – heck, we may even decide to stay ourselves if anyone'll sponsor a couple of space aces. But I promise you, you're not gonna be abandoned. Cause we're all Denebians now - members of a very select club: the Mayflower Clan."

Then reaching up on tiptoes, Erica kissed Daniel softly on the cheek before the entire crowd gathered around her, wrapping her in hugs.

"They should get going," Dashawna said to Erica, breaking the circle of love and pointing to the movements of the twin suns whose shadows began to touch the planet below with their dusky fingers.

The courageous young pilot nodded and with Dashawna and her husband Dodzi, watched as the refugees from the *Mayflower* stepped into the awaiting shuttle, Hoshi ready at the helm. Daniel waited patiently while Abeiku and Reeta paid their goodbyes to their parents who turned to slowly make their way into the cockpit. Daniel tried unsuccessfully to summon a smile to his lips.

"You be real careful on the way back, okay? Erica..." he continued, clearing his throat, "I know that if your dad were here, he'd tell you this himself. But since he's not, it's up to me. I've watched you break your ass competing with Fynn. And let me tell you something – you're every bit as good as he is and you've got nothing to prove to anybody. You're brave, smart, and independent. You'd make any parent proud and you're going to make the best mother any kid could have. So... you get yourself back to Deneb ASAP and then send me some pics the minute your little girl takes her first breath, okay?"

Tears fells down on Erica's cheeks as she threw her arms about Daniel and squeezed him with a surprising strength. "Thank you Dr. Radu, I'll always think of what you said."

Disengaging from her arms, Daniel smiled over his shoulder at Erica, her long blonde braids frazzled but her smile as wide as the space that would soon separate them. Stepping into the shuttle, the door zipped closed behind him and he took his place at the controls. Hoshi waited until Erica climbed clumsily up into the Meganeur's cockpit before engaging launch protocols. As the ramp to the big transport ship slowly retracted, the shuttle began its hover and just as in the simulator, Hoshi nimbly guided the craft from the gaping maw into the depths of space.

Daniel looked back and pondered the sight of the great beast hanging in space, a whale shark about to feed. *I guess she's leaving the ramp open till we hit the atmosphere, in case there's a problem.*

The engines roared to life as the shuttle fought to break its orbit from the blue planet below. Unable to rip himself from the past, Daniel forced himself to look back until the Meganeur receded into a mere speck in the dimness of space and a pall of sadness fell ever so heavily on his shoulders.

"That's it then," Hoshi announced, laying back in her seat and cracking her knuckles with a loud pop. "We just sit back and relax and let automation do its work."

"Except of course if there's an emergency…" Daniel replied with a look of dejection. Ignoring her co-pilot, Hoshi closed her eyes and let the weightlessness of space tame the inner tension. The inky blackness gave way to vivid hues of red, orange, and yellow, flames licking the surface of the shuttle as it entered the Cepheusian atmosphere.

Parental instincts kicking in, Daniel swivelled in his seat only to be amused at the sight of his sons staring in awe at the fiery beauty that engulfed them.

Down the shuttle descended, now ever so slowly, through a violet mist which gave way to delicate lavender skies that kissed the brilliant turquoise waters of the Cepheusian seas. A golden band traced the long fingers of land that plunged into the oceans. Minutes passed into hours and with the setting of the twin suns, the sky was graced with the appearance of a string of moons that rose like pearl-white swans in the night, seeking their evening roost. Beneath them, the pale moonlight danced off an infinity of tall glass structures that stretched across the narrow margins of land, sprawling into one immense megatropolis that blanketed the entire surface of the planet. Or almost. For the shuttle was making for a patch of open water that lapped upon the shores of one of the rare islands where nature had retained her reign.

Finding its repose in the warm shallow waters of the Bay of Besarina, the skin of the shuttle began to shimmer a delicate pale yellow while the sound of rushing air filled the interior.

It's time, Daniel thought as the raft deployed, ready to transport the refugees to their new home. *But there's one last thing I have to do.*

Daniel unhooked his harness. "Can you get everyone onboard while I let Erica know she's good to go? Just keep an eye on the boys for me, they've never been around water before," he asked Hoshi.

A rush of warm, humid air greeted them as the shuttle door slid open. He could just about make out the shoreline from the shuttle in the moonlight and suddenly an urge came upon him.

"I'll set in motion the ditching protocols. And Hoshi? Don't wait for me. It's a lovely night for a swim."

**

"That's her alright." Pallav rolled his eyes while his son watched transfixed as the inane hololog brought Bafa to life before their eyes. Flipping her thick black hair and pouting seductively, Bafa chirped in a completely moronic voice about her vacation.

> *"Hi Everybody! So just in case you were kinda like wondering... we all hear that Siddi Oasis is like... ...super exciting and all... but yeah... it's not just dune surfing and... like... desert hang gliding... y'know, there's a lot more... like...I wasn't planning on going shopping while I was there... but you know what, I decided I needed to check out the deals..."*

"Okay Luke, that's about all I can take," Pallav growled and reached for the control. "No dad, this stuff's great. Check out the haul she scored. Isabella, Jolanta, you two have gotta see this." As his sister raced into the living room followed by the young Wessel fosterling, Pallav threw his hands in the air in exasperation.

> *"And honestly, y'know, I thought it was like, gonna be empty at the shops an'all, 'cause I thought that everybody'd be like, sipping Lesh or chilling at the water, but like... no, not the case. It's buzzing! Like, if I could I'd stay here forever. Hahaha! Like, and dance for a living! Hahaha! And I gotta warn 'ya, most'a the stuff I got's bathing suits, cause, like, I live on a desert planet, right. And now I'm gonna show you just how cute they are..."*

A bellow tore through the air. "That's enough!" Grabbing the controls, Pallav terminated the transmission with the result that Isabella flounced out of the room in a huff with Jolanta running after her while Luke looked at him with confusion.

"But Dad, she's giving us tons of clues."

"Uh-huh. Got nothing to do with the fact that she's about to try on bathing suits, right?"

Resigned to the passions of teenaged boys, Pallav hid a grin and shook his head while his son tried in vain to hide the blush colouring his cheeks. "A wounded animal usually goes to ground, Luke. They find someplace safe – like a burrow or high up in a tree. But that's the wrong choice, it's the first place to look. To survive, you need to take risks. And that's what Villutomi has done."

Opening his light tablet, Pallav punched up the security log for the Great Plains HQ compound. "See here, she accessed her office two days ago at 0230 hrs. Then, her Hover-V was clocked going over the speed limit at the intersection of Baffin and Clark in Nida at 0315 hrs; later that morning the same vehicle was found abandoned on the outskirts of Khulan ASW. Now, look at this map son and tell me what you think."

Luke furrowed his brows, his blue eyes pensive. "She's making for the border? But why Dad? Wesselan's at war with Fyjerlan."

"Let's not worry about the why yet Luke. Look at this."

Pulling up a schematic on the light tablet, Pallav handed it to his son. "See the satellite image there? Even though we're at war, if you know where to go, a whole busload of tourists could slip across the border. And you know something else? The easiest place to hide is usually in plain sight. A girl like that, she could be confused for a Geiten couldn't she?"

Luke blinked. "How would I know Dad, I haven't seen many of them. But I doubt she looks Geiten, they're filthy disgusting vermin and she's…"

A strong hand gripped Luke's shoulder, making him wince. "Enough. Forget what you learned in school Luke; your mom could pass for Geiten. Half the people on the *Mayflower* could too."

Pallav sighed, disgusted at the propaganda that his children were being force fed. "I've got a hunch – that she stole across the border and made her way to a city where she can blend in. Then just disappeared into the crowds."

"No way Dad, you're wrong. Listen to her hololog!" Grabbing the control, the image of Bafa once again jumped to life while Pallav gritted his teeth in anger.

"Dad, look…"

The sound of her voice grated on Pallav's nerves while he could feel his blood pressure rising from the constant hair flipping and idiotic smiles.

"Listen Luke… she probably could've made it from Khulan to Phost in about 2 hrs. So, if we pull up satellite data from yesterday morning, then we may be able to find her."

Images beamed from the light tablet onto the living room wall as Pallav began to zoom in to scan the city outskirts. A few Hover-V's plied the empty skylanes while down below, workers in freighters delivered goods to big box stores. But the autowalks rolled on empty throughout the streets. "Hmmm…" Pallav scratched his head while Luke sat cross-legged and bored, the lad flipped open his comms device to check his friends' social media sites.

"Wouldn't she have entered the city from the east?" Pallav scanned the streets, one by one, to no avail. "Hmmm… Luke, how'd you like to check the northern quadrants while I tackle the south?"

Luke shook his head. "Dad, you're not listening to me." The young man stood ramrod straight in front of his father, his hands defiantly on his hips. And then he thrust his comms device in front of Pallav's face, who blanched at the sight of a scantily clad dark-haired woman jumping merrily in a wave park while being sprayed with water. "This's her, isn't it?"

Pallav swallowed and raised an eyebrow, looking every inch the disciplinarian. "Luke, get off Villutomi's feed." Grabbing his son's device, he held it at arm's length. "If you don't want to help, that's okay, but you shouldn't be looking at this stuff."

"It's a live stream Dad. I found her. She's in Siddi Oasis."

Raising the other eyebrow, Pallav smiled and proudly ruffled his son's hair. "Tara, kids… get your bathing suits ready, because we're heading on vacation."

CHAPTER 10 - GOODBYE – HELLO

You can never cross the ocean unless you have the courage to lose sight of the shore.
– CHRISTOPHER COLUMBUS

A red light blinked in the now empty cargo hold. On and off it went, trying to draw attention, shouting out for anyone to take action. The cavernous belly gaped like an open wound that without treatment would become deadly, sucking the life from the Meganeur. The vacuum tore at the controls, bursting them in great blossoms of glass and graphene whose crystal shards floated off into space. The great beast groaned and creaked but its cries for help went unheeded as those in the cockpit intently watched the descent of their colleagues to the Cepheusian surface. The magnification function of the bridge windows captured the transit in stunning detail and as the shuttle gently touched down in the moonlight, a tear glistened in the corner of more than one eye.

When the moonlit raft washed up on the shores of the Bay of Besarina, Dashawna and Dodzi cried out in happiness as they saw little Teuvo and Lark jump from the raft into their mother's open arms. They could make out tall fronds blowing in the sea-breeze that flirted with the indigo waves, caressing them into tiny white caps. Dodzi shook his finger at the display screen in surprise, pointing at the figure that expertly plowed through the water, arms rhythmically rising and falling as it neared the shoreline.

"That's got to be Daniel," Dashawna chuckled, recognizing the bare muscular torso that rose from the waves before walking ashore. "Will we ever see them again?"

Her words ached throughout the small space and Dodzi plunked himself down on the console to sit beside his wife. "It's in God's hands Dashawna. But you and me? We have to make sure Erica gets back safely now."

But the pilot's attention was entirely on something else and she bent over in agony, a powerful contraction gripping her abdomen. Sweat beaded on her forehead and she sucked breath in greedily before it subsided. "Well guys, I think it's time we slip the bonds of Cepheus-9. I got a date with an obstetrician."

Reaching into her flight suit pocket, Erica pulled out the pre-flight checklist she'd had since pre-NASA days. Long since modified for interstellar travel, she quickly began to check the flight controls, instruments and gauges. "Doors and windows – locked. Fission thrusters at full power. Ok, I'm lighting her up. All systems good for leaving orbit."

Dashawna began to shiver and tremble and with wide eyes stared at her husband. "Our son, our grandbabies – they're down there Dodzi – will the babies remember us?"

Her husband clucked sympathetically and petted his wife's arm who unbuckled her harness to be enveloped in his arms. "It'll be alright," he whispered. "The war won't last forever. I promise we'll visit them on the first transport out of Deneb."

Hugging his wife, Dodzi pecked Dashawna's cheek as Erica began to erase the data log, removing any trace of extraplanetary travel from the Meganeur's data banks. All the while, a blinking light bathed the aft end of the cargo hold in a red glow, unseen and unnoticed, a vivid testament to the damaged ramp control. Its cockpit counterpart glowed like a fiery brand on the console, a second fail safe measure that was a life-line to safety. But the Meganeur was anything but safe – for perched atop the blazing warning light was Dodzi, glued to the console with nothing but pain in his heart at the loss of his family.

With the loading ramp gaping open, Erica fired up the powerful fission engines to tear the leviathan from its orbit. One last glance at Cepheus-9, then with a sigh, she swept her hand forward across the console, engaging the forward thrusters and sealing their fate.

***

Ravenna's face gave nothing away as she sat in the Department of Defence's Operations Centre, although beside her the nervous energy of the new Commander of the Aerospace Force could be cut with a knife. Francis had been an ally of hers for years; they'd served together as peacekeepers during the First Denebian War that had pitted the Fyjers against the nomadic Geiten and she'd come to think of him as an old friend. But today was all about her, so she turned a shoulder to him and inhaled deeply, waiting for Gomalan and impatient to get the show on the road.

Her thoughts turned to the big alien who had wormed his way into the High Commander's confidences, and she narrowed her eyes, unconsciously giving evidence to her dislike of Colonel Pallav Kóbor. Every fibre of her being screamed to her that he was misleading them, and she wanted to unmask him for the traitor that he really was. But first there was a war to prosecute and today she would earn her stars once more.

Francis nudged her as Gomalan strode into the room followed by President Meryx. *Now this is a surprise*, she thought, scraping her chair across the floor, she jumped to her feet. *I wonder why he's here today.*

Taking his seat at the head of the conference table, Meryx nodded at Ravenna. "Start," he said without preamble, his voice gruff and heavy.

Smoothing down her tunic, the general flicked on the holodisplay and while the arms raised from the floor, Ravenna stifled a smile in an attempt to control her pride. "Sir, I'll let the images speak for themselves."

She could see Meryx turning to Gomalan and whispering in the old warrior's ear before the High Commander nodded and pulled out a message for the president who pocketed it quickly. Then their attention was fully taken by the hologram that played out before their eyes. Rounds sang through the air, hammering into the enemy battle tanks while artillery fire rained upon the hapless Fyjers. Down swooped three Fenris warbirds, pouring death onto the fleeing enemy. Gomalan jumped as one of the Fyjer tanks was blown sky high, its flaming hull crashing apart before seemingly landing at his feet.

RAITs streamed across the holofield in the wake of a battle detail of Acoustic Levitation Light Tanks. They could hear Fyjer infantry soldiers screaming for ammunition while the nerve-wracking shrieks of the advancing robotic soldiers curdled the blood of those poor devils who faced no escape. The ACOLEVs poured over the field spewing flames from their muzzles; death sped on air cushions into the enemy ranks. Fyjer tanks lit up; tongues of fire dancing like demons of destruction, their crews tumbling out to stumble like the half-dead until they were dispatched by ever vigilant RAIT forces whose robotic sights never failed.

The landscape metamorphosed into a macabre canvas: smouldering craters, mangled equipment, trees torn from the ground, tossed and discarded like children's toys after a birthday party. And scattered here and there, the corpses of Fyjer warriors lay - blackened and burned, unrecognizable for the most part, their final resting place a scene out of hell.

Ravenna watched the president whose stony features concealed any emotion. But not Gomalan. The High Commander was reliving his youth when as a young man he had tasted the bite of battle. And she understood, touching the scar that ran the length of her cheek, remembering the day that shrapnel had ripped across her face marring her youth forever. After all these years, it still burned.

Now such sweet revenge played out in front of her eyes and a smile snuck across her blood-red lips. Fyjer soldiers crawling out from under smouldering vehicles threw their hands in the air and walked towards the RAITs. Tripping over their dead comrades, skirting the burning wreckage, they were taken into captivity.

The scene shifted as Ravenna changed to satellite imagery. A tranquil canvas floated before them: the Zamyr River flowing rapidly from the Northern Ice Cap, its steep rocky banks blanketed in a carpet of early spring flowers merrily peeking out from between the crags.

Meryx stared in surprise at Ravenna and before he could question, Gomalan patiently stayed his hand. He felt as if he were a pybar, soaring high above the river then swooping down and down, closer and closer until he could make out the hardened shelters of a Fyjer Air Base, where Starhunter warbirds and Teratorn Transport airships reposed in orderly lines along the apron. Aviators plodded between the hangars, swinging their arms nonchalantly, enjoying the returning warmth of the fiery Breath of Ru.

A shrill scream broke the stillness of the day and the sky darkened as a squadron of Stryker Skykillers plunged downward from the heavens. Strafing the airfield with rippling electromagnetic pulses, they banked sharply before soaring into the upper reaches of the troposphere where they circled like birds of prey, ready to dive into action in the blink of an eye. The Ops Centre was filled with a low throaty rumble. Growling like a pack of hungry bloodwolves, Firestorm bombers roared overhead, unleashing their deadly cargo to devastating effect. The room was suddenly transformed into a sea of carnage – the Fyjer's Massita AeroSpace Wing was obliterated when waves of flames rippled and washed over the airfield.

Shielding his face against the fiery blast, Gomalan shuddered. "By the gods! Nothing could've survived that…" In his mind, he was once again a young Captain. He could feel the sweat stinging his eyes as he led his company up the Pacoretti Ridge, the blistering heat of the Breath of Ru suffocating them when suddenly the mountainside erupted in a carpet of flames. Fyjer infantry with flamethrowers stormed down from their aeries engulfing his little group in a sea of molten fury. His breathing quickened as he recalled how he threw himself between two boulders and found himself falling, falling… away from the flames… while dirt poured into his dry mouth. He stayed in that hole for hours fearful of the fiery death, battling an unquenchable thirst and breathing the stale musty air until he slipped out into the fresh night air to a scene straight from hell. The smell of roasted flesh overcame him, and he vomited until his stomach was sore and his throat raw. And now once more before him, the flames leapt again and he closed his eyes to escape the horror.

But Ravenna knew, for she understood. Her scar stung and she rubbed it again while Meryx sat impassively, one leg crossed over the other, patiently waiting. Air Marshal Francis broke the silence, "It's not over yet, Sirs."

As the flames licked the sooty corpses of the once powerful Fyjer airships, the roar of the raging fires mingled with the moans of the wounded. Before their eyes, Meganeurs charged down from the clouds, their ramps opening to disgorge plane loads of RAITs that roamed the still burning grounds, dispensing final rites from their steely bodies. Gomalan felt the blood pounding in his temples at the horror, but he knew: war ate up soldiers; it was their fate.

"The POW cages are full Sir," Ravenna declared proudly, ending the transmission. "Over thirty thousand prisoners taken on that day alone."

Meryx turned his reptilian eyes on the general and his mouth cracked into a grin. "Well done General Ravenna! The Army of the North has proven itself again. And Francis, your airships acquitted themselves honourably in the battle."

The president's bony hands gripping the table were white, and slowly he rose on creaky joints. "A victory against the Fyjers! I want to see them begging for mercy… Premier Lowena on her knees before me. Broken and without hope."

Ravenna curled her lip in disgust as the men in the room began to chuckle at the thought of the proud Fyjer woman debased. Rolling her eyes at their juvenile suggestions, she coughed loudly, bringing their attention back to the only thing that mattered: defeating the Coalition.

"Gentlemen, if I could have your attention once again…"

The wall shimmered, Ravenna commanding its transformation into a giant satellite image of the northern regions of Fyjerlan where the towering Promina Mountains held sway. Snaking far below their snow-capped peaks raged the Zamyr River, foaming and boiling as it cascaded through the narrow gorges and deep canyons that characterized the tall jagged peaks. Crawling up a low foothill, a blur of grey and beige appeared – the grubby mining town of Zelayna. Clustered on the mountainside straggled a series of rectangular enclosures from which tall smokestacks jutted, belching their offensive fumes into great billowing dark clouds.

Ravenna focused in on a web of tracks that snaked along the towering hills of gangue, remnants of the discarded mining spoils. Between tall spiky conifers, wagons bulging with ore could be discerned, travelling on their way to processing plants where their contents were to be crushed and smelted before being sold for profits that fueled the Fyjer economy. But now the mines of Zelayna transformed the raw materials of the mountains into weapons of war: weapons fixed against Wesselan.

The satellite continued in its tracking across a landscape where mountains and the river held sway, past vast fields of tall golden blossoms that turned their brown faces to the Denebian sun before giving way to the outskirts of the massive city of Massita that sprawled across the banks of the Zamyr River. Ravenna's brown eyes darkened with pleasure and she arched an eyebrow while turning to Meryx. "The northern strongholds are now utterly defenceless … it'll take months to rebuild the damaged bases and even longer to replace their warbirds and train new personnel. The powerhouse of the north," she purred, "the mines of Zelayna and the million-strong population of Massita… are now exposed and at our mercy."

A smile graced the High Commander's face and he broke the satellite transmission, knowing that the message had been neatly hammered home. "Compelling the Fyjers to transfer forces from the south for protection," he added.

The general's dark eyes glowed with satisfaction, and she nodded ever so slowly, acknowledging Gomalan's perspicaciousness.

"And we'll be ready for them," Ravenna promised.

***

The racket was intense, beating into his brain, pounding, vibrating, and irritating... oh so irritating. He pulled a T-shirt over his bare torso and pushed his feet into a pair of sandals before burrowing in his duffle bag for something... anything to dull the noise. He could not face it otherwise. But his attention was pulled away by the sight of his wife traipsing across the cool marble floor, her dark skin aglow against the white of a tiny monokini.

Pallav's eyes dilated, at first in pleasure, then in shock, as she reached for the door of the cabin that they had rented in the cheapest all-inclusive resort in Siddi Oasis.

"My God Tara, you're not going outside like that are you?"

It was then he noticed his teenaged daughter, whose long golden-brown hair brushed against her bare chest, a minuscule amount of material wrapped about her slim hips.

"What the...? Isabella, get back in your room this instant and put on something decent!"

Tara watched as her husband's normally pale skin was transformed into a blazing shade of red and she knew the bull would soon be loose in the china shop. Reaching for his arm, she was shocked when Pallav pulled away and loomed over Isabella whose body was rigid with defiance.

"I know what you're going to say... and don't waste your breath young lady. You are not Denebian and you will not wear that... whatever you call it...in public."

Fuming with self-righteous anger, Isabella flounced away while Tara rounded on her stubborn human husband.

"Listen here Mister... it's not like we brought bathing suits with us when we fled from Earth. This is what they wear here, this is all we could find, so you better get used to it."

Pallav gritted his teeth and grabbing the ear defenders that he had the sense to pack, stormed out of the cabin, on the lookout for his son.

This place drives me crazy, he grumbled while men and women half his age staggered around the resort to the ever-present mind-numbing beat of the latest Fyjer noise that passed as music.

If it weren't for the people, the noise, the jackasses trying to sell you stuff you don't need, the plastic palm trees... this could be a nice place, he admitted to himself while a cloud passed overhead, blocking the bright sun.

And then he laughed. *God, I'm getting old. I'd rather be back home, a good horse underneath me, trekking through the Black Hills. Or just prowling about, hunting with my Old Man. Those were good times.* But the blaring noise and the incessant laughter from half-naked drunks made him feel that the good times were all behind him now.

With a grunt of disgust, Pallav scanned the immediate surroundings for Luke and realized with horror that he'd have to venture further into the den of iniquity to find his son. Sighing in resignation, he watched as a pack of teenagers staggered by, reeking of booze and laughing at the antics of one pimple-faced munchkin who balanced two glasses of some odd violet concoction in the palms of both hands while walking backwards.

Stepping off the stone-lined path to avoid the oaf, he felt himself being shoved by one of the drunken buffoons and cringed as the icy cold drink spilled down his back to the raucous tune of their laughter.

"That's it," he bellowed at full volume, picking up both drunken louts and venting all his built-up frustrations and anger, he tossed them into the wave pool.

At the feet of Captain Bafa Villutomi, whose eyes went wide with horror at the sight of the burly alien Colonel Pallav Kóbor.

"You," he seethed through closed teeth, grabbing the topless monokini-clad dancer by the wrist. Ignoring her struggles Pallav pulled Bafa off her feet and dragged the unwilling woman from the wave pool to a chorus of hoots and hollers.

Digging her bare heels into the sand, Bafa threw her weight forward in an attempt to knock the big man off balance. Pallav stopped in his tracks, turning around and raising an eyebrow at the futility of the young woman's antics but was caught off guard by a stinging smack across his cheek. She could see green fury in his eyes and felt her wrist being crushed in a tightening vice.

"You want to do this the hard way then?" Grabbing her by the waist, Pallav threw Bafa over his shoulder, ignoring her thrashing fists and kicking legs. "You and I, we're going to have a little discussion."

From her upside down perch, Bafa could see the confusion in the quickly gathering crowd. Her only hope of remaining alive was to stay concealed, far from the deadly reach of the Black Hide, and she knew a return to Wesselan and her death would be in the cards if she couldn't escape from Kóbor. And so, Bafa threw on the theatrics.

"Let me go! I said no! Someone help me!"

Punching, kicking and screaming, she realized in horror that her efforts only spurred on the throngs of drunken revellers who began to cheer the big alien on.

Deciding more drastic action was required, Bafa twisted in Pallav's arms and taking a deep breath, planted her lips firmly on his and with his grip loosening, she quickly dropped to the ground. *Result!*

Pulling away, she was surprised to see shock and confusion in his eyes. *Damn, he looks so innocent...like a little boy but with the body of a statue.* And without thinking, Bafa ran a hand along his jawline and caressed his cheek.

Pallav blinked in horror and confusion at her touch as she reached up to stroke his hair. Taking a deep breath, he pushed her hand away and she noticed the determination returning to those soft green eyes.

He is so repressed! And kinda adorable in a way...I actually hate to do this to the big guy, she thought, before taking a step back with a smile on her face and viciously ramming a knee into Pallav's groin.

He went down like a ton of bricks and Bafa leapt to her feet, her mind planning the next move that would see her live another day. Until she fell, tumbling to the ground with a hellcat of a woman on top of her, spitting fire into her face, pinning her shoulders to the ground so that Bafa lay helpless and at her mercy.

"No one screws with my husband," Tara announced as Pallav slowly limped over, a look of revenge marring his handsome face.

Zanne Raby

CHAPTER 11 - THE SHOOTING STAR

The freedom of the soul-bird death cannot take away.

– SRI CHINMOY

Crumpling the message into a little ball, Meryx let it fall to the ground. "So that confirms it, doesn't it?"

"Correct Sir." A troubled look passed over the High Commander's face. "But we still don't know what she was doing at Farb. And why would she be at the controls of a Meganeur? None of this makes sense."

Meryx sank in his chair. "Does it really matter now?" In his mind he could picture Erica with her bright blonde braids bouncing as she walked, eyes the colour of the summer sky. "I needed to be 100% sure before I spoke with Fynn."

"I toured Farb afterwards with Francis. And by the gods, it looks like Deneb opened her maw, fire spewing from her very core before chewing everything to shreds and vomiting it back up."

The grizzled head shook, and his opal eyes stared blankly at the vision of destruction that still danced before them. "There was nothing left – no remnants of buildings, no sign of airships, and certainly not survivors. Never, never in my four decades of military career, have I seen anything like this."

The sound of a chair scraped across the floor and brought Gomalan back to the present. Clearing his throat, Gomalan's shoulders slumped. "I had to make sure, you understand. If there was even the slightest possibility that we could've been wrong, that somehow Erica was still alive... well, I needed to explore that."

Meryx nodded, a look of despair on his face. "And I thank you for that, old friend. But it's time now, isn't it? Time for me to destroy Fynn's world."

100

Gomalan placed an arm about the stocky man's shoulders. "Why don't you let me send for Magdar? My wife's always liked young Fynn and Erica. She can…"

"She can what? Bring back the dead?" Meryx shook his head. "No my friend, thank you for the offer. But there's nothing that anyone can do for Fynn now, except to tell him the truth."

With that the two men walked in silence through the Parliament's corridors, the sound of their footsteps echoing across the empty halls. As they exited the tall ornate building, the engines of two aerocars roared to life, the vehicles dropping down to the docking pad where the drivers vaulted out and opened the doors for the president and his High Commander with sharp salutes. Meryx watched as Gomalan pulled away and his heart grew heavy with sadness. "Take me to Lieutenant-Colonel Vogel's residence," he directed, his aggressive voice dull with pain.

That young woman was like a daughter to me, he reflected as the aerocar skimmed across the darkened city of Styria. He smiled at the memory of her almost crashing the first time she tried to fly, the look of surprise on her face as the airborne vehicle disobeyed her untrained touch. *And yet… she showed us all. Taking to the Meganeur like she'd been born to fly them. By the gods, I don't know what I'm going to say to Fynn…*

A light burned at the entrance to Fynn's residence, a lodestar left blazing in the darkness. For him. For Erica. He did not know. Heavy footsteps shook Fynn from his vigil, and he opened the door with a look of hope on his weary face. But all was dashed as he beheld the tear that slid down the old man's wrinkled cheek. His face was as pale as the moon of Haldane that hung like a sickle in the Denebian sky. Fynn stared into Meryx's tear-bejewelled eyes. "How…" was all he said, his voice as soft as a whisper on a spring breeze.

Composing himself, Meryx walked into the kitchen and thrusting a glass under the dispenser, watched listlessly as the water filled the crystallite glass. "She didn't suffer, if that's what you want to know." Handing the glass to Fynn, Meryx watched as his young charge took a sip with trembling hands. "She was at Farb, strapped into a Meganeur and ready to launch when an explosion leveled the base."

Meryx shepherded the dazed man to the couch where they sat together. Fynn's hazel eyes seemed more vibrant in his pale freckled face as he took in the news. "But why was she there? She was desk-bound, working in Flight

Ops & Plans until our baby was born." Pulling away, Fynn rubbed his eyes with the palms of his hands. "No! No, I'm not having any of this. There's got to be some mistake. She wouldn't have gone to Styria… she just wouldn't have."

Meryx threw his arm around Fynn. "Son, there's no mistaking it. She was on that base when it went up in a cataclysmic explosion. Air Marshal Caydnn was killed in the attack as well. Nothing's left of Farb."

Throwing his head back, Fynn groaned in anguish. "You told me you'd take care of her! You promised me!" Abandoning Meryx, he walked to the window to stare at the moon hanging low in the sky, its reflection painting the River Panni in shimmering waves of silver. He remained as still as a statue, not able to trust, to believe the old man who sat on his couch with one leg neatly crossed over the other.

"Fynn…" Meryx let the alien name hang in the air while he fought for the words. What could he say to let the young man understand that he'd checked in on Erica every single day, running errands like a servant, bringing her meals… but words would never be enough. And so Meryx sighed and slowly pulled himself out of his seat.

Perhaps I did fail him, he reflected as he made for the door. Guilt washed over him – blame for confining Fynn to quarantine while his blood was harvested; anger at Erica who wanted one last chance at touching the stars before the baby was born; and fury over his inability to protect the young couple who meant more to him than anything in his life. *But I won't fail him now*, he thought, and changing his mind Meryx crossed the floor to take his place beside the young man whose face was ravaged with pain.

"I don't understand, Meryx. I should be laying in bed with Erica beside me right now, and our baby girl sound asleep in her crib. Look…" Grabbing Meryx by the sleeve, he pulled the old man through the hall. "Erica even finished decorating the baby's room. No… This can't be real…this isn't supposed to be happening."

Picking up a stuffed toy, Fynn looked at it despairingly as Meryx turned off the light to the nursery and shepherded the young man to his bedroom. His gruff voice was gentle as he spoke to Fynn like a terrified creature, run to ground by bloodwolves that circled eagerly for the kill.

"Let me tell you what we're going to do, son. Tomorrow you and I are going to head over to Gomalan's office where you can review the data of everyone who went in and out of Farb on the day of the attack. Then we're going to fly over to Farb and walk the grounds together. And there's the broadcast a rebel group made… you should look at that too. I hope the pieces will come together after that. But first, you need to get some rest."

Meryx fished in his pockets for a bottle of sleeping tablets he'd brought with him and shook one out. Handing a little yellow pill to Fynn, he watched while the young man nodded despondently before swallowing it and crawling into the big empty bed, still clutching the little plush toy.

"Meryx?" The sound rasped with pain and the elderly man turned on his heel to see Fynn regarding him with misguided hope. "Erica left me a strange note before she left." Retrieving the crumpled paper, Fynn handed it to Meryx who without a glance, pocketed it.

"I'll make sure General Ravenna gets it in the morning; she can have her staff follow up on it." Meryx took a long look at Fynn's ravaged face and pulled the blanket over the young man's shoulders. "You get some rest now."

Then the sounds of Meryx's heavy footsteps retreated in the distance while Fynn closed his eyes, the darkness wrapping him in its heavy pall.

***

The water was warm and caressing as Daniel made his way to the shore, and purposely he slowed his strokes, revelling in the long forgotten joy of gliding through the ocean surf. It was not long before he planted his toes firmly in the powdery sand of the beach. With a wide smile on his face Daniel strode to where the others huddled about a small fire awaiting his arrival.

Angelo beckoned him over and shoving a cold drink at him, pointed to where the children lay curled like cubs on the sand, sound asleep under the tall palms that bordered the beach. Daniel's old mentor raised his eyebrows. "So here we are. Another few years older, another planet to explore."

The fragrance of flowers wafted on the warm tropical breeze and Daniel leaned back on his elbows and looked into the heavens. "We've come a long way from Earth, that's for sure. One of those stars up there is Deneb – Tara'd be able to point it out to us if she were here – yeah…what a ride we've had."

"Let's hope we don't have to repeat it again," Hoshi handed Daniel his clothing and sat beside her shuttle co-pilot. The three looked across the water at the string of lights that glittered on the horizon.

Rifling through his pack, Daniel pulled out three blue cards bearing the emblem of the Interstellar Collective for Peace and Security, over which was stamped the Seal of the Denebian Union. "This time we're better informed and armed with the right stuff."

But his lips twisted suddenly in disgust. "That bastard Kóbor used the worst picture he could find of me and check this out." Handing the card to Hoshi he pointed in disgust at the information. "The only stuff he's got right here's my name!"

"Hmmm... normal info isn't it... birthday... oh, I see he made you a lot older ... place of birth – Udoli, Geitenia...well, that's in the middle of nowhere..." Turning over the card, her eyes grew wide. "Occupation: exobotanist? Marital status: three-time divorced?"

Grumbling, Daniel grabbed the cards and threw them all back into his pack. "Yup, but the joke's on him. I actually did study botany in university so I can handle my own there, especially when you consider that earth's an exo-planet to these people."

Angelo clasped Daniel on the shoulder, his eyes sparkling with mirth. "But at least he got us out of there before the Wessel forces liquidated the village, my very divorced friend."

Shaking his head, Daniel watched the flickering flames and felt his eyes growing weary. *It's been one helluva day*, he reflected, knowing that this night would be the last that his group spent together. He stared over the black velvet of the ocean at the necklace of dancing lights arching between clusters of shimmering brilliance.

"It sure is different from Deneb, isn't it?" Barb plunked herself down beside the fire, the glow casting flickering shadows of flame in her red hair. "Reminds me of the Overseas Highway back home before the ocean took it, doesn't it?"

Dom sidled up and joined the group and soon the adults were reminiscing about their old lives back in Florida while the young crowd slept peacefully under the starlight.

"From the details Tara left us, it looks like we should be able to integrate pretty well here," Daniel interjected. "The geography's a bit unusual though. The entire planet's one big ocean dotted with an archipelago of islands spanned by bridges."

Carmen reached over to tap Angelo on the shoulder and motioned for him to follow her to the treeline where a blanket lay in the sand. "Sorry guys, looks like it's time for me to turn in. See you all at daybreak."

Poking at the dying embers Daniel raised his eyes once more to the stars while Dom and Barb sat companionably beside him. Suddenly a blaze of dazzling brilliance streaked across the sky. Pulling Barb close to him, Dom whispered softly into her ear, "A shooting star; it'll bring us luck."

The tail of the interstellar visitor slashed through the heavens like a flare, bathing the Bay of Besarina in an eerie glow before it fizzled out – a child's sparkler consumed and spent. Daniel looked on in awe, wondering about the beautiful play of lights, then closed his eyes and let sleep carry him away.

***

Dodzi lay at her feet, limp and lifeless, his face smashed to a bloody pulp while Erica fought like a lioness to regain control of the Meganeur. Bucking like a wild bronco, the leviathan vibrated as it spun madly while Dashawna screamed out in pain, her body broken by the violent assault that the vacuum in the cargo hold had wreaked on the massive airship. But it all meant nothing to Erica, who in concentration had blocked everything from her senses, everything except the blinking red light that had been concealed by Dodzi's bulk before she fired up the fission engines to rip them out of Cepheus-9's orbit.

"Damn!" She could feel the airship slowly being ripped apart at the seams, the pressure having built to enormous levels while in vain she tried to close the damaged ramp. A pool of blood sloshed about her booted feet, making the pedals slippery and unresponsive and overcoming her revulsion, she pushed the body of Dodzi away while Dashawna's sobs grew ever more weak.

"Think." Willing herself to concentrate, Erica fought the monster's death throes. She visualized a storm at sea, ploughing into the bow of the ship, throwing it about like a cork, the mast crashing down with its great sails billowing about. She could not steer, she could not fight it; she realized she had to ride out the storm and hope that it took her gently to the surface of the watery planet. But she knew that her hope was misguided as the sound of the rivets popping in the cargo hold resounded throughout the airship.

The Meganeur spun like a top and Erica could feel her sight growing dim, a humming echoing in her ears.

"No! I won't let this happen!"

Pulling herself upright, she willed herself to stay alert but the blackness closed in like a tunnel. Snapping back, a warmth washed over her and the stench of bile burned her nostrils. *What a time to be sick*, she reflected as she shifted her weight, the vomit pouring down her flight suit, and she kicked down on the pedals in an attempt to stabilize the beast in its death throes.

A robotic voice burst her bubble of concentration. "Denebian Meganeur, this is Cepheus-9 Space Guard. We've detected your ship is in distress. You are requested to ready your ship for clamping procedures. Acknowledge."

"Space Guard, this is Flight Officer Erica Rosendahl from the Denebian Meganeur. Enabling clamping protocols." A wave of relief flooded over the young woman as she shut off the fission engines and disabled her mission's coordinates.

I'll have to let Pallav know when to pick me up. I'm not going to be on schedule, she thought, wiping the sweat from her forehead.

The Meganeur began to float like a dead fish through space as a powerful gravitational clamp locked onto the damaged airship. Breathing a sigh of relief, Erica looked on in horror at the bodies of Dodzi and Dashawna, realizing that their deaths were on her conscience for having neglected to ensure the couple's security before ex-orbit.

Her guilt was forgotten as a spasm more fierce than any before ripped across her swollen belly and throbbed up her back. Breathing deeply, Erica was horrified as another cramp followed quickly on the heels of the first.

"Ohmigod, I'm having the baby now!"

Gritting her teeth, she groaned as the contractions took hold of her and she curved back in agony while the wild gyrations of the Meganeur rocked the ship back and forth, playing havoc with the gravitational clamper. Back and forth, side to side, the beast bucked while Erica fought the contractions.

"Meganeur, you need to stabilize the stern of the airship ASAP to allow the clamper to perform its function. Acknowledge."

A death defying howl broke across the cabin as the pain became unbearable. "Meganeur? Meganeur? Acknowledge."

Panting like a beast of prey cornered by its predators in a life or death struggle, Erica moaned in agony to the Space Controller, her pain mounting with every second. "I'm helpless."

The voice on the other side was calm. "Hang in there, we'll do what we can to give you a soft landing. Rescue'll meet you at the surface."

That is, if I survive, Erica thought as her body cramped and arched. A tug of war pulled the airship like a saw tearing into a tree. She could feel the air about her growing warmer, hotter than anything she'd ever experienced as the hull of the Meganeur glowed a silvery white while it streaked across the dark Cepheusian skies.

Almost there Rosendahl, she said to herself, resisting the urge to push as the ground loomed closer and closer. *Almost there. Millions of women give birth every day, you're going to be alright.*

The impact was far greater than she expected, ripping her from the safety harness while great blossoms of flames erupted across the cockpit floor. Something warm and sticky coursed down her chest and she screamed in agony as another contraction rocked through her pain-wracked body. "Oh God, oh God, oh God! FYNN!"

Shattering through her pain, she could hear the sounds of cracking and banging when the cockpit door burst asunder. Yellow garbed rescuers pulled her from the Meganeur and she felt her body floating in a sea of agony as the waves came closer and closer together.

"We need to stabilize her or she'll bleed out." The words floated over her, and Erica's muddled mind pondered on their meaning. "Don't let me die, please..." she murmured, weak and groggy.

A gentle face smiled at her and took her hand in his. "We're going to pull out all the stops to keep you and your baby alive. Just stay calm. You got a name for the little one?"

The long silver dart punctured her arm and she shuddered in surprise. "Danica," she said, her voice a whisper as the darkness swirled about her before it took her on her final flight into the heavens.

"Tanika," the medic repeated as the little girl baby screamed in the darkness of the night while light years away, a cold breeze passed over Fynn, ruffling his sandy brown hair before resting as gentle as a butterfly on the tip of his freckled nose. Then he knew; she was gone.

CHAPTER 12 - BAFA BEFUDDLED

Those who plot the destruction of others often perish in the attempt.

– PLATO

"Ouch! Damnit!" Flinching from the pain, Bafa tried to pull away from him, but the ropes were unyielding, pinning her tight against the chair.

"Sit still; stop squirming! You're worse than my kids."

Extracting another fragment of stone from her back, Pallav dabbed at the bleeding wounds with disinfectant to another chorus of swearing and a futile bout of thrashing while Tara stood in the doorway breathing fire.

Bafa sagged, fearful of retribution now that the colonel knew her to be a member of the rebel group. "How'd you find out?"

"The ring." Bending down to face her, he grabbed her arm in a vice grip and held it up in front of her. "If you ever plan on making a rebel broadcast again, which I firmly advise against by the way, I'd recommend that you not make your identity so blatantly obvious."

Watching the interplay between the two – a teacher to a stunned pupil – Tara bristled. "So *she's* the real reason you took us on vacation? Not that you might've wanted to spend some time with your family? I should've known when we crossed the border in the middle of the desert in the dead of night that something wasn't right. But no, I went along with your hair-brained scheme and now you tell me we're leaving after, what, an hour?"

Pitching clothing into suitcases, Tara picked up Pallav's ear defenders and threw them across the room. "I find you chewing the face off a half-naked woman and you act as if nothing happened! Are you going to tell me what this's all about?"

Pallav silently glared at his wife, his nostrils flaring. "You've got it backwards," he snorted, returning his attention to the abrasions on the young woman's back, the after effects of Tara's panther-like reflexes. "She attacked me. You saw that yourself."

Walking up to Bafa, Tara narrowed her eyes at the young woman then rounded on her husband. "No Pallav, what I saw was you all over that woman and she was defending herself."

Breaking off the universal translation device, Pallav shouted at his wife in plain English. "You think for a moment that I'd throw myself on this person? C'mon Tara, you know me better than that." He could feel a headache brewing and instinctively he rubbed his temple. "She's a member of the Black Hide, the rebel group that claimed responsibility for the explosion at Farb and I need to bring her in for questioning. That's all there is to it."

"You are *such* a liar and a hypocrite," Tara responded, her voice shrill while Pallav raised an eyebrow and caustically reflected on her long-running affair with that asshole Radu, but he let the moment pass. Not so Tara. "You yell at me and Isabella about our 'indecent' bathing suits and then I find you pressing yourself against this half-naked wave dancer…"

The sound of laughter rose above Tara's tirade, making husband and wife turn in surprise. "How charming!" Almost choking on her laughter, Bafa giggled. "A domestic in an alien language! Can I have subtitles please?"

Furrowing his brow, Pallav pursed his lips. "My wife thinks that I… well… that I…" Stuttering in embarrassment at Bafa's heaving naked chest, he turned away to rummage through his duffle bag. Pulling out one of his T-shirts, Pallav threw it into the young woman's lap.

"Now both of you listen to me." Ignoring the twin looks of disgust from both women, Pallav craned his neck to glance outside where chaos continued to reign. "Tara – you get the kids packed and ready to leave and keep an eye on her. Villutomi – you are going to give me access to your room while you wait here nice and comfy. No discussions. Got it?"

The two dark heads nodded almost in unison, while Pallav glowered. Bafa chafed at the ropes biting into her wrists and ankles and she indignantly endured the stolen glances and leers from Kóbor's teenaged son who loitered outside. "Room 451, in the Palm Quadrant. Now will you untie me so I can cover myself?"

"No," he hollered, startling the sleeping Jolanta who looked up in surprise. Growling in anger, Pallav retrieved his ear defenders and quickly plodded off.

A mirror image of the young woman, Bafa's room was an explosion of clothes scattered about on every surface while makeup lay strewn atop the bathroom countertop. "It figures," he said aloud and he scoured the room for holochips. *But what the heck's this? Oh, you can't be serious? She's gone to all this trouble to disappear and then she's kept a picture of her family... and her boyfriend?* Grabbing her meager possessions, Pallav pitched them in Bafa's duffle and with a second thought, scooped up the mementos before slamming the door behind him.

I need to tread carefully here, he realized, making his way through the mine field of drunks who bobbed and weaved throughout the resort. *Otherwise, she'll get us all killed. Hmmm...*

The crushing wall of humanity seemed to rush in at him and needing a respite, Pallav stopped in his tracks beside a tall frond tree. The sun beamed down on his upturned face and his thoughts wandered back to boyhood days when he'd wait in anticipation for the spring sunshine to melt away the snow and he chuckled. *How I'd love to go snowshoeing again! Feel the crunch under my feet; see my breath in the cold mountain air!* Clouds of dust rose around him, far from the pristine snow of his reverie, settling on his skin, filling his throat and making him cough.

Sandboggans! That gives me an idea.

Hitching up Villutomi's duffle bag, Pallav sauntered off once again into the thick of the crowd before retracing his steps to their cabin only to find Bafa bearing a red welt across her cheek and the tiny Tara arms akimbo towering over their seated son, whose face bore a look of utter shame.

Running a hand over his forehead in exasperation, Pallav waved his wife off. "I do not want to hear about it." Sighing, he sat down beside Luke. "But what I do want is for the kids to have a bit of fun before we take off."

Luke looked hopefully at his father, anxious to be away from the scene of the crime. "Here," Pallav said, thrusting three bracelets at the lad. "You take your sisters on the sandboggans and be back in about an hour."

Quick as lightning Luke made for the door while Tara looked on in wonder. "Okay mister, now what? You've got a very cunning creature tied up in there."

Tara closed the cabin door and glared at Bafa while Pallav picked through the AWOL captain's duffle, shoving the holoimages towards her. "Your family, I presume? Tara, untie her." Pallav stood at the door while his wife loosened the knots. "Now for God's sake, cover yourself up and act decent for a change."

Swallowing in fear at the look in the big man's face, Bafa meekly obeyed. Staring about the cabin, she recognized that escape was unlikely and would only lead to another beating by the small woman. So shrugging into Pallav's massive T-shirt she stayed rooted to the spot while her mind pursued various courses of action.

Squatting down, Pallav lowered his voice to a hiss. "You value your family, don't you? So much so that you're going to tell me everything that I ask, aren't you?"

When she said nothing, he grabbed her by the hair and forced her to look into his eyes. "Aren't you? Nod like a good girl now."

Dropping her head, he stood in front of Bafa who began to whimper in fear until she remembered. *If he was going to kill me, why would he tend to my cuts?* She looked up at him from under her long eyelashes and hid the hope that rose within her. *No, he's soft. He won't do anything.*

But in that glance, Pallav could sense the defiance and he hoped that Tara would understand. Grabbing the Captain by the throat, her eyes bulged in fear as he snarled, "Don't underestimate me, Villutomi. I will do anything for the honour of my country."

Searching his face for the softness that she'd seen earlier but finding none, her golden-brown eyes dilated in terror and she nodded in earnest.

"Good. So let's start with this guy here." Shoving the image of Tax'n hugging Bafa in front of her nose, Pallav wiggled the holoimage back and forth and stared into her eyes for any sign of deceit.

Tipping her head back, Bafa groaned loudly. "That's my ex-boyfriend, Tax'n."

"You think I don't know that? He's with the Black Hide, and a Geiten, just like you," Pallav bluffed, keeping his narrow eyes focused on her. Slumped in the chair, he was surprised to see the young woman fighting tears and standing up, he ran his hands through his hair in exasperation while Tara coolly surveyed the scene. His wife clicked her tongue and shaking her head walked up to Bafa.

"You think tears are going to help you now? You little bitch!" With all her might, Tara backhanded Bafa who fell hard on the floor, her lip cut open.

"He is! He is with the Black Hide," she moaned, pulling herself up from the ground. "But I'm not Geiten." Taking the proffered handkerchief from the big man, Bafa dabbed at her torn lip. "I swear! I'm Wessel…I was born and raised at the forks of the Wessla, in the town of Labutta. But I met him, Tax'n, at university in Styria, he was a Geiten exchange student."

"So you fell in love with a foreigner, is that it?"

"Yeah. I mean, no. I mean… we were both on the Hiking and Mountaineering Club at uni and not that long ago, I bumped into Tax'n again. We kind of hit it off; he seemed supportive of my career – you know, that's sort of odd for a Geiten come to think of it – and before long, yeah, we fell in love. I mean – I guess, I fell in love with him." Bafa curled her lip at the memory of Tax'n and covered her face with her hands in shame.

She could feel electricity pulsing from Pallav, as if he were a Tagarian snake about to pounce and she looked up, a frightened girl facing a very angry alien and his terror of a wife. "Go on," he said, his voice coaxing her along the path of dishonour.

"When the Wessels began to segregate the Geiten, Tax'n railed at the injustice. He'd been with me one of the nights that they rounded up the Geiten, and it was just his luck to be on the way home when he saw Sarpa assault vehicles roaring into the neighbourhood. He hid in the shadows and watched his elderly parents stumble from their home, his father bleeding from a gash on his forehead. His mother, clutching her housecoat about her frail body, faltered in the darkness and then a guard viciously slashed at her with a baton. He could see the blood rising from the welts, even through her gown. Some of the Geiten, they tried to run, but the Sarpas' electromagnetic pulses vaporized them, poof, into nothing but a wisp of smoke, wafting in the night sky."

Tara shuddered, thinking of Daniel and the others forced to live with the Geiten, and thanking the Lord that they were spared a similar fate, she quietly left Pallav to further uncover the nightmare of treason.

Breathing a sigh of relief, the big alien held out a cup of water to Bafa. "Go on," he said softly, aware of the emotions welling up in the young officer.

She looked straight ahead, as if she were alive to the horrors of injustice that Tax'n had used as bait to draw her in to the rebel camp. "Tax'n melted into the darkness while his mother was dragged by the arm and thrown into a transport. Tax'n's father – he shouted at the police to stop. After all, they were going willingly – as if they had a choice. The words made Tax'n's blood freeze; the police spat at his father, 'Vile, filthy vermin. You suck the blood of our country and pollute it with your existence. Parasite scum.' And then he watched as his father was struck off his feet. You see, the police had a baton and he hit the old man over and over again until all Tax'n's father could do was crawl on his hands and knees. Even then, they shouted and taunted him like savages, 'Crawl like the worm you are!' And all Tax'n could do was watch… watch while his elderly parents were probably driven to their deaths to one of the notorious Collection Centres."

She blinked and took a sip of water again while Pallav squatted down beside her, his face an inch from hers, his voice contained a whisper of venom. "And then, Captain Villutomi, you decided to become a traitor."

Bafa shrugged, unable to meet his glance. "I did what I thought was right. The Wesselan government needs to be overthrown. It's a nest of demons, bent on genocide. Don't you see?" Pausing, she searched his eyes but the cold blue stare gave nothing away.

"At least you believe in the cause." Standing up, Pallav paced behind her and placed a heavy hand on her shoulder. "So tell me then…why'd you disappear?"

Silence greeted him as Bafa contemplated her choices, for to confess to her part would lead to her execution, either by the Wessels or the Black Hide.

He flicked a copy of her leave pass in front of her. "Your grandmother is dead… hmmmm… perhaps she could be…" Turning in the chair, Bafa stared in horror at his impassionate face.

"My grandmother's a crippled old woman. She's never harmed a fly. She knits sweaters for orphans on Cygnus-Morea. She donates her time to help out at the animal shelter. Leave her alone for pity's sake! She's a good person."

Pallav crushed the leave pass in his hands before letting it drop to the floor where he ground it under his heel into dust. His eyes were like daggers as they bore into her, and she cringed.

"They were going to kill me afterwards, the Black Hide and Tax'n," she blurted out, images of the efficient way the colonel would dispatch her poor grandmother giving her tongue a mind of its own. *Bastard would probably politely knock on the door, have a cup of boricha with Grandma before checking out her porcelain collection then vaporizing her.*

Seizing on the admission, Pallav struggled to contain his surprise. "The Black Hide wanted to dispose of you afterwards? After what exactly?"

"He never loved me."

Pallav sat down facing Bafa and readied himself for the tale of woe that he figured would follow. "No," she sniffled, "the Black Hide used Tax'n to get to me. You know how men are…yeah, telling me how special I was, how he'd never met anyone like me… well, that part's true. A gullible idiot like me! He said he'd buy us a little place in the foothills of the Tagar Mountains where we'd live after we were married. Have kids and grow old together. You know – happily ever after. Such bullshit!"

Cupping her eyes, Bafa's shoulders began to shake followed by the hollow sound of laughter that rang piteously through the little room. "They needed a stooge, yeah, and that was me. I forged their passes to Wessel military bases. I got them weapons. I am such an idiot! But I was willing to be, if it meant putting an end to the suffering of my fiancé's people. Except, by the gods, I meant nothing to him… nothing…"

Her sobs began again, and Pallav sighed, realizing he was getting nowhere in determining the extent of the spread of the rebel faction within Wesselan. Reaching out, he gently touched her arm and tried a different tactic.

"You know I'm foreign, from a planet so distant that it took years of travel to arrive here. I didn't want to leave Earth. It was everything I loved. I wish you could see it: beautiful grasslands where the plains are so open they reach up and touch the skies, majestic ice-capped mountains, and oceans so blue and wide. Giant trees that reach up to the heavens. Water, ice, snow, forests: they framed my life and gave it meaning. But we left because of war, people being abused because of who they were, what they looked like, and where they came from. I was forced from my home because of it – who would want to raise a family in a place where people are culled because of what they are. My own ancestors had to flee persecution over a century ago. And now I see it happening all over again here on Deneb. I never knew. They kept all that from me. But now I understand."

Sniffling, Bafa wiped her nose on the sleeve of the oversized T-shirt she wore while Pallav made a mental note to give it a thorough washing afterwards. Bending down, he took both of her hands in his and willed compassion in his eyes. "Let me help you Bafa."

Misunderstanding the colonel, Bafa brightened up at his touch. "It's planned for Friday; I should say, I planned it for Friday. We worked together, me and Tax'n and the others. The Black Hide himself congratulated me on a job well done. Then he and Tax'n went out back to 'have a smoke'– oh, did I forget to add, and for some clandestine bromance."

The snivelling started again and in frustration Pallav put an arm around her quavering shoulders. Between sobs, Bafa continued. "There was a part of the plan that I wasn't aware of that I overhead that night – yeah, they forgot to mention it to me –Tax'n was supposed to kill me later that night. Yeah, after one last fuck… just dump my body in the desert and let the bloodwolves feast on my remains. The bastard!"

Bafa began to sob more fiercely. and Pallav patted her shoulder sympathetically. Disgust welled up within the big human and he fought to swallow the revulsion. "It's going to be alright," he soothed, while inside he seethed with disgust. "Tell me though, there's something I don't quite understand… you said 'it' was planned for Friday?"

Her eyes grew wide. and she nodded, suddenly trusting this man against all her instincts. "Yes, that's the day the president always visits his sister."

Picking at her nails nervously, she hiccupped like a child after a bawl. "He normally strolls through the streets of Styria and chats with the people with his security detail following in his wake. But he's old and slow so he won't be a hard target. Tax'n's gonna be in the crowd and when Meryx walks by the Ellys Grocers, he'll cut in between the president and his guards with a baby carriage – I was actually supposed to be there with him. Well, that's when the Black Hide'll have a clear shot at him. It's all planned out, it's sure to work. And then we'll be rid of the corrupt Wesselan government, and the Geiten can be freed."

Grabbing her by the shoulders, Pallav pulled Capt. Villutomi roughly to her feet and shook her. "You stupid girl! What have you done?"

She collapsed against him, blubbering like a child and threw her arms about him while the storm of emotions raged over her. Yet Pallav stood stock still, balancing the disgust of the traitorous young officer against the horror that was Tax'n. He felt her trembling body next to his, and the thought of her unaware, delightfully pleasuring this Geiten scum only to be executed once he sated his lust made his stomach churn with loathing.

What a stupid little fool, he reflected, *sticking her neck in the noose for this evil creature. So much in love that she'd risk everything – her career, her reputation, her very life – for a man who was ready to dispose of her like trash. But if I breathe a word of her involvement, she'll be put to death for treason. And for what? For being loyal to her man. I just don't know…*

Pallav understood that he should unmask Villutomi for the traitor she was. But then he hesitated. He thought of Tara and the ease with which she betrayed him with Dr. Radu, and the unfamiliar sensation of conflict surged over him. For no one had ever loved him to the point of laying down her life, and here was this young woman, stupid he had to admit, but ready to forgo all for the love of a low-life scum. *I'll deal with that later*, he decided, and pushing aside his inner conflict for the moment, Pallav came to a decision.

"Listen to me Bafa… you trusted Tax'n and you'd have done anything for him. You planned this assassination to save his people, didn't you? To rid the world of a monster whose blood-stained hands are destroying the lives of untold numbers of Geiten. But you were wrong. By killing the president, you'll only make a martyr of him, of corroborating and confirming the Wessel's beliefs in the justice of Meryx's point of view. That the Geiten can never be trusted and that they are worthy of annihilation. You see?"

Taking her chin in his hand, he tilted her tear-stained face up to his. "So I'm asking you now to trust me. Because Bafa, you see, the best way to fight evil is from within."

CHAPTER 13 - MY NEW JOB

It is never too late to be what you might have been.

– GEORGE ELIOT

The horizon stretched out before him; endless blue seas lapped against a violet background while the twin Cepheusian suns hung in the sky. Aerocars and aerofreighters soared through the air while down below, ships plied the waterways delivering their goods to the upscale shops of Dopang. Miles and miles of suspended autowalks and translucent tunnels looped between the sparkling glass superstructures that housed the powerful head offices of interstellar businesses that rippled with energy.

The Cepheusian government, aware of the virulence of the latest strain of the Denebian flu, had taken every precaution against the accidental import of the disease and the little group of pseudo-Denebian refugees had been quickly ushered into quarantine. Another round of inoculations and thirty days of isolation in paradise where they acclimatized to their new surroundings and their new identities. But now, as Daniel sat on his terrace and sipped his coffee while watching the denizens of Dopang shuffling along on their way to work, a sense of loneliness overtook him. It had been weeks, and he hadn't heard hide nor hair from the others, leaving him with a feeling of isolation.

"Denebian proprietary communication rights," he'd been told when the realization that his comms device had stopped functioning. The nice lady at the Immigration Refugee and Citizenship Office checked his Denebian comms device, then with an apologetic shake of her head, casually threw it into a shredder. With Daniel protesting loudly, she cheerfully issued him its Cepheusian wristcuff counterpart, uselessly devoid of his precious contact information. Shaking his head, he realized his Mayflower colleagues would all remain off-the-grid until they were finally settled.

He wondered how his friends fared while he sulked in the upscale residential housing unit that had been assigned to his family. And his boys missed their playmates, growing bored with outings to the museum and the art gallery where he hoped to garner some understanding of the planet which was to be their new home. The dark mood descended even deeper – for soon he would be even more alone.

Sighing, Daniel rested his chin in his hands, while he mulled over the interview his case worker had secured for him. A shadow of despair hung over Daniel from which he could not retreat, even in the knowledge of an exciting new assignment. For he had surpassed all expectations at the Ministry of Agriculture and was offered a job on a team of exobotanists. His heart plummeted at the need to leave his sons behind while he traipsed about alien planets on the hunt for new crop sources, and in despair he opened a link to his case worker before realizing that she could accomplish nothing. And so he quickly shut it with a groan and took another sip of the now cold coffee.

That asshole Kóbor screwed me over once again. I'm an astronautical engineer for God's sake – not a bloody botanist. And now I have to live this lie for the rest of my life. All because I was desperate enough for affection to play house with his wife.

Finishing his cold coffee in one swig, he slammed the cup down in anger, causing both Lewis and Max to look up at him quizzically. A little blonde head popped up beside him. "What's wrong Dad?" Lewis's blue eyes looked soulfully into his and Daniel ruffled his eldest son's hair.

"Nothing, son. I'm just thinking of you guys heading off to boarding school," he lied, pushing the thought of Tara from his mind. "I'm going to miss you, you know."

Lewis hugged his dad and beamed a gap-toothed smile. "But you get to rocket all around the galaxy dad! Hasn't that always been your dream? To see new worlds? It'll be so cool! I wish I could come along, just like last time, when we left with Mom."

Wow, that just made me feel even worse, Daniel brooded and stared off into the distance, ignoring the warmth of the sun on his tanned face before returning Lewis's smile. "Yup, I get to travel all over the place," he admitted with false cheer.

Max ambled up and joined his brother at Daniel's side. "Will you go back to Deneb, Dad?" The child threw out his lower lip in a pout, dark eyes as large as saucers. "If you do, can I come along? I miss our home back in the village."

Lost in thought, Daniel was silent. *Our village. Urkyn. Maybe it'll be rebuilt one day. Maybe the wind turbine still stands. Maybe the cistern survived the bombing. A ton of maybes! But there's no way I'd choose to live on Deneb... that damned place filled with hatred and prejudice, sand, and wind. Kóbor and his family can rot there for all I care. But I wonder how Erica and Fynn are, their little daughter... and Dashawna and Dodzi.*

Seeing the hope in Max's eyes, Daniel knew he couldn't crush the young boy's dreams. "Maybe one day son, but now this is our new home."

A smile from his youngest son rewarded Daniel. But then like two gazelles his boys were off, sprinting between the flowering planters and under a canopy of sprawling greenery, leaving him once again alone with his thoughts. A rustling alerted him to the presence of something and Daniel turned, hoping to finally come face to face with one of the tiny, scaled creatures that regularly raced along the stones of the terrace only to hide in the shrubs.

"Hey neighbour!" The man was tall and angular, his narrow eyes hidden behind round spectacles, thinning grey hair slicked back on a high-domed skull. Daniel hated him at first sight.

"Hope you don't mind me barging in like this. Name's Seb. The wife sent me over to see how you all were doing."

Picking up Daniel's cup, Seb sniffed at it gingerly before pulling a face and depositing it as if it contained explosives. "Whew, that must take some getting used to," he declared and pulling out a metallic case from his tunic, he flicked it open. To Daniel's surprise, a row of neat cylindrical rolls lay within and grabbing one of them, he thrust it between his lips before lighting it and inhaling deeply.

"Jewelweed," he instructed, watching the smoke coil towards his surprised neighbour. "You never tried it, right? Well, of course not!" Seb laughed, a high-pitched cackle. "You're Geiten! How silly of me... I forgot. No fermented drink, no jewelweed, no fun before marriage, did I miss anything?"

Your manners, Daniel seethed as the rancid sickly-sweet smoke filled his terrace, but in an attempt to seem neighbourly, he nodded and grinned, the smile not quite reaching his eyes. "That about sums it up: we Geiten eschew all pleasures."

"Well then my Denebian neighbour… my wife's invited you and your little tribe to dinner tonight." Seb said, flicking the ash from his jewelweed onto the cobbles. Climbing through Daniel's hedge, Seb looked over his shoulder. "Six o'clock sharp."

The stench of the jewelweed lingered in the air, pungent and oily. From the adjacent terrace, Daniel could hear Seb's nasal whine describing their encounter with great hilarity to his equally loud wife. Suddenly the idea of intragalactic botanic explorations seemed far, far better to him and this time, the smile that curved on his lips was indeed very genuine.

***

She was perfect: a tiny elfin creature with wisps of tawny hair and big blue eyes framed by long dark lashes. Her little hands pawed at the air, searching for her mother. Taso Samandr watched as his wife carefully took the baby in her arms and smiled up at the counsellor, her eyes moist with joy.

"She's perfect," Fadiya breathed and cuddling the little creature she dropped a soft kiss on the child's head while the proud new father hugged his wife.

The counsellor warmed at the couple's happiness to the beautiful little being but she also knew of the tragedy that had befallen its birth mother. "Before her death, the mother named the baby Tanika."

Taso's furrowed brow was etched with worry that the baby they so wanted would be taken from them. "And the father? Have the inquiries turned up anything?"

Shaking her head, the woman placed a reassuring hand on the man. "Sadly, nothing. The mother was probably Denebian. Space Guard identified her ship as a Wessel-built cargo vessel, but a verification of the flight plan database determined no Wessel ships bound for Cepheus-9 – so she must've been travelling under a different planetary flag."

"Wouldn't it be possible to track the origins of the flight? I mean, if her father's alive…" Leaving the sentence dangling, Fadiya put baby Tanika back in her cubby.

"Rest assured Mrs. and Mr. Samandr, the Adoption Agency's run this to ground. Unfortunately, even the transmission from the cargo vessel was garbled to the extent that it was impossible to unscramble the mother's name. In any case, the spacecraft sustained major damage upon entering the atmosphere. Of the three people aboard, she was the only survivor. I was told she was a beautiful young woman, tall and slender with silver hair. The poor woman died almost immediately after giving birth so there was no way to obtain any information concerning the father."

Relaxing, Fadiya looked on adoringly at the tiny beauty while Taso picked her up and held the cooing baby even closer. "Don't worry little Tanika, you've got us now and we'll keep you safe and love you. Forever."

***

"Forever," Fynn whispered as he stared at a photo of Erica. "I swear to you Erica; I'll love you forever." Kissing her image, he placed the photo inside his breast pocket, and touched the spot where it lay safely nestled over his heart. But the softness in his eyes evaporated as the door to the presidential office slid open and he stepped in to confront Meryx who pulled his bulk up from his seat, shepherding his young protégé inside.

Meryx gritted his teeth; he hadn't expected that Fynn would pay him a visit this morning and leaving a queue of ministers outside his office, the president gestured for the young man to accompany him to the terrace that ran the length of the building. Fynn draped himself over the railing and stared out over the quick flowing waters of the river towards the Geitenian border.

His hazel eyes dripped with hatred and without introduction he launched into the crux of his visit. "You said that the Black Hide was responsible for the explosion," he spat venomously. "They killed my Erica and our baby. Everything that I cherished – they robbed from me – I did all this for her you know – left Earth, abandoned my parents, travelled across the universe – all so that she could be safe."

Meryx remained still as a statue, knowing he could not lance the poisonous wound that festered within the young man. Yesterday had been traumatic for Fynn – that he understood. As they flew over the remnants of Farb ASW, Fynn had blanched at the smouldering remains of hangars and buildings, beams twisted and gnarled jutting from the scorched earth like the ribs of a carcass, picked over and left to bleach in the sun.

121

They had walked together in silence, side by side, through the rubble. Clambering over broken walls of buildings and skirting the tall, twisted girders, they arrived at the site at which the departing Meganeur was last reported. Nothing remained, not even ash, to testify to the firestorm that had consumed Fynn's family. Pulling a tiny stone out of his flight suit pocket, Fynn held it up to the sky, the sun reflecting on its iridescent green surface, before he touched it to his lips.

A voice as soft as a summer breeze carried to Meryx across the blackened ground. "The first time I took Erica home to meet my parents, we all went camping on Isle Royale. While we were out walking along the water's edge, Erica picked up this stone… an Isle Royale Greenstone."

He turned it over in his hands as the memories washed over him. "She told me it'd bring me luck and I've carried it with me ever since. It was the first gift she ever gave to me, other than her heart." Kneeling down, he laid the glowing green stone to rest on the scorched earth. "Beautiful like her. But now my luck is gone."

Turning on his heel, Fynn strode back to the waiting airship and as he climbed aboard, the president reached down, unseen, to pocket the lustrous green stone. Within minutes, they were airborne again and a shell of a man sat beside Meryx, hunched over in pain and lost in thought.

And now the next day, here Fynn was, standing tall and straight and with fire in his eyes. *Good*, Meryx thought, *let the flames of anger burn away his grief.*

"I've lost her forever," Fynn raged before he grabbed Meryx's arm in an iron vice. "But her death will not go unavenged. I swear to you, I'll find the Black Hide and crush him with my own hands… but first I will destroy everyone and everything he holds dear."

The president's next words surprised even himself. "Fynn, son, this isn't the way. You'll be caught up in a vortex of spiralling retribution and reprisals where there cannot be a winner. Is this how Erica would want you to live? In a miasma of hatred and anger? Let me offer you an alternative."

"And will that bring Erica back to life?"

Meryx let his head drop to his chest in response and the stocky man lowered his eyes. "No, but…."

"That's right," Fynn interrupted. "Nothing can. So I want to make that son of a bitch understand how it feels. I'm going to look him in the eyes as his life flows away and laugh while the devil escorts him to Hell."

Taking Fynn by the shoulders, the president forced the bereaved husband to face him. "If you go down that path, it'll be you who ends up in the Netherworld."

Collapsing against Meryx, Fynn suddenly let his emotions carry him away and he sobbed uncontrollably on the old man's shoulder, the futility of his action plan materializing in front of him. Struggling to contain the black shadow that filled his life, Fynn looked despairingly to his mentor. "I feel so powerless Meryx. I don't know what to do!"

Ushering him back inside, Meryx guided Fynn to a chair and sat beside him. "But I do. General Ravenna's reviewed the letter you gave me. Colonel Kóbor already had a lead on the Black Hide and he's following up on it. Trust me, we'll catch whoever's responsible and then Wessel justice will prevail. In the meantime, you're going to draw on the strength inside of you. And it goes without saying that I'm always here for you. You know that, right?"

Rubbing his red-rimmed eyes, Fynn nodded while Meryx snarled, unleashing his malicious energy. "It doesn't end with the Black Hide's demise. It's the filthy Geiten; we've already begun rounding up those cockroaches and sending them to Collection Centres to contain their pestilence, but I can see that it's not enough. Those scum harbour the Black Hide and his horde of vermin. Wesselan needs to be free of the Geiten infestation; the contamination has to be eradicated within our borders and the terror stemmed; root them out and rid ourselves of this loathsome race."

His craggy face exuded hatred as he turned to his young protégé. "I suppose you guessed that I was behind your promotion and appointment as the Squadron Commander to 19 Fighter? Well son, when you're ready to get back in the saddle, I want you to unleash fire and brimstone across the border; make them pay for birthing the traitorous rebel group by sending them on a one way journey to the Netherworld."

Sporting a halo of fanaticism, Fynn jumped to his feet. "I'm ready for it Meryx. My squadron can launch within the next 24 hours."

Shaking his head, Meryx motioned for the young man to sit beside him once again. "No, you're full of rage right now and that's not what you need to lead the mission. You'll end up blindly sacrificing your airships and your crews."

Taken aback, Fynn blustered with impatience until he noticed the old man holding something back, waiting for him to be more receptive. Turning in his seat, the president took Fynn's hands in his.

"I'm an old man and I've lived through war before. I've seen commanders squander the lives of their troops for nothing more than a few square feet of soil that even the lowest geiten herders wouldn't fight over. Bloodthirsty, intent on winning medals and accolades, focused only on themselves like school children - their needs for praise and glory above all. But you're better than that Fynn. I see so much natural talent in you. Strength mixed with compassion; technical skill augmented by leadership and initiative. So I've been thinking… and you can say no to this… I have no children of my own. But you've become like a son to me Fynn. Now I can't run this country forever. So I'm offering you a new role - that of my heir and successor."

Fynn's jaw dropped, and he clenched his hands together to stop them from shaking. Unable to speak, his simply stared wide-eyed at the president.

"Oh, you'll still fly and command, Lt-Col Vogel – by the gods, you were born for that. But if you agree, I'll start slowly bringing you into the decision-making process." Meryx chuckled as the light began to grow in Fynn's eyes. "But don't you worry… I'm not so old yet that I need to turn in my president's badge."

The big door slid open and Meryx's secretary peered in anxiously. "Sir, you're behind schedule for a meeting with the Minister of Science followed by your weekly holo-conference with the Standing Committee on Interplanetary Trade." With a sideways glance at Fynn, the secretary continued, "Shall I show the Minister in?"

Meryx pulled himself out of the seat and smoothed down his tunic. "Tell them all I'm out of the office."

Then, extending a hand to Fynn, he winked. "Why don't you let an old man take you on a boat ride down the Lower Sirga River. The fish are always biting this time of the year."

CHAPTER 14 - WHOSE IN TROUBLE NOW

It is not a matter of what is true that counts, but a matter of what is perceived to be true.
– HENRY KISSINGER

The two officers waited at the ready outside General Ravenna's door, impatience evident on their faces, while inside they could hear the rustle of papers and the clicking of a keyboard.

"You got any idea what we're doing here?" The diminutive Lieutenant Colonel Summer Filiponi leaned against the wall, her hands jammed in the pockets of the tunic that proudly bore the deep green patch marking her kinship to the Targa ACOLEV Regiment.

Col Hudson Lott, Commanding Officer of the 2nd Battalion of the 17th Mechanized Infantry Brigade shrugged and picked a piece of lint off his uniform. "No better than you Summer. Except something the Old Man said yesterday in the Mess. About Urkyn."

"Not that again!" Summer rubbed her boot against the back of her leg and groaned. "How many times d'we gotta to go over this? You'd think that the Old Man could've briefed Scar Face!"

Suddenly the door slid open and a sour-faced General Ravenna glared at the two officers who threw crisp salutes before marching into her office. The Commander of the Land Force gestured to a leather couch and rising from her seat, strode over to sit opposite them. Her eyes narrowed to dark slits, she stared at LTC Filiponi before running a finger down the scar that blossomed across her cheek.

Let her sweat, Ravenna thought as she glared while LTC Filiponi squirmed uncomfortably before her. *May she be so lucky as to never understand.*

Pushing a thin folder towards the Armoured Officer, Ravenna directed her attention to the younger woman. "According to this report, you spearheaded the attack into the village of Urkyn. Tell me Filiponi, where were you during the incursion?"

Summer swallowed nervously, her pale eyes wide with confusion. "Ma'am, I was in the third ACOLEV" … *What's she getting at?*

"The report states that you entered the village at 0130 hrs. Tell me what you saw."

Her mind spinning, Summer racked her brains to recall what she'd drafted in the Post Ops Report. It was all still so clear to her: how she'd briefed the Regiment on the mission earlier that day and then personally ensured that all the vehicles were fueled and ready to roll by dusk. The ACOLEV drivers had flashed cocky smiles as she walked the lines, the young soldiers encouraged by her presence. She could picture the troops cleaning their weapons, the peculiar odour of gun grease wafting in the air. She could still taste the exhaust fumes as they rolled out of their lager on the eastern banks of the River Panni with the setting sun on their backs.

They had breached the border with no resistance, for the Geiten had concentrated their forces closer to the Glodati Mountains in anticipation of retribution for the earlier attack on the River Panni Dam. Gentle rolling hills, easy ground to manoeuvre, her light tanks accompanied by the Panni Guards had made good time.

"Ma'am, is there something missing in the report?" The instant that those words slipped from her tongue, Summer regretted it.

"I asked you a question, Lieutenant Colonel. Is it too difficult for you to provide me with an answer?"

Blushing to the roots of her hair, Summer looked away from Ravenna's frown trying to collect her thoughts.

"What I saw…" she began, wondering how to tell the battle hardened woman who sat stony-faced in front of her that she quailed as her tanks rolled into the unprotected village, shells exploding amongst the fragile dwellings, those who had somehow survived the firestorm of the bombing now running in fear, mere shadows amongst the hungry flames. A pointless exercise in death and destruction of innocent people, and Summer felt sickened by her role in it.

"Ma'am, we leveled the village. We razed it to the ground."

Ravenna nodded, her eyes swinging to Col Lott. "And you Lott? Tell me. You went in with your soldiers. You cleared the village…house to house. What did you find?"

"Very few Geiten, Ma'am. I'm not sure what the population of Urkyn was before it was eradicated, but we came across less than 30 bodies in a village that had hundreds of dwellings."

"I see. No humans?"

"No Ma'am. A positive identity on every single body was completed. The remains were all Geiten."

She smiled at Lott and her tone became warm. "You've done well Lott. You've confirmed my suspicions. Why don't you head down to the cafeteria while you wait for your colleague."

Her gaze then turned to Summer who blanched as the older woman's stare bore into her. "LTC Filiponi and I have a few things to discuss."

***

"The younger generation have no manners whatsoever," she moaned to Reyhart, rubbing her scarred cheek as the memory of the insult suddenly interrupted her train of thought. For the handsome pale man had been staring at her intently, unnervingly. Looking sideways at him, she wondered if he too considered her repulsive, that jagged silver memento marring her otherwise sculpted features.

Vanity is weakness; power is strength, Ravenna reminded herself – the daily balm she applied ever since the bandages had been removed.

Reyhart crossed his long legs, unconsciously smoothing out the wrinkles in his impeccably tailored trousers. "If I may offer an alternate point of view Ravenna? Take it as a compliment." His smile was as wide and white as the powdery beaches of Lacerta. "The scar is a symbol of survival, of fortitude and the ability to overcome. Something to make you even more interesting. And furthermore, that woman is an ass."

A delicate flush blossomed across Ravenna's cheeks and Reyhart tucked the knowledge away while resisting the urge to smile again. *What an amazing woman! So powerful, yet so feminine. And so dangerously deadly*, he mused, enthusiasm causing a heat to spread within him.

"Well…" Ravenna took a sip of water and watched intrigued as Reyhart mimicked her movements. "I need you to do something rather… distasteful…"

His laugh was deep and sonorous and took the general aback. "Of course you do." A twinkle played in his pale eyes and a smile lingered at the corners of reptilian-thin lips. Seeing her discomfort, Reyhart leaned forward until his lips almost brushed Ravenna's ear. "And tell me, my dear General, what do you need from me?"

She pulled back as if stung by a sand scorpion and raised an arched eyebrow at him. Grabbing her light tablet, a hologram of Colonel Pallav Kóbor suddenly materialized in front of them. A strange emotion filled Reyhart that he quickly analyzed and was surprised to find jealousy rearing its ugly head.

"An ex you want me to dispose of?" he asked, silently hoping he was wrong for once.

Ravenna blinked and the look of shock dissipated the green haze clouding Reyhart's vision. "Colonel Kóbor? No, I don't go for the tall, strong and alien type. Furthermore, he's happily married with children and I do believe that duty is his only mistress. But I want something from him and he's even more secretive than…" Hesitating, she had the tact to look embarrassed.

"I will take that as a compliment too," he added, wondering what this giant alien had to do with the general. "So, how can I offer my services?"

Ravenna reached down and pulled out a copy of the last letter that Erica would ever write to Fynn and handed it to Reyhart. "You're obviously aware of the destruction of Farb ASW by the Geiten rebel group that calls itself the Black Hide. Well, the day of the explosion the author of this letter, a young Flight Officer named Rosendahl, was at the helm of a Meganeur that was vaporized in the attack. Problem is, she wasn't supposed to be flying. Actually, she was due to give birth within days. But before she went to Farb, on a mission that only the gods can fathom, she left this message for her husband, and it refers to the man in the hologram: Colonel Kóbor."

Reyhart quickly scrutinized the note before handing it back to General Ravenna, his fingers lingering on hers for just a second too long. His touch was like fire pulsing through her veins and Ravenna pulled back as if burned. Dismissing the unfamiliar sensation, she looked up at the tall pale man through sooty dark lashes.

Her voice atremble, she continued. "I believe he's the key to a mystery I need to solve."

Reyhart looked questioningly at her. "And you want me to interrogate him for you?"

Her silky blue-black hair flowed about her as she shook her head. "No. He's the kind that'd die rather than talk. I need information. I want you to kidnap his family so I can use them as leverage."

Ravenna took out an image of the big alien colonel with his arm wrapped around a gorgeous willowy creature half his size while a dark youth and a budding young beauty stood beside them. "The family." She pointed at the image she'd taken from Kóbor's desk. "Will you do it? I can assure you, you will be well paid."

This time it was Reyhart who raised an eyebrow while a pearly-white smile spread across his thin face, one that made Ravenna's heart skip a beat. "Oh I usually am Ravenna." Lowering his voice, he reached out to gently stroke her scarred cheek. "But this time, I believe that we can mutually enjoy the compensation."

***

He was amazed at the waterworks she could put on: tears streaming down her face, caterwauling as if she were being racked and then the heaving and hiccupping. *My God, she's good*, he thought, watching Bafa reeling Tax'n into their planned web of deceit.

The air in the closet was suffocatingly hot and Pallav tried hard not to sneeze as the overpowering scent of perfume that lingered on Bafa's clothing swirled about him. He watched intrigued as the woman blubbered on about her grandmother's fictitious death, how she'd been raised by the old woman who was like a mother to her and how everything she learned came from her sweet granny's wisdom. And now she was bereft, unable to sleep, to eat. Hurt and alone in her room, she needed him to come to her.

Tax'n's hologram cast its malevolent eyes on the woman huddled in the fetal position on her bed. "You left for her funeral without even telling me. What was I supposed to think?"

But his acting was nowhere near as convincing as his one-time fiancée's and his feigned hurt was evident even from Pallav's darkened refuge.

See through him, he willed her, thinking of the enjoyment he'd get breaking the man's legs – that is, unless he talked. *But fanatics seldom do*, he mused with an aura of anticipation at the upcoming task.

"If you trusted me, you'd've come to me when you found out so that I could be at your side, consoling you. Not calling me up on a hololink days later. Nothing was stopping you, you just chose to forget about me. How convenient I am when it suits you. But maybe this doesn't suit me Bafa... I'm in the midst of business right now, and that takes priority. Especially over a woman who doesn't trust her fiancé enough to make him part of her life." Rubbing his dry eyes until they were red, Tax'n pretended to cut the transmission, ever so slowly, while he observed his prey closely.

"Wait!" Bafa reached towards the hologram, her eyes pleading. "You're wrong Tax'n. I do trust you; I'd do anything for you. Let me prove it to you."

A twisted smile slashed across his face and a mouthful of jagged teeth were on display, lending him the appearance of a ravenous piranha. "I'm tired of the way you prove it to me. Why don't you just stay in your miserable little barrack room and cry in your pillow. I've had it with you."

Pallav could see Bafa repressing a shiver as her mind wandered back to her nightly couplings with the hideous Geiten whose true image danced before her. "If that's how you feel..."

Two can play that game, she thought, realizing that she possessed far too much knowledge about the rebel group's plans for him to let her go. And so, secure in her ploy, she turned her back to the rebel before smiling and playfully winking at the colonel in her closet.

A pitiful voice rose up. "Bafa, I'm sorry."

When she faced him again, all traces of the prior merriment had fled her countenance and Pallav was astounded at the transformation. Pain radiated from her eyes and she curled in a ball and rocked herself.

"No Tax'n, I'm the one who should be sorry. I love you so much and right now I need you here with me. I'd do anything to prove myself. Let me be the one who distracts the security detail; let me take the risk. Don't let us end it like this."

His dark eyes bore a strange light as he replied. "I can't risk a visit to the Base this time of the night. Why don't we meet at the river, say, in an hour? Then, you and I can walk the route that Meryx takes and I'll show you where you'll have to cut him off. And maybe we can make up afterwards. How's that sound?"

No, no, no, no, no! Pallav hoped his thoughts conveyed to the young woman – for a clandestine meeting at the river in the darkness was setting off alarm bells in his mind.

"Maybe you can pick me up Tax'n? I've been crying so much I don't have the energy to fly."

Good girl, get him here.

"You said you wanted to prove yourself to me – so do it. Meet me along the river path. The second bench north of the bridge. One hour Bafa, don't screw it up or we're through." And with a flick of the wrist, Tax'n cut transmission.

Unfolding himself from the closet, Pallav sneezed, waving away the stale air. "The river path? You settled for a poor location."

Opening a window, Pallav inhaled the fresh air of a beautiful evening, trying to rid his lungs of the stale perfume.

"What else was I gonna do? Your idea didn't work."

Folding his arms over his chest in exasperation, Pallav grimaced and then motioned for her to grab her jacket. Opening the door, the two walked to the docking pad where Bafa's mini Hover-V sat. "Keys," he ordered, but ignoring him she vaulted into the driver's seat and rolled her eyes at him.

"How's it gonna look if you drive me to the river path and he's already there? So Colonel, I recommend you fasten your harness and make yourself invisible."

Soaring towards the Lower Sirga River Valley, Bafa watched out of the corner of her eye as the big alien struggled to conceal himself in the tiny vehicle. Twisting and turning, grunting and wiggling, he only managed to elbow her in the head and bang into her arm with his knee. Not able to take the spectacle or the bruising anymore, Bafa burst into laughter. Raising a sandy eyebrow, Pallav frowned at the young woman and gave up, instead silently staring at the shadows playing across the desert beneath them.

"Are you always this way? So cold and distant?" Pallav jumped as a hand touched his thigh and he took her arm by the wrist and pushed it away.

The harshness of his tone overrode the immense surprise and shock he felt. "Just fly, Captain. And keep your hands to yourself; I don't play games. Now concentrate on our next steps."

Bafa repressed a giggle. "I don't play games either Colonel; you take things far too personal. But as to our next step, I do believe I'll be letting you out a few kilometers away. There's no way you can conceal yourself in here and we don't need to take any unnecessary risks."

Grudgingly he had to admit that there was logic in the idea. "Agreed. Fly over the RV point to allow me to get my bearings and then set down about a km away; I'll get out there. Give me a time appreciation of when we should arrive."

"I estimate our arrival in a few minutes. Far in advance of Tax'n."

As Pallav lapsed into silence, Bafa fiddled with the in-console touch pads, and the sounds of music soon reverberated through the tiny cabin while she hummed to the tunes. Shaking his head in irritation, Pallav did his best to ignore the ear-splitting noise, concentrating on the stars twinkling in the ebony sky and as his thoughts turned to Erica he wondered why he'd had no news from her.

I'll hail her first thing tomorrow morning, he thought as the Hover-V began skimming over the Lower Sirga River.

"There," she said, pointing to an empty pedestrian bridge that crossed just below the forks of the Sirga in the Wesselan capital city. "That's the place. The area's usually deserted at this time of the night."

Circling above the bench, Bafa pulled up and soared above the riparian trees making her way to a meadow where she put down in a mist of sparkling dust, shimmering in jewel-like splendor. The young woman watched as wonder lit up the colonel's face and she smiled at the alien's enchantment.

"Every year," she explained, while Pallav gaped wide-eyed at the mist that shimmered like the breath of a fantasy creature, "between the Cooling and the months of heat, the glowwings swarm in great clouds around the waterways. It lasts two, maybe three days at the most and then, like a rainbow, they're gone."

Pallav watched in awe as she swirled her hands through the kaleidoscope of colour that rose and fell like the tide. "I wish Tara and the kids could see this," he breathed and spell-bound, his hands began reaching out into the cloud of tiny insects, unaware of the sinister presence that lurked in the shadows.

For the first time in months Pallav felt a freedom lifting him up like the tiny winged creatures flitting about him. The choking dust of the desert, the insufferable heat, the betrayal of the only woman he'd ever loved, all fell away as the magical creatures danced about him. He smiled at Bafa through their iridescent splendour and he flung his arms out wide, allowing the glowwings to surround him in an aura of resplendence. Blissfully heedless of the malevolence in the depths of the undergrowth, he felt at peace, a peace that robbed him of his normal vigilance.

Vicious teeth were bared in a narrow dark face as Tax'n watched the giant man and his Bafa laughing and playing amongst the twinkling glowwings. "She lied to me, the slut. I'll make her pay. It was gonna be quick, painless. But not now. And when I'm done with her, I'll take great pleasure in dispatching him to the underworld. Ah yes, I'll make them both pay."

Grinding his heel into the dirt, Tax'n turned and skulked back to his aerocar and noiselessly lifted off into the night sky, his thoughts contemplating the destruction of the traitorous bitch while far below, a brilliant twinkling cloud continued to dance.

CHAPTER 15 – BETRAYAL

The mills of God grind slowly.

– LORD ACTON

One leg folded over the other, her black boot swinging, swinging, swinging – it was driving Fynn insane – that plus the waiting. And Lt Col Amber Anjit wasn't helping matters by fidgeting. Reaching over, his arm pounced on her thigh, a heavy thud accompanied by a grim face. "Stop it," he intoned, his mind running over the bombshell that Meryx had dropped earlier on him.

The Commanding Officer of the 37th Bomb Squadron rolled her eyes, weary of the special treatment and praise that was constantly spoon fed to the alien sitting beside her. And then she remembered Erica. "Sorry Fynn." Swivelling away from him, she pulled out her light tablet and suddenly immersed herself in a world far away from the dusty tent that in the pre-dawn darkness served as their Wing Operations Centre.

Fynn sighed at his churlishness and closed his eyes where a vision of Erica joined him. *I know babe, I'm as prickly as a porcupine these days.... Yeah, I know she didn't deserve it...No, no...don't you worry I'm not going to forget what I promised you... that's right...I am considering what Meryx said, I just don't know...*

A spray of sand blew into the Ops tent as Col Stanford, Commander of Air Detachment Iluzija strutted in, interrupting Fynn's reverie. Throwing his light tablet on the table that almost ran the length of the tent, Stanford stuck his elbows out and for a small man, Fynn thought, the Commander sure monopolized a lot of space. The assembly grew quiet as Stanford stabbed at his tablet with stubby fingers and everyone waited with bated breath for the Mission Brief. "Commence," he barked and suddenly the air shimmered before them as a live satellite image coalesced in the darkened tent.

He'd heard it all before, since Meryx had briefed him over supper last night. But Fynn listened politely to the speaker, jotting down the obligatory notes although the mission was already burnt into his memory.

"The first phase of Operation Golden Thunder has succeeded in pushing across the River Panni Valley and capturing the village of Urkyn with little resistance. Today begins the second phase that will result in the carving of a large swathe of destruction throughout Northern Geitenia and Fyjerlan.

"Your mission, that of Strike Force Viper, will focus on Air Base Irtusch, in the northern plains of Geitenia. Irtusch is believed to be used as a training grounds for the Black Hide rebel group which has launched successful incursions against our bases and on key strategic Wesselan infrastructure. As well as being an intermediary staging point for Fyjer warbirds, it is also a choke point that denies our forces access to the mineral-rich Tagar Mountains and the northern gateway to its coalition ally, Fyjerlan. The capabilities of Irtusch must be neutralized."

Fynn wearily looked on at the images floating in front of him, already knowing what was being asked of his squadron of Skykillers as the tall, lanky Meteorological Officer ran through the weather conditions. *It's going to be a glorious day for a spin. Hot, sunny, light winds…a good day to take to the skies… and sow the seeds of destruction."*

Glancing outside, the dim lights illuminated the gravity-defiant protective netting that surrounded the desert-bound camp and then he came face to face with the lethality of the enemy as a terrifying holographic display bristling with weaponry surfaced before him.

Whoa! Those look like the ancient Patriot anti-missile batteries of Earth! He stared in wonder at the lineup of dun coloured vehicles, each sporting the rectangular missile launcher that sheathed the deadly projectiles. The throaty roar of Fyjer drones echoed through the tent as their holographic depictions prowled the airspace like hungry guard dogs, providing constant surveillance against enemy air attacks while far below on the ramp lurked the real danger: Fyjer Starhunters, the deadly warbirds lined up and ready to launch against any incursions.

Fynn grunted impatiently, ready to get on with the battle, until the Weapons Briefer cut the projection and the room fell quiet.

"You can also expect this," the captain said, picking up a long tubular weapon and hefting it to her shoulder. "The Wasp's not the most effective, but you can bet it's lethal at short range. Picks up a heat signal and hones in on it; the Geiten Armed Forces have been using them for decades now. Best defence is to keep high: they got a limited range. Chaff and flares – best friends in case you run into Wasps. Lastly, we've got intel that the Fyjers have brought along gravity-webs – stay well clear of them by remaining high. Gravity knows no master; once you've been ensnared, there's no escape."

Fynn nodded, recalling his own experiences on the *Mayflower* as the briefer passed the Wasp around before pulling up a schematic on the holoscreen.

"Now, reviewing what you'll be carrying... Ma'am, your 37th Bomber Squadron's Firestorms are loaded with satellite-guided precision missiles complemented by an array of cluster bombs. Old school, but deadly." The Weapons Systems Officer's fingers traced a pattern on the holoscreen, resulting in a suspended mass of lethality sparkling before the assembly.

"The very latest in technology's being loaded onto 19 Tac Fighter's Skykillers. Backed up by old school guns and missiles of course."

Fynn chuckled as the captain held up what reminded him of a hockey puck. Canting her head questioningly at Fynn, she continued when he shook his head apologetically.

"This seemingly inoffensive disk's an Air-to-Air Electro-propelled magnetic-tipped radiation missile. Once the ELPROMATIR's fired, it clamps onto the skin of the enemy aircraft and bores inside the cockpit where it unleashes a deadly dose of radiation, killing the pilot instantly. Recall that they must be deployed within short range, from 1 to 20 km. In case of air to air combat, rotary cannons are loaded with 20 mm explosive rounds, firing rate 20,000 rounds per minute. Tracers every 5 shots. You can switch between rotary cannons and electromagnetic pulse guns. These systems are augmented by the more standard long range Beyond Visual Range Air to Air BVRAAM Thruster missiles with lock on after launch ability and an array of short to medium range heat seekers. You're riding an ammo-depot on wings, ladies and gentlemen.

"Lastly, a quick reminder of the Skykiller's cam-skins vulnerabilities." An evil-looking hologram of the warbird suddenly materialized into sight, then shimmering briefly it disappeared before the trained eyes of the audience.

"While this technology is, let's face it, amazing… many pilots put too much faith in the concealment ability of the cam-skins. The billions of scale-like mirrors making up the skin of the Skykillers reflect whatever's in the surroundings, making the aircraft virtually invisible to the eye. And if you kill your radar, you may think that your opponent is blind in the battle. But remember one thing: with the cam-skins activated, you lose hypersonic speed. And you still have a heat signature. Something to think about."

Colonel Stanford nodded at the young woman and stood up. Small puffs of dust floated about him as he dismissed her from the briefing. His face was stern as he turned to the aviators who were chomping at the bit to get underway. "Ladies and Gentlemen, are there any questions?" As the seconds droned on and silence held reign, Stanford looked to his team before announcing in his barking tone, "Stations at 0530 hrs. All crew at airships with pre-flight checks done at Station."

With an image of Erica in his thoughts, Fynn threw his light tablet into his pocket and strode out into the wee hours of the early morn. *Well babe, this is it. I'll be counting on you, just like I always have – the best wingman in the whole US of NA. Riding in on one of the four horses of the apocalypse and sending those Geiten bastards straight into the deepest abyss of Hell where they'll burn for all eternity after what they did to you. To us.*

Off in the distance, Amber and her team were scrambling to their hulking Firestorms while Fynn was surrounded by his crew, all eager to taste blood. They were mostly neophytes, having never engaged a ruthless foe who'd be waiting, just waiting, for the slightest error to pounce, to dispatch them from the skies in one roaring, deadly fireball.

But Fynn had faith in them. He'd drilled and exercised his team to exhaustion, imparting the skills he'd acquired during the earlier Refugee Wars of Earth when he and Erica flew side by side, roaming the borders of countries whose nations were imploding, interdicting the desperate men, women, and children from invading Fortress USNA. And when the remnants of those nations rose up in anger, they were there – Vogel and Rosendahl – destroying the enemy forces in a short, bitter conflict.

Back then, he found it distasteful to neutralize so-called threats who were simply downtrodden people looking for a safe haven. Doubts lingered in his mind as he strafed the columns of combatants turned refugees and watched as they tumbled under a hailstorm of lead. *Orders are orders*, he'd always tell himself to the taste of bile that rose in his gorge.

But those days were long gone, and this time he had faith. He believed in the message: the Geiten must be eliminated. As he looked into the eager faces of those he'd lead into battle, Fynn was sure he saw Erica's image shining amongst them. And it gave him comfort, for he knew he would never be alone.

"You all know the mission." Fynn scanned the eyes of his team while butterflies fluttered deep in his belly for only a fool knows no fear. He grinned as a group of heads nodded in unison: Inara, Matt, and Nicki – all keen and eager to taste blood.

"A swarm of jammer drones are going in first to disrupt the Coalition warning systems. Keep your eyes open for them, they're slower and not as manoeuvrable; the swarm might still be in the Irtusch airspace when we arrive, depending on their success. We stay high, covering 37th Bomb Squadron. Fyjer warbirds are in the vicinity, and you all know what to do. Engage and destroy. Show no mercy. Once the bombing mission's complete, we disengage and return to base. All clear?"

Three heads shook in unison and Fynn smiled. *Okay babe. 0515 hrs. Time for me to earn my keep.*

All about the camp, the desert sand began to glow, first orange and then pink, as the sun kissed the horizon. Dazzling white rays burst through the clouds as the Denebian sun began its journey through the skies. The big Firestorms began to rumble down the runway as a swarm of drones buzzed through the low-lying clouds and flew off into the sun. Fynn lined up with his team behind him, the sound of brakes shrieking as they stopped on the button of the runway, their engines revving and ready to lift off.

And then they were airborne, hovering above the lumbering Firestorms, ready to engage at the slightest hint of opposition. A surge of exhilaration filled Fynn as he scanned the horizon. The River Panni shone like a silver ribbon below as woolly clouds drifted by. *Such a lovely morning.* Approaching Geitenia, he could make out giant flocks of brightly coloured birds soaring under his wings, riding the early morning winds, unaware of the peril overhead. *So tranquil and peaceful… yeah, peace… Am I going to give those bastards peace… yup, Rest in Peace, Geiten scum.*

***

Light pooled on the pathway, spilling over onto the bench upon which Tax'n sat, a dagger gripped in his hand as he waited for the traitorous Wessel officer. *The little fool. As if I could ever love a Wessel*, he fumed as his mind played over the words with which he'd slice her before plunging the dagger into her disloyal heart. He could hear footsteps in the distance echoing across the pavement damp with the evening dew and he turned to cast a glance at the slut who he'd seduced into betraying her own kind. *And now she's betraying me with that big aurox.*

He could see the phony smile on her face and his stomach turned, thinking of the times when that actually meant something to him.

Or did it… he reflected, and remembering the burning touch of the Black Hide, he shivered in anticipation of their joining once this inconvenience was resolved. And then she was at his side, all smiles and hair flips, her big golden eyes moist with tears.

The treacherous phony.

His hand had a mind of its own as it stayed glued to his side, the long jagged blade concealed under his thigh. With horror he realized his courage was slipping away and he grimaced at the young woman who stood before him, his mind casting back on the betrayal that seared his being, hunting for the hatred that would reignite the burning desire for the traitor's death.

"So you dragged yourself from the Base then, did you?"

Bafa blinked and frowned. "What'dya mean Tax'n? I told you everything over the link. It's been horrible for me, you couldn't understand." Tears coursed down her cheeks.

Crocodile tears, he thought. The blade was cold and heavy and uncomfortable under him, but it did not yet budge. Her hand reached up, tucking a strand of dark hair behind her ears and in the pale light of the lamppost the blood-red ring shone like blood.

I gave that unfaithful whore that ring!

The knife warmed in his hand, rising like a serpent from its subterranean den, ready to strike. But first, he decided she must feel his poison, for the wrath bubbled up uncontrollably inside of him. Jumping to his feet, he caught Bafa by the throat and he saw the fear reflected in those expressive eyes. "You little slut! I saw you. You and that big man, carousing at the edge of the trees."

Bafa struggled against Tax'n, but she was no match for the enraged rebel. Under his grip, she could feel her sight growing dim. Then the ground rose up to take her, the wind knocked out of her, and she gasped. "No, you've got it all wrong!"

She could see the dagger poised above her and Tax'n's face like a mask of hatred looming above. "You were never any good. Bafa the stupid little whore. Betrays her own country for a fuck."

Her legs encircled him, kicking and flaying, trying to rid herself of the horror above while the blade shone like the moonlight on the river, inches from her throat.

"And I've got nothing wrong," he spat. "You betrayed the oath you took to Wesselan, then you turned coat on the Black Hide and ran. You're untrustworthy and now you've worn out your usefulness."

Her screams pierced the darkness, carrying across the still of the night to the meadow through which Pallav now raced, his legs pumping and his heartbeat in his ears. He could see them now locked in mortal combat, the Geiten's weight on Bafa's chest, a menacing dagger ready to strike, only being thwarted in its deadly descent by the struggling woman's fading resistance.

Pallav leapt through the air, a thunderbolt of fury, his shoulder smashing into the smaller man's frame who staggered under the punishing blow. Rolling on the ground, Tax'n clung obstinately to the jagged knife and nimbly jumped to his feet to face his attacker. The blade whistled through the air and Pallav lunged backwards on his heel to avoid its steely edge. Bafa watched helplessly as Tax'n threw himself at the Colonel, who sidestepped the blow and grabbing Tax'n's arm in a vice-like grip, wrenched it from its socket.

A blood curdling cry rose up from her one-time lover while Bafa lay helpless on the ground, pain coursing through her chest and constricting her throat as she gasped for breath. His arm hanging limp at his side, she watched as Tax'n charged Pallav head on, landing a blow to the alien man's abdomen. Stumbling backwards, Pallav looked on in horror as Tax'n vaulted to where Bafa lay fighting for breath and grabbed his erstwhile fiancée by the hair.

"The bitch dies if you try anything," he snarled, pulling Bafa roughly to her feet, the blade in his good hand pressed hard against her throat. His eyes were pits of darkness, furtively seeking his escape route while twisting the helpless woman into a chokehold.

Pallav shrugged and stared deep into Bafa's terrified eyes. "She's told me everything already. Villutomi's expendable: a traitor to her country. You'd be doing me a favour by getting rid of her. Less blood on my hands."

One millisecond of doubt and a fraction more as Tax'n's guard dropped in surprise. And Pallav closed the distance between them in the blink of an eye, tearing Bafa from his opponent's grip while he threw himself onto Tax'n, pinning the rebel to the ground.

He could hear the man's crooked teeth gnashing as he pressed his face hard into the wet dirt, spittle frothing in little bubbles from his lips as he attempted to breathe. Bending down, a knee pressing hard onto Tax'n's spine, Pallav growled into his captive's ear, the threat clear in his voice. "If you value your life, you're going to lead us to the Black Hide. Otherwise, I'm giving you over to Captain Villutomi. And believe me, she's just itching to try out some of the new tricks she's been learning."

The rebel's eyes bulged in his reddened face, a thin gurgle escaping his pursed lips.

"So be it."

Grinding the Geiten's head into the ground, Pallav fished in his pocket for the double zip ties and pulled Tax'n's arms roughly behind his back, resulting in an ear-piercing scream of agony. Tax'n's body began to spasm in shock as a flood of pain coursed through his injured shoulder and he thrashed like a landed fish at Pallav's feet.

"Stop squirming," Pallav directed, sitting on the Geiten rebel in an attempt to halt the thrashing. He'd succeeded in securing one hand while the smaller man continued to buck uncontrollably when the comms device he loathed came to life and a holographic form of a hysterical Tara appeared in front of him.

"I need you here now Pallav. It's the kids!"

He could see her face, white as winter's first snow and etched with fear. Pallav grunted and sat on Tax'n's arms, a hand on the rebel's cheek pressing him down. "Darling, can you call Gomalan? This is not the time."

It was then that the burly figure of the High Commander came into view, an arm thrown about Tara's slight shoulders while Jolanta slept in his wife Magdar's arms. "Kóbor, listen to me. Your kids have been kidnapped…"

His world collapsing around him, Pallav's mind began to spin with the horror of the situation, wondering if the creature beneath him had orchestrated the wickedness. Mindful of the distraction, Tax'n jerked his body upwards and with all the strength remaining in him, rammed his knee into the big man's abdomen.

"Kóbor?" Gomalan's voice broke through the darkness. "Kóbor, did you hear me?"

Scrambling to his feet, Pallav remained rooted to the spot, indecisive, his vigilance deadened by the fear he felt for Luke and Isabella while Tax'n raced towards the shadows. His stomach in knots, Tara's hologram crying on the elderly High Commander's shoulder while he waited for a response, Pallav watched in dismay as his prey scrambled down the slope towards the River Panni.

A quick glance at Bafa proved the young officer still incapacitated by the ruthless attack, a blossom of purple and violet mushrooming across her throat.

This moment will never repeat itself, he told himself, cursing the conflict raging within. In a flash, Pallav picked up the fallen dagger and raced towards the vanishing figure, the cries of his wife pounding in his head.

Launching through the scrubby bushes that lined the steep slopes of the river, the rebel was perfectly silhouetted in the dim light. Clinging to the trunk of a gnarled tree that jutted from an overhang with his one good arm, Tax'n swayed in the night breeze below which the dark waters of the river boiled.

I can't let him escape… we need him…

Dropping the dagger, Pallav eased himself down the scree slope and lay flat on his stomach to extend an arm to the stricken man. "Here, take my hand." Reaching out, he anchored himself to take the weight of the Geiten, but instead only the wind took his fingers in their grip.

Tax'n's dark eyes were filled with hatred as he snarled and spat like a caged dune-lyon. And then, he smiled. Jagged teeth cropped up over bloodless lips before the rebel relaxed his grip. Pallav watched in horror as Tax'n tumbled down the river bank, the sounds of the Geiten being dashed against the rocks followed by a splash, proof that the rebel was now truly out of reach.

A fine-boned hand reached out above him and Pallav took it. The red-ruby ring cut into his skin and he could feel the warm wet blood flowing down his hand.

"You saved me," Bafa said, her voice raspy as the big alien clambered up the rocks to stand beside her. "I thought you were going to…"

"He's dead Villutomi. Dead. He can't provide us with any information on the Black Hide. And he's no longer my prime concern. My wife," he said, pain twisting his voice as he scanned the wet grass for his comms device.

"Is safe with the High Commander and his family. And you, Colonel, have a date with General Ravenna ASAP. She's received information on the kidnapping that can't be transmitted outside of secure means."

Pallav wiped his bloodied hand on his trousers and swore softly. "In cases like this, operational security needs to take a back seat. Dealing with blackmailers, kidnappers, and scum of their sort calls for immediate and decisive action. Not office calls in the middle of the night, wasting precious time." His voice rose in anger. "Give me that comms thing, I don't have time to lose."

Bafa walked to the river bank as Pallav linked in to General Ravenna's office. Light from the river path danced along the current of the swirling dark waters and she scanned the river for any signs of her one-time lover. The still of the night was broken by the maddened shouts of the colonel; she could hear his threats and the general replying in a slow and lazy cadence before being replaced by an eloquent male voice.

"☐What an enchanting daughter you have Colonel Kóbor. So sweet and innocent. Isabella, isn't it? A lovely name for an exquisite young woman. Shame that such beauty will go to waste, don't you think? And your son… my my, a chip off the old block, isn't he? Quite a little fighter. But I was ready for that, for a son of yours wouldn't be taken without some blood shed, now would he? Oh don't worry, it's nothing serious. At least, not yet. Now if you want to see your precious children again, you'll do exactly as I say.'"

Bafa stood still as the recording paused and Pallav's agonized voice rose over the gurgling of the river. "Tell me, General. What does he want from me?"

Ravenna cleared her throat. "Patience Colonel. It's a ransom note, they always end the same – in a demand for money. Let me read it to you: 'In two days, proceed to the abandoned quarry located fifty kilometers west of the Sirga Delta, via the old stone road south east of the settlement of Kharsh. You'll come across a rusted gate. On the left post, you'll find an old metal box. In exchange for the safe return of your son and daughter, place a chip loaded with 2 million Krowns in an envelope into the box. Your son will pick it up and bring it to me. If you follow these instructions exactly, your children will be released unharmed. But if you deviate from them, you can expect to retrieve their body parts at your leisure.' Now, you understand why I wanted to tell you this in person."

Sucking in her breath, Bafa kneeled down in the shadows. *This doesn't make any sense — anyone with half a brain in their head would know that the colonel's a man with almost nothing.* She could hear Pallav swearing and she wondered how the general would view this insubordination.

"Listen to me Colonel," Ravenna cut in, "I can help you. I can find that amount easily. But I need something from you in return. Are you willing to trust me?"

Over the lip of the riverbank, Bafa could see Pallav's hunched shoulders as he sagged in frustration. "What choice do I have?

"But you do have one," Bafa whispered so softly that the wind picked up her words carried them feather-light, far across the waters.

"Then tell me, Colonel Kóbor, all about Urkyn." Ravenna's voice was taunting and Bafa heard the colonel groan.

That wicked bitch! Bafa guessed at his involvement, and grabbing a stone, she skipped it to where Pallav stood agonizing over his decision. Although she was unaware of his part in the betrayal of the Urkyn mission, she could somehow sense his involvement and knew that this would bring down the fate of the dishonoured. *Something the Colonel does not deserve...*

Pallav could make out the look on Bafa's face as he turned to the riverbank, her lips pursed, her eyes narrowed as she shook her head and reaching into her tunic, pulled Tax'n's comms link from her pocket. "Trust me," she whispered, seeing the confusion shadow his pale green eyes.

Raising an eyebrow at the woman hidden on the riverbank, he snarled back at the general, "I've told you everything already, General. I've nothing further to add."

With his heart in his throat, he broke the transmission and turned back to her, hoping with all his might that this had been the right thing to do.

But Bafa knew. She'd heard it through the grapevine how late one evening, a certain man whom the Red Tabs hired when they needed to clean up their messes had left arm-in-arm with the female general in charge of the Wesselan Land Forces. It was Reyhart, the cold-hearted murderer. And she knew exactly how to resolve Colonel's Kóbor's dilemma.

CHAPTER 16– GUNS ABLAZE

He who loses sight, loses the fight.

– ANONYMOUS

"You got the hang of that fast," Daniel's partner Meera commended him as their compact space-transport landed on the tiny planet of Aditi. Daniel smiled, the corners of his blue eyes crinkling in his deeply tanned face as the memories of Erica's tutoring of the landing shuttle were revived. *I wonder how she's doing now? I bet they're over the moon and Fynn's spoiling his girls beyond belief.*

Pushing himself away from the nav console, Daniel stretched his legs. "Glad to be here finally." Glancing around, he noticed Meera accessing the weapons lock up.

"Do we really need those?" Pointing to the interrupters, he shook his head in dismay. "I mean, we're meeting with Aditi Government officials to purchase a few containers of seaweed."

Rolling her eyes, Meera checked the charge levels and engaged the safety catches. "Better safe than sorry," she replied, handing Daniel an interrupter.

The door to the spacecraft opened onto a rocky beach where a wooden pier overlooked a vast blue ocean, and lugging out a small rigid hull inflatable boat, they threw in two large blue containers and breathed in the tang of the ocean.

"It's nice to be on terra firma again, isn't it?" Meera said, her steel grey hair ruffling in the wind. "But where are they?" Perplexed, Daniel ran a hand over his bleached flat top, for there was not another soul to be seen in the vicinity.

"This is the right spot… the right time…" Meera said, scanning the horizon.

Pulling the RHIB along the rocky shore, Daniel stared out over the crystal clear water. "Well, Aditi's seaweed's one of the answers to Cepheus-9's carbon emissions, so I guess we just gotta sit tight and wait for our contacts."

His colleague looked at him quizzically. "What surprises me most is how a guy from a desert planet's an expert on seaweeds."

Smiling at the spectacled Cepheusian scientist, Daniel chuckled to himself, his false identity having been accepted without a question throughout the Department. Then he saw them, silhouetted in the morning sun: two forms on a distant dock floating alongside rows of brightly coloured buoys.

Pointing out to sea, Daniel nudged Meera. "I think that's them… they've been waiting for us at the seaweed farm all along. C'mon…"

Grabbing the rungs of their RHIB, the pair launched their boat and opening up the motor, they skidded across the tops of the waves. Sunbeams sparkled in a brilliant dance as Daniel guided the little boat through the shallow waters. Tiny fish darted amongst the brightly coloured corals and he dangled a hand in the warm sea, feeling the silkiness of its watery caress. *This is a much better job than I expected,* he reflected as the warm sun kissed his face. *Probably the only thing I can ever thank that dick Kóbor for.*

Tall forests of kelp rose up from the shallow ocean bed like watery medieval cathedrals, waving slender fingers in the tides, their brown and green tendrils stretching upwards in their quest for the sun. Cutting the motor, Daniel heard an angry buzz zip by the boat, like the sound of a swarm of bees furiously intent on chasing off a marauding foe, followed by another.

"By the gods," Meera exclaimed, "they're shooting at us!"

Swinging the RHIB about, Daniel raced to put as much distance between their attackers and the little boat as possible. Meera flattened herself and held on for dear life as Daniel swerved and turned erratically, water spraying in great fountains concealing their efforts at escape. Yet the attackers maintained a constant volley of shots to the amazement of both botanists.

"Enough of this!" he screamed.

Changing course, Daniel sped directly towards the floating dock while Meera looked on in alarm. "You're going to get us killed!"

146

Pulling out his interrupter, Daniel sprayed the dock with a deadly volley and watched as one of the aliens fell head first into the water while Meera took control of the RHIB. Now close enough to see the two, he realized that both aliens had the distinctive features of Aditians with their characteristic green-scaled skin, hairless bodies and bulging fish-eyes.

Thrashing about, the injured man called out to his colleague, who grabbed a large container and vaulted from the dock into a waiting seacraft. Without even a backwards glance the seacraft sped away, leaving the injured Aditian crying out for assistance. Slowly he began to lose strength and slip under the waters.

Pushing the RHIB's motor to its limit, a steep wake rising from behind the little boat, Meera sped to the assistance of the injured Aditian. A widening blossom of yellow swirled about the alien – blood leaking from his wounded torso that would soon draw in vicious predators.

Pulling off his shoes and shirt, Daniel dove into the water as the Aditian bobbed up before sinking again under the rising tidal waters. Grabbing the cold scaly torso, Daniel felt himself being pulled under as the stricken alien bucked in panic. Cresting to the surface, Daniel gulped air and kicked the injured man away while in the distance the triangular shape of fins appeared, slowly meandering forward, zeroing in on the scent of Aditian blood.

"Daniel!"

Meera threw a flotation device to him, but he ignored the proffered lifeline and treaded water while the Aditian fought against the pain of his wound and began to give in to the beckoning voice of the deeps. As the wounded creature slipped under the surface again, Daniel saw his chance and raising the alien up, knocked him unconscious before dragging the bleeding Aditian into the RHIB.

The fins circled their little boat in wide sinuous curves, slowly closing the distance to the blood meal that they had been recently denied. Meera revved the motor, leaving the sea-wolves far behind, and began the journey back to the shore where a group of lab-coated Aditians congregated. Pulling out a first aid kit, Daniel turned the injured man on his back and began to bind his wounds while the little boat raced over the waves. "There's one thing that confuses me Meera…kelp poachers?"

"Don't be so naïve! There's a black market for this seaweed; so many planets, and not only those in the Collective, face challenges in balancing the environmental impact of their activities. It's as rare as an honest politician. And the only place this specific kelp is found, is here on Aditi."

Biting his tongue, Daniel remembered raking mountains of the strong-smelling brown algae from the beachfront where he and Poppy vacationed when they were first married.

Had I known better, I'd have brought tankfuls of the stuff from Earth and live a life of leisure as a rich man on Cepheus-9!

Beaching their boat, the pair was greeted by their Aditian contacts. Pulling the wounded man from the RHIB, Daniel deposited the still unconscious poacher at their feet who groggily moaned and opened a set of protruding white rimmed eyes.

Trying hard not to stare at the Aditians, Daniel was astonished at how fish-like they were and he marvelled at their inability to swim. One of the Aditians scrambled forward and brusquely shook the injured man, pulling him to his feet and pushing him towards the government seacraft. The Aditian closest to Meera offered a scaly hand and a smile in greeting, a row of tiny serrated teeth glistening in his pale mouth.

"I'm Dr. Pilo and I have to apologize for our tardiness. But I see you've unfortunately encountered the underworld of Aditi."

Dr. Pilo was in fact indistinguishable from the other Aditians other than the nametag on his lab coat. About the size of a pubescent Earth child, but broad and fleshy, the Aditians all crowded around them. Friendly and cheerful, their oversized jaws clicked as they introduced themselves, bubbles frothing from lipless mouths and Daniel looked away in revulsion.

"That one there," Meera said, pointing to the injured man, "had an accomplice who escaped with a crate of kelp."

She seemed immune to what Daniel regarded as hideous and conversed freely with the alien officials while he pointedly inspected the tops of his shoes.

"Unfortunately, Dr. Meera, it's becoming more and more frequent. The efforts of the poachers have become completely brazen, and most confrontations do not have such a fortunate ending. And we are grateful that you managed to capture this thug."

Dr. Pilo bowed to Meera who returned the courtesy before turning to Daniel with a flourish.

"It was rather my colleague, Dr. Radu, who was responsible for that." Nodding his fishy head, Dr. Pilo threw a scaly arm across Daniel's shoulders who barely succeeded in repressing a shudder.

"Then perhaps you will both join us in a meal once the purchase is concluded?"

Never had Daniel experienced such stomach cramps and nausea as on that day. Even after returning to Cepheus-9 with the precious kelp, he could feel the rumbling and gurgling assailing him. And Meera was no help whatsoever, as the Cepheusian scientist pleaded a blinding headache, leaving him no alternative but to lug the containers home by himself for the weekend. Tired and still queasy, Daniel deposited the heavy kelp tanks on his deck to the grating bray of his neighbour Seb's laughter that soared over the hedge.

Trudging back inside, the flashing green light of the holocom greeted him. Ignoring its message, Daniel poured himself a glass of water to which he added a few ice cubes before throwing himself down on the couch.

"Home at last," he sighed as he sipped the icy beverage, closed his eyes and breathed deeply. *Serenity! No one's going to be chomping on shelled molluscs, slurping slimy strings of seaweed, or drinking the gore from sea-cucumbers. No more Aditian food! Give me an hour and it'll just be me, a burger, fries, and a coupla fingers of Buffalo Trace.*

Peace descended upon him. He felt his body floating on waves of relaxation and Daniel began to drift off to the realm of dreams. Hands interlaced on his chest, he could feel his breath rising and falling rhythmically and a smile spread across his broad tanned face. Peace! Drifting in warmth; relishing the feeling of serenity… tranquility…when suddenly the voice of Angelo Morelli stole into his space – *what was it he was saying – only a dream* he told himself – until two heavy thuds landed on his tender abdomen.

"Welcome home Dad!"

***

That's funny… I got this weird eerie feeling…like I'm wrapped in an ice cold blanket of the creeps…

A hundred thousand feet above the Denebian planet Fynn checked his angles; nothing but blue sky punctuated by thin wisps of cirrus clouds riding the breezes below. *Just a feeling... like electricity coursing around me...*

Shaking his head, he checked the in-console sat-tracker. All normal: three white bricks glowed, shadowing the progress of his team's Skykillers as Nicki, Inara and Matt trailed at a respective distance. He could make out the chunky signals of Amber's squadron of Firestorms chugging along far behind their deadly escort. Like the heavy winged dragons of ancient legends, the bombers were poised to spew fire and destruction on the enemy coalition.

All's in order. Still, I can't shake that feeling... and just clearing the Panni Valley – approaching enemy airspace. Ready to switch to combat frequencies.

The radio crackled to life, cutting him off before he could relay the change. "Watchdog; contact at 140, 350 kilometers. Looks like two Starhunters. Angels 50."

A wicked grin spread across Fynn's face as he listened to the heads-up from Satellite Early Warning System. Then two red bricks blinked onto the periphery of Fynn's sat-tracker, exactly where Watchdog indicated: bearing 140 degrees from him, now 150 km away at 70,000 feet...just a touch out of missile range.

Pay back time's about to start. Tick tock you bastards, your clocks are about to run out.

"Falcon 122; Concur. Cam-skins on and let's take 'er up now, heading west. Speed 1200 kph. Angels 45, now in the ascent."

Everything faded in the background as concentration overtook him. The red bricks tracked across the top of his screen before banking smoothly to the left. "Contacts appear to be heading south, heading 250. Speed 1630 kph. Angels constant at 50. Let's accelerate."

The voice of Inara punched through his dogged determination to throw his machine into the breach. "Falcon 127. Speed restrictions for cam-skins at 1235."

Snorting in irritation, Fynn pushed his warbird into a steep ascent to rise above the Starhunters.

Damn! We'll never catch 'em cloaked.

Jabbing a gloved finger at the console, Fynn disengaged the cam-skins that concealed him from the enemy warbirds. The two red bricks swung their noses in a tight arc, bearing directly on him while Fynn gently ran an anxious finger over the master arm switch.

"Inara, take over lead and maintain top cover for 37ᵗʰ Bomb Squadron. I'm … going to… get these bogies away from the drop zone."

A button as white as the Denebian sun glowed on the left eyebrow of the cockpit and Fynn punched it off, deactivating the Thought-Melding Interface of his warbird.

Sorry gang, but I'm going solo here… and engaging the backup hoverfans, Fynn pushed the Skykiller into a vertical ascent.

Nicki watched in dismay as Fynn climbed ever upwards, gaining altitude over the Fyjer Starhunters and came to a decision. "Inara, I'm going after him. Earth Boy's going to get himself killed."

"You stay put girl. That goes for you too Matt. We've got a mission to see through – those bombers need top cover. Earth Boy's got his fangs out – let him exorcise his demons by himself."

But Fynn could hear none of this, his eyes scanning between the controls while he reflected on his plan of attack.

Bogies at 200 km, closure rate 1330 knots on collision course – good stuff! Within range for Thrusters… but I'd rather see their ugly little faces when I send 'em to hell…

A squeal grabbed his attention momentarily as the Radar Warning Receiver chirped to life.

And now the fun begins, they're tracking me…

Twisting his warbird to the left, Fynn banked abruptly and dove towards his opponents, his finger poised above the weapon release button.

"Beep… beep… beep…"

A high-pitch noise sounded intermittently in his helmet, the audio launch warning him that a missile was rocketing his way and Fynn shook his head.

Tsk, tsk, tsk. Mistake #1 guys, firing too soon.

Jinking sharply to the right, Fynn accelerated and pushed the Skykiller into a tight curve and a series of rapid, erratic turns while the missile gradually lost its acceleration and ability to track, plummeting to the ground in a great fireball.

Christ, it's that feeling again. I can't seem to lose it…

Another chirp caught his attention as a second missile sought to tear him from the skies. He could see its white smoke trail before peeling off to increase his distance from its deadly embrace. Breaking into it, his warbird's steep angles threw off the missile which couldn't hack the turn and instead lost control, free-falling into the desert floor below.

What the hell was that?

It felt like a breeze wafting over his face, flowing under and across his cheeks before touching the point of his nose.

Get it over with, a little voice said. *This isn't a playground in the sky, Freckles.*

"Christ! Erica?"

In that one second of distraction, a hail of bullets rained past his warbird as the Fyjer Starhunters thundered past him in a deadly duel. Fynn snarled. Pushing the madness from his mind he switched on his targeting pod and toggled to the AAM ELPROMATIR mode.

"Ok assholes, I've quit playing games. Except maybe... follow the leader..."

Switching to dogfight override he shot upwards, twisting right and left while pushing his warbird to the limit as the quarry continued in their pursuit, guns ablazing. "Idiots...falling into the trap nicely...altitude 52 nautical miles... ...effects of gravity minimal... air thinning to minimum for engines...right about now..."

Tensing his body, Fynn shoved the stick forward and the Skykiller plummeted nose down towards the horizon. With gravity assisting and afterburners lit, his warbird was now far past hypersonic. Fynn ignored the greying at the peripheral of his vision and pushed himself to the limit. Unleashing a roar through the cockpit, he held down the trigger for a snapshot.

Let's go for the throat.

A torrent of high explosive bullets tore through the belly of the lead Fyjer warbird and Fynn eased back on the stick before banking left and engaging the cam-skins while the second warbird catapulted downwards in search of its prey with its cannons blazing.

Shooting blind, he admonished as the bullets pounded into the Geiten base below, *tut tut tut, blue on blue.*

It was still there; he could feel a cold tingling on the back of his neck and he shook like a dog shaking off water after falling into a pond.

For a split-second, he contemplated keeping the cam-skins activated until his RWR squawked again.

This imbecile just won't give up! Now a heat-seeker, coming my way.

Off went the cam-skins in an attempt to outrun the infra-red missile and Fynn initiated a sharp course change, hiding his hot jet pipe from it before he pointed his warbird directly at the Denebian sun. Pulling hard left, he could track the missile's path duplicating his every move.

No worries, that little bugger'll run out of juice before me!'

A quick flip disengaged the warbird's wing hoverfans. Reflexes kicking in, Fynn banked hard and enacted a rapid succession of erratic turns, keeping the heat-seeker off to his starboard side while popping off flares. Confused the missile shook and shimmed like a lemming in a hawk's talons before it exploded harmlessly into the air far behind the racing Skykiller. Wingfans roared back to life and he chuckled, "Good riddance, piece of junk! Now back to that Starhunter…"

Suddenly, Fynn noticed a second red brick appear on his screen. *Steady up, that idiot's got backup…Okay…120 for a 33 offset, 85 km... Target entering ELPROMATIR range…Locked on…*

"Falcon 122. Fox 3."

From the Wessel warbird, a slender cylinder dropped and hung suspended in the crystal-clear blue sky for a split second before racing forward, faster than the eye could follow. A brilliant white tail was the only clue to the projectile bearing the seemingly innocuous disk, one that to Fynn resembled a Frisbee-hockey puck hybrid. And one that would latch onto the doomed Fyjer warbird, dissolving through its hull while fatal levels of radiation obliterated the life of its occupant.

In less than the time that it took for Fynn to exhale, the warbird was falling from the sky in a graceful arc while its counterpart finally understood the danger from the maverick Wessel pilot.

Pulling his nose up in anticipation of a third kill, the powerful wing fans spun the warbird around in a tight circle and engaging his afterburners Fynn raced across the sky in search of his final target. The white bricks of the 37th Bomb Squadron beeped on his screen, shadowed by his teams' Skykillers and Fynn understood the urgency of his mission for in mere moments it would be too late for him to enact his revenge. Pushing his airship, Fynn raced until he was neck and neck with the enemy warbird.

Let me see your face before I blow you out of the sky…

For a second, it seemed like the enemy pilot could read his mind. Pivoting in the cockpit, she pushed her long brown hair to one side before raising a fist to him in anger and surging ahead in a deadly dance above the desert plains. Except Fynn had no more time for games. Looping to the right in a tight curve, he watched as she attempted to follow him. But the Starhunter was no match for his warbird and swinging wide, she overshot.

Sorry Sweetheart today is not your day… he whispered, a clear shot at her starboard side materializing before him. As his finger plunged down on the trigger, he felt nothing; nothing at all.

What the…? No fucking way! Blockage…

He could feel his heart pounding in his chest.

"Falcon 122 onboard computer, manual override. I repeat, manual override…"

Grabbing the emergency stick in his hands, Fynn grinned. *Never liked that crazy eyeball-posture control shit anyhow… This is me now Sweetheart. Say your prayers.*

Red warning lights from the onboard computer blared off and on in the cockpit and with afterburners cooking and hoverfans spinning furiously, Fynn surged ahead past safe maximum speed, depressing the trigger repeatedly. Click, click, click… click, click, click… BANG! The pounding of his guns etched lines through the clouds.

Ah, there you are my friends. Now let's get back to business.

Rising higher and higher, he pushed the powerful Skykiller until it rose almost to the Karman line, then crested inverted. A snap half-roll and upright again, and suddenly he was swooping downwards, picking up speed like an avenging falcon in a dive.

Out of the corner of his eye he could see them approaching, the chubby Firestorms, and he watched as the remaining Starhunter hung seemingly motionless, its pilot torn between the courses of action in front of her.

Just for a second the Fyjer pilot was conflicted, for she could see Fynn approaching at breakneck speed while the bombers droned towards the base which she was sworn to protect. Unaware of the shield of Skykillers high above the Firestorms, she hesitated for one second before turning, fleeing from him in an attack on the bombers.

But it was too late. Zooming down in a high-speed pass with guns ablazing, the world ceased to turn for Fynn as he unleashed a deadly shower of bullets that tore through the Starhunter, transforming it into a fireball streaking across the sky before it spiraled to the desert floor where it exploded in a burst of greasy black smoke and billowing orange plumes.

"Woo Hoo! Nothing like a guns kill!"

Pulling back, he breathed deeply, feeling his muscles relaxing as he plugged back into the warbird's system. Reactivating the Thought-Melding Interface, Fynn banked and began to ascend to fall in with his team, high above the rapidly approaching bombers.

"Falcon 125. Welcome back…Good kill… *Earth Boy*…"

"Glad to be of service, Nicki," he laughed, shrugging at his newly acquired call sign. Until a blinding flash from below caught his attention. "Christ, gravity nets!"

Deployed in a great burst, canopies thundered about him, their powerful tentacles reaching out to pull him in and bring him down. And as they closed on the Wessel warbird, he could feel the same eerie electricity surging about the cockpit mocking him, and he thought he could hear a laughing voice whispering in his ear – *Gravity knows no master.*

CHAPTER 17 – WE'RE AFTER BIG FISH NOW

Let your plans be dark and impenetrable as the night, and when you move, fall like a thunderbolt.

– SUN TZU

"Will you just give me that thing!"

Bafa looked on exasperated as Pallav fiddled with the Universal Translation Device, unable to change its frequency. "Let me look at it," she reiterated while he waved her off, his browed furrowed in frustration. The Wessel Captain sighed, watching the Colonel's big hands fumbling with the delicate device pinned to his collar.

Nerves on edge, Bafa dreaded making contact with the Black Hide and this delay was only adding to her anxiety. Finally, she couldn't bear it any longer.

"Come here."

Grabbing the big man by the collars she caught Pallav off guard and pulling him towards her, she reached up and deftly removed the little button.

By the gods he's tall, she thought as her hand brushed against his chest. *And with eyes as green as the River Panni.*

Pallav pushed her away, his face flaming red and his eyes flashing fury. And when he spoke, she smiled, for she understood not one word.

Waggling the UTD in front of him, she smiled before retiring a safe distance. "You, Colonel Kóbor, need to start learning our language…" Turning her back to him, she flipped open the top of the button and squinting under the dim light of her barrack room, tinkered with its frequency. But instead of handing it back to him, Bafa hooked it up to her tunic.

"So what's this language you speak? How'd I sound?"

His face now flushed with thunder. "Now is not the time Villutomi. My children are in danger. The president faces an assassination attempt. Unfortunately, you are my only hope in resolving these situations."

One eyebrow cocked, Pallav then extended his hand while the chastened woman handed over the UTD. And watched as his big fingers once again fumbled with it, pricking himself and cursing in his strange alien tongue.

"Oh, and by the way, it's English."

He glared at her menacingly and reflected momentarily on his decision in trusting what he considered a slip of a girl and a traitor to boot. Shrugging his shoulders, he realized he was in too deep now to turn back.

"So, you say that the Black Hide remains anonymous." Pallav's eyebrows raised in surprise at the sound of his modified voice. For he sounded exactly like the man who had plunged to his death last night in the Sirga River. "But would he be to Tax'n, if, as you purport, they were lovers?"

Her dark head nodded. "The Black Hide's never been unmasked. His identity is a closely guarded secret, and even Tax'n had no clue. And before you say anything, yes, I asked him because I was curious. You see, the Black Hide has an accent when he speaks Geiten. It's like he's learned the language later in life. I don't think he was raised Geiten."

"Good to know…" Pallav saw a smile light up Bafa's face so like his daughter Isabella when she handed him a good report card that it made him uneasy. "Now then… let's review this once more before we go live. Cause if this fails Villutomi, make no mistake, it's your neck in the noose."

He flinched at the look of shock and hurt on her face, and the feeling of uneasiness spread even deeper as he eyed the mottled purple bruises colouring her slim neck. Bafa looked up at him with eyes moist and trusting.

"I won't fail you. I promise." Her voice trembled as she met his gaze. "Just make the call, Colonel."

Tax'n's comms link was cold in the palm of his hand as he scrolled through the call log with Bafa peeking over his shoulder. That's it," she said, poking at the screen to disable holographic transmission.

He sat across from her. The room so tiny he had to bend his legs beneath him to avoid contact with the young woman who, perched on her bed, was now nervously swinging her feet like a child.

Rolling his eyes, he heard a crackle on the line as the Black Hide engaged. The voice on the other end flowed melodiously like warm honey.

"Tax'n… you never showed up last night… I waited… is she…?"

A series of explosive coughs resounded through the little barrack room.

"I've got it now. I'm in quarantine at the Grace. By the time she arrived…" Pallav coughed again, deep and loud until he was out of breath. "She flew me to the hospital. I didn't have the strength to…"

"It's okay, it's okay." The other man's voice was filled with fear and the connection was silent until Pallav faked a wracking cough that ended with him gagging for real while Bafa struggled to contain her amusement.

Catching his breath, Pallav cleared his throat. "Listen, we don't have to scrub the mission. Bafa can do it, she'll find an excuse to get off work on Friday. And what's more natural than a woman with a baby carriage…"

The Black Hide grunted his displeasure, the tone now cutting and sharp. "There're others who I'd rather rely on… those who'll gladly take your place."

"No… no…" The pleading in his voice turned his stomach and Pallav swallowed nervously. "I swear you can rely on her. Bafa's a good girl when it comes down to it. Maybe we should just let her be, she doesn't deserve…"

Pallav coughed again until tears ran from his eyes, and he took the tissue that Bafa offered with a wink.

"By the gods Tax'n, you crazy? You must be sick to be thinking like that. Bafa's a liability; she knows too much and we can't trust her. You can never trust a traitor."

The disgust in the Black Hide's voice was plain and dripped with disdain for his ailing disciple. "And now I have to sort out your mess. But don't worry…Friday I'll take care of everything. And Tax'n? Save your strength, forget about calling till you're better, you understand?"

The shock was apparent in Pallav's face when the transmission was suddenly cut. His surprise was evident, even as he spoke to the Wessel Captain in Tax'n's shrill voice. "And that is the man you betrayed your country for? Someone so self-absorbed and uncaring that he hung up on his dying lover? I'm actually speechless."

Her big amber eyes blinked as she studied her hands and with a twisting motion she jerked off the blood-red ring and threw it against the wall.

"Bastards! Both of them… He was using Tax'n just as that piece of filth was using me." With a look of defeat upon her, she lowered her head in shame and covered her face with her hands. "I wasn't able to locate him either. He was jamming the signal from his comms device."

Pallav shifted to the small bed and sat beside the young woman. "It's alright, Villutomi. We know where the Black Hide's going to strike, and we'll be there and ready for him."

Her slight shoulders began to shake and Pallav could hear her muffled sobs. Against his good judgement, he took her in his arms and held her close. He could feel her hot tears staining his shirt and her body trembling as she broke down weeping.

"There, there…" he said soothingly, using his softest Dad-voice. "It's going to be fine. It's all going to work out."

Suddenly she reared up with anger in her eyes and tore at him like a wildcat, ripping his shirt and leaving a red welt across his neck.

"What the hell!" Backing away, he tried to calm the frantic woman who flung up an arm protectively.

"I'm sorry Villutomi," he started, "if I've offended you in some way…" She shook her head, not comprehending the words from the big man.

"English," she replied in a lispy foreign accent. And then he understood when she motioned to him before reattaching the UTD on his tear-stained collar.

"I'm sorry Colonel, but I couldn't stand to hear that son-of-a-bitch's voice anymore. Not one second longer." Surveying the angry red scratch rising on his skin, she looked away sheepishly.

He exhaled deeply and glared at her. "Listen, there's something I have to ask you. The Black Hide mentioned he'd sort everything out on Friday. You understand that means you too, don't you?" His face was grim as he continued. "Villutomi, if you want to back out of it, I'd understand. You don't need to put your life in danger…"

"Colonel, I'm in. No need to go any further. You said it'd be alright, didn't you?" A pair of serious green eyes met her gaze and she smiled as he nodded ever so slightly.

"Good. Because I trust you."

Glancing at the time, Bafa raised an eyebrow. "And now, how about we get ready for the Club? If you want me to catch a big fish, I'm going to need the right gear."

***

159

"Fynn!" Nicki's voice pierced Inara's ears as the gravity nets slammed down from the sky, while Fynn's warbird hung immobile, hovering beneath.

"Falcon 125. Requesting permission to break formation."

"Negative Falcon 125. Keep your mind on the mission."

A raspy voice broke in. "Inara, if we disengage cam-skins and rake the nets from above with cannon..."

"No go Matt," she replied, her tone calm and bereft of any emotion. "Stay the course, both of you. We're going to watch Irtusch go up in flames. And that means Earth Boy's on his own." She winced as Matt cursed over the Thought-Melding Interface while Nicki snorted irritably in exasperation.

But Fynn was unaware of his team's anguish as a sense of weightlessness overcame him. For a millisecond he could feel himself floating, being lifted up from the confines of the Wessel warbird's narrow cockpit and transported back through time to the *Mayflower*. He was sitting at the helm, rocking the ship furiously in a futile attempt to dislodge the gravity net that had snared the mighty star-traveller in its gossamer-fine web. He remembered the ship's thrusters ready to burst into flame while the great Space Ark bucked and pitched like a bronco at a rodeo and how he slowly brought her down upon the Denebian desert sands, avoiding a catastrophic failure. His first failure. And now again, history was repeating itself and he was powerless.

Electricity pulsed all around him, engulfing him with prickly cold fingers that probed and prodded. Time stood still while the pulses crackled about him, sharp like the sound of a whip.

Not yet Freckles. You can find the way. Find the way...

"I'm too low babe, I'm going to thunder in. It's curtains for me."

Bracing for impact, Fynn closed his eyes and waited for the jolt that would send his spirit to the heavens.

This is it, he breathed, while the crackle rang louder and louder in his ears. And then it struck him: *Gravity has no master. But by God, it has a mistress!*

Hoverfans reversed, Fynn plunged to the ground at hypersonic speed, his warbird concealed in a giant bloom of sand and stone that lacerated through the crowd of soldiers manning the anti-air defences. The gravity nets sliced through the sand vortex, closing faster and faster upon the doomed warbird while Fynn worked at maniacal speed, flipping open the cover on the Skykiller's light-speed drive. In less than a millisecond, a blinding flash of light tore through the sky and with a thunderous roar, the warbird broke across the desert floor mere centimeters above the barren rocky ground. In the blink of an eye Fynn was weightlessly rocketing through space, the powerful Stryker Skykiller in full gallop along the edge of the envelope.

The graceful warbird was built to rule the skies, to demolish any who dared challenge her, but never meant to traverse such a punishing environment. Yet it soared on, proud and strong, ready to serve the man behind the controls who dared to lead it far above its domain. And as the Denebian planet receded to a little brown point in a black velvet canvas, Fynn remembered the days on the Space Ark when he and Erica dared to dream together.

We did it Babe! We kicked ass! Fynn laughed, his heart bursting with pride. *Never thought I'd actually use anything from high school physics… the speed of a gravitational wave equals the speed of light… but babe, you've always been my light, my Erica.*

Circling the Moon of Haldane, he decelerated and hovered between the two celestial bodies, so alien to him with their seemingly lifeless, barren surfaces. But he knew from Deneb that the determination of life triumphs even against the most austere situations.

It was then he realized that it was gone: the crackling sound, the air wafting under his warbird's canopy, the feeling of electricity that had jolted him into action. It had abandoned him. She'd left him. Again. His eyes narrowed and sighing in disappointment, he turned the warbird's slender nose back towards the Denebian planet.

For he knew that he was not alone – he had his team and a mission to complete. His thoughts crystallized and with a parting glance at the beautiful black canvas of space, he rammed the warbird into action, allowing his Skykiller to plunge back through the atmosphere, while a ripple blossoming behind him gave testament to the speed of the Wessel warcraft. A powerful boom erupted as his warbird fell from the heavens and dropping back to subsonic speeds, Fynn engaged the air brakes and joined his team.

"Fynn!" The cheerful voice of Nicki rang through Fynn's Thought-Melding Interface and out of the corner of his eye, a Skykiller surged forward to join him, flying alongside his now battered and blackened warbird. He smiled as she threw him a quick salute and waved in return while bursts of brilliant yellow and orange erupted beneath them in a carpet of flames. It seemed like all his Independence Days combined as Irtusch Geiten Air Base exploded under the destructive powers of the Firestorms' bombs.

Chaos gripped the base. From his vantage point, Fynn watched as the warbirds so neatly lined up on the runway burned with a fierce intensity, while hungry flames leapt between the buildings, demolishing everything before them in their fiery maws. A great pillar of greasy black smoke swirled skyward, momentarily obliterating the scene below.

But he needed to see, to make sure that the desolation was complete. Rising up through the ballooning clouds of ash and soot, the heavy Firestorms surged before leveling off and banking. The lumbering beasts were on their way back to base, their mission completed, their duty done.

And so it should be for the Stryker Skykillers, yet Fynn hovered above the scene of carnage, transfixed, his team awaiting his call to join their unwieldly brethren. But trouble was brewing below where ant-sized beings were descending from Tonka toy-like trucks, bravely battling the flames before comprehending the futility of their actions.

"Falcon 122. Nicki with me. Inara, Matt… escort the beasts home."

A voice rushed over the Though-Melding Interface, its tone almost taunting, biting in sharpness, as Inara responded. "Falcon 127. Roger, returning to base."

"I'm with you," Matt replied and the sound of the two Skykillers roared across the desert vista as they peeled off in quick pursuit of 37th Bomb Squadron.

Blinking in wonder, Fynn marvelled at the brilliant shades of oranges and gold that painted the skies, deadly in their fiery beauty while cleansing the Tagar plains of the Geiten filth and their Fyjer allies. And down below on the planet surface the doomed began to flee, like a stampeding herd of cattle raging across the barrens in an attempt to escape their fate. But like the hapless bovine, they too were bound for slaughter as Fynn readied for a ground attack.

"Let's mop this mess up Nicki. No mercy. Hear me kiddo?"

"Roger Falcon 122."

Accelerating her warbird in an attempt to keep pace with Fynn, Nicki questioned the morality of gunning down defenceless Denebians who terror-stricken were throwing themselves to the ground, heedless of the sharpness of the stones underfoot, powerless to escape the vengeance of her Squadron Commander. Hovering above the throng of Geiten soldiers, she could see the fear in their eyes, almost taste the scent of blood seeping from their wounds. The acrid smoke rose up in tendrils to enshroud her cockpit and in her imagination she could smell the stench of roasting flesh, making her gag. She watched horror-struck as Fynn swooped down amongst the survivors, his cannons ablaze as bullets sang their melody of death, finding their way to end the suffering.

Powerless to halt Fynn's blood lust, Nicki realized with dread that suddenly his warbird hung back, rising until he was at eye level with the young woman. "Hey kiddo, you want in on the fun and games?"

Ashamed to admit to her weakness, Nicki spun the warbird around and with her heart in her throat, plunged down to race across the desert floor. It seemed as if the ground rushed by her feet as she passed over a mixed group of Fyjer and Geiten survivors cowering for cover behind the low scrub. And then just as she feared, it happened.

Dressed in drab brown, a solitary figure rose from behind a clump of thornbushes, brandishing a shoulder-held surface to air missile. Nicki could see the white of the soldier's eyes as he aimed the deadly MANPAD at her and she froze, just as Fynn sprayed the ground with high-explosive shells before pulling up hard. With trembling hands Nicki followed his lead and the two warbirds soared once again above the clouds.

Fynn cursed, recognizing his mistake. For other than Inara, neither Nicki nor Matt had ever flown a combat mission. He remembered his first time. The feeling of absolute power when he had defeated the enemy, a sensation that lifted him up higher than his fighter jet, above the clouds and into the stars. It had come natural to Fynn – the angles of attack were like a well-travelled path while his body, mind and fighter melded into one unit as he scored his first aerial combat victory. And then in the blink of an eye, he engaged again. And again. And again. He was insatiable. He wanted the kill, he longed for the feeling of triumph that rose up within him as an enemy canopy opened, the hapless pilot ejecting from a doomed aircraft, its hull a blazing torch. He was born to fly, he lived and breathed for the battle.

Grandma always joked that I could fly before I walked, he thought with a smile, momentarily relaxing and letting the warbird chart its course home. But in the Skykiller streaming along his starboard side, he could make out Nicki's slumped figure hunched at the controls and he reflected that sometimes the best combat aces were the ones who had to work the hardest.

Damn, I'm such an asshole, he chided himself, *asking the kid to gun down soldiers fleeing for their lives. I should've let her fly on my wing...one of those Starhunters could've been Nicki's first kill...that would've made it easier on her...*

Little white bricks flashed in and out of the in-console sat tracker as the cumbersome bombers were safely escorted through enemy airspace on their way back to Wessel Air Detachment Iluzija.

Forget about them... the kid's down in the dumps because she froze... she's a damn good pilot. Otherwise I wouldn't have thrown her into the breach, he thought as he looked over at Nicki.

A picture of dejection, her eyes were fixed straight ahead, uncaring about maintaining situational awareness. Fynn swivelled his head in the direction of what had been Irtusch – and grinned at the sacrificial immolation that they'd left behind. Then he remembered... it was what *they* did after combat, when Erica was on his wing.

Perhaps...

"Hey Nicki," he intoned into the Thought-Melding Interface, "you want in on an old Earth tradition? I mean, so ancient my Great-Grandma initiated me..."

Struggling to remove her helmet, a sea of deep mahogany hair fell in waves about her shoulders. Fynn could see the look of hurt in her eyes as she shrugged. "Can't hurt... can it?" she replied, her voice husky with sadness.

"So," he started trying to keep the banter light while pushing away a tinge of disloyalty to Erica's memory, "it was something my Great-Grandma used to do after a mission... oh, but that's a long, long story."

They'd made it just for these occasions, he and Erica. For celebrating a good kill, for coming back alive.

"It's like an opera," he said to a confused face.

"A what?"

"Forget it, kiddo. It's in two parts. Now for Act One."

Nicki flinched as the pulsing beat of *Loving Every Minute of It* reverberated through the two Skykillers.

"Fynn," she shrieked, covering her ears, "what the hell's that noise?"

"Listen to the words kiddo. And now for Act 2. Get ready for it."

She wiggled her wings to get his attention and he could see her nose crinkled and a light in her eyes. *It's working,* he thought, stifling a laugh.

"If it's as bad as this song, then I don't want any part of it!"

"Nah, this's truly what it means to be human. My Great-Grandmother's end-mission-tradition." He laughed and then, raising his voice he yelled out as loud as he could, "Last one back to base buys the other a drink."

Fynn watched as a plume of flames erupted from the rapidly retreating warbird that only milliseconds ago had been limping in the shadows of his wing. Now whipping past him was one very competitive woman, back in the saddle once again. Fynn eased his Skykiller in her wake while he sat back, a smile spreading across his freckled cheeks.

Mission accomplished, he breathed and pulling a victory roll he headed back to base.

CHAPTER 18 – IN THE SHADOWS

A door once opened may be stepped through in either direction.

– MADAME DE POMPADOUR

The blood seeped down his forehead, across his nose and dripped from his chin into a pool of coagulated gore at his feet. Head slumped on his chest, Luke Kóbor moaned and opened one swollen eye. A darkness, blacker than night, spread its stygian pall over him. His head throbbed horribly and he ran his tongue over parched lips with fear stealing over the normally cool-headed lad. Blinking, Luke tried to dispel the panic that raged through his mind. And then he remembered his sister.

"Isabella?" he whispered, praying that she was safe and unharmed and far from this nightmare. He trembled as a tiny whimper sounded from across the room followed by a choked sob.

"Bella, I can't see. My vision… everything's dark…I think the bastard blinded me."

The whimper grew louder and he craned his neck towards it. "Bella? Is that you?"

He recognized her crying and tried to straighten his broken body to reach out to her. But the clanging of the chains sounded like laughter to his vain attempts.

"I'm over here," the tiny voice sobbed. "I'm so sorry Luke." He could hear the rattle of the shackles over her sniffles and in the grips of fury, he raged against the iron that bound his wrists, pulling and thrashing until he could feel its icy grip tearing into his young skin.

Collapsing in exhaustion, Luke sagged against the damp wall and spat out a clot of blood. He conjured up an image of his father and tried to think what he would do, but his head throbbed and his ribs felt as if an elephant had trampled on them.

Dad'd tell us not to expend our energies on futile acts but to seize the first opportunity to escape, Luke thought and with a sigh, he slowly lowered his battered frame to the ground. He knew he could take it - whatever that fiend dished out – but he worried about his younger sister whose silence hung heavily in the dank stale air.

"It's me who should be apologizing Bella. It's all my fault, I let him in… Did that bastard hurt you?"

His sister snorted and yanking on the cold iron digging into her wrists she snarled. "A lot less than you. I thought he was going to kill you."

Breathing a sigh of relief, Luke whispered in the darkness, worried that the demon would return. "He doesn't work with Dad. That's for sure."

Her laughter caught him by surprise. "By the gods Luke, where'd you learn to fight like that? If he hadn't tazed you, I think he'd have been a goner. But he's left us now and after he brought us here, well, he wasn't taking any chances."

"Here? Where's here? Did you see anything?"

Isabella shook her head, "No. I screamed and kicked and tried to fight back… I tried to break away… to run for help. But… well…" She rattled her chains and slumped down. "You can see how that worked…"

A tear snaked down her cheek as she remembered how the man had slapped her cruelly across the face cutting her lip, and how she had fallen in a heap on the stone floor. She could still smell the cologne he wore, see the steel in those cold eyes while his fingers bit into her skin as he pulled her to her feet and dragged her across the room. And how in a flash she had rammed her knee into the man's groin and leapt away, only to see the glint of the blade clasped in his hand, poised to strike her brother's battered and inert form.

"I had no choice. I went with him." she continued, trying to exorcise the memory. "He threw us both into the back of a beaten-up old white aerovan, trussed like turkeys and blindfolded. I couldn't tell where he flew us but when we arrived, we were already underground in the basement of some sort of compound. It's soundproof, here, this room we're in. Custom made for that devil. Shackles on the wall, grated floor… no windows, no lights. But at least there's no rats here."

"That's cause there're no rats on Deneb, Sis." The two shared a stilted laugh before Isabella turned serious.

"He told me he was holding us for ransom money. A lot of money. Like the kind Mom and Dad don't have."

Sighing, she pushed herself away from the damp wall. "But Dad'll find us," she said softly. "And when he does, that bastard'll be on his knees praying that it would've been you who'd finished him off."

***

Reyhart groaned. "Yes, yes, they're fine." Ignoring the hysterical voice on the other end, he reminded himself that his damned aerovan had deactivated the holo function again. Shrugging, he made a mental note before casually inspecting his trousers and flicking a piece of lint from an otherwise immaculately tailored suit. *That's now torn*, he gruffed to himself and remembering the wildcat man-child of Colonel Kóbor, rubbed a bruised cheek before gingerly probing his broken nose.

He'd left the captive brother and sister pair secure and safe in heavy chains before flying off to the Grace Hospital where he now waited, still in his van, while Ravenna nattered at him.

"Uh-huh... uh-huh..."

Long ago, he'd learned the art of tuning out distractions, and so he turned his attention back to his battered face while the general maintained a constant stream of inconsequential chatter.

It's not so bad, he admitted to himself, tilting his chin from side to side and scrutinizing his chiseled features. *I'll survive. A bit of bruising here and there, breathing through the mouth for the next few weeks. Wasted trip...*

"So what should we do?"

Now that caught his attention. Startled from his distraction, Reyhart turned to a familiar phrase that always seemed to work with women. *Even powerful women like General Ravenna*, he reflected.

"Do, my dear? What do you recommend?"

"Well, I certainly don't want you to kill them. But I can't see any way ahead."

Reyhart could think of several, all involving Ravenna, fluffy pink handcuffs and a king-sized poster bed, but that would only infuriate the already testy woman.

"Besides," she continued, "Kóbor's not talking. Reyhart... I think I may've made a big mistake... maybe he had no involvement in the Urkyn fiasco. He's always banging on about the Black Hide rebel group having infiltrating the WAF."

Reyhart tapped his fingers angrily on the aerovan's dash. *This is all becoming so tiresome*, he thought, looking again at himself in the mirror. Raising his eyebrows, he grimaced at his reflection and then tilted his head, perplexed at the Colonel's intransigence.

"So you mean to tell me that Kóbor's refused our demands?"

"That's right Reyhart. He snapped at me. Said he already told me everything he knew. And then cut transmission. Can you believe it? But then again, he's Gomalan's pet and basically immune from discipline."

His brows furrowed in frustration and Reyhart contemplated his next steps. For he knew the second he walked into that darkened room to free his captives, he would open himself to another brutal attack. *And whether it be the Colonel's powerhouse of a son or his lovely young lass, the first to move against him, he decided, would be the first to taste cold steel.*

"My dear, what do you propose I do then with those two terrors in my basement?" Reyhart's voice was soft and caressing as he continued, his mind glossing over two quick deaths and back to Ravenna's bedroom. "Getting rid of them would really be the easiest solution. We could toast the end of our first fiasco before celebrating our new... friendship."

It was the last thing he expected – Ravenna exploded. "Have you lost your mind? Killing innocent children!"

Rubbing the bridge of his battered nose, Reyhart blinked in shock, speechless.

"You free those two! You hear me Reyhart? Drive to that deserted quarry you mentioned and leave the kids there. Then let me take over ... Once Kóbor's kids are home safe, I'll pay you what you're owed and then consider our business concluded. You understand Reyhart?"

Stunned, his mouth gaped open while his mind churned. *Play with a tiger and you're bound to get mauled. Except*, he realized with wonder, *I rather like it.*

His battered old aerovan purred to life as he engaged its hoverfans and skimmed over the squat Grace Hospital, contemplating the unpredictability of women. Shaking his head, Reyhart felt the frustration building up inside, like a coiled snake ready to strike, and he slammed a fist against the dash.

Damn if I'll ever understand women. Now Ravenna... there's a woman worth the effort. But think Reyhart, think of the complications...Ah, a nice drink, and see who's on the menu tonight...that should take care of these pointless complications.

169

A golden sky unfurled before him as the sun kissed the horizon while a sliver of the Moon of Haldane ascended and Reyhart sighed.

Such a beautiful night. For once, wouldn't it'd be nice to just go home to a good meal, a glass of wine and a cuddle on the couch?

Clearing his throat, he raised an eyebrow and smirked. "Hi Honey, I'm home. Just let me hang up my garrote and clean my blaster. Oh and don't worry sweetheart, I won't be getting any blood on the carpet tonight... yes that's right Baby, it was a long-distance kill. Yes, I do prefer close up and personal, but this way we get to spend more quality time together." His laughter rang through the old aerovan before he bellowed, "As if!"

Shrugging, he flew the familiar sky route towards the Starlight Club before he'd return back to his base near the confluence of the Upper and lower Sirga Rivers. He hardly considered it a home. Hidden at the end of a dusty dirt road, overgrown bushes covered in thorny vines concealed the entrance to the subterranean dwelling that was custom-built to satisfy Reyhart's unique profession. How ironic that all those involved in the construction had somehow perished shortly after its completion. As the sun started its trek below the horizon, he flew past isolated farms where lights burned bright: parents watching sitcoms while children ran about bare-legged and carefree in the warmth of the summer's grand finale.

Curiosity bubbled inside him at how these average people lived their dull lives: tilling the earth, tending their crops, selling their produce for a pittance. Yet the children played and laughed cheerfully, unaware of the destiny that awaited them – one of back-breaking toil from first until last light, tumbling into bed with the hope of a few hours of sleep before the never-ending cycle of daily drudgery would recommence. Unconsciously, he decelerated and descended, intrigued by the scene before him, one of merriment which he himself had rarely enjoyed in his life.

A little girl waved at him from one of the impoverished farms and a boy who Reyhart assumed was her brother ran alongside the low-flying aerovan, his tunic having come untucked and blowing in the wind, the rays of the setting sun casting a glow on the boy's cherub-like face.

Was I ever like that – trusting and innocent? he wondered as he pulled back up. Shaking his head, he recalled the horror of being an orphan, of others laughing at him and a fury grew in his eyes.

For Reyhart had been abandoned by his mother, unwanted and unloved. Alone in the world and never the recipient of any kindness, Reyhart wondered what it would be like to have been part of a family. He stared at his reflection again and thought how easy it had always been to have a woman.

Never more than one night; never in his home: that had been his maxim. Everything in his life had its own box, their contents neatly divided and packed away on a shelf only to be pulled out when required. It had made life simple. The overflowing chapters of his professional life never mingled with the bare essentials residing within the folder summarizing his sparse personal affairs. Business was never tinged with pleasure, for he took none whatsoever in what was simply a means of existence. Of saving himself from the fate that awaited all orphans who could not find their way in the heartless, cruel world.

But neither did sympathy cross his path when he severed the thread of life of those begging under his blade with their last breath. Efficient at his profession, accepting of the solitude, Reyhart survived.

But what would it be like, his analytical mind pondered, *to be needed; to be wanted?* And with an image of the luscious General Ravenna playing in his thoughts, Reyhart contemplated how it would be if he crossed the line, if he tore open those boxes to mingle their contents, and for the first time in many years, the unfamiliar spectre of fear rose up.

Damn that Ravenna, he cursed, angry for allowing himself the luxury of that one night of passion with the powerful general who commanded the entire Wesselan Land Forces.

She's enticing, that damn woman! Powerful, beautiful, sultry… independent… and ruthless…but would she care for who I really am? Or is she just like the others, in need of me only to save her from her mistakes?

The crackle of the in-craft communication system shook him from his reverie, and Reyhart almost jumped out of his skin. Not only had the unreliable holoimage module flickered back to life, but the object of his curses and desires coalesced beside him. He blinked, then taking a deep breath to erase his confusion, turned to the holoform and raised an eyebrow.

"My dear General, you flatter me… two calls within less than an hour. Whatever is the occasion?"

Her face portrayed a tapestry of confusion. "Reyhart? What the hell happened to you? Your face…"

He himself was surprised as the reins of calm took control of his voice and he chuckled. "Occupational hazards, my dear. All in a day's work."

She stumbled over her words, the uncertainty making her even more delightful in his mind and he thought of the two children at the farm. "Have you... Reyhart, have you released them yet?"

A feeling of light-headedness passed over him as he docked just outside the club: never near a lamppost, always hidden in the shadows. His features neutral, Reyhart sweetened his acid-tongue in response, betraying the disappointment that coursed through him.

"My dear, I have not yet returned to the whereabouts of the two Kóbor children. Nightfall is almost upon us; it would not be in their best interests to be set loose in the quarry at this hour. Trust that they are safe for the time being. Perhaps..."

He wavered, reflecting if he should break his rule, just this once.

Arms crossed, Ravenna scowled, looking as fierce as a bloodwolf and Reyhart felt butterflies fluttering about in his stomach. "You were saying..."

The stars were peeking out from behind the curtain of darkness, their silvery light radiating down from the heavens as Reyhart stared in rapture. "Yes, the boy and his sister are both resting and at the moment safe. In the morning, I shall take them to the quarry where they can be reunited with their parents, if that is what you desire. But in the meantime, I have no other... clients... and can provide you with all of my personal attention. And whatever else it is that you desire."

Reyhart shivered in anticipation recalling their previous engagement. *There... fool that I am... I've leapt into the breach...*

The second it had left his mouth, he knew that he had made a fatal error for in her eyes he could see the approaching storm.

"Reyhart..."

Keen judge of body posture, he could see the unease in every inch of the woman. But she surprised him.

"Reyhart, you know my position. We're in the midst of planning operations against the Coalition. I've been burning the candle at both ends... you can't imagine... and the Kóbor kids... they were the last straw for me."

She smiled a sheepish smile apologetically and a flame danced across her scarred cheek. His heart pounding in his chest, Reyhart realized that for the first time he could remember, he felt hope: there, under the dark skies in the docking lot of the Starlight Club where he conducted his business.

"Of course, we all need some distraction to get through these terrible times," she continued with a flick of her lustrous black hair. "You could always come over tomorrow night – I've got a bottle of Lesh that's been gathering dust. You and I could conclude our deal, that is… if you're not too busy?"

His mouth felt dry while Reyhart's palms began to sweat. *What is it with women?* he thought, *a few hours ago she wanted nothing more to do with me. And now… oh bother! But the opportunity may never present itself again.*

"My dear Ravenna, there is nothing that would give me greater pleasure. Now may I suggest that I pick you up for dinner beforehand? I can get us a table at the Three Lyndins; breath-taking views…I promise you."

A corner of his mouth curled up as Ravenna gasped. The Three Lyndins: the most exclusive restaurant in the capital city was perched high on the chalk cliffs overlooking the Sirga River valley, and where reservations for mere mortals were as rare as hen's teeth. But the Maître D' owed Reyhart and Reyhart was not one to forget.

A shuffling sound behind her drew his attention to someone approaching and Ravenna pulled a face. "I have to go. Just text me the timing and I'll be ready."

"No need my dear. I'll pick you up at Set -1." He winked at the soft blush that coloured the general's cheek and she smiled at him before cutting the link.

On winged feet, Reyhart traipsed through the door to the Starlight Club and without a second glance at the seedy surroundings, padded to his usual spot. Pulling out a chair in the darkest corner of the sleazy bar, he nodded to the bartender. His mind was racing as the manager waddled towards him.

"Sir, there's a man wanting to discuss business with you tonight. Shall I show him over?"

Shaking his head, a wild look came into Reyhart's eyes as he stared at the man across the room who nodded in response. "No Kristofer. Please convey my apologies to the gentleman, but I'm debating whether to take down my shingle. You see, I'm contemplating retiring from the business."

The shock on the manager's face was quickly replaced by a blank stare. "Very good Sir. Shall I have one of the girls bring you your regular?"

For the first time, the manager saw the suave cold man smile. A brilliant smile, he realized, one filled with happiness. "That would be kind Kristofer. But tonight I'll just have a drink. I'll be going home early."

Retiring from the business! Really Reyhart, what's gotten into you? Oh well at least for tonight... until I see which way the wind blows. Who knows, maybe it's my profession that interests her...

The thought somehow bothered Reyhart who looked casually around the club, watching the half-naked women parading across the floor with drinks and menus. His eyes became hard again as he realized that he'd had them all over the years – and each and every one of them was only interested in one thing: his money. Gold diggers, every last one of them.

But Ravenna... no...she doesn't need me at all. Ravenna... she simply wants me.

Through the smoky window he could see his aerovan docked safely in the shadows, but in his mind he was flying along the sky route with Ravenna beside him, his hand caressing her rock-hard thigh. Dreaming about her silky skin quivering to his touch, the man in the impeccable suit with the bruised face did not notice an aerocar that silently slid beside his vehicle. And as sweet hope arose within him, Reyhart was rendered blind to the dangers lurking in the shadows.

CHAPTER 19 – THE GIRL IN THE GOLDEN G-STRING

When I'm good, I'm very good. But when I'm bad, I'm better.

– MAE WEST

It had always been a mysterious process to him: how a woman could transform herself from the girl next door into a total vamp, a luscious seductress who, like the Lorelei of legends, coaxed her enthralled victims to their doom. Tara always attacked the transformation with the precision of a military operation. Dress: skimming every curve, ordered well in advance with coordinating accessories: check. Nails, perfectly filed and lacquered to a high gloss: check. Hair, fresh chocolate highlights dancing through her bouncy dark hair: check. Shoes, nosebleed high stilettoes –a grin on his face as the tiny waif-like beauty barely reached his shoulders: check. And then of course, the magic of makeup completing the metamorphosis. The Tara of the Bare Face, Astrophysicist- extraordinaire, suddenly re-appeared looking like a miniature version of a lingerie model.

All this while Pallav waited patiently on the couch thumbing through the latest edition of his Security and Intelligence journal. Ten minutes before launch, he'd brush off his old navy blue suit and pull it on in mere seconds to wait by the door, keys in hand, ready for the annual Christmas Ball. Bowing his head, Pallav concealed a smirk, remembering all the times she'd burst out from the bedroom, twirling in high heels so that her dress flowed voluptuously about her, while he stared at his wife with admiration, mesmerized by her ageless beauty.

But never before had he witnessed the process first-hand. And certainly, he reflected, never had he intended to with another woman. Pallav scratched the back of his neck uncomfortably while Bafa pursed her rouged lips, and from heavily kohled eyes threw him a saucy wink before turning her back to him.

"You mind?" she asked, handing a stone-encrusted necklace to him. Sucking in his breath, he fumbled with the clasp and as his hands brushed the hair from Bafa's neck, he could feel himself blushing with embarrassment. The heavy scent of her perfume reminded him of spring time in the mountains after a heavy rainfall and he could sense the heat marching across his cheeks as he swished the heavy fall of hair back in place.

Sit on your hands idiot, he chided himself as she turned to face him.

Her nervous smile caught him off guard, and he could hear the tremble in Bafa's voice.

"So, will I do?" Hesitant golden eyes searched his for an answer, but the icy green eyes were cold and distant.

Clearing his throat, Pallav nodded tersely but seeing the light in her face extinguished, the big man quickly realized his mistake. *The fragility of the female ego. Even when she'd put Aphrodite to shame,* he reflected in amazement.

"Captain Villutomi, you look absolutely stunning. If I were single and twenty years younger…"

A girlish giggle stopped him from saying anything more incriminating as she slid out of the aerocar. A mischievous look on her face, Bafa reached over and kissed Pallav's blushing cheek before closing the door on his shocked face.

"Well Colonel, if you were twenty years younger, you'd be jail bait. And I've never liked them young anyhow."

Her stilettos clicked on the hard pavement as Bafa strode with her head held high towards the Starlight while Pallav futilely called after her.

Villutomi… Captain… Bafa…! *Dammit! That girl's never serious. If she doesn't succeed, I'll see her up on charges of desertion and treason.*

Scrubbing the lipstick from his cheek furiously, Pallav could only wait in the shadows and watch as the young woman flounced away. Through the back door of the club Bafa snuck and into a tiny locker room where the dancers and waitresses changed away from prying eyes.

Quickly discarding her tunic, she shrugged out of the leggings to reappear in a barely-there gold lace G-string sporting a tiny diamond below a saucy bow. The gem-encrusted necklace that Pallav had secured about her neck now nestled boldly between a set of firm round breasts. Raising an eyebrow, Bafa critically surveyed her image in the mirror and with a toss of her lustrous dark hair, she confidently strutted out into the dimly lit bowels of the Starlight Strip Club.

A large-jowled man rose and walked towards her, a look of confusion on his red-veined face. Extending a ring-bedecked hand to him, Bafa smiled seductively. "You must be the manager? You see, I can always tell who's in charge, and you have the look of power…Uh-huh, I'm right, aren't I?"

His hand was sweaty and his handshake limp.

"I'm Bafa, the new girl? You remember, I was hired yesterday to take up some of the slack… Well, here I am!"

Standing back from him she struck a pose trying hard not to laugh as images of Basic Training came flooding in: chest out, stomach in, stand tall Villutomi! Except this time, red-lacquered toes were peeking out from six-inch heels, feet planted far wider than shoulder width apart.

The man hesitated. "I don't recall…"

Bafa towered over him and bending down giggled, ensuring he had a bird's eye view of her most appealing assets. "No, why would you? A man like yourself's far too important to be concerned with hiring. But I'm here now," she said seductively, her voice husky and low. "Why don't you try me out for the night?"

The manager's reply was cut short as a bellow from the grey-haired bartender caught Bafa's attention. "Where's your belt? Grab a belt and serve table number six. Thornleaf-chasers."

Across the bar came a drink-belt and grabbing at it, Bafa smiled at the old man before hitching up. Spinning on her heels, she sashayed across the room while the ear-splitting tones of the latest music pounded through the air. A group of middle-aged businessmen crowded around Table 6, eyes agog watching at what Bafa could only guess was a woman from Cygnus-Morea who gyrated wildly in tune with the beat. Hair black as the night, her pale skin glowed in the darkness of the club as Bafa interrupted the group worshipping at the pretty alien's feet.

"Line 'em up boys," she shouted over the music, bending over the table while the men pushed their glasses towards her. Now all eyes were on her while the Cygneusite continued unabashed in her dance. A devilish grin on her face, Bafa arched her back, her perky breasts on display. "You want me to dispense, or you want to push my buttons?"

Keeping a smile on her red lips proved to be a challenge, even for a woman who had hid her identity as a wave dancer. The men groped her shamelessly while pouring their shots from the drink belt slung over the tiny lace G-string. While they ran their hot sweaty hands over her body, Bafa's mind was elsewhere. Surreptitiously the young woman surveyed the club for the real prey – the big game she'd come to hunt.

Everyone knew that he'd be found here, night after night, as he waited patiently for clients. For there were always those who needed his services, however repelled they were by his profession. Those who wanted someone to go missing – perhaps a rich husband looking for a cheap way out of a dying marriage; perhaps a businessman wanting to eliminate the competition; and sometimes, maybe even a bit too frequently, one of the Red Tabs looking to crush some dodgy issues without getting their lily-white hands stained. That, she reflected, was how word got out within the higher echelons of the WAF: that he was the go-to man when things went south. Reyhart: the man without a past, without compassion, scruples, or morals. But most importantly, the man who'd get results.

She saw him there, sitting alone in the corner, with a dreamy look lighting up his chiseled features, a quizzical expression playing in his narrow eyes. Slapping away the prodding hands, Bafa quickly scanned their payment chips and made her way past the tangle of bodies and chairs towards her mark.

Lost in thought, Reyhart stared at the ceiling as Bafa passed by, her hips swaying, her breasts bouncing as she pressed her body into his table. Red lips parted, revealing a row of even white teeth as she smiled at the elegant assassin whose eyes looked blankly at her. Wincing insincerely at the damage to his handsome face, Bafa bent over the table and with eyes full of faux compassion, leaned down over him.

Her voice silky and seductive, she hitched up her dispensing belt, showcasing the minute strip of gold lace that she'd earlier coaxed the burly alien colonel to buy for her.

"Ouch…" She grimaced, slowly tracing a line down her own nose and across her cheek, her eyes aglow with feigned lust. "Looks like you could use a stiff one."

Leaning over, her perfumed breasts skimming against his arm, Bafa whispered, "This one's on me…." And before he could protest, she threw him another seductive smile and disappeared into the sea of grinding, pulsing bodies.

Losing sight of the topless waitress, Reyhart shook his head in wonder before inhaling deeply of the pungent liquid and closing his eyes. The delicate balance of smokiness mingled with the scent of freshly baked lava cake, the kind he and Ravenna had shared last night. Lost in contemplation, he let the velvety elixir roll over his tongue, its heat tickling his mouth and tipping back his head, he reveled in the sensation before reality reared its ugly head.

Those Kóbor brats...By the gods if it wasn't for Ravenna, I'd throw their lifeless bodies to the bloodwolves.

He followed her with his narrow eyes: the girl in the golden G-string strutting about the Club, winding in and out of the crowds, giggling as she pushed away the sweaty hands and passed overflowing shot glasses to the muddled drunks. *Always in view*, he reflected, wondering how he could not have noticed her before. *The girl seems to be genuinely enjoying herself, not like the others whose faded smiles never light up their eyes. How could I ever have missed her?*

Savouring his drink, Reyhart relaxed and took a deep breath. The corners of his thin lips raised as pleasant thoughts once again expelled the dark clouds that normally overshadowed his life-or-death existence. With surprise, he eyed the empty glass and pushing it away, rapidly surveilled the room. His would-be client had long since moved on, and he knew that it was now time to depart. That is, until Golden G-string arrived again.

A smile played over her cherry-red lips and with a toss of her lustrous hair, the young woman bent over to retrieve his shot glass. Her dark eyes smouldered as she licked her lips suggestively before pressing a strong hand into his chest.

"Uh-uh, you can't leave yet. It's my birthday and I want everyone here to cheer me on."

Sensing his reticence, the woman flashed a saucy pout before putting her luscious body on display that normally would lead to her legs on his shoulders in the back of his aerovan. Toying with the idea, Reyhart allowed the lithe creature to push him back in his seat and he felt his body respond to her touch. Raising an eyebrow, he watched intrigued as she fumbled with her dispensing belt, a look of embarrassment flooding over her features.

"Damn thing sticks at times."

So captivated was he by the bouncing of her breasts as she shook the drink belt vigorously, that he failed to notice how Bafa crushed a capsule into the glass before pouring his drink. She smiled again, her eyes aglow before setting the glass into his hands, allowing him to caress her wrist suggestively. "This here's made from toasted peekans. On the house."

Winking at him, she flounced to the stage and momentarily the music ground to a halt. Bafa stood there, her long legs splayed, and her arms glued to her sides while she stuck out her chest.

"Ladies and Gentlemen..." Giggling like a schoolgirl, she continued. "Well, let me correct myself... Mmmmen... yeah, I like how that sounds!" Squealing in delight, Bafa ran her hands down her slender torso. "And...drum roll please...today I'm turning 25!"

Around and around the stage spun, rotating so that she was on display for all the Starlight Club to see. Bafa was in her element, all eyes on her and she preened and posed.

"So what you guys think? You up for celebrating with me? Ok, let's raise our glasses and drink to birthdays."

The roar exploded throughout the club and the music began to pulse as the girl in the golden G-string gyrated with the lovely Cygneusite in tune with the beat. The enraging noise banged across the parking lot to where Pallav waited.

Cued by the furor, the big man casually made his way to the battered white aerovan hidden in the shadows. A spark of blue electricity erupted from his hands and surged over the craft. Covering his eyes protectively, Pallav waited as the intense burst twisted violently and arced like a creature in its death throes. Patiently he stood back until the glow from the vehicle began to fade, its theft-deterrent system now fried. A tiny click and he was in.

The scent of expensive cologne permeated the aerovan, compelling Pallav to leave the door ajar. Jabbing a transfer device into the homing protocol port, he turned his attention to the propulsion system as the little clip sucked Reyhart's details from the van's memory. Popping the hood, he bounded back into the darkness of the night and pulling out a small pen knife, began to work feverishly.

Within minutes, the sturdy wiring of the propulsion system was shaved within millimeters, rendering it fragile and brittle and ready to spark from the heat generated from the aerovan's exhaust manifold. The battered old van, now crippled mid-air, would plummet to the ground. A perfect crime he thought, his green eyes cold with unabated fury, as he gleefully visualized the aerovan falling from the sky lane and crashing in a ball of flame in the desert below with Reyhart immobile at the controls.

A fitting end to a murderous fiend… untraceable and an understandable accident in such an old jalopy.

Stealing to the rear entrance, Pallav sat himself down on the stairs and sank into the pall of the evening, a predator lying in wait for his prey to emerge. And there Reyhart was, visible through a narrow window in the dim light of the club, his back against the wall with a look of desire playing on his thin sculpted face.

Pallav's target was unaware of the fate that awaited him, sitting patiently on the stairs to the back door. For mesmerized, the assassin analyzed his lust and staring at the gutsy girl in the golden G-string, he was surprised that these feelings should emerge after a night with the hungry Ravenna.

Maybe I was wrong after all… he pondered, thinking how ridiculous it would be to abandon his lucrative profession while at the height of his career. Then he shook his head and stared down at his sleek hand-crafted balmorals. *But all things must run their course I suppose… and the time to capitalize on change is when one is on top. And she can help me, Ravenna, the General in charge of the Army… yes, certainly… with a war going on, for there can never be enough arms dealers on the scene.*

Reyhart closed his eyes and with the beat of the music straining in the background, he visualized a new empire rising from the ashes of his old profession – all with the patronage of the beautiful General Ravenna. Turning the liqueur over in his mouth, he savoured its deliciously toasted nutty flavour, when suddenly he was struck by a strange sensation that was possessing him.

Molten rivers of pain ran down his throat before cascading to his stomach. The burning spread like a flame amongst dry tinder, searing while it coursed along his legs and arms. With his head spinning, Reyhart quickly made his way to the exit.

He barely noticed the beautiful woman in the golden G-string coming to his aid, holding his near-lifeless body in her shapely arms, and ushering him from the club. The voice that croaked from his mouth was garbled and in shock he realized his limbs were quickly going numb. His eyes were pleading for help as he stared up into what he remembered as the face of an angel. But a metamorphosis had brought him into the arms of a demon, replacing any hope he may have had for salvation.

Paralysin, he registered with detachment. *Tasteless, odourless, reacts within seconds to render the victim incapable of movement or speech while retaining brain and visual functions. Of short duration, useful in abductions.*

The she-devil in the golden G-string dragged him down the stairs and there Reyhart came face to face with Satan, as an enormous alien tore him from the naked girl's arms.

Kóbor, he realized, the pieces to the puzzle falling into place when he recognized the burly alien from Ravenna's holoimage. Try as he might, his limbs would not obey him and he sagged under the grip of the alien whose strong hands closed tighter and tighter about his throat.

"Stop it!"

It was the woman, her voice no longer seductive but commanding interlaced with a sprinkling of terror. For a millisecond, hope sailed in golden lace before his eyes until it crashed at his feet.

"You want to draw a crowd, Colonel? Cause that's what's gonna happen if you keep this up!"

The big man grunted and Reyhart felt his body being smashed against his battered old aerovan while iron-like fists slammed into his defenceless body. *That will definitively hurt later*, he thought before adding, *if there is a later.*

He could see the hatred radiating at him from those icy green eyes, but Reyhart held the alien's stare. Quizzically, he analysed the bronzed face dispassionately before arriving at the unfortunate conclusion that his life was indeed over. For Reyhart recognized the storm in the eyes that burned into his own: the eyes of a man tipping on the edge of murder.

He himself had never felt the passion of a kill, but there were others – those who he'd briefly crossed paths with and discarded as too fervent – whose eyes had betrayed their thoughts. And Reyhart knew, as only a man whose profession revolved around killing, that the longer Kóbor was held back from the kill, the more chances he had of regaining possession of some motion. And he would not waver.

Drawing on his experiences, Reyhart attempted to lure the young woman into hesitation using the same tack that his victims had tried on him; it was all in the eyes – sad eyes, pleading eyes, eyes that begged for mercy.

Women are sentimental. And this one is young, still naïve and pliable. A perfect combination.

Her golden eyes bore no trace of pity as she grabbed Kóbor by shoulder and tore him away. With a voice like thunder she bore down on the alien Colonel. "Stop it, stop it! By the gods, you'll kill him! That's not the way."

Reyhart felt a silent laugh bubble within him as the naked girl stared Kóbor down, her chest heaving and her slender arms restraining the giant man. Nostrils flaring in fury, Kóbor nodded silently in agreement before hoisting the assassin in his arms and flinging him into the sabotaged van. His head nodded before he stalked away silently.

With shock, Reyhart realized the girl was in the van beside him and gently she buckled Reyhart into the flyer's seat. She motioned into the night with her slender arm; Reyhart could see the beautiful necklace dangling between her breasts, a ruby-red ring on her delicate finger and he pondered the meaning of this.

Her smile was so sweet, so innocent. "It's such a lovely night, isn't it?" Her voice was once again filled with promise. "Can you see the stars? Of course you can. You can still see; but you can't move and you don't feel a thing right now. Oh, but you will. Trust me; you will. You'll be taking a little flight tonight – yes, but not to where you think. You see, that man is the father of the two children you kidnapped. And the only thing between you and death, is me. Now you blink for me, okay? Blink, Reyhart."

Obediently, the man blinked, intrigued by the little game being played out. Reyhart knew this was not going to end well unless the effects were to wear off before his assailants carried out their plan.

Buy me time my dear, he thought hopefully, relishing in his mind the ways he could use to bring an end to the woman's existence.

"Good, good. Now Reyhart, I want you to blink once for yes, and twice for no." A smile lit her face up and she reached over to brush his hair back into place. "Are the children alive?"

They are mere amateurs, he reflected, *to try to get anything out of me in a parking lot*. Racking his brains, he scanned methods of increasing the elimination rate of the paralysis agent while he blinked once. "Good. You understand. Are they at your house?"

He recalled reading somewhere that rapid eye motion combined with deep breathing held some promise. But not yet, not while she was hovering over him. One blink. Another smile from the girl in the golden G-string.

"Thank you Reyhart." Taking the man's face in her hands, she caressed his bruised cheek. A shocked thrill coursed over him as her soft lips hovered over his, kissing him deeply while he could only sit there immobile under her gentle touch. Her golden eyes stared into his and she whispered.

"Goodbye Reyhart, enjoy your final flight."

There was nothing he could do as she leaned over his body, her breasts nuzzling against his cheek while she lifted his inert hand and pressed his index finger against the ignition button. The fans whirled to life, and she blew him one last kiss before disembarking to stand beside Colonel Kóbor.

It was then that Reyhart realized that the young woman was wearing his jacket – a well-won trophy for her night of big game hunting.

CHAPTER 20 – I GOT IT WRONG ALL ALONG

Everybody, sooner or later, sits down to a banquet of consequences.

– ROBERT LOUIS STEVENSON

Across the universe, over the vast distances of time and space, there is one thing that every civilization holds dear – one that transcends nationality, race and even species: the ubiquitous aroma of bacon sizzling in a hot pan that signifies the coming of the new day. Whether the epicurean delight comes from pig, cow or turkey, from vegetable or animal source, bacon rules the breakfast table.

And so it was that sunny Denebian morning when Fynn awoke to its smoky essence wafting through the air, his temples throbbing, his throat parched. Raising up on an elbow, he scrubbed at his eyes with a closed fist before squinting into the brilliant sunshine that streamed through an open window.

The sounds of a heady brew percolating mingled with the distinctive crack of eggshells; the steel brush of a whisk transforming yolks and whites into a creamy melange ready for its conversion into a fluffy omelette. He registered the fact that it smelled divine, while his stomach churned and he fought the rising nausea.

Untangling himself from the sheets, Fynn stumbled to his feet and foraged for his clothing amongst the piles that littered the floor next to a strange bed, in a strange room. Grabbing his crumpled uniform, he tugged it on with shaky hands. The stale stench of smoke and the noxious brew that he'd been quaffing last night still lingered, and he raced to the window to greedily gulp of the fresh air.

Sweet Mother of Jesus, he intoned, looking at the display of holo-frames adorning the pressed wood dresser. *Dear God, please! No…*

Picking up a frame, he guiltily replaced it as if his fingers had been singed. Turning around gingerly, he felt his head pounding as a cheerful voice belted out a cutesy melody at full volume in the kitchen.

My cue to wake up I suppose, he thought abashed.

Padding to the ensuite, Fynn stared at the stranger in the mirror; a man whose red-rimmed hazel eyes betrayed the shame he felt within. Splashing his ashen face with water, Fynn raked unsteady hands through his tousled sandy hair and ran a tongue over the furry coating on his teeth. He stared into those eyes in wonder, pouring over the events of last night.

How has it come to this!

He had returned from the bombing raid on Irtusch a hero – he and Nicki racing in to a photo finish, their air brakes shrieking in protest as they dropped onto the runway nose to nose. Yet she was a millisecond ahead; he had planned it that way.

He remembered her pulling off her helmet, the shock of mahogany hair spilling out as she looked up at him adoringly. That he was used to. It happened all the time to the best jet jockeys.

Same as back on Earth, he thought, although then he would brandish his magical wedding band – that little piece of gold that kept him safe and sound and reserved for Erica.

Women, yeah…they love the tough guy, the bad boy. Except I'm not. Bad, that is. Not really. Fynn groaned and rubbed a hand over his forehead in disgrace. *Not till now.*

Slumping over the sink, he tried to block the happy tune emanating from the kitchen to no avail.

Gotta get this over with… this awkward morning after thing… and then back to the Squadron… my God, everyone's gonna talk.

Fynn rounded the corner just as Nicki was bouncing on the way to the balcony, hands full of steamy mugs of what passed as Wesselan coffee. Mere seconds before collision, she stopped in her tracks, a cheerful smile lighting up her face.

"You almost wore this Earth Boy," she joked, swerving around her red-faced Commanding Officer. "Made us bacon and eggs. Figured you needed the energy after last night. Sit, relax; after all, we got the day off."

With a chuckle, the young woman spun around and returned to the kitchen where plates of crisp aurox bacon rubbed shoulders with fluffy kyttel eggs.

Gosh, what am I gonna do? Fynn sighed, pulling out a deck chair and adjusting the umbrella to keep the sun from burning his freckled face.

She swished back out, hands full and a grin on her face. Shoving a plate in front of her queasy Commanding Officer, Nicki dug in with gusto. Begrudgingly, Fynn had to admit that his young accomplice made a mean omelette. Mouth full of creamy, buttery eggs, he pointed to the culinary masterpiece and nodded appreciatively; a good breakfast always starts the day right. And so it should have been until Nicki broke his bubble of hard-found happiness.

"You were magnificent back there, Earth Boy."

Coyly looking up at him through dark lashes so long that they brushed against cherubic rosy cheeks, Fynn quailed at the thought of hurting such a sweet young woman. He shrugged nonchalantly, ignoring the elephant on the balcony, stuffing his mouth to avoid conversation.

"I mean, I've never even seen it done like that before! Up and down, in and out. Wow, you were like a man possessed. Amazing! I know I don't have a lot of experience... I hope I didn't disappoint you too much?" Timidly, she peeked at the man who suddenly dropped his fork to grimace.

"Oh by the gods, you don't like it do you? I mean, I don't know what humans like for breakfast, I just assumed..."

Reaching over, Fynn brushed Nicki's hair out of her eyes and gently took her hand in his. "Nicki. There's something I need to say."

He squeezed her hand, more to give himself courage than to console the junior officer, ignoring the questioning look on her face. "It's about last night. You're a beautiful woman – any man'd be proud to be with you. You're smart, funny, and hey, you can cook like a five star Michelin chef. But listen, about last night. You and me last night... it can't happen again. I'm still getting over Erica. You understand?" ... *There, I've said it. And I feel like a cad.*

He was ready for anger, he was ready for tears. But he was not ready for her to burst out laughing.

"Oh by the gods Earth Boy, you got an ego the size of the Milky Way galaxy. You think that me and you...?" A peal of giggles resounded like machine guns thundering into his disgrace.

Fynn furrowed his brow as Nicki tried unsuccessfully to hide her merriment at his embarrassment.

"Listen up Vogel, you were staggering drunk last night in the O-Club. I saved you from a face plant in the docking lot. Yeah, you were incoherent by then. You were slugging back the Vulpeculan brandy like water. Never a good idea, but hey, I thought – Earth Boy can handle it."

His eyes were glued to the table in humiliation while she railed on. "Boy was I wrong…You don't remember do you, how I held your head while you were praying to the porcelain goddess in my bathroom? After cleaning up the mess you made, I dragged your lifeless ass to bed and spent the night on the sofa."

Fynn found the crisp bacon suddenly rolled around in his stomach like a ship in a typhoon. *Or is that my ego being bruised?*

Shame flushed his face as he sipped at his ersatz coffee while Nicki's stare bore into him. "I just assumed…" he stammered before allowing a crooked grin to wash away his dishonour.

"That's okay Earth Boy. You don't know our ways yet. You teach me those hot-dogging stunts you pulled up there, okay? And I'll let you in on the Wesselan way of life. Which, by the way, doesn't include jumping the bones of your Commanding Officer when he's in a drunken stupor. Deal?"

She stuck out her hand human-like and Fynn shook it then wiped his mouth on the sleeve of his rumpled flight suit.

"Don't think me rude kiddo, but I got to head over to Colonel Kóbor's place – we got some unfinished business to mull over."

Over and over he'd thought about the last letter that Erica had written without ever grasping the link between Kóbor and his wife's disappearance. It was not something that he'd let lie. Getting up from the table he took one last swig of coffee before throwing a casual salute to the woman who he thankfully hadn't slept with last night.

As he made for the door to her little apartment, Fynn suddenly stopped and turned in his tracks. "One last thing Nicki… a friendly word of advice from your CO … try not to drop-kick the next guy's self-esteem outta the solar system, will you?"

***

The girl was a mistake, Kóbor. Chatty, talkative, but quite delicious! All the while the paralysin was being eliminated from my system.

Reyhart exhaled, then filled his lungs while the hands of time continued to turn. Another deep breath. Narrow eyes scanned his surroundings while his brain continued to ponder the complexities of life.

My, my… Ravenna was wrong about that man. Happily married, ha! Oh my dear fellow, you will indeed have your hands full with that cheeky little monkey! Had I known of your vixen of a mistress, this blackmail endeavour would have led to a far more satisfactory outcome – at least for me. Children are always the riskiest of kidnapping targets. Oh yes, they lead to all sorts of melodramatic scenes. Quite distasteful.

Hope still swam within him, circling like a shark through the dark, dangerous waters. Filling his lungs to their capacity, he continued to scan the night skies for the safety of his home. Limbs refused to obey Reyhart's steel will; instead, his efforts exhausted him. Frustrated with the futility of neutralizing the toxin coursing through his body, he could only sit helplessly at the controls as his clunky old aerovan sped across the starlit countryside.

Reflecting on the probable hopelessness of the situation, he cursed his stupidity in breaking his number one rule – never to let emotion enter into the equation – and this he had broken in spades with General Ravenna. The small thin boy who no one had loved had built a shell so impregnable that light could never touch his soul. Until he came face to face with the general with the scarred face, the woman whose stormy past was blazed for all to see across her tanned, broad cheek.

But he saw, Reyhart did, far past the puckered blemish and the fierce exterior to the real woman within. A woman who conquered a once fragile sense of self-esteem to wield the supreme power of the Wesselan nation. A woman who lived behind a mask, camouflaging her sensitive spirit with the combativeness of a bloodwolf.

That jagged silver line that wound its way down her cheek had penetrated into her very being, festering and growing in malignancy until it rendered her one whose only solace lay in the uniform that she donned each morning. A wound that he could understand – a kindred spirit through whom he had discovered something new, something that he had never felt before, something, he reflected sourly, that would soon take his life from him.

He raged against the injustice until he experienced an epiphany of sorts, finally acknowledging his role in the world and accepting the responsibility for ripping his victims from the arms of their loved ones, forever shredding the fabric of their lives. His would be a fitting death, he acknowledged.

Of life he had no regrets – it had been his creed – to live without analysis, reflection or remorse, and until tonight that had remained true. Except now Reyhart commiserated that he would never again revel in unwinding the layers of complexity of the intriguing General Ravenna, the one woman who could breach the defences of his broken soul.

Another series of full, deep breaths left Reyhart at more peace with himself, accepting of the death that he had so frequently dealt unto others. For death held no fear: he had seen it reflected in the eyes of his victims so many times. Never believing in the gods, he wondered what lay beyond the dark world in which he tread.

He sucked life-giving oxygen into his lungs and sighed. There was marvel in the thought that soon, upon this beautiful night, he would cease to exist in one supreme burst of pain and that the fabric of his being would be consumed in a wreath of flames. Breath after breath he took, until his head spun. *Hopeless indeed*, he thought wistfully, and sighing in a dismal recognition of his fiery destiny, he simply watched the tableau unfolding before him.

There was the seedy motel far below where he had found himself on so many a night with one of the loveless but money-grubbing Starlight dancers. And just beyond, he could see the impoverished farms where mothers and fathers were now relaxing after putting their beloved children to bed, watching the news or some dreary holo-show that had gone into syndication. Pathetic barns stood in barren fields with their chipped paint and broken boards that did little to shelter the shrivelled livestock from the hot winds that blew endlessly across the desert steppes.

The sounds of the hoverfans sputtering along choppily made him aware of the impending final moments of his existence. A vision of the girl in the golden G-string flashed before his eyes.

This Kóbor, what a strange fellow. A dour type – that is indeed certain. How can that playful little chit be part of his colourless world? Ah well, I have never comprehended the choices people make. But he should have understood – a man with his background. I would have imagined that Kóbor could tell that it was nothing personal. Of course – his wretched brats would have been safe had he left things well alone. But now... death of starvation, of thirst, chained in the dark... horrible...terrifying. Ah, I do grow soft towards the end.

A tiny noise escaped from Reyhart's thin lips as he dwelled on General Ravenna. *And yet Kóbor's no fool – an amateur assassin he may be – but no fool.*

He'll shortly unravel Ravenna's involvement in this botched endeavour and with his children at stake, there's no doubt he'll unleash a terrible revenge. For she has no knowledge that could lead to their freedom, and no knowledge equals no use – time expired. No, the little Kóbors will perish cruelly in the dark, never knowing that it was their father's witless bravado that led to their demise. And Ravenna, well my beauty… may you bravely meet the death he deals to you.

And suddenly, there was only silence. The whirr of the hoverfans had faded and Reyhart was only left with the whistling of the rushing wind and the sound of his breathing.

Rapid, shallow, he noted as fear replaced the indifference of short moments before. *Hmmm… at ten thousand feet, it shouldn't take too long.* He found his brain was unable to calculate although the air speed and altitude display sat just beneath his broken nose. Panic began to overtake his normally calm demeanour, his chest rising and falling with short quick breaths.

Mumbling to gods to which he had never ascribed, Reyhart sped off his final prayers. *If I've offended, it was at the will of others. I was only a tool, paid to resolve the problems of those too weak to seek their own solution. I've never taken pleasure from my work, I've never reveled in causing undue pain – death has always been quick, professionally done. Consider this when you take me, oh God of Fire. Grant me a second chance, and I promise by the Fires of Ru to put this behind me. To morph from murderer to protector. And if this is not in your wishes, then I beseech you: grant me a speedy death as I have done to those who knelt before me in supplication.*

In his panic, Reyhart did not notice his lips which began to move to his garbled appeals; the twitch of an eyelid was lost in the intense fear that gripped him.

Oh by the gods! 5000 feet… 4000 feet…This cannot be happening!

Tumbling from the sky, the earth seemed to rise up to meet him, except it was not the barrenlands, the kingdom of the sand scorpion and dune-lyon, where Pallav had intended.

Instead, Reyhart recognized the little farm where short hours ago two innocent children had run alongside his van, joyfully waving their chubby hands at the sight of him. Little did he deserve it, he thought. And little did the poor family asleep now on their scratchy straw pallets deserve for their pathetic home to be destroyed in a ball of fire.

It was then that a second regret surfaced within Reyhart's panicked mind. That his death, so merited, would inflict such senseless carnage on the innocents and at that moment his silent prayers were heart-felt.

Deneb, Mother Goddess, hear me now. Send me to my death but spare the family below.

Only the rush of the wind answered his call and unconsciously Reyhart covered his face with his arm as he plummeted earthward. It was then he became aware of the answering of his limbs to the commands emerging from his brain and in that moment, Reyhart sprang to action, valiantly trying to regain control of the dying aerocar. Pitching madly, the battered old beast shivered and shuddered, attempting to respond to the sudden erratic commands that taxed its ancient frame. Violently it spun out of control, twisting in the air like a demon tormented. With every last ounce of strength, Reyhart clung to the controls trying to spring the bird from its swan song.

His mind had stopped functioning; it was only the animal instinct deep within the assassin that kept him going, stopping him from meekly accepting his death. His efforts were not without success, for the van wheeled away from the old farmhouse, twirling like a top as it tore into the broken-down barn where it shattered into pieces. It was the last thing that Reyhart accomplished and a smile tugged at the corner of his thing lips, knowing that he saved the family with the two sweet children from their deaths. And then, all was suddenly black for the man in the impeccable suit.

CHAPTER 21 – ON THE HOUSE

Mistakes are the portals of discovery.

– JAMES JOYCE

The banging of music throbbed across the parking lot and Bafa watched the battered old aerovan skim over the Starlight Club as it veered off to the east while Pallav sat in his vehicle, his fingers drumming impatiently on the dash. Already the hoverfans were roaring to life, the aerocar ready to pursue the doomed assassin on his trip to the netherworld.

And yet she remained immobile, a statue in stiletto heels and gold lace, under the dim lights of the parking lot. Pallav descended from his vehicle, his long legs carrying him to where the young woman stood, her head tipped back as she watched the taillights of the doomed man fading in the distance.

She turned to him then, lipstick smudged, mascara coursing down tear-stained cheeks. With golden eyes the size of saucers, her bottom lip quivering, Pallav wondered if he had asked too much of her.

She's a foolish creature, one who never thinks things through… jumping from one bad decision to the next. Still, without Villutomi I shudder to think of how this would have turned out.

That was where his sympathies ended, for Pallav did not wish to be robbed of witnessing the death of the man who had kidnapped his children. Who had tried to blackmail him. And who was somehow linked to the vicious General Ravenna at whose orders the village sheltering his human compatriots had been destroyed. Ignoring her tears, Pallav took Bafa by the arm and spun her about.

"Save the waterworks Villutomi and let's get going," Pallav growled, omitting the satisfaction he would feel at watching the swine who harmed his family crash and burn.

But the force of her resistance took him by surprise. Rearing up like a wildcat Bafa spat fire, rounding on him. "Let go of me!"

Pulling away, her screams pierced the night. "You think nothing of it, do you – you cold-hearted bastard! I just drugged a man and sent him to his death. And all you want to do is push me around and tell me what to do."

The sound of the heavy metal door creaking open caused Pallav to pull Bafa into the shadows, but it was too late. A roll of jewelweed between his fat lips, the manager had waddled outside for a quick smoke but instead saw his new waitress being accosted by a giant of a man. Reaching behind, he pulled out a blaster and with Pallav in the cross-hairs, motioned for Bafa to step away.

Hands in the air, Pallav grinned. "It's okay, just a simple misunderstanding." He chuckled as if it were a normal everyday thing – to be faced with a deadly weapon pointed at his chest. "I don't want my daughter working here. You understand, don't you? My wife's been crying her eyes out since she found out. I had to do something."

One arched eyebrow arched even further as Bafa stared at Pallav, her mouth agape. The blaster stayed level at his chest as Pallav griped, "Kids, eh? We paid for her to go to university, and this is what she does with her education. Can you believe it?"

Shaking his head, Pallav slowly lowered his hands. "Now, there's no need for that. She'll give you back that drink belt and I'll be taking her home."

A questioning look came over the man's face as he lowered the blaster and pointed to Bafa. "That's on the level then, is it? He's your father?"

With a shrug of her shoulders, Bafa frowned. "This. Is. So. Humiliating," she moaned to Pallav, stripping off Reyhart's jacket to unhitch the drink dispensing belt before handing it back to the manager. Glaring at the red-jowled man, she stuck out her hand, "My pay. I worked two hours; I want my pay."

Dumbstruck, Pallav grabbed her by the arm and forcefully pulled her back to the aerocar. "Put that damn jacket back on and get inside now," he seethed while the manager only shook his head in commiseration, happy to have sired only boys.

She stared at him dejectedly, not noticing the grim line of his mouth as he engaged the hoverfans and flew off into the night. A green light illuminated the dash, the little chip with Reyhart's data flashing as the aerocar found its way along the now abandoned sky lanes that would lead to the assassin's home. Sighing sadly, she looked down upon the desolate farms and wondered how far he had travelled before his life had been extinguished.

"What have I done…" she whimpered, unable to staunch the pain inside. "Because of me, two men have met their deaths. One man I loved, who I thought I'd spend my life with… his cold body's now floating face down in the river. And this Reyhart – what's he done to deserve this? Your kids are safe, Colonel. Safe and sound in his house. And because of me, he's riding to his death."

She sobbed like a child, sniffling and hiccupping, but Pallav's thoughts were far away, searching through the hidden nooks and crannies of his mind, reflecting on the time when he was young and tasted first blood.

True, he remembered, *a smidgeon of guilt had welled up inside of me, but then the USNA had been at war – a war to save my country against the unwashed hordes surging at our doorstep, aiming to destroy the American way of life. And the Refugee Wars, they were so long ago – it was in another life, on another planet, and worlds away.*

Shaking his head, he dismissed the thoughts abruptly. *My cause was just. Same as now.*

Over the abandoned fields and empty terrain they flew in silence. Crumpled against the door, Bafa sulked while Pallav massaged his temples, wondering how to break through to the suffering woman. The stillness of the night crept through the vehicle, suffocating the two in a thick quilt of unspoken emotions. Sensing the remorse stretching out its poisonous fingers, he glanced over at her guiltily – the young woman so unlike his logical wife – and reaching out took her cold hand in his.

"Listen to me Villutomi… two men are dead. Two evil men. One who would've snuffed your life out without a second thought; the other, a murdering bastard without a conscience. The world's a better place without scum like that.

"What you did before, you know, with the Black Hide? Turned your back on your own kind. Playing the good little captain on one hand, all the while sabotaging military security systems and colluding with the enemy while your nation's at war? That's treason. But it was easy for you, wasn't it, to feel removed from it all when you acted at arm's length. Forging security passes and stealing access codes. You kept your hands clean, right?

"But thousands of innocent people died because of the part you played. And now, you've experienced death close up and personal and you realize that you don't like it."

The grip on her hand tightened while his voice dripped with condemnation. "Is that it then – you can stomach betraying your comrades in arms but not wiping out evil?"

His mind told him that she would rage at him with unjustified sentiments of saving the downtrodden, of freeing Deneb from the corruption of the Wesselan government and how the soldiers whose deaths she caused were only implements of destruction, casualties of an unjust war. That the reign of terror perpetuated against innocent Geiten civilians had to be countered with actions, making her part in the destruction of the Wessel military bases justifiable. And Pallav was ready with a rebuttal to these arguments, but what he was not ready for was Bafa collapsing in tears into his arms.

Nuzzling her head into his shoulder, the young woman sobbed uncontrollably and instinctively Pallav cradled her against him, dismayed as her tears soaked through his shirt. There was no military manual that could help Colonel Kóbor navigate the stormy waters of a young alien female acting in a very unofficer-like manner and so Pallav awkwardly switched to the familiar Dad-mode.

Patting her back sympathetically, he made small comforting sounds like he would to his children when they were little and had scraped their knee or survived a trip to the feared dentist.

"Shhh. There, there. You were only doing what you thought was the right thing." *My God, I sound like a complete ass! She lost her fiancé and that's the best I come up with!* "Bafa, listen to me… you know that Tax'n never loved you, you know he only used you… he wanted to kill you for God's sake."

The sobbing stopped and she stared up into his face with tear-stained eyes, uncertain, willing for him to go on. Pushing her head back into his shoulder to avoid those puppy-dog eyes, Pallav softly stroked her hair.

"And Reyhart… Reyhart was an assassin who was going to kill my children. Villutomi, you protected my family and me from some Machiavellian scheme that originates from God knows where…"

Her voice broke as she shrugged out of his arms and arched an eyebrow in confusion. "Machia-what?"

Fishing a tissue from his pocket, Pallav smiled at the unintelligent earth-references that peppered his speech. "What I'm trying to say Villutomi is that because of you I'm not going to be bringing my kids home in body bags. You did real well. Now pack up that guilt Captain, I need you fresh and alert when we practice our break and entry protocols into Reyhart's lair. You lifted an iris-scan and his prints, right?"

A bob of the dark head confirmed that the young woman had, and leaving the feelings of guilt behind, she reflected momentarily on the distractive powers of a kiss. Yet for Pallav, the anger continued to bubble up within him: that he was not able to protect his children, that his family had been senselessly targeted. Until those dark clouds were replaced by a feeling of angst for his actions had led to the death of the one man who could have provided insight as to the true culprit – the one upon whom he should also have sought revenge. Feeling the fool for having allowed the passion for retribution to cloud his normally logical mind, he flew on in silence, knowing that danger still stalked him, dark and menacing, from somewhere, from someone, on Deneb.

***

A pile of dresses sat crumpled in a bundle on the bleached wood floor and in frustration Ravenna threw herself down on the corner of her bed, her hand on her forehead.

I'll never be ready in time, she moaned, her eyes stealing over to the khaki coloured uniform that hung neatly on a hook. *What'll Reyhart think if he has to wait while I decide what to wear? Or what to do with my hair? Or… or…or… oh by the gods I should never've agreed to have dinner with him!*

Sitting up straight, Ravenna arched an eyebrow as a fantastic idea popped into her head.

Magdar!

Jumping up, she pushed the gloom aside as her HomeLink System transmitted into Gomalan's dining room. Astonishment blossomed on the general's face as the High Commander's form coalesced, a ladle in one hand as he served out the evening meal to a table that included the wife of that alien Colonel Kóbor. She could see that the surprise was not one-sided as he paused, ladle mid-air. It was then that she remembered her state of half-dress and grabbed a towel with flames colouring her cheeks.

"General Ravenna," the silver-haired general coughed. "I take it this is urgent?"

Twisting her lips in embarrassment, Ravenna screwed up her face. "For me it is," she mumbled before turning back to the High Commander. "I was wondering if your wife could spare a few moments of her time. I need some… ummm… women's advice."

The sound of a chair scraping across the floor caught her attention as Magdar stood and smoothed wrinkles from her spotless shape-fitting tunic. "Of course, Ravenna. Any time. What can I help you with?"

Silence filled the rooms as Ravenna stared at Gomalan. "It's a bit private, if you don't mind."

Ravenna waited while the elegant woman sailed across the stone pavers onto a sun-filled terrace. Out of earshot of her husband, Magdar nodded conspiratorially. "Coast is clear; go ahead."

Minutes later, Gomalan watched questioningly as his wife calmly took her seat at the table and wordlessly began to spoon the fragrant kyttel stew into her plate while miles away, Ravenna shrugged into a silk blouse and pencil skirt. Tugging the hem into place, she once more eyed the comfortable combat uniform ready for the new day and groaned, "How the hell do women wear this stuff day in and day out?"

A quick glance in the mirror showcased the silver scar that ran down her cheek while the sunlight cast shadows on creases that spread in a fine web from the corners of her eyes. Surveying herself critically, she curled her lip at the sight of silvery threads winding their way through her dark mane.

By the gods, who am I kidding? Old and wrinkled and past my prime. I wonder… Pausing, she ran her hands down the sides of her skirt, before blackening her lashes and running a deep shade of blood red over her lips, *what exactly does Reyhart want from me. The Three Lyndins! The most romantic restaurant in all of Deneb… What is that man up to?*

The sound of her alarm startled her from her thoughts and Ravenna padded into the sunroom on bare feet, activated the entrance screen and gingerly sat on the edge of the couch awaiting Reyhart's arrival with anticipation. Cushions had spilled onto the plush carpet and Ravenna retrieved them along with memories of the elegant assassin tumbling onto the floor under a sea of colourful pillows while she held him down, helpless, as her hostage.

His infectious laughter still echoed in her ears as flashbacks surfaced of him writhing under her while she bit, licked and kissed her way down his long, lean torso. The smile that beamed up at her had shocked Ravenna for it lit up his pale eyes and instantly transformed that cold sculpted face into one of pure blissful innocence.

Like an angel, she thought, revelling in the pleasureful delights of his attention that brought out the devil in her. *This man of murder and bloodshed who can be so gentle, so eager...by the gods, he's so intriguing! And I could use a little bit of fun right now – something light and amusing – nothing too involved.*

Crumpling under the thoughts of day-consuming briefings by cretins and cowards who failed to comprehend the true threat of their Geiten foe, Ravenna's happy-bubble was momentarily burst until her eyes lit on a brilliant splash of orange underfoot. There a tumble of withering petals lay forgotten, casually discarded by her ardent lover who had delicately traced the contours of her face with their silkiness before descending lower and lower.

That's the kind of distraction I could become accustomed to!

The powerful warrior in her evaporated and she melted under the memories of the prior evening until a quick glance at the time revealed that her knight of the dagger and death was half an hour late. Doubting herself, she checked again before hailing the HomeLink System; but getting no response, Ravenna tried Reyhart's aerovan.

Hmmm… Crossing her legs, Ravenna smoothed down her skirt while she wondered what to do. *If they're anything like their father, those two mini Kóbors are probably holding him up. I'll be glad when this is all over – it didn't help one bit, I still don't know how the humans slipped through the net.*

Checking the time again, Ravenna stared into the sky, willing herself to see Reyhart's aerovan until she remembered. *That damn old jalopy of his has always had problems with the hololink. I'll leave him a voice message instead and meet him at the Three Lyndins.*

The Three Lyndins. Prices into the next solar system. Waiters so snobbish that their noses grazed the stratosphere. Artistically crafted food measured in centimeters. But the ambience – divine; a little slice of heaven in Wesselan. The plebs could only dream of such a place. Secluded alcoves were carved into the steep chalk cliffs overlooking the lush Sirga River Valley where tables nestled under the guttering light of fragrant torches. Flowering vines cascaded over the rockeries, while the gurgle of a nearby waterfall that tumbled into the mighty river below ensured clandestine whispers retained their spell-like charm.

And tonight – it'll be all mine, she thought as she slipped off her panties and discretely pushed them into her clutch while in front of her house, her driver jumped out of the military aerocar to open the door.

A quick salute and a questioning look on his face caused the general to raise an eyebrow. She could see the confusion on his face and she snarled as he impudently stared at her bare legs.

"Drop me off and don't bother waiting for me Sergeant," she snapped. "I'll see you tomorrow morning – Rise -1, sharp."

Stomping off, Ravenna almost lost a heel in the docking lot and chided herself, trying to recall how to walk in anything but combat boots. The crunch of the pea gravel under her heels mingled with the twittering of song birds that darted along the tree-lined path leading to the stately building. Pausing half-way, Ravenna took in the large stone planters overflowing with a riot of colourful flowers standing as if at attention on either side of the broad twin red doors.

Loud buzzing caused her to stop in her high-heeled tracks as two black and white clad drones ushered out to greet her. Hovering inches from her face, one scanned Ravenna while the other maintained a watchful guard.

"General Ravenna. Welcome to the Three Lyndins," Drone #1 intoned mechanically. A nod from the woman acknowledging their vigilance and then she confidently led off with the left foot until the second drone buzzed alarmingly near her.

"Madame, it does not seem you have a reservation. May we provide you with information on the next available slots? In seven months' time, we could fit you in for… 1400 hrs perhaps?" The two drones took up position, side by side, blocking access to the restaurant.

A smile on her blood-red lips, Ravenna brushed aside the pesky creatures. "It'll be under Reyhart," she replied casually, again trying to bypass the metal sentinels. "He made the reservation last night I believe."

The hovering automatons seemed uncertain, maintaining their vigil while Ravenna's patience grew thin. "Get the manager," she seethed, her feet beginning to wish she'd found alternate footwear. As Drone #1 whizzed away, its alter-ego advanced and retreated, like a watch dog at the end of its tether trying to decide whether to fight or flee against an invading threat.

"Finally!"

Never one to act conciliatory, Ravenna strode up to the tall bespectacled man whose long nose reminded her of a race hound. Words rushed out of her mouth as she thrust her hand forward in greeting. "There's a reservation for Reyhart and guest at Set -1. He's running late. I'm the guest and I'd appreciate being seated." An angry glare at the drones made them skitter away while she could sense the manager's unease.

Rubbing his forehead, the man exhaled loudly, a look of distinct discomfort on his narrow face. "General, there's been a misunderstanding. Of course there's a table for you and Reyhart waiting. Please accept my apologies, and if you'll follow me, I'll take you to your table."

She could still hear the drones buzzing angrily while the manager seated her under the shade of a magnificent lyndin tree whose waxy-white flowers perfumed the air. The roar of the waterfall covered her grumbling against the ineptitude of the robotic staff until one of the metal-bodied waiters floated over with a virtual cart of offerings.

Waving him away testily, Ravenna checked her comms link to no avail. *What's keeping him? No answer at home; nothing from his crazy van's communication system. What gives?*

The dying rays of the day painted the Sirga River to a lovely rose gold and Ravenna tried to appreciate the beauty of the evening. But her mind drifted far from the paradise surrounding her, to the empty trip to the abandoned quarry that morning where the Kóbor kids were no-shows. Hours later, she heard through the rumour mill that the alien colonel and his wife were somehow, once again, one big happy family.

We must've got our wires crossed, she brooded, while the drones scurried about lighting the torches amongst the dinner tables. Pulling out her comms link, Ravenna began to mindlessly scroll through tedious holo-mails, her stomach growling and her thoughts running wild.

A light touch on her shoulder caused Ravenna to look around in surprise, her face aglow until she noticed it was the long-nosed manager and her features crumpled in disappointment. "General, I apologize for this, but this table is reserved for Gil Hum in an hour…"

The disappointment morphed into anger and giving him a sour look she hissed. "Unbelievable! An entertainment star trumps the General of the Wesselan Army and your very dear acquaintance, Reyhart! And exactly what type of establishment is this where a dinner reservation is for an hour? I get better treatment at the Mess Hall."

She was surprised when Long-Nose straightened his shoulders and stared her down. "There was no reservation for Reyhart tonight. I haven't heard from him in months, not since… well… If he were here, I'm sure we could arrive at some sort of an understanding. But it's obvious he's not coming. So I suggest you have a drink on the house before your departure."

Setting down a crystal goblet of amber liquid that glowed like the setting sun, the manager lowered his voice and whispered into her ear. "Within the hour, General."

Low clouds hung over the river like a string of grey pearls while inwardly Ravenna seethed. The heavens opened up in an uncharacteristic summer downpour and drones raced about in panic, deploying protective canopies over the richly-clad diners. Yet the general was oblivious to the water soaking through her silk blouse and pooling in puddles beneath her heels.

Kóbor! It's that bloody big aurox, I'm sure of it. Somehow, he's to blame for all of this! Where was he last night anyway?

Angrily, Ravenna grabbed the goblet and draining its contents, slammed the glass down on the table before throwing a credit-chip to the hovering waiter-drone. "Tell the manager I don't do on the house."

CHAPTER 22 - VISITORS

All a man has is pride. Sometimes you have it so much it is a sin.

– ERNEST HEMINGWAY

It hung with pride above his desk, its dark frame contrasting sharply with the white walls of his study, alone except for the obligatory family portraits. A brunette beauty seated at the foot of a moss-festooned oak looked out from the celluloid while dreamily contemplating the tiny bundle in her arms.

That was the day we brought Lewis home, Daniel reminisced.

And then there was the beautiful golden frame taking prime position on his desk. It was to be a reminder for their children of who they really were, for Daniel had snapped that shot the day before the *Mayflower* had blasted from the Earth. He picked it up and a bittersweet smile crossed his face. There she was, his Poppy, her face lit up like an angel. The bump that would become Max was barely visible while their son Lewis wore a devilish grin as a younger Daniel enveloped his family in his arms.

Poppy would be so proud of us, Daniel thought as he straightened the frame, remembering the moment as if it were only yesterday.

His eyes flew once more to the certificate with its accompanying holo-image and he relived the surprise when he and Meera were called into the Director's conference room where the Aditian Ambassador stood patiently awaiting their arrival. Repressing a shiver as a cold scaly hand gripped his, Daniel had shot a puzzled glance at Meera who had simply shrugged her shoulders in bewilderment.

"For Courage and Bravery", he read, sighing wistfully. For he'd had many other awards over the years – from High School Athlete of the Year to Outstanding Academic Achievement at university and the more prestigious and coveted international award for Innovation in Scientific

Research – but those were tucked away and never talked about; awards from a planet once unknown to the Collective until the Denebian pandemic, and whose recognition could only lead to catastrophe.

He hadn't heard them enter, the beat of the music hiding the normal pounding of their little feet on the tiled floors. Max pushed up against Daniel's leg and wondered, in the way the young often do, how a piece of paper could so captivate his father. Other than a massive blue seal embossed in gold, the paper seemed so very ordinary to the lad.

Staring up at Daniel, his tiny face smudged with sauce and his little hand curled around a fish taco, Max's questioning look was so reminiscent of his mother that Daniel was speechless. Until he noticed morsels of spiced fish and splotches of sauce underfoot.

"Hey buddy, why don't you and Lewis go outside and hang with Teuvo and Lark?" Pushing his sons from the office, Daniel felt the resistance as Max spun around, dripping sauce on the second T-shirt since that morning.

His dark eyes sparkled with confusion as he pointed to the holo-image of his father gripping the Aditian ambassador's scaled appendage. "Dad, is that fish you caught what we're eating? Why's it wearing clothes and how can it be standing up?"

Lewis choked back his laughter as Daniel frowned. "That is actually an alien ambassador, and he's presenting me and Meera an award." Pointing to the holo-image, Daniel read the citation to his sons with pride swelling inside him.

> "Dr. Daniel Radu is awarded the Aditian Commendation of Valor for demonstrating conspicuous bravery on the 18th of Brumaire 1799. While under withering fire, and without regard for his personal safety, Dr. Radu came to the rescue of a wounded Aditian citizen, leading to the subsequent dismantlement of an interstellar smuggling ring. For his courage and bravery, Dr. Radu is presented with the Order of the Cobalt Wave."

The sauce-covered face stared up at him with big dark eyes, impressed by his hero-father. "Now c'mon guys, let's get back to the party." Ushering his sons outside, Daniel was surrounded by the sounds of talk and laughter that rose above the glissando of the slide guitar as strains of the blues sailed clear and bright over the stone-paved terrace. He saw Meera with a drink in her hand chatting with Hoshi and Barb and joining them, Daniel threw an arm about his colleague's shoulders.

"Well partner, you enjoying yourself with my Geiten-gang?"

Squirming out from under his embrace Meera chuckled, "Categorically," she replied before winking, "and the food's a lot better than the Aditian buffet!" As the three erupted into laughter, Daniel recalled the assault against his stomach and shaking his head, left the trio to debate the follies of alien food.

All about him the crowd mingled and chatted, yet Daniel felt alone. *There's so few of us left now.*

His mind wandered to the three Space Arks that had fled from Earth, two meeting their end in the vortex of the wormhole that brought the *Mayflower* to Deneb, until now only a shadow of the original team remained on Cepheus-9. *And we owe it all to Erica*, he thought, and an image of the courageous young pilot, smiling and happy in anticipation of the new baby, floated before his eyes.

And then it happened, like it always did at the functions back at NASA: Marco began to sing in his deep rich voice, making up the lyrics as he went along with a chorus of Pat, Olivia and Lucia adding their vocal talents. Chuckling at his friend's antics, Daniel felt a pang of envy that his one-time disciple had landed a plum engineering job with the government until he remembered the coffee-fueled, stress-laced hours analyzing reports until his eye balls felt like they'd been scrubbed by cotton balls.

No way; never again! Kóbor did me a massive favour when he faked my résumé. Who'd have figured we'd luck out on Cepheus-9…

Ambling over to the buffet table, Daniel grabbed a plate and piled it high with veggies straight from his garden and topped them with the fragrant spiced fish. With the twin suns warming his face, he grabbed a glass and poured himself a few fingers from his ample stash of Buffalo Trace. Slowly sipping its velvety sweetness, the peace of finally being at home filled him.

But a rogue wave threatened his calm… Tara: both friend and foe. Without her, they would never have succeeded. Yet she held within her power the promise of a love-filled life that was never to be. The wave quickly crested and rolled over him, no longer threatening to drown him within its depths, for he had learned to conquer the waves of denied love that had tormented him so, robbing him of sleep during the long Denebian nights. The woman who had possessed him, body and soul over the years, who he had desired with an aching so deep that he believed the void could never be filled, had joined the ranks of ghosts who flitted on stormy wings through his dreams. He was free at last.

"Penny for your thoughts." It was a sweet voice, one he couldn't place that shook him free from his musings. It had always surprised him that a cantankerous old man like Dr. Vance Nolan could have fathered such a sweet child. Except Olivia was no longer a girl. Twenty-five years old, skin as clear as porcelain and with her mother's vibrant red hair, the young woman was a reflection of dignity and composure.

Daniel shrugged. "Not much. Just that I like it here." Seeing the doubt cloud her blue eyes, he tilted his head inquiringly. "And you? You ever think about life back on Deneb?"

Face flushed from the singalong, Olivia shook her head and stared into her hands. "Not really, but it's a good thing we left when we did. Pat heard from Renzo a few days back. He and Lila were halfway to the Glodatis when they heard from some refugees that Urkyn had been levelled by a Wesselan attack. So they struck out into the barrens, you know, just in case, but the going was real rough."

Olivia tugged at her sleeve nervously as the wind off the Cepheusian Sea breathed softly through her hair. Shielding her eyes against the glare of the waves, she paused for a moment. "They doubled back. Back towards the River Panni, until they came to an old ford. Believe it or not, Renzo and Lila crossed into Wesselan and made their way to Bâcha. Pat talks like it was just a great adventure, but my brother's safe and sound, day in and day out banging away at the computer. What's he know anyhow about life anyway?"

Her mouth turned up at the corner as Olivia stared at Daniel hesitating, while his stomach growled with hunger. "But you know about life." Her face flushed with emotion, she looked up at him with glistening eyes. "Dr. Radu, you've got experience. I mean… what would you tell a woman to do, I mean, a much younger woman, who's found herself in a very strange position."

Reluctantly putting his plate back on the buffet table, Daniel took Olivia by the arm and led her away from the crowds and back into the house. The tone of her voice led him to believe that some trouble was brewing, and habitually he reached for a glass and pouring a shot, handed it to her while her face burned as bright as the hair on her head.

"And would this young woman be in need of some of the smoothest bourbon in the universe to tell Uncle Daniel what's troubling her?

Dear God, I hope she's not pregnant by some Cepheusian Lothario!

Swirling Daniel's precious Buffalo Trace, Olivia stared intensely into the amber liquid as if searching for an answer before taking a huge gulp. "Thanks, it's really awkward what I need to say. I mean, there's a man who I've known for years now. Well, at least since we left Earth. At first, I thought it was just a silly crush, but now I know it's not. I mean, he's perfect for me – a brilliant scientist, warm, funny – he's even got a great job with the Cepheusian government. He's older, but then age really isn't a big deal, is it?" Smiling shyly, Olivia looked up at him with hope lighting up her face. "And I think you know who I'm talking about."

Daniel gulped and ran a hand through his hair, his mind wildly running down the list of *Mayflower* passengers on Cepheus-9 as Olivia's cornflower blue eyes bore into his.

"I'm not sure..." Daniel sputtered, wishing he'd poured himself a drink as well and reached over for the bottle.

But Olivia grabbed his arm, her nails digging into his skin as she pulled him close to her. Her voice was nearly a whisper as she breathed secretively, "I'm not a kid you know. But I'm guessing he thinks I'm still the girl who cried the day the *Mayflower* lifted off." Her eyes darted back to the terrace where Angelo and Marco were vying for the Karaoke championship.

"You understand what I'm talking about, don't you?" Her voice was pleading while her hand squeezed his arm with greater pressure. "I mean... how could I make it any plainer?"

When the only response that she received was a look of panic on Daniel's face, Olivia burst into tears and threw herself into his arms. Her head fit perfectly against his shoulder as she sobbed, while Daniel froze in terror.

"I'm such an idiot. You must think I'm crazy. But we'd be perfect together, don't you see?" She looked up at him with tear-stained eyes. "I could make Marco happy; I know I could. But Dr. Radu, any time I get close he pulls back. You're his friend... can you help me?"

"Ahhhh... well...that I can do." Panic floated away as a radiant smile lit up the young woman's face. "I'll have a little chat with Marco and see what I can do about getting this train moving on the right tracks."

Squealing with joy, Olivia threw her arms around him and bestowed a big kiss on Daniel's cheek while hugging him appreciatively.

It was at that moment that the room began to glow, and a large menacing hologram emerged from the sparkling mist. Icy green eyes opened wide in shock at the sight of the young Nolan girl in the arms of the despised Radu.

Jumping back like a scalded cat, Daniel reeled in surprise. "Kóbor! What the hell!"

The surprise on the big man's face was replaced by a sour look. "Ms. Nolan, I must say that I'm rather shocked." Glaring at Daniel, Pallav narrowed his eyes. "But then again, I suppose it's something I've come to expect – there are always surprises with Dr. Daniel Radu."

Indignant with anger, Daniel turned on Pallav while Olivia, reading the situation, quietly slipped from the brewing conflict and back to the party. The holoimage snorted and Pallav raised an eyebrow in disgust.

"I'm not here to comment on your love life or judge your lack of morals, Radu. You can do whatever you want, just so it doesn't involve my wife anymore."

Daniel could feel his temper flaring at the unwanted intrusion. "I don't give a damn what you think. This is my home and I don't remember inviting you here. So state your piece and get out."

With the temperature rising in the room, jealousy struck Pallav at the sight of the tastefully decorated rooms, the sumptuous furnishings, tapestries and artwork that led his eye to a sun-drenched terrace packed with friends. Even after all the efforts he had made to sabotage Dr. Radu's future on Cepheus-9 – Daniel had somehow still managed to come out on top.

And then there was the Nolan girl love-flushed in his arms, far too young and innocent to be hitching her wagon to a man with Radu's track record. Glancing into the study, green envy overtook him as he squinted to read the citation proudly displayed over an imposing desk. Pallav grunted in frustration, realizing his ploy had failed miserably.

The bastard landed squarely on his feet, he scowled.

Shaking off the disappointment, Pallav tried his best to look conciliatory. "Listen Radu, it took me a while to figure out the protocols to synch our HomeLink System to Cepheus-9's HIVE – and I don't have the time to bicker with you. I need your help."

Daniel snorted and laughed in his face, "You expect me to help you, after all the bullshit you threw my way? Go to hell!"

Swallowing the furious retort that threatened to tumble from his lips, Pallav threw up his hands in exasperation. "This isn't about Tara. You see, it's Fynn and Erica…"

"Erica?" Screwing up his face in confusion, Daniel wondered how he could be of help to the couple to whom he owed so much.

"She never returned."

The reply was like a blow to him. "What? That can't be," Daniel interrupted. "When we put down on Cepheus-9, she turned back. You should be able to track down the Meganeur!"

Daniel felt his heart pounding at the thought that something ill had befallen the woman who had saved their lives. His face ashen, his mind raced through possible scenarios. "Listen Kóbor, Dom's a nurse at the Dopang Precinct Medical Centre – between the two of us, we can check out the local hospitals to see if a pregnant woman fitting her description was admitted. I'll get back to you…"

"Dr. Radu, wait. Tara hacked into the Wesselan Aerospace Force tracking systems – I know that was risky, but I wanted to keep it away from the prying eyes of the authorities in case they discovered that Erica was involved in your escape from Urkyn – and Tara was able to determine the exact timing that the Meganeur went off-line….it was the date of your arrival."

Pacing the room restlessly, Daniel suddenly stopped in his tracks. "You know, she's probably still in hospital, snuggling up to the new little Rosendahl-Vogel princess, wondering where're the balloons and stuffed toys. Don't worry Kóbor, we'll find her."

The light of hope shone in Daniel's eyes as Pallav allowed himself a brief smile. "Listen, Fynn believes she died in the explosion on Farb ASW, the one that masked her departure. I don't want to raise his hopes until we're sure, you understand? And the fewer people who know about this, the better. I mean, there's not only Erica, but the Nuakos who are also missing."

"You can count on me to keep it quiet," Daniel replied as the growling of his stomach reminded him of his forlorn plate of food, waiting for him outside.

"Yes, I imagine I can count on you to keep secrets," Pallav glowered before turning in surprise, the sound of footsteps interrupting the sword-play of words between the two men.

"Bafa? I told you I needed a few moments to myself. Are the kids okay?"

Cocking an eyebrow, Daniel surveyed the scantily dressed woman who sauntered over to Pallav and casually placed a hand on the big man's shoulder before turning her amber eyes his way.

"Your brother?" she asked in a sultry voice. The eyebrow went higher as Pallav shook his head vigorously in denial. Ignoring the questioning look from Daniel, Pallav pushed Bafa's hand from him.

"Are they okay?"

With a shrug of her shapely shoulders, Bafa stared at Daniel. "So you're not going to introduce me then…"

When thunder crossed his face, Bafa blinked, suddenly all serious. "They're fine. Luke's all cleaned up and Isabella, well, seems Reyhart has a thing against hurting the ladies."

"Had a thing," he corrected as Daniel watched the interplay with curiosity. "The bastard's dead now."

The one-time *Mayflower* Captain could see a shadow play across Pallav's face. Bafa pulled on his sleeve, pointing to Daniel through the Home Link System.

"How's he linked to this?"

"He's not. This is something separate."

Tired of the mystery, Daniel piped up. "And the 'he' is Dr. Daniel Radu, Project Manager and Chief Engineer for the Space Ark *Mayflower*, now masquerading as an exobotanist residing on Cepheus-9."

He could see the veil of confusion being lifted as Bafa turned to face him. Her eyes scrutinized Daniel as if memorizing each feature and detail, questioning the veracity of the information. Then her voice boomed across the room as she screwed up her face. "So that's the man who was having an affair with your wife!"

Pallav winced, aghast at the one time he let his guard down with that foolhardy confession, while Daniel looked about in embarrassment feeling his face burn with shame. Smiling as if uncovering one of the great mysteries of life, Bafa's holoimage approached Daniel. "Count yourself lucky that all he did was send you to Cepheus-9; you should see what happened to the last guy who crossed his family."

Turning her back on the flustered man, Bafa tugged on Pallav's sleeve impatiently. "I need you. So if you're finished here, c'mon upstairs."

She glided out of view while Pallav grimaced seeing the smirk on Daniel's face. "What're you waiting for Kóbor? The woman said she needs you."

The big man eyed Daniel and snarled menacingly, "Be my guest killing yourself by jumping to conclusions. But first check back in about Erica, will you."

With a gleam in his eye, Daniel noted Pallav's discomfort as he stared after the woman while unseen from behind the sofa, Max slowly got to his feet and snuck back onto the terrace in search of his brother with a secret burrowed away in his young mind.

Smirking at the awkwardness of the situation, Daniel nodded. "Just give me a few days and I'll get back to you, that is, if you can tear yourself away from your little piece of arm candy."

Rolling his eyes, Pallav terminated the transmission and wandered down the walkway to the barracks where he had dropped off Bafa with the instructions to clean up Luke and Isabella. The sight of his son covered in blood had made the big man wish he'd torn the throat out of Reyhart, and even though the wounds were only superficial, he knew he couldn't bring the kids home in that state.

And then there was Bafa. The woman who seduced Reyhart before drugging him with a quick iris scan and fingerprint lift to secure their entrance to the murderer's abode.

No way could I ever explain bringing home a half-naked woman, he thought, wondering why she had left Reyhart's jacket inside her barrack-room. *Oh well, she certainly took Luke's mind off his pain.*

Off in the distance, Pallav could see that the arduous task of debris removal from the recent Coalition attack to the Great Plains Army Base had been completed. Now surveyors were floating about on hover-packs in anticipation of the construction of a new hospital and fire hall, styluses in hand as they poked at light tablets. Climbing the stairs, Pallav avoided colliding with a barrack rat, hands gripping the standard issue mesh laundry bag as he trudged downstairs to complete his weekly washing. Otherwise, the entire block seemed deserted – more than half laid low with the pandemic and the others deployed to Forward Operating Bases.

Following the racket led him to Bafa's room where he spied her usual lack of orderliness, causing him to shake his head in wonder that she could ever find her uniform amongst the clothing heaped in piles on the floor. But immediately he realized this was more than the Bafa-messiness he had come to expect – the slashed mattress, the broken holoframes, the mirror over the sink hanging by shards – the room had been the site of a targeted attack. And in the middle of it sat Luke, his head bandaged, his bruises slathered in healing ointment while his sister and Bafa combed their way through the wreckage.

"Dad!" Slowly rising to his feet, Luke limped to his father, his arm in a sling. Pallav cringed at seeing his son bravely fighting the pain as the teen shoved a message into his father's hands. "It was nailed to the wall," he explained.

Fumbling in his tunic pocket, Pallav took out the glasses that he loathed to wear, but before he could read the scrawl, Bafa tore the message from his hands. "Leave it," she ordered, "There's nothing to worry about. They didn't find it, cause it doesn't exist."

Isabella stifled a laugh as her father twisted his mouth and cocked an eyebrow. "That," she pointed, "means Dad's not impressed."

"Not overly," he replied, rubbing his pounding temples, "so start telling me what's going on Villutomi."

Looking chastened, Bafa clapped her hands and the music stopped. Pointing to Luke, she indicated for him to close the window before brandishing the note in Pallav's face.

"They came looking for a list of agents within the WAF. You do know that I'm not the only one, right? There're thousands of citizens who oppose President Meryx's thirst for Geiten blood; hundreds working within the Wesselan government, and dozens planted in the Armed Forces. And I have that list, the one that would provide them with the name of every single Wesselan soldier working for the cause."

Raising her hand, she tugged off her blood-red ring and twisted the stone in her fingers, revealing a tiny chip the size of a pea. "Officers in the highest places too," she continued at the look of utter surprise on Pallav's face. "That's right, I recruited them all. And their names are here, safe and sound, where no one will ever find them."

Pride beamed from the young officer at the key role she played in the Black Hide until Pallav wiped the smirk from her face.

"Have you gone mad?" Ripping the ring from her hand, Pallav screwed it back together and threw it down on the bed. "How do you know that whoever did this to your room searching for the list, hasn't planted a hidden camera? You never learn, do you Villutomi…"

His anger was quickly replaced by guilt as he saw Bafa crumble and Luke place a consoling hand about her bare shoulders.

"Listen…"

Removing his son from the scantily clad woman, he steered her to the window. "You're just eager, I understand that. If I come on a bit strong it's because I know how very capable you are. But Villutomi, you sabotage yourself by being too impetuous. You've put yourself in a very serious situation by crossing the Black Hide and at the same time, you've betrayed the oath you swore to your homeland."

He could see her bottom lip quivering and he patted her on the shoulder before raising her chin to meet Bafa's golden-brown eyes. "You're not safe here anymore. Get dressed and grab a few things. You're coming home with us."

And heaven help me when Tara sees who I've invited to dinner.

CHAPTER 23 – PHOST IS LOST

It's not what you look at that matters. It's what you see.

– HENRY DAVID THOREAU

The deafening thunder of hoverfans echoed across the broad Wessla Valley as the powerful Stryker Skykiller skimmed mere meters above the placid surface of the river. Serrated blades whipped the languorous water into peaks as Fynn dipped his wings in greeting to a column of ACOLEVs racing beyond the riverine embankment and onwards to breach the Jundar Mountains of Fyjerlan. Banking his warbird, he streamed off over the border, climbing steeply over the countryside until below him the Fyjer capital of Phost finally peeked out from under the early morning cloud cover.

Beneath him the charred remains of the city smouldered. Exhausted citizens scurried for cover as the four-pack of enemy warbirds buzzed overhead. Wretched and miserable, the Fyjers clutched at their meager belongings as they leapt into the shadows while about them the fires of defeat burned. Pity momentarily fluttered across his soul for he had no bones to pick with them – these tragic Fyjer souls who in their foolishness had supported their Coalition partner. In his mind, their Geiten ally was no more than a race of murderous scum, a backwards misogynistic plague that spread its contaminated tentacles across Deneb and Fynn believed in his heart that they needed to be eradicated.

Sensing the anger, Fynn's passenger clasped a heavy hand on the space ace's shoulder and earned a contrite smile in return. "Sorry Meryx, I was a thousand miles away." The older man stared into Fynn's hazel eyes and recognized the pain-flecked hatred bubbling once again to the surface.

"Take us down, Fynn. I need to see Phost for myself."

Barrelling through clouds of oily smoke that coiled sickly across the sky, the warbird hovered above the wreckage of the city that huddled in the shadows of the Jundar Mountains. The fighting had been frenzied: wreckage lay all about them as a testament to the vicious combat. But it could only have ended one way in this uneven battle.

The Wessel commanders had been aided by Goffa, the diminutive Minister of Information, who had prepared a campaign of subterfuge that had been simply brilliant. Fabricated images of massive troop build ups in the northern reaches of Wesselan had been beamed across the nation in the knowledge that the falsehoods would spread like wildfire throughout the Coalition. With painstaking attention to detail, the Wesselan Army had erected massive screens of ultra-light camouflage netting over the terrain of the rolling foothills of the Promina Mountains, concealing only rocks and trees from detection by enemy satellite and sensors.

Holograms of non-existent soldiers could be seen milling about the foothills snaking up from the southern ice cap – their images being lifted from the actual ongoing activities east of the Wessla and cunningly transmitted into place. Tapping deviously into Fyjer satellites, Goffa's minions in the Ministry of Information had carefully manipulated the images: Great Plains Wessel Army Base – a burnt out hulk, blackened cadavers littering the smouldering ground; Wesselan's Khulan Air Base – reduced to rubble; fabricated evidence of mass burials outside its perimeters showing as light patches on satellite images. And the Supreme Commander of the Fyjer military had taken the bait, redeploying her southern forces to the northern reaches of her nation, certainty abetted by a false sense of security that Wesselan's might had been neutralized.

Working around the clock, the most effective defensive weapon ever to be deployed on Denebian soil had been developed by Wessel scientists and engineers. Behind the deception of camouflage nets and holographic images of troop buildups, mining equipment had been eating away at the base of the foothills of the northern Promina Mountains, carving a vast arena deep underground.

Buried within, the root of the terrifying device was laid. A powerful magnetic field, acting as an invisible stem, tethered a series of globes – all coated in multi-millions of reflective crystallite scales – to the base buried below. They floated about overhead unseen while deep within the underground compound, a team of operators waited – working and eating and sleeping in the cavernous structure, ready for the signal to activate the machine.

By the time the Wessel warbirds streamed across the border towards the Fyjer capital city, it was already too late. Recalled to fight the threat, the Fyjer armed forces were immobile, stuck as if trapped in quicksand. For the crystallite globes had been called to action, sending out powerful acoustic disruptive vibrations that destroyed the sensitive electronics of the war machinery – Fyjer Starhunters careened about wildly before bursting into flames on the ground; armoured vehicles immobilized, nothing more than tons of useless metal. The vibrations hit the troops like shock waves, bruising and punishing, deafening and bone jarring. It was like nothing the Fyjers had ever seen before, and it shaped the battle before it had even begun.

And as his forces rolled past the start point, Meryx waited, safely ensconced in his bunker deep within Styria and watched in captivation as the Wesselan armies converged on Phost, the ancient capital of Fyjerlan. In the dim pre-dawn light, wave after wave of Firestorm bombers roared out of Dilem Aerospace Wing to surge above the besieged city and dropped their lethal cargo, while far overhead Fenris warbirds patrolled the enemy skies, deadly guardian angels flying in a protective screen.

Then the big artillery guns spoke, flames arcing from their blackened maws as they spewed forth death upon the hapless city. Thunderous roars deafened the terrified populace as hour after hour, magnetized plasma shells rained down with ferocity, pulverizing the capital into the dust. And suddenly, an eerie silence prevailed.

Breathing a sigh of relief, the hesitant survivors tentatively peered from their sanctuaries and slowly dragged themselves wearily through the rubble, stopping to search for the remnants of their lives. Ashes floated down from the heavens, a snowfall of cinders that fell about them, fluttering on the breeze like grey petals. Yet the wind carried with it a new threat; the Phostians would remember the sound of a heartbeat, growing ever louder in intensity until the thumping became mind-numbing. And then they were on them, the ACOLEVs and the RAITs, pouring into the city, vaporizing any living creature that crossed their sights.

Digging out from under the rubble, the Fyjer soldiers left behind to guard the city bravely stood their ground while Premier Lowena and her senior ministers were spirited away by the Supreme Commander's battle staff. Gwynne's hair streamed behind her like a blood red pennant as she guided a stunned Lowena onto the premier's nano-crystal armoured Teratorn transport airship. Rising into the air amidst the puffs of deadly gunfire, the dun-coloured craft hovered for a heartbeat, spinning and whirling on its axis before it melded seamlessly into its surroundings.

Staunching her tears, Lowena stared in horror as the Wessel ACOLEVs broke through the Fyjer lines, soldiers crushed underfoot as the acoustic levitated armoured vehicles leap-frogged about the wreckage, disgorging infantry troops. Fyjer drones buzzed about like angry wasps, firing impotently at the well-armoured Wessel warcraft. Gwynne growled at the pilot, her brown eyes flashing as her premier sniffled, "Get us the hell out of here. Now!"

As the Teratorn streaked through the sky like an arrow, its tawny hull concealed within its magnetized cloak, Lowena sighed. "Our capital's destroyed, our army in tatters. It's all falling down around us. Was it all worth it Gwynne? I just don't know anymore."

The battle-hardened general shrugged, irritated by her leader's sudden lack of determination and gazed out into the darkened morning sky. Stygian tendrils of oily smoke clawed their way upwards, seeking to strangle the fleeing airship as it zipped to the safety of the Blue Star Emergency Command Centre deep within the Jundar Mountains. Reaching out, Gwynne switched off the view ports and snapping her fingers, she motioned to the young flight steward who scurried off to return with two glasses of sparkling aamfruit juice. Handing the crystallite tumbler to the premier, Gwynne watched as Lowena dutifully took a sip of the frosty pink liquid.

"Ma'am, if I may say so... the Wessels may have taken Phost but the government will make it to the Jundars. We can ride it out there; rule in safety from the distance, hidden from the enemy." Gwynne reached over and took the premier's cold hand in hers. Her eyes were like flint as she peered into Lowena's reddened face.

"We must stay resolute Ma'am. This is just a setback, giving us time to regroup and consolidate our forces for a counterattack when the time's right. When the tides of war turn the other way, the recapture of the Wessla River Valley will be an achievement of great strategic importance."

Seeing Lowena's chin rise up defiantly gave hope to the Supreme Commander and she recognized that the possibility of victory called for a new tack. "Perhaps allying ourselves with the Geiten was a grave error," Gwynne assayed. "Against so formidable a foe, to form a Coalition with such an ill-disciplined, poorly armed and incompetently-led military power was bound to fail. But without them, perhaps…"

Leaving the thought dangling, Gwynne paused to see if Lowena would take the bait. Yet the premier shook her dark head forcefully and her golden eyes narrowed as she spat out her disdain for the idea. "I'm not about to betray Geitenia! I gave my word to Redlan, may the gods keep his soul. Bakril's floundering, that's true; but the Geiten forces have been neglected through no fault of his. So you see Gwynne, that would make it even more odious for us to abandon our ally."

As Lowena sank into silence, Gwynne padded away and ducked into the cockpit, leaving the premier alone with her thoughts. Thoughts that boiled and surged like water coursing through a narrow gorge, tossing the Fyjer Premier mercilessly against the rocky shore of her conscience. For Lowena had heard about the attack on Urkyn, that grubby nomadic Geiten village, where the Wessels had ruthlessly exterminated every living creature in their savage hunt for the humans. She had seen the holograms of broken corpses being savaged by wild bloodwolves and relief flooded through her that no humans had entered her country.

Disgusted with herself and her lack of compassion for the Earthlings who had sought refuge on Denebian soil, she realized that in herself lived a creature not far from those Wessels who waged war against the Coalition. She knew in her soul that she was too weak a being to fight against the selfish creature within, one that would push the others into the abyss while clinging to the edge of that dark cliff. The fight must be left to the Geiten and to that nation alone she realized, for Lowena longed for the sweet fragrance of peace for her people while it was still wafting fresh on the morning air.

As the Fyjer Teratorn winged its way onwards to Blue Star, negotiating the twists and turns of that rugged mountainous terrain, the premier's heart had turned and her thoughts were clear. And so while off in the distance, the Wessel ACOLEVs from the 16th Armoured Regiment streamed through the mountain passes, Lowena found her determination, and now, as the airship's skids touched down onto the pad hewn deep into the mountainside, the premier had made up her mind – she now knew.

***

A sharp elbow broke him from his reverie. "Take us down, Fynn. I need to see it for myself," Meryx repeated, his voice gravelly.

"Roger that Sir!"

Following Meryx's gesture, Fynn flew towards the Fyjer Parliament. Its blackened façade and blown out darkened windows reminded Fynn of a ghostly ship surging through stormy seas, its crew long dead and forgotten. Leaning back into the seat, the warbird's postural controls kicked in, its nose dipping in response as Fynn cut the hoverfans. The camouflaged metallic outlines of the RAITs were barely visible as they swarmed over the ground, locusts on a feeding frenzy while infantry soldiers prodded and pushed the surrendering Fyjer prisoners of war into long lines as they began their long march into captivity.

Boy, this sure looked different at 50,000 feet, Fynn reflected as he surveyed the damage. It had been an uneven battle, for the Fyjers had been taken completely by surprise. Phost now lay before them in ruins, buildings a jumble of shattered steel and masonry, while the bridges that once arched over the irrigational canal twisted and lurched into the empty air.

The National Parliament docking pad loomed beneath him, somehow having escaped damage from the aerial bombardment and the artillery barrage and Fynn guided his Skykiller and his team through the throng of drones while gradually losing altitude.

"Falcon 122. Let's take 'er down team. The President wants to stretch his legs."

Beneath them, Wessel soldiers raced about under the shadow of the noble warbirds, clearing the pad for their landing while Fynn could make out the silhouette of a Helocruiser tied down near the outer perimeter of the building. Meryx grumbled as the skids touched down, for he would not be the first to inspect the conquest. He could see the profiles of the High Commander and the Commanders of the Land and Aerospace Forces, the old general's muscular frame bowed as he appeared to listen to a group of captured senior officers who were gathered about them like a swarm of bees.

Cutting his engines, Fynn deactivated the Thought-Melding Interface and exhaled sharply as he came face to face with fresh evidence of the recent battle. Men and women, who had recently emerged from the relative safety of the bomb shelters, had already begun to wind their way to where once their homes sat, filing past mountains of shredded steel and shards of blood-stained glass, most quickly shaded their eyes as they bypassed the already stiffening cadavers piled obscenely in neat rows, while a few gaped open-mouthed in horror.

Jumping from the Skykiller, Fynn extended his arm to the president. The smell of burning flesh mingled with the acrid stench of the spent battle and caused him to gag. Meryx patted his back sympathetically.

"C'mon son, let's take a walk – just you and me." Glancing over at Gomalan, Ravenna and Francis, his grey eyebrows knit together conspiratorially. "Do you think we can avoid the brass over there?"

The thuds of docking warbirds shook the rooftop, momentarily taking Fynn's mind off the devastation that dominated the landscape. Inara bounded out of her Skykiller, followed by Matt, Nicki and three close protection operators.

Grumbling in disgust, Meryx pulled Fynn aside. "I don't need those goons hovering around me, telling me where I can and can't go. Shielding me from stuff they think I can't handle. By the gods, I served as an officer during the First Denebian War. Now that was brutal. This," he growled, his arm sweeping the landscape, "this was a quick victory. Nothing more than a Fyjer bloody nose. Now let's get going, son. I don't have time to waste."

Swallowing hard, Fynn stared at Meryx before blinking and turning to Inara. His voice was a whisper as he addressed his 2IC. "Make a distraction. Do it. Now."

In a millisecond, a shocked Matt was flying across the rooftop to land hard on his backside next to the High Commander's Helocruiser while Inara shrieked at him. "You bastard! Call me that again and it'll be the last word you ever say!"

Jumping on the unfortunate soul, Inara began to wail on him with all her might. Bruised and battered, Matt stifled a laugh and cooperated in the subterfuge.

"Someone get this crazy bitch off me," he yelled, earning a new round of slaps and punches.

Meryx chuckled as the close protection agents launched into action, and grabbing Fynn by the cuff, the duo bolted into the parliamentary building. Files had been torn from their folders and parchment littered the floor. Portraits were ripped from their wall-anchors, the images of Fyjerlan's premiers broken and smashed. Chairs had been thrown through windows and desks broken where the bureaucrats once had sat with styluses in hand transcribing laws and ordinances. Upended, their contents spilled from opened drawers onto the cluttered floor. And amongst it all, to Meryx's anger, were Wessel soldiers. Caught in a blood lust of destruction, they were blithely looting and destroying everything of value, of beauty and grinding the labour of the parliamentarians into dust.

Seeing the fury in the president's eyes, Fynn quickly shepherded him past the soldiers gone mad and out into the open air where clouds of smoke billowed past them, concealing them from searching eyes. Wordlessly, Meryx walked the streets with Fynn at his side and memories flooded back to the old man from his youth: the rioting and looting that followed the fighting, the hollow-eyed children silently starving while their mothers begged and sold their bodies for a scrap of cheese, a loaf of kyorn bread. And it was the mothers who had to bear the burden, as the men had given their lives for a lost cause or had disappeared into the fog of war, leaving a generation of women to fend alone for their families.

Fynn walked silently beside Meryx, his eyes following the devastation seemingly impervious to the suffering all about them. But while his tongue remained silent, his mind played back the scenes from earlier days when he and Erica had flown side by side into battle. He could almost see the vicious smile erupting on his wife's face as they jumped down from their fighters, callous to the carnage they had wreaked from the skies during Earth's Refugee Wars. The second their vehicle hit the gravel driveway and the wheels stopped turning, she'd pull him from the car. Throwing herself into his arms and wrapping her legs about him, Fynn would effortlessly pick Erica up and carry her into their tiny, crowded apartment where they didn't even wait for the door to slam shut before they'd be ripping off their flight suits. Grinning at the memories, the scent of Erica's warm skin wafted through Fynn's mind as he strolled beside the President of Wesselan, his thoughts anywhere but on the destruction before him.

But the smile was torn from his face at the sight of a young woman lurking within the shadows, her bright blonde braids hanging down her slender shoulders.

"Erica?"

A rush of wind flew by his cheek, a bright red gash sprouting from the graze and Fynn flinched, his hazel eyes widened in confusion.

"Get down, son!"

Pushed to the ground by the elderly president, Fynn looked up in surprise as Meryx grabbed the woman by the arm. He stared into a face filled with hatred and sighed. *She's just a frightened girl trying to defend herself.*

"Go home, lock the doors, and stay inside. By tomorrow this'll be all over. Now go!" Meryx turned to help Fynn to his feet as the woman regarded them with hatred and rose up to face them.

"You're wrong. It'll never be over. Never. Not until we rid ourselves of the very last of the Wessels and take back our land." Looking them up and down with disgust, the woman sneered and scampered away, a leaflet falling from her tunic pocket.

Picking it up, Meryx quickly scanned the crumpled page and grimaced at the troubling image of a dishevelled Geiten woman, her gore-stained mouth sucking the blood from a struggling kyttel while a bevy of filthy children scrambled at her side, waiting for their fill with widened angry eyes. Turning it over with his gnarled fingers, his lips twisted angrily as he read the print almost too small for his ancient eyes.

" 'Fyjers: you give your lives for this: the parasites of Deneb...' hmmm... this has got the scent of Goffa all over it."

Throwing the offensive leaflet to the ground, Meryx scanned the environs for signs of danger and finding none, the old man relaxed his guard.

"You know... that knife...," Fynn said, dabbing at his cheek. "It was meant for you. We're just lucky her aim was bad. Now if that'd been Erica, you'd've been a dead man..."

Meryx clapped Fynn on the shoulder. "But it wasn't. And it's going to take a lot more than some skinny kid with a knife to stop me... Well, well, will you look at that, someone's remembered us!"

Seeing his close protection team running towards them with Gomalan following closely behind, Meryx slapped Fynn's back and laughed. "Looks like our private party's about to be busted."

Fynn chuckled. "I was wondering how long it'd take them to find us." Meryx winked and together the two men walked companionably to meet their anxious entourage.

CHAPTER 24 – LET THERE BE PEACE

People, even more than things, need to be restored, renewed, revived, reclaimed and redeemed.
– AUDREY HEPBURN

It was small and sparkly and soft and elicited a series of high-pitched squeals, and Bafa had never seen anything like it before. Luminous pink eyes dominated a narrow head that was crowned by a silver spiral rising above its lustrous creamy mane. And it was not alone. A speckled golden and brown creature with glowing green eyes was flanked by a pointy-eared brown baby beast with a long bushy tail.

"By! The! Gods! You've got the cutest creatures in the universe on Planet Earth!"

Isabella laughed as Bafa picked up the beanie babies that Tara had spirited aboard the *Mayflower*.

"I mean, these are absolutely adorable," she enthused. "While all we got here are icky crawly things and predators that'd rip your throat out."

Clutching the stuffed unicorn to her chest, Bafa almost floated out of Isabella's room into Pallav's office where she found the colonel deep in thought. Clearing her throat, she waited impatiently for Pallav who looked up at her from under his hated reading glasses. A sandy eyebrow rose at the sight of the stuffed animal in her arms and his face froze in confusion. Before he remembered… this was Bafa. Crazy, kooky, gutsy Bafa and he stifled a laugh before donning his serious face.

"Captain Villutomi, whatever is it now?"

On the holoscreen before him floated the route between the Wesselan Parliament and the president's sister. Building by building he had been analyzing the various egress points and potential arcs of fire, considering where he would station himself if the presidential assassination were his assignment to carry out.

Motioning her to sit, Pallav rubbed his eyes in exhaustion. "I've been over this a thousand times. Look here… President Meryx normally stops to chat along the way, and my analysis has determined that the majority of his interactions take place right here, a natural choke point outside the Naraan Tull Marketplace. Now I need to be sure… the Black Hide said here?"

Pointing to a tall glass building, he searched her face for any sign of treachery. Any indication that within the depths of her soul, that she still harboured a yearning to overthrow the legitimate Wessel government. Bafa blinked under the intense scrutiny of those cold green eyes but her gaze remained steady.

"That's right," she replied, the unicorn forgotten in her arms. "The plan's for the Black Hide to take a room on the upper floor of the Esfara Hotel. One with a window overlooking the promenade and the marketplace. That'll give him a clear shot at the president when he walks by the grocers."

"But it's also packed with people at that time of the day. Chances of hitting bystanders are high."

Bafa shrugged, knowing that collateral damage meant nothing to the Black Hide. "He'll be there, you can count on it. And with President Meryx finally out of the way, the Black Hide figures in the ensuing chaos, our agents will be able to take advantage of the power vacuum and overthrow the murderous regime."

Standing up suddenly, he overturned the light tablet that had been resting on his thigh and towering over the woman, Pallav growled a warning.

"Our agents?"

Retreating a pace, she shot back. "You forget, I was part of the Black Hide for years. It isn't as easy for me to change sides as it was for you. You know, like, when you turned on your crew mates and abandoned them to set you and your family up in Wesselan." Hiding the smile that came to her lips, Bafa placed a restraining hand on Pallav's chest. *And cue the self-righteous, indignant anger…*

Count to ten, Pallav…how does she manage to enrage me so much?

Batting away her hand, he took a deep breath and hissed, "And you… you forget your oath of allegiance, Villutomi. The one where you swore on your life to be faithful, loyal and obedient to the president and the Wessel people." Pallav could see the fire in her eyes, her chin raised defiantly and he sensed that there was more. "And you're leaving something out."

The golden eyes smouldered at the well-placed barb and she remained tight lipped until her shoulders were grasped in a steely grip and with his face mere inches from hers, he dropped his voice to a whisper. "Who're you protecting Villutomi? Because it's not yourself. These people see you as disposable, you were a dupe…"

By God, I think I care for her! Hmmm…. I'm far too old for some stupid boyhood crush and the woman is hardly more than a child. Child… That's it!

The realization floored him, and he stared open mouthed as she struggled against him.

She reminds me of my foolish, impetuous baby sister, that's all!

 Relief flooded over him and he shook with laughter.

Surprised, Bafa shrugged from his grasp. "Then I'll be betraying another vow I made. To those who fight for equality… but I suppose you need to know if you're going to put your life on the line. 'Cause make no mistake colonel, the Black Hide is a dangerous man."

"Go on."

His tone was emotionless once again as he waited for her to elaborate. Bafa twisted her head about as Tara walked by, her bare feet silent on the warm stone floor.

Pallav glanced at his wife and knew that she'd been watching silently and listening, angry at his insistence that the captain stay with them until the plot had been foiled.

"Ignore her," he said, frowning at Tara while thinking that it was now his wife's turn to have jealousy as a shadow. Inclining his head, Pallav tried to dispel the image of his little sister that kept clouding his mind.

"There's a cell within the WAF that are ready to jump into action the second the president's dead. It's all arranged… I have the list of the collaborators and you'd be surprised. Officers of the upper echelon who disagree with Meryx's war, with the way the Geiten are being treated, who want peace."

A wan smile crossed her face. "I know, I know…you think I'm being naïve. That I've betrayed my country. But this isn't a just war. To use the Denebian plague as an excuse to cut off the water to the Geiten was only a ploy to weaken the tribes, so that Wesselan could absorb Geitenia … They had every right to demand that the floodgates to the River Panni dam be opened. Without water, there's no survival for them. And we both know that the plague didn't originate in Geitenia. They've been made convenient scapegoats for a problem that the government can't solve. You know…deflect from the real issue; refocus the anger to another party to save their skins."

For a split-second Pallav almost flinched, but years of experience threw a mask over the doubt that floated through his mind.

Impossible that she knows anything about the true nature of the pandemic, he thought.

"Bafa, listen to me."

Taking her hands in his, he forced her to sit next to him.

"Now is not the time for us to be having this conversation. Tomorrow, President Meryx will be facing a life or death scenario, into which you and I are to be playing major roles in countering the threat. Against a legitimately elected head of state. The Black Hide must fail. If Meryx is killed, the result will not be an overthrow of the government like you believe, but a more resolute effort to annihilate the Geiten who will bear the blame for the assassination. You understand? Is that what you want? Never lose sight of your aim, remember?"

Hesitation clouded her eyes and she shook her head. "You're right. I know you are. But you never grew up in a world where people living just a stone's throw away from your borders were looked upon as lower forms of life, impure and polluting our nation just through their mere existence."

Repressing a shudder, Pallav reflected on the Refugee Wars that had plagued the United States of North America and shaking his head, he conveniently left those memories behind him in the past where they would remain safely boxed up.

"None of that matters right now Villutomi. We have our mission. Now, my question to you is, are you going to help me or you want to play with my daughter's unicorn?"

***

Its words carried the weight of the world with it, yet the parchment – so rare in these days of holograms and mind-links – was feather-light in his gnarled hands. Removing his reading spectacles, Gomalan grunted irritably. "But this is preposterous!"

Sunshine streamed through the doors of the balcony to the presidential office, a halo of light illuminating the ancient man sequestered behind the long broad desk as he pulled himself to his feet and walked over to the tall windows. He ignored the carping; during the long years of his leadership, he had come to rely on his High Commander as a confidant and a friend, but now it was as his leader that he turned to face the weathered soldier. He could see the confusion on the drawn, lined face mirrored in the eyes of the others. "Read it. Aloud this time," he ordered as the others fidgeted nervously.

Gomalan shook his head in wonder before donning his spectacles and with surprise still etched on his face, took a deep breath.

> "The Honourable Meryx, President of Wesselan, and representing the peoples of the Wessel nation, is extending an offer to the Fyjer nation for the immediate cessation of hostilities.
>
> "In recognition that the military power of the entire Wesselan Armed Forces has taken control of your capital city and southern provinces and is poised to strike deep into the heart of Fyjerlan, I call upon you to consider this proposition very carefully, allowing reason to be your guide, for to ignore our overture for peace will result in the total and utter devastation of your homeland.
>
> "I call upon you to carefully consider your collusion with the terrorists of Geitenia, who having deceived the people of your nation, led Fyjerlan into an unjust war in the quest for planetary domination. I call upon you to carefully consider our terms, which are both reasonable and just.
>
> "To ensure the restoration of peace and stability, the area from the southern ice cap, bound in the east by the Wessla basin, to the north by the Motzen irrigation canal and extending west to the foothills of the Jundar Mountains shall be occupied by Wessel forces.
>
> "Fyjer military forces are to disarm immediately and to surrender to the occupying forces.
>
> "The Fyjer government shall maintain sovereignty over all the lands not included in the occupation zone, including the districts of Blaut, Massita and Zelayna as well as those lands within the Empty Quarter under her jurisdiction.
>
> "I therefore instruct the government of Fyjerlan to acknowledge the unconditional surrender of all military forces under its command and control. Failure to do so will result in a resumption of hostilities which will only lead to the ruination of your nation."

Gomalan slapped the parchment onto Meryx's desk to a chorus of hushed groans. A coughing fit erupted as Goffa choked on the boricha he had been sipping to calm the knots twisting his guts. Tentatively picking up the document as if it would burst into flames in his hands, Foreign Minister Talyx trembled with apprehension as he slowly reviewed the wording, his opal eyes bulging in their sockets.

Ravenna pursed her lips and stared accusatorily at Fynn, believing him to be the culprit behind Meryx's sudden lapse into weakness before turning her attention to the Supreme Commander. Rooted to the spot Gomalan seemed lost, unable to comprehend the twist and turns in the mind of his old friend. But Ravenna, still stinging from the disappearance of Reyhart, had no patience for such faintheartedness. As the Foreign Minister and the Minister of Information reviewed the document with a mixture of shock and disgust on their faces, Ravenna's voice carried across the office, cutting through the disbelief.

"The Fyjer armies and aerospace forces are now powerless, far off in the northern province and immobile on the ground. Fyjerlan is on the cusp of total defeat. Why now offer the branch of peace? We can crush them under our feet! So much more can be accomplished! Our victorious forces can wrest from them their entire northern province, with its rich resources and temperate climes."

Buoyed up by her opinion, the Commander of the Aerospace Forces joined in the attack. "We mustn't lose our nerve at this important juncture. To do so, to show compassion, will only be seen as weakness."

His head nodded in agreement, and with the hated Denebian Peace Declaration brandished in his hand like a torch, the Foreign Minister stoked the flames of dissent. "The Fyjers betrayed the covenants of the Denebian Intertribal Union by forming a Coalition with the Geiten with the express purpose of conquering our nation. We need to push them down and hold them down – so far down that they will never again be able to rise to mount an attack on our lands." Talyx looked about the room for support and a crocodilian smile snaked across his broad face as the heads nodded once more in unison.

"Mr. President, this is not the time for peace," Goffa interjected while Meryx raised an eyebrow in tired response to his senior advisors. The Minister of Information's thin arms gesticulated wildly in the air, his agitation apparent as he continued. "Rather we must remain steadfast in the pursuit of our aims: pushing the hostile Fyjers back to the inhospitable desert regions from where they will languish, weighed down in the knowledge that their paltry attempt at the destruction of our country has brought them nothing but blood and tears."

The old man twisted his mouth sourly and turned to Fynn. "Son, you're the only one who hasn't spoken. As the heir-designate, I'd like your thoughts. Are you in agreement with my generals and ministers?"

Fynn scratched the back of his neck and his cheeks flamed with colour yet he raised his chin defiantly and faced the group of dissenters. The president watched his young protégé with those bright hazel eyes brimming with confidence, and pride overtook the old man.

"I'm just a simple fighter pilot. I get assigned a mission and I scream across the skies to annihilate my adversaries. I don't land until I've mopped up the last enemy warbird. I won't come back until the bombs are dropped, the bases blown up and the enemy neutralized. Unable to strike back; impotent; finished. That's what I do." His gaze was challenging as he continued. "But I'll tell you what I don't do. When the enemy bails out of a burning warbird at 80,000 feet, I don't strafe them as they plummet to the ground, with their parachute blossoming above them. After their bases are turned to dust, and the fires of defeat are burning, I don't return for one last strafing round to knock off the injured. And yesterday when I flew into Phost with the president and saw the pitiful survivors scrambling about in the remnants of their homes, digging through the smouldering piles of bricks for some lost toy, a pot to cook their food in, or a blanket to keep them warm and dry, I knew that it needed to end. The Fyjer people are defeated and demoralized. The Wessels are secure, safe from attack. It's time to end it. It's time for peace. Peace with Fyjerlan."

Meryx narrowed his eyes, for there was an unspoken message hidden within Fynn's speech. For he knew that for Fynn, the war with Geitenia would never be over; the young man thirsted for revenge for the deaths of Erica and their unborn daughter. Blinking, his milky white eyes surveyed the gaggle that had formed around him and he clasped his hands behind his back.

"It's a relief that one of you agrees with me. I see I've chosen my successor well." Patting Fynn on the shoulder, Meryx walked over to his desk and plopped himself down.

"Now, let me tell you all how it's going to work. Talyx, open a channel with the Fyjer Foreign Minister and present this offer to her. Make her understand that there will be no exceptions. It's either this or complete destruction – they have 48 hours."

Turning to Goffa, Meryx addressed the Minister of Information. "And I want this broadcast all across DNN. Read it yourself. I don't care if you have to drop flyers over their cities. I want the Fyjer people to know what we're offering." He winked before continuing. "That way, they know who to blame if this's turned down. Now, you both have your marching orders. Let's move it gentlemen; the clock is ticking."

The duo were about to leave when Goffa cocked his head questioningly. "Pardon me Sir, if you'll permit one last question? Do we have a proposal drafted up for Geitenia?"

Out of the corner of his eye, Meryx could see Fynn stiffen and his nostrils flare and the president waved the young pilot off.

"Not at the moment. Let's see how the Fyjers play the game. Will they leave their ally high and dry or will they honour their commitment to the Coalition."

"But it's a good question Meryx." Not to be put off by the President's basilisk stare, Fynn continued. "So let's say the Fyjers take the offer – where does that leave us with the Geiten? We've got the power to knock 'em out of the ballpark."

"We play the long game, son. We draft up a similar proposal to the Geiten. We offer them peace in return for the lands east of the River Panni to the Tagar Mountains. They can keep that shit hole Urkyn, and their irrigational canal. You understand?"

The blood drained from the young pilot's face and he curled his lip in distaste. Yet he refrained from replying, for he knew the explanation would come later, when he and Meryx were alone and they could speak the unadorned truth to each other.

Ravenna turned to Gomalan, looking for support and finding the grey-haired warrior mute, she voiced the opinion of the others. "Let's go for the jugular. Finish them off, once and for all!"

Goffa twisted his face in derision. "So, we're to offer the Geiten a ceasefire? After their attack on the River Panni dam installation that led to crop failures for our farmers? And how many lives were lost because of the plague they brought down upon us through their filth and bestial ways?

Should we forgive them for this? And all you are asking for is a thin strip of land across the north of their territory? What'll we tell the orphans – that their parents died for a few hundred kilometers of rocky, useless land?"

"You're dangerously overextending yourself minister," Meryx warned, his gravelly voice low and menacing.

Like a puppet on a string, Goffa's waif-like frame shook as ire overtook caution. "The Geiten have been our misfortune for years now. They've sowed the seeds of misery in our nation, polluting us with their poisonous presence like a pustulant boil. Who can deny that their very essence devalues our cities and lands? Refusing to work, clinging to archaic traditions that are an insult to our civilization, citing religion as an excuse for idleness. It is us, the Wessel, who support them. Make no mistake, the Geiten are parasites – they have never contributed to our society. Takers. Leeches. Bloodsuckers. Mr. President, let us destroy them and rid the planet of this cancer."

A fist slammed on the presidential desk as Meryx jumped to his feet, his purple cheeks labouring like bellows. "How dare you question me," he roared while Gomalan cleared his throat nervously and the others stared about uncomfortable at Goffa's outburst. Fynn placed a restraining hand on Meryx's arm while the president regained his composure.

"Very well, I suppose it isn't obvious to you." Looking down his nose from under a thick pair of reading glasses at the diminutive cripple, Meryx slowly returned to his seat.

"Now if you're all finished, I'll enlighten you because I want this to be crystal clear in everyone's mind," the president growled. "It's just optics, you see. To absorb the Fyjer and Geiten territories without economic sanctions by the Interstellar Collective for Peace and Security, Wesselan must be seen as the aggrieved party who was provoked into carrying out a war of defensive action. By reaching out to our enemies and making an offer of peace, we appear magnanimous in the eyes of the Collective. And let's not forget, that useless strip of land you spoke about Goffa: the one rich in minerals that the Geiten are too lazy to exploit – scandium and mica – oh and by the way, bordering on Fyjerlan so we can keep a close eye on our new ally?"

Meryx paused; he could see their eyes lighting up and he knew he had them. "Now… there can be no dissent amongst us; we need to present a united front before the people. Do I make myself clear?"

Heads nodded as comprehension finally dawned on the presidential advisors. A bright light bathed the room as Meryx powered up his holoscreen and the president seemed deep in thought while the never-ending parade of documents, ready for his review, floated before him. A cough caught his attention, and looking up, he blinked absentmindedly.

"What're you all still doing here? You're dismissed." As his senior advisors shuffled out of the office, Meryx sighed and collapsed in the high backed chair. "Fynn, you too. We'll catch up later."

Hesitating at the threshold, Gomalan waited until the office was clear. Turning on his heel, he closed the door and retraced his steps until the High Commander stood facing the president. "You and I, Meryx, we need to talk."

"I was expecting this," he replied, motioning for his senior general to take a seat. "Two old warhorses, saddled up and ready to ride into battle. Except, Gomalan, the war's already been won."

The High Commander sighed, his shoulders slumping with fatigue. "I understand your rationale, but do you really fear the Collective? When have they ever followed through on a threat? The most they'd ever consider would be feeble economic sanctions. Meryx, I say grind the Coalition into the dust so hard that it'd take a thousand years for them to rise up again. Make our nation so powerful that no other race on Deneb could ever rally against us. Only that way can Wesselan truly be secure from outside threats."

Reaching deep into his desk drawer, Meryx fished around until he struck the motherlode. An ancient hand blown glass bottle lovingly reposed like a precious newborn in his gnarled hand. Uncorked, an evocative fragrance redolent of fresh fruit tanged with a smoky essence wafted on the afternoon air and Gomalan's eyes grew wide as Meryx poured out the clear liquid.

"Halo-dew," he whispered as the president slid the glass across the desk.

Every five years on the planet Cygnus-Morea, the barrel-shaped halo-bush blossomed high on the rocky slopes of the Aspero Mountains, its pungent fragrance perfuming the air for miles. Jealously guarded through the centuries by the Nevi Family, it was a well-established tradition for the younger members to climb into the carefully tended groves before sunrise to collect the glistening dew that emanated from the flower buds before they evaporated under the rays of the Cygneusite sun. And the resulting priceless liqueur could only be described as liquid ambrosia. The glass beckoned to the High Commander who took it in his hand and swirled its fragrant contents appreciatively.

"To us Gomalan. Survivors, you and me. We've been through battles, in and out of uniform, and we're still standing." To the sound of glass clinking, the two men sipped at the intoxicating infusion.

"Ahhh…divine…"

The president held his glass up to the sunlight and was rewarded with a sparkling rainbow of colours shimmering within the clear liquid. The colours coalesced and a vision of angelic-like beings suddenly took shape. Swirling and twisting, the shimmering colours snaked into a dark nightmare of demons before cascading into a dancing kaleidoscope of brilliance.

Meryx tilted his head at the whirlpool of colours swirling in the glass. "Who could think that something so wondrously alien could prove so dangerous? Deadly, in fact, if one does not take the proper precautions."

The president set his glass down abruptly, drops of the beverage spilling in prismatic gouts onto the desk. "I'm talking about the humans, of course. The very ones who fled a dying planet and journeyed through space to land on our Deneb. Scared, exhausted, and pleading for a chance to make our planet their new home. And we were so sympathetic. So compassionate to their plight. We took them in; gave them a chance at a new life. And they repaid us, didn't they? They brought it to us, our so-called Denebian flu, and now we're paying the price by spilling the blood of our kin. Denebians are being killed; pitted against each other – the entire population of Urkyn was destroyed – all because of the humans and their disease."

The sunlight streamed across his desk, motes dancing in and out of the brilliant beam that burnished the dark wood before cutting across the holoimage of Fynn and Erica. Gomalan stared at the frame of the happy couple and his thoughts were of Pallav, who was risking not only his life but those of his family to uncover treachery within the ranks of the WAF and his mind was clouded with doubt.

"But how were they to know?"

Meryx shook his head dismissively. "Whether knowingly or not, innocently or with guile, they were the source of this carnage. And we're the only two people alive who are aware of this. But now, it's gone on for long enough. We can take what we want from the Coalition to make us stronger, but let's not destroy fellow Denebians in the process."

Tipping his head back, Gomalan drained the glass. Wavering in his thoughts, the scales tipped between agreement and the belief that the president was losing his nerve. The High Commander analyzed his old friend for any trace of weakness and in its stead came across only certainty and strength.

"Your judgement is sound, as always. And," he added with a wink, "I appreciate the Halo-Dew."

Although the hand was veined and leathery, the grip was as strong as ever as Meryx squeezed Gomalan's shoulder. "Any time, my friend. Any time. Now let's bring peace to our planet."

But as the High Commander left the presidential office, Goffa's insidious mantra that had been repeated over and over began to chant to him, softly at first, and then so powerful that it raged like a torrent: "The Geiten are a curse upon Deneb… The Geiten are a curse upon Deneb… The Geiten are a curse… A curse…" And then he felt it surging up within him and he knew it in his bones, it throbbed angrily through his veins – there could be no place, no matter how remote, desolate enough on that desert planet for the Geiten.

CHAPTER 25 – THE KING HAS LEFT THE BUILDING

The silence and the emptiness is so great that I look and do not see, listen and do not hear.
– MOTHER TERESA

The paint was faded and chipped, the lino on the floor buckled and warped in the stuffy little room where a rickety chrome table was centred. On its surface, tucked under an ashtray overflowing with half-smoked jewelweed butts, was a tumble of maps and papers filled with thin black scrawl. Digital media left tracks, while paper – well paper could be consumed with the flick of a flame – removing any incriminating trace of illicit activity forever.

They had sat up long into the night, setting out strategies for the future and debating on policies before turning their attention to the undertaking of the morrow. From his pocket, the older man had pulled a dark square and stretching it out, he handed it to his young protégé who tugged on the material. Splaying it between his fingers, he looked on in marvel before pulling it over his head: a black mask.

His high pitched voice trembled with emotion as he voiced the anticipated words. "I'm not worthy." But beneath the honeyed phrases, the young man hungered for the power. If it came to that, if the masked man before him failed in tomorrow's enterprise.

Ah, but what are the chances? he thought irritably while the leader laid a long case on the battered table.

"Open it," the older man ordered, savouring the delight in the eyes of his accolade as the weapon came into view. Lovingly, the young man caressed its long grey barrel before assembling the powerful 38L-42 disrupter. In two strides, he was before the window and wielding the weapon towards the empty promenade, he closed one eye and stared through the scope.

The clarity and precision astonished him as he scanned the shop windows. "Ah… laundry detergent's on sale this week – 3.59 for a liter. And Aamfruit juice…"

The Black Hide pushed the barrel down and out of sight from any late-night revellers who might be returning home after a night on the town. "Laser-guided, accurate to over a kilometer. You can't miss with that."

Taking the weapon from the young man's hands he reverently laid it on a blanket and secreted the bundle under the steel-framed bed before lighting another fat wad of jewelweed.

"Now listen, it's crucial that you not lose sight of the objective. It's the president who's brought this cursed war to our people. He is the one who authorized the roundup of the Geiten, who permitted them to be treated as no more than flotsam – mere waste to be eliminated from within the borders of this wretched police-state.

"Meryx is the true leader of the Wessel Armed Forces – he directs their every move. Without him at their head, they will fall. The country will be in chaos. And that is our time. When we will rise up and seize power, restoring our people to their rightful place in society."

The young man nodded in agreement, his black eyes filled with admiration and pride at being chosen as the successor-in-waiting. But a slight hint of doubt also tip-toed through his thoughts, for he was young and not yet of an age to grow the flowing beard of which the Geiten males take such pride.

"Now Alonz, you won't forget, will you? Under no circumstances will you give your position away by a thoughtless act." The Black Hide stared at the teenager whose eyes registered comprehension and the masked man reflected on his choice. The young man was vicious and the anger bred inside of him had molded Alonz into a fearless fighter for the Cause.

The blood of his veins flowed only for one purpose: to rid Deneb of the rule of the Wessels, so that his people, the Geiten, could once more live free from tyranny and oppression. And his hatred burned so bright that he had fled the safety of his family tribe to undertake the arduous journey across the blistering deserts and over treacherous mountain passes.

Arriving near the tumble of seared poles that once secured the pehas of Urkyn, Alonz had hid amongst the chaos of the torn down scaffolds of death with their grisly possessions strewn about irreverently. She was not there: Brynn, the perky little Geiten girl who was to become his bride and for that he mouthed a pray of thanks to the gods. Then, with infinite care, and forging out only by nightfall, Alonz had finally succeeded in finding the entrance to an abandoned labyrinth of tunnels that led to Wesselan.

Following ancient dirt pathways, the teen had trekked on to Bâcha and to the market stall where a black geiten hide waved in the feverish wind. His quest satisfied, Alonz gave himself up, body and soul, to the Cause.

And now the honour dangled before him, repayment for the sacrifices that he had made. All he needed was patience until the mantle fell on his shoulders. Someday. But until then, his obsidian eyes would follow his mentor's every move, memorizing his actions and deeds in the hope that one day he would prove to be a worthy successor.

"You hear me? Remain vigilant," the Black Hide repeated impatiently.

Alonz nodded, angered by the apparent lack of trust while the Black Hide sucked lazily on the smouldering roll of jewelweed before passing it to the teenager. He waited until the smoke curled from the boy's nostrils and perfumed the air with its sweet scent.

"Come now." Standing he led Alonz back to the window and pointed into the dark of the night. "Down there," he said with a broad sweep of his hand, "will be Wessel citizens going about their daily business, trudging in and out of the market. Uncaring and callous of the fate of those born of a different race, they live their pathetic lives hiding from the truth. Do not concern yourself about them. They are as inconsequential as the birds of the sky."

Grabbing Alonz's chin in his hands, he stared deeply into the young face. "Look for me on the seventh floor of the Esfara Hotel at Zero Hour. We will have a clear view not only of each other, but more importantly of the president as he limps down the Promenade. Focus only on me; keep me in your sights. If something should go wrong, do not attempt to save me. If I fail to accomplish our aim, only then are you to take the shot. One shot – then you know the rest."

His dark head nodded, but the Black Hide could see the questions on his disciple's tongue. Squeezing Alonz's cheeks, he patiently waited for his protégé to come to terms with the heavy task that he was assigned. The young man swallowed nervously, breaking the spell, casting off the Black Hide's grip.

"I do and I will never let you down. But surely it won't, it can't, come to that!"

Through the mask, the Black Hide's ebony eyes glistened. "There is nothing certain in life except death Alonz. And if it is my cup to drink, then

I shall empty it to the last dregs, sure in the knowledge that you will lead the movement."

He wrapped a paternal arm about the teen's slender shoulders. "My boy, there's nothing to fear – Drex'n is ready and able to assist you if I am gone. He'll be loyal until the last drop of blood flows from his veins. But he's no leader. Use his knowledge, take advantage of his experience to guide you, let him activate the call-out on your orders. Although that turn-coat bitch Bafa has the consolidated list of trusted insiders – may the Daevas curse her soul!"

Pacing the small room, the Black Hide stopped suddenly and grabbed Alonz by the shoulders. "I trusted Tax'n to get rid of her and recuperate the microchip, but only the gods know what happened to them."

Sneering at the thought of his one-time lover playing him false and fleeing with that insipid wretch of a Wessel, the Black Hide released the young man and pondered on the implications, for no search could find a trace of the two traitors. He could sense the nervousness rising up within his young charge and he resumed the slow pacing on the worn-out linoleum.

"But not to worry if you must assume the black mask, for I've put Drex'n in touch with my contacts in the WAF and they're ready to pounce once the president is dispatched."

Alonz's face was impassionate as he stared at the older man. *And if he should fail tomorrow, then I alone will wear the black mask! The Wessels will learn to fear, as our people have tasted the bitter tears of despair. I'll stop at nothing to bring justice to the Geiten tribes.*

The sound of laughter shook the teen from his reverie of power and the Black Hide squeezed his shoulder.

"But I don't plan on taking the trail to the ancestors yet! You'll have to walk in my shadow for many years before I pass the torch to you."

***

A delightfully cool breeze swirled about the crowded promenade ruffling Pallav's hair, and he shivered in the happy knowledge that the scorching desiccating days would be soon over, washed away by the cleansing storm bursts of the Cooling. For all life depended on the precious, life-giving rains on the desert planet without which famine and misery would be born. At least to the Geiten, for the irrigation canals which supplied them with that essential source of all life were now shut off, dry and dusty, in retribution for the war. All along the Promenade in Styria, people stopped in their tracks and looked to the skies in anticipation. The hot season had been a long one, ripe with death and disease, war and plague. Now their enemies had been rendered powerless and the Wessels waited impatiently for the death blow to descend on those who had dared to make war on their mighty nation, allowing a sense of normality to resurge into their lives.

Yet today was anything but normal for Pallav, and he steeled himself in the knowledge that on this day he would end a man's life. Either by force or through capture, for the Black Hide would be vanquished before the setting of the sun – finished and destroyed – and all that would remain of the murderous wretch would be a footnote in the history of the River Panni conflict. Shading his eyes from the sun, Pallav mumbled half to himself as he searched the rooftops before his attention was drawn back to the scene playing out below.

"He'll never be able to take the president down with all these people milling about."

But Bafa shook her head knowingly. "I don't think you've ever come across a 38L-42 disrupter, have you? With one of those babies, you can hit the eye of a pybar in flight at 500 meters. And don't think for a moment that the Black Hide would care if others were to fall. He always told us that in the end, results are the only things that count, regardless of any fallout of your actions. So collateral damage, yup, he's okay with it."

Before them stood the Esfara Hotel, its stately façade rising imposingly over the busy promenade. Pallav knew they were prepared. They had walked the route, familiarizing themselves with back alleys and hidden doors. They had meandered along the red-carpeted narrow corridors of the Esfara and taken the skylift to the room in which the assassin would lurk. His logical mind was telling him that they could not fail, yet the butterflies dancing in his stomach seemed to taunt him.

Craning his neck, Pallav could make out the window below from which a slender dark-grey tip projected. Shoving his hands in his tunic's pockets, the big man gestured with a jerk of his head. "That's my cue… looks like I'm up."

"Pallav." A light touch on his arm halted him in his tracks. "If something happens today… if I don't come back…"

Taking her by the shoulders, Pallav recognized the concern in his protégée's blanched face.

"Listen Bafa, nothing's going to happen to you. Have faith in me. I'm not going to let the Black Hide or any of his thugs hurt you. You'll be safe."

She lowered her head and took a deep breath. "You listen to me for a moment." Staring straight into his eyes, Bafa reached up to cup his cheek and saw a spark of confusion light up his broad face. "You've taught me so much over the past few weeks. I can barely tell you what a difference you've made in my life."

Gently, Pallav removed her hand and squeezed it in a comforting grip. "And you've been a great help to me too, Captain Villutomi. Because of you, the ring of traitors within the WAF will be rooted out and the war can be brought to a close without more bloodshed."

She shook her dark head. "I'm not sure you understand. You see, I was lost and treading down the wrong path. You set me straight; you made me face the truth. But now I need you to do one more thing for me."

Her golden eyes narrowed and suddenly Bafa, the woman of smiles and giggles, became deadly serious. The change in her surprised Pallav and he raised an eyebrow questioningly. "If I don't come back, you got to promise to forget that I ever existed. Got it?"

"Bafa…"

"Got it?"

"It won't come to that."

Over her head, he spotted the elderly president and Fynn meandering along the promenade in the distance. Time was of an essence to their success, but patiently, he attempted to coax hope into his accomplice.

"Trust me, we've been over this time and time again. Stick to the plan and by this time tomorrow we'll be enjoying a cold drink on my patio. Now, let's get it done."

Turning on his heel he strode off, only to be pulled off balance and whipped around, Pallav found himself staring directly into the stone-cold serious face of Capt. Villutomi. There was no light dancing in those golden eyes of hers as she hissed in his ear. "Forget me."

And then, pulling a hood over her head, she spun him around like a top before disappearing into the crowd.

Christ, that was spooky, he thought regaining his composure. Brushing off the incident as nerves, he casually made his way into the Esfara. By the time he'd reached the rooftop, the entire scene had been forgotten. Leaning over the steel and glass railing, he squinted against the sun to see Meryx and Fynn slowly making their way along, while down below a hooded figure seemed to be window shopping in front of the Naraan Tull Market.

Good, she's in position.

Down the skylift, around the corner and a quick stroll along the corridor and there it was – the door to Room 74 loomed before him. Fishing about in his pants pocket, Pallav pulled out a miniature, yellow-coated card and ran it over the door lock. Shielding his eyes, a blue burst flared over the lock cover and silently the door swung open.

An open window. A masked figure leaning out, immobile, elbows propped against the windowsill. And silence. Total silence as the Black Hide waited, deep in concentration for the perfect moment. Through the open window, Pallav could see the crowded promenade; a flock of birds swirled down from the sky and the skylanes were crammed with traffic. A normal Friday afternoon.

And there was Meryx, just coming into view with Fynn at his side. Pallav held his breath lest the assassin sense his presence and studied the man for a heartbeat before making his decision.

"Room Service…" he growled.

The Black Hide flinched and jerked the trigger as Pallav launched at him, knocking the disrupter from his hands. Small and wiry, the Black Hide dodged the larger man and rammed an iron fist into Pallav's stomach. Impervious to the blow, Pallav grappled with the Black Hide, pinning him to the ground, but he gasped in pain when the masked man's teeth sank deep into his forearm, drawing blood. Wresting himself clear, the Black Hide scrambled for the disrupter and took quick aim, but before he could squeeze the trigger the big man charged and knocked the deadly weapon out of the Black Hide's hands to tumble from the open window.

It was then that Pallav became aware of the throbbing in his forearm, pulsing with every beat of his heart. It grew stronger and stronger until it entered into his consciousness, demanding attention. But his knees were on the Black Hide's chest and his hands on the man's throat, and he could feel the struggle growing weaker and weaker as the masked man's thrashing diminished. Reaching down, Pallav grabbed the mask and pulled. And gasped. His eyes widened in surprise at the identity of the man lying underneath him.

Pulling the traitor to his feet, Pallav seized him by the throat and held him in the air, his eyes ablaze. "So General, this is how you serve your country? By betraying the sacred oath you made? By causing the death of your own soldiers and now by attempting to assassinate your president?"

A great roar bellowed through the room. "You know nothing Kóbor – Gomalan's lackey. You're a stooge to a criminal regime."

The grip on the Black Hide's throat tightened and the rebel leader choked, clutching at his neck with frantic fingers. And then a sound rang out, like the popping of a cork, echoing throughout the maze of tall buildings while screams rose to fill the air.

"You're too late you fool," the Black Hide hissed before hauling back and spitting into Pallav's eyes. Breaking free, the traitor mounted the narrow window sill, balancing precariously before turning to Pallav. "The Black Hide can never die, he will be re-born."

One step into the nothingness and the general tumbled through the sky to the cobbled promenade below, where his lifeless body lay broken and mangled. Unable to resist the urge to peer over the window sill, Pallav stared in horror at the scene below. For what he saw froze the blood in his veins.

***

But now it is mine, the young man whispered, as the sights of his powerful disrupter zeroed in on the frenzied jump of his mentor. Above him, an alien giant with chestnut coloured hair peered over the windowsill and for a second, Alonz contemplated the destruction of the man whose interference led to the death of his master.

Remembering the Black Hide's words, he re-established his focus, now following the descent without passion until the masked man's body lay in a puddle of blood and gore on the promenade. It was only then that he swivelled the barrel of the weapon. Taking a deep breath, he held it for a second before exhaling half-way and then gently, as if he were stroking a cub's soft underbelly, he depressed the trigger. A lick of flame shot from the disrupter and the recoil of the weapon threw Alonz flat on his back. And in that moment, he knew his life was no longer his own. Leaving the window open behind him, Alonz grabbed the flimsy black cloth from the chrome table and shoving it in his tunic, the young Black Hide calmly walked out the door.

***

The bright rumble of laughter belied his rough demeanour; it was infectious, charming – none of the attributes that one would equate with the President of Wesselan.

"You'll get used to it son!" Meryx chuckled as Fynn craned his neck to check on the security detail that trailed in their wake. Like baby geese following their proud parents on their first foray into the water, they chugged along behind the two as they strolled nonchalantly along the promenade.

Every few feet, the couple stopped. Hands shaken and heads nodded as the president and the one who he had named his successor listened to the trials and tribulations of a people bent by the weight of the war and weakened by the scourge of disease. A galleon under sail, Meryx wound his way through the crowd while, like a patient father, he passed on the wisdom the younger man would need when it was time for Fynn to step into his shoes. And so it was, companionably enjoying their walk along the promenade with the promise of hot cloudberry pie while a cool breeze caressed them that they were oblivious to the danger lurking above.

But she was anything but inattentive, waiting outside the Naraan Tull Market. An older woman, her head wrapped in a pale-yellow scarf, watched and waited. The Black Hide had recruited her for the task, and honoured to have been selected, the older woman was ready to give her life in the fight for freedom. Beside her, a shopping cart was full of the necessities of everyday life: a loaf of bread, a basket of fruit and vegetables and some biscuits. Blending into the background, she waited for her moment to pounce.

Crack! Stunned she looked around but relaxed as an old aerovan stuttered its way across the skylanes. But the explosive backfire was not the only thing to come from above – the heavens were to produce a very peculiar downpour as suddenly a body plummeted to the ground, crashing on the cobbles with a sickening thud.

Ignoring the remains of the mysterious man, unaware that is was he who she had idolized, the one who was to lead the Geiten to salvation, she pushed her way forward. As the crowds rushed to and fro in their panic, she saw her chance. Stampeding with the masses, pushing the shopping cart before her, she threw herself between the president and his security detail. Then she stood, frozen and immobile, a flesh and blood barricade, and stared vacantly into the sky, unaware of the direction from which the blow of liberty would be struck.

The slender hooded figure looked upwards and caught a glimpse of a head over the edge of the window and with rapid steps, she closed the distance between herself and the president. She saw no evidence of a young couple pushing a baby buggy. The Black Hide was dead. The president was safe. Breathing a sigh of relief, Bafa relaxed her guard momentarily until a woman in a yellow scarf pushing a shopping cart slid behind Meryx and stopping in her tracks, began to survey the tall buildings.

By the gods, it's Ramina! Leaping into action, Bafa pushed her way through the crowd, weaving in and out of the masses of onlookers who had thronged about the dead man. In one bound she cleared Ramina and threw her shoulder against the elderly president while a sound of an explosion pounded into her ear. Meryx landed flat on his back as Bafa shielded him from the assault.

"Thank the gods you're safe," she whispered unaware of the blood pooling beneath the president. But Bafa was anything but. Grabbing her by the shoulders, Fynn threw her off the wounded man and pinned her to the ground. Meryx's adopted son held Bafa in an iron grip, his fingers tearing into the flesh of her shoulder and he shook her fiercely in his rage.

"What have you done, you bitch?"

Above her, Bafa could see Pallav's shocked face as he leaned from the window before her vision grew ever more grey. The freckled young alien who loomed above her was like a wild animal in his rage and she was helpless in his grasp. She stared into those maddened eyes and was reminded of a desert oasis, while the tiny brown spots that danced across his face were like the stars in the night sky.

Her killer was beautiful to her – an avenging angel – for Bafa believed she deserved to die. For she had killed without a conscience – first in the name of the Cause when thousands of Wessels who like her served their country had died due to her treachery. Her mind drifted over the death of Tax'n, her one-time lover, before sailing past the part she had played in the demise of Reyhart. Peace flowed over her like a mountain stream and Bafa let herself float on its currents, for she felt that the wrongs for which she was responsible were now being expiated.

A stream of blood spouted from the elderly statesman's mouth and his eyes opened wide in shock as realization set in.

"Fynn," Meryx muttered, a gurgle of blood spouting from gore-stained lips. With all his strength, the old man struggled to raise his stocky frame but collapsed back earthward with the effort.

Shoving the young woman hard against the cobbles, Fynn raced to the dying man's side. Gently cradling the president, he supported his foster father's head in his arms. Tears flowed down Fynn's cheeks as Meryx smiled weakly before reaching for his hand. "Let it go Fynn. All the anger inside, let it go."

A fit of coughing wracked the elderly man and Fynn could feel the warm life blood soaking through his trousers, carrying the president away on its red tide.

Immobilize the victim… apply direct pressure… raise his head… Pulling off his shirt, Fynn carefully placed it behind the elderly man and tied it in place, trying to control the bleeding.

"Hey, stay still Meryx. Save your strength. Help is on the way."

The corner of the president's mouth rose in a feeble attempt at a smile. Already, his body was becoming numb and cold, and Meryx recognized his fate as he felt his life force slipping away. Reaching up with a shaky hand, Meryx wiped the tears from Fynn's cheeks.

"Fynn, I need you to be strong, to stay the course that we plotted, you and I. You've been a god-send to me; a son in my old age. But Fynn… don't fail me now. Promise me…" The old man's voice cracked with emotion. "Promise me, Fynn, that you'll follow the path of peace."

The sobs that racked the young pilot brought Bafa out of her stupor and she pulled herself to her knees, sadness overwhelming her as she witnessed the alien's grief. She heard the choking rattle as Meryx's life-thread was severed. Then silently and slowly, Bafa rolled under the legs of the throng of onlookers who had gathered about the dying president.

As the emergency medical teams arrived by air ambulance, sirens wailing, lights flashing, Bafa tore off the oversized hoodie and slipped away unseen through the confusion of bodies and the labyrinth of buildings. A howl of anguish ripped through the air, a lament that like an arrow pierced her soul with its suffering.

Riveted to the spot, she turned to witness the remains of the elderly gentleman, his tunic blood-spattered and torn, being lifted onto a stretcher while the solitary figure of the young president-designate of Wesselan sobbed inconsolably.

CHAPTER 26 - LONG LIVE THE KING

Pity for the guilty is treason to the innocent.

– AYN RAND

There it was once again: that annoying little twitch. Drex'n blinked, trying to stamp out the tick that always appeared when he was under stress. He first noticed it the day that Tax'n, his master's inamorato, had slipped away with that Wessel whore, Bafa. Expecting to slide into his shoes, Drex'n was further dumbstruck when the Black Hide announced to all that a beardless youth would be groomed as his successor.

"Alonz?!" The name curled forth from Drex'n's tongue like a foul breath and he spat. For all the years that he'd stood by his master's side, never too proud to carry out the most heinous of crimes in the name of the Cause, always waiting for honours to be bestowed upon him for his steadfast loyalty, and now he had nothing to show for it.

The twitch shattered his concentration again and Drex'n cursed under his breath. Once more, he was being called upon to soil his hands while others would reap the rewards. But this time for a pimply faced youth whose voice was still breaking. He could still hear it cracking as Alonz linked in to him, informing him of the death of their master. Alonz: the new Black Hide, the mask-wearer. But a vow sworn is a vow sworn and the words played over and over in Drex'n's embittered mind.

I swore that I'd be prepared to risk my life in support of the Cause…that I'd give my unconditional obedience to the Black Hide...

Rubbing the transgressive eyelid, Drex'n sat on his haunches in the command post and snorted.

I won't be a filthy oath-breaker, he concluded miserably and putting the terrible thought out of his mind, Drex'n switched on the tiny device to engage his first contact.

"General Diti Cavell." The voice on the other end was soft and mellifluous, belying the steel spirit within the older woman.

Drex'n cleared his throat, for the message that he was to pass on was paramount. The words, like pybars skimming over the desert sands, flew from his throat. "Ah General, the Cooling is upon us… and relief is now at hand."

As the burner comms device clicked off, the Vice Commander of the Wesselan Armed Forces felt a flush of heat surge over her. *They've done it — the president is dead!* Wiping off the sweat from that trickled down the front of her tunic, Diti Cavell hesitated. *Qislen'll be back soon… the honour should by all rights be his.*

But the thought of seeing that old warhorse Gomalan restrained in cuffs was too delicious. Drumming her fingers against the highly polished desk, she allowed a congratulatory smile to crease her elfin features before swiping to access the Minister of Internal Security. A smile played at the corners of her pale, almond-shaped eyes as the holoimage of Nestor shimmered into her office.

Vain and arrogant, the minister's ebony hair was slicked back revealing a high sloping forehead underneath which his deep-set golden eyes shone with intensity at his summoning. Silently, he waited for the words which would guide his next move. And the light from the handsome woman's face told him everything.

Her soft, sweet voice brimmed with excitement and exultingly Diti raised her chin under the serpentine glare of the nation's chief of security. "Nestor, the time is ripe for us to hunt."

He raised an arched eyebrow before erasing all emotion from his narrow pallid face. "Indeed it is Diti. All preparations have been made." She nodded once and began to wipe the connection but was shocked when Nestor continued, breaking the agreed protocols.

With eyes like flint, the minister challenged her. "Let us see who can bag the most game today, shall we?"

Suddenly, Diti's throat felt dry and she swallowed nervously as the amplitude of the undertaking that lay ahead of her became crystal clear. For Ravenna had been her ally over the years. Pushing the dark clouds from her mind, the steel returned to her and Diti narrowed her eyes at her co-conspirator.

"You're on," she grinned and then, before Nestor could utter another word, she wiped the connection clean and reached into her desk drawer.

The Adyms Mk II blaster glowed as it came to life and slapping it into her hip holster, Diti marched into the hall with her head held high. Into the Ops Centre she strode, disrupting the young captain whose face was buried under comms devices and holoscreens as the fall-out from the assassination rippled around the planet.

At the sight of General Cavell, the Duty Officer pulled himself away from the devices, jumped from his seat and came to attention. Any misgivings she had were instantly dismissed at the sight of the red patch on his sleeve proclaiming him a member of the Presidential Guards.

So young, so innocent… she thought at the full head of wavy hair and clear complexion, unmarred yet by the lines of worry. *I was like that once. Believing in the system, that it would take care of me like a benevolent parent. Ha! How wrong I was! But now I'll no longer be forced to serve a criminal regime.*

What a strange sight for the captain: a General Officer in the Ops Centre, and not just any general, but the second in command of the Wesselan Armed Forces. He stood stock-still at attention under the intense scrutiny of General Cavell, not moving a muscle and holding his breath. Diti could see the confusion in the young officer mirrored in the face of the Duty Sergeant who tumbled in unceremoniously from the other room.

"Gentlemen. Today, we've been bowled over by a tragedy." Her brilliant pale eyes jumped between the two who would become mere extras in a scene that was about to play out. "But on this day, you and the men of the Presidential Guard will achieve immortality. For through your actions, your names will be forever on the lips of school children and written in the history of our proud nation. The death of our beloved President Meryx was no act of simple terrorism."

Pausing for effect, Diti's gaze passed over the reports that danced on the holoscreen and noted with trepidation the actions that the keen young officer had already taken to secure the government in the aftermath of the bellicose leader's demise.

It can all be overturned, she coolly reminded herself as she stood unflinchingly at the threshold of the bridge to treason.

"Subversive actors have taken steps to overthrow our government. Officers at the highest level within the WAF, trusted and highly respected by our dearly departed Meryx. They banded together in collusion to destroy the man who was leading our nation to glory, all so that they could wrest the leadership from the rightful government and wear the cloak of power. Do not be unnerved by what I am about to tell you, for it is truly frightful. Abominable even. But take courage in knowing that your actions will save our people from the calumny that has befallen us."

With cheeks afire, the Platoon Commander of the Presidential Guards hovered over his work, scrolling through the holoscreens as a testament to his abilities. "Ma'am, all protocols have been adhered to, the Guards have been recalled and are assembling as we speak. My Commanding Officer…"

With a wave of her hand, Diti cut him off, impressed with his courage. *Ah, a young lion! This bodes well for us…* "Irrelevant!"

Her soft voice now forgotten, her commands rose like the consuming flames of a funeral pyre. "This cannot wait for the arrival of your CO. Does the O Plan take into account that the nest of vipers springs forth from the office of the High Commander?"

A gasp escaped from the Platoon Commander's lips and he mopped his forehead with the back of his hand. "But ma'am, not ten minutes ago the High Commander…"

"Needs to be arrested," she finished for him. Then seeing the shock cloud his youthful features, she surged forward, taking another step along that precipitous arch. "As well as the Commanders of the Land and Aerospace Forces. All conspirators in this ungodly plot. Now…"

Approaching the holoscreen, Diti flicked it off and as the images faded into the ether, like stars in the dawn sky, she motioned to the door. "Let us brief your assembled troops."

The very cream of the Wesselan forces faced her: identical in height, square-jawed, muscular and ready for battle. She could hear the nervous joking as the last ones waited in line to draw their weapons and ammo. Memories, yellowed by the passage of time and blunted of their raw emotions, flooded over her. For she and Ravenna had both frolicked with handsome Guardsmen in their younger years.

Silence dominated the halls, only broken by the rhythmic clang of metal cleats against the polished floors of WAF HQ. A pall of shock and sorrow had fallen over the building as Diti, flanked by the young Platoon Commander and his 2IC, led the troops to the Inner Sanctum.

Iris scanned, finger print activated and the door whirred open. Heads swung about as General Cavell marched with the shock troops into the SCIF housing the WAF Command Suite which hummed with activity. Gomalan's Executive Officer, the very robotic Colonel Jillian, crashed her booted foot down to attention at the sight of General Cavell and waved the posse in to the High Commander's office without the slightest air of concern.

There he stood, with a look of disbelief on his face at their arrival: his mouth agape, eyes wide with shock. At his side General Ravenna tilted her bronzed face in a mixture of bewilderment and reproach while Air Marshal Francis stood bolt still as if frozen in time. The Guards moved about the room swiftly, placing themselves like boulders between the commanders, denying them escape. Diti threw her shoulders back and boldly issued the command. "Arrest them!"

Then it happened like a bolt of lightning. A hand crept ever so stealthily to the tunic hanging on the chair on which Francis rested his arm. Nonchalantly, he dug deep into its pocket, the feel of the metal cool in his fingers. Grasping the blaster, he inched his index finger towards the trigger. But the captain was fast, quicker by a hair. In the blink of an eye, Air Marshal Francis lay dead, a vacant stare on his face, while the red glow of discharged weapon in Captain Sartaj's hand slowly faded.

With a quick nod of his head, the captain signalled for a pair of burly soldiers to come forward while their partners covered them off, weapons at the ready. Gomalan bristled and looked down his aquiline nose at the diminutive Cavell.

"Under whose authority are you acting," he snarled as his wrists were encased in cold, hard iron. But his question went unanswered as Diti revelled in the High Commander's fall from grace.

Her face burning in shame, Ravenna flinched as a soldier young enough to be her daughter slammed a set of cuffs on her and shoved her against the wall. With the blood pounding in her temples, she glared malevolently at her one-time friend whose eyes flitted like butterflies about the room. But those brilliant eyes couldn't avoid the corpse that rested in a pool of blood, one arm still dangling from the pocket of his tunic.

Idiot... she thought without any hint of mercy for the dead man who until recently had sat across from her during the Commander's briefings. Silently Diti motioned for the Platoon 2IC to dispose of the body. As Marshal Francis's remains were being dragged ignominiously away, Diti stared out the window into the lovely sunny day. She could hear birds chirping as they flew by and sound of the wind rustling through the trees. *A good day for the start of a new world order*, she thought callously before turning to the two generals standing impotently before her.

"On behalf of the nation of Wesselan, I place you under arrest for plotting and organizing the assassination that took our president's life. High treason, High Commander. You will be taken from here, from this cursed room where you gathered like common criminals to plot the murder, to the holding cells where you will be detained until your trial."

Reacting in anger to the shepherding by the Presidential Guard, Gomalan swung about to face his deputy and the Platoon Commander at her side. With a voice like thunder, he bellowed. "Guardsmen! I order you to stop; these charges are fabricated and have absolutely no basis in reality. Halt this madness! Sartaj, we spoke only minutes ago; you know the truth. Release us! Now!"

Like a fish out of water, Captain Sartaj's mouth opened and closed as he stared from Gomalan to Diti. But the indecision lasted only as long as it took for him to draw a breath, and aware of the error in judgement that he had made in the heat of the moment, the captain strode to Diti's side and addressed her in hushed tones. "Ma'am, I'm going to have to ask you to provide me with further proof."

At that moment, Sartaj wished the ground could open up and swallow him for the diminutive elfin general had been transformed into a creature from his darkest dreams. A flush of red discoloured her pale skin, her brilliant eyes glowed with fury while the rosebud lips curled in fierce derision. There was no doubt in his mind that this woman had fought her way to the very top, fearless and with an iron will.

But the fury was all part of an act that the Vice Commander played and her once sweet voice was as sharp as a whip as she pulled out a miniature wafer before glaring at the shocked Guards.

"Display," she hissed and the tiny device lifted from her outstretched palm. Glowing like a firebrand, a beam of light emanated from its golden metallic surface and reassembled choppily into a holographic display of General Ravenna and Marshal Francis coming to their feet as the High Commander entered the situation room a few days earlier.

"Did you make any headway with him?" Ravenna questioned.

Gomalan sighed, the taste of Halo-dew still on his lips. "No, he's as obstinate as ever."

Arms crossed angrily in front of his body, Francis stared menacingly at the High Commander. "Then we need to force a decision."

The old warrior looked uncomfortable and pursed his lips while Ravenna fumed. "So, he's going to ignore everything we recommended. If all he wanted were people to snap to attention with their heels together, then he should've found corporals to do his bidding. I can't take much more of this. We've got to do something, we can't let Meryx push us down this path."

"Ravenna's right!" Francis slammed his fist on the situation room table. "You're the High Commander. You should dictate how the war is waged, not the president. He keeps referring to his service in the last war, but what was he anyhow, a junior officer? He knows nothing about military strategy! Only if we band together can we save Wesselan from this insanity. Gomalan, listen to us — Meryx has to be stopped. At any cost."

His face contorted with the thought of betraying an old friend, the High Commander was seen wavering between loyalty to his oath or his beliefs in what was the true course of action. Ravenna placed a hand on Gomalan's forearm. "You know it's the right thing to do, my friend. We need to take action against the president if Wesselan is to remain a strong, proud nation. History will prove us right!"

His greying head slumped on his chest, Gomalan slowly nodded. "You are both correct. I personally will see to it that this is taken care of."

Out of the corner of her eye, Diti maintained a close scrutiny of Captain Sartaj and saw the anger suffuse throughout the junior officer's body as the damning testimony played before his eyes.

"There," the Vice Commander shouted as she interrupted the incriminating evidence that General Qislen had taken such care to obtain. But then, the Provost Marshal always kept his secrets locked up tight next to the black mask that concealed his identity from all but General Cavell and the Chief of Police. Diti smiled inwardly at the thought of their masterful leader, for with Qislen as the Black Hide, the evil regime that had poisoned Wesselan would finally be overthrown.

Glowing with righteous rage, the sylphlike woman grew in stature as she closed on Sartaj. "There Captain, for all to see… there is your proof. General Qislen had caught wind of a plot and installed surveillance to gather evidence. And what did he find? To his horror, three generals, disgruntled with our president, conniving in this very room. Plotting to rid themselves of the leader so beloved by our people! And it seems the traitors acted before he could close the noose."

Gomalan groaned and pulled at the restrictive chains. "No! Diti, this is all a misinterpretation of our conversation! A simple misunderstanding. Listen to me…"

Waving a dainty hand in the air, Diti dismissed the High Commander's remonstrations. "I've heard enough already," she bellowed. "Captain, escort the traitors to the cells where they can reflect on the sins of their actions."

The butt of a disrupter struck the High Commander in the small of his back and he stumbled forward, while an overly keen Guardsman shoved him from behind. The big man halted in his tracks and turned on the soldier who recoiled in surprise, for not many would dare challenge the elite of the WAF. But this was the High Commander, not just any officer. His voice calm, Gomalan muttered resignedly to his escort. "I know the way, no need to shove."

Beside him, Ravenna walked leadenly. For to struggle was useless; she realized that. Yet somewhere deep inside that vitriolic creature walking behind her was a friend of old. The Diti with whom she'd shared secrets, clothes and men. Years ago…it seemed like only yesterday. Scanning her one-time friend's face, she understood that all that was in the past. There would be no reprieve from the trumped-up charges that would lead to a traitor's death. And so, lost in thought, Ravenna let herself be led to the cells in the subterranean vaults of WAF HQ. Hopeful that the truth would come out, she marched resolutely at the side of the High Commander to whatever fate awaited them.

As the iron doors creaked open, the two generals balked as their senior staff rose to attention from inside the dimly lit crypt, while a dark figure waited patiently in the shadows.

Relief filled Diti at the arrival of her co-conspirator. *Qislen! Finally…*

Slowly, the shape slid from the darkness into view and the smile left her face.

"General Berkan?"

In two steps, she was beside the Commander of WAF Communications and taking him by the sleeve of his tunic, Diti pulled him into the corridor and away from prying eyes. With quick steps, the duo walked past the troops, the Vice Commander leading Berkan into a small alcove.

Concealing the disappointment from her face, Diti raised an eyebrow. "You were certainly efficient. You must've got word from the Black Hide first?"

Berkan rubbed at his chin, perplexed. "It was Drex'n." With a nervous sigh, he continued. "But it seems like we made a clean sweep."

She nodded, lost in thought. "Now all we have to do is wait to see if Nestor got his little pigeon. Do you have the media release?"

Slipping a knife from his tunic, Berkan tore open a concealed pocket from which he unfurled a printed script. "I took the liberty of committing it to writing," he said, offering the paper to Diti. "You never know, do you, when things go south. This way," he continued as she surveyed the proclamation, "there's no lasting evidence and it's so easy to dispose of."

"Well then," she said with determination, "let's get on with it. There's no going back now."

And from an alcove deep within the bowels of Wesselan Armed Forces Headquarters, the voice of treason victoriously gurgled across the airwaves.

CHAPTER 27 - JACOB'S LADDER

To fight aloud is very brave - but gallanter I know Who charge within the bosom the cavalry of woe.
— EMILY DICKINSON

He ran to the window, a scrap of black cloth dangling from his fingers. In two hurried steps he had closed the distance and ignoring the throbbing in his arm, he held out a hand. But he was too late. Horror-struck, Pallav watched as General Qislen flailed about in mid-air, his face now sporting only a mask of contempt, before he plummeted to his death.

And then the roar of a disrupter resounded over the tall buildings lining the Promenade. Leaning over the windowsill, Pallav stared in shocked silence at the mangled figure below, while from the corner of his eye he spotted a blur of colour as Bafa leapt onto the president. From his vantage point, he saw the flare of the weapon rip into the old man's back. She was too late. They had failed. He hung there, suspended in time, while down below Fynn launched a deadly attack on the woman who so reminded him of his kid sister, and Pallav gasped in fear as her dark face slowly began to purple.

His feet had wings as he charged down the stairs and raced through the reception hall, pushing aside the patrons in his haste to save the young woman's life. But as Pallav ran out into the street, she had vanished, the crowds swallowing her up. He could see Fynn holding Meryx in his arms while the security team held the crowd at bay, and he hesitated for a heartbeat. Then like a ship under full sail, Pallav cut through the crowd of onlookers. He knew that he had to find her, for they had failed and her life was now in peril.

Shoving the black mask into his front pocket, he continued in the hunt. But as the minutes ticked away, Pallav knew he had run out of time. Bafa's words came back to him now, and he paused in the shade of a tree flush in new bud with the memory of her warning resurfaced.

Officers in the highest places…could it be?

Grabbing his comms device, Pallav opened a link to Gomalan and groaned in frustration as his Executive Assistant replied. On his tiny screen he could swear that the stout Colonel's face was tear-streaked, but Pallav pushed the idea from his mind for he knew the woman to be collected even under the withering verbal fire from the deadly duo of Ravenna and Francis.

"Jillian, what's going on? I'm downtown and I've just heard the president's been shot."

Pulling out a tissue, Gomalan's loyal assistant dabbed at her eyes and took a deep breath, transforming herself into the formidable creature who the High Commander could trust to deal with any issue.

"President Meryx is dead, Pallav. And I can't believe I'm saying this, but the High Commander as well as General Ravenna and Air Marshal Francis are the lead conspirators in his assassination. Half the senior officers have been placed under arrest. And we haven't heard anything from the Provost Marshal. But at least the nation's in safe hands. General Cavell's assumed leadership of Wesselan until the president-designate can be sworn into office."

He stood there silently while a cool wind blew through the budding branches and Bafa's voice played over in his mind. He could trust no one. Not Jillian. But Gomalan? No, he dismissed that idea as impossible, for he knew that the power-hungry High Commander would never willingly place himself under the command of General Qislen, the Black Hide. No, Gomalan was no traitor, of that he was sure. Silently he waited, wondering for whom the woman's tears had fallen.

"Pallav?" Two red spots burned in her cheeks and Jillian narrowed her eyes as she watched him suspiciously. "You must get here on the double. With Qislen missing, you step into his shoes."

"On my way," he barked and breaking the link, Pallav cursed. *Damn! I have to find that girl! Her ring is the only proof I have that this is a coup d'état by the Black Hide.*

Scanning the horizon, all he could see was a tide of dark heads, already resuming their daily business, as if the death of a president and the suicide of a top general were daily occurrences. The skylanes hummed with activity, the streets throbbed with the masses trudging home after a long week at work. But nowhere, no matter which way he looked or down which alley he searched, could he find a trace of Capt. Villutomi. For she had gone to ground.

He knew he had little time before the conspirators would be firmly entrenched and the overthrow of the government a reality. "Gomalan's creature," he had heard them call him behind his back, and Pallav realized that his life hung by a thread should the plotters prove successful. Retracing his steps to his aerocar, Pallav's fingerprint accessed the vehicle, and jumping inside he threw himself into the driver's seat and began to fish about in his front pocket for the fob. To find nothing other than the black mask that had so recently concealed the identity of the Provost Marshal.

"Damn!" Knowing that backtracking would lead to nothing, he cursed himself and threw his head back against the seat in frustration. And that was when he saw it, neatly folded in the back seat: Luke's hoodie. But what he failed to notice was the woman standing nonchalantly in front of a shop window, staring into the glass at the reflection of the big alien in the small aerocar who was playing out his role in the drama.

Bafa watched as Pallav pawed through his son's hoodie's pockets and a smile curled on her face as he pulled out the fob and a blood-red ring. She stood there motionless when he linked into his comms device and watched as he spoke animatedly while the powerful hoverfans activated. She could glimpse him scanning the city as the aerocar lifted from the ground. When his head dipped in sorrowful resignation, Bafa wanted to cry out and run after him, but her feet remained glued to the spot. And long after Pallav had entered the skylanes and his vehicle became just a dot on the horizon, Bafa stayed by the shop window, whispering a silent prayer to the gods for the safety of the big alien who had been like a brother to her. Then turning on her heel, her golden eyes darkened and taking a deep breath, Bafa Villutomi confidently marched down the sunlit alley, the fob to Reyhart's Dune-Rider dangling from her manicured fingernails.

***

The wail of the ambulance shrilled through the Promenade as Nestor looked on in astonishment at the corpse laying in a pool of blood and brains, their gore-splatter trickling down the little gaps between the ancient cobbles. A crowd of onlookers milled about, pushing and shoving to get a better glimpse of what remained of General Qislen, the one who had secretly worn the black mask. Nestor pondered on the fact almost casually: the Black Hide was dead, and now a new man would rise to the challenge – for the rebel group would never cease to exist until justice had been achieved.

Trying hard to maintain an impartial appearance, the Chief of Police watched as the mangled remains of the man to whom he had sworn allegiance was peeled from the stones and ignominiously stuffed into a black plastic bag on a gurney. His tall lean body stepped purposefully up to the constables who had been assigned the distasteful duty and he waved a long-fingered hand in blight indifference, as if flies had descended upon a forgotten morsel on his dinner plate.

"Control the crowd," he spat, and pushing his way to the gurney, he peeled back the dark shroud. Donning a set of disposable gloves, Nestor showed no emotion as he ran his hands over the corpse. Great clots of congealed blood coloured his hands as he searched the body, looking for the evidence of Qislen's treachery.

Nothing. Pausing momentarily, Nestor stared in confusion at the blood-stained cobbles.

But where could it be?

Wrist-deep in gore, he continued his search but to no avail. The symbol of leadership had fled, and not only from the mangled face of the man who was Nestor's military counterpart. The black mask, the badge of leadership, had been carried off. Just like the soul of the man who had once been the living embodiment of the Black Hide movement.

Staring at the carcass within the black plastic bag, Nestor reflected coldly on the fate of his one-time leader. *You played your part well; and what more could any of us ask for than to die a noble death. For is it not better to pay the ultimate price, than to live bowed under the yoke of tyranny?*

Then stepping back from the gurney, and with a wave of his gloved hand, Nestor signaled to the air ambulance driver to rid the crowded street of what remained of the Black Hide. Cautiously the gloves were peeled off and Nestor irritably rubbed at an offending stain on the cuff of his tunic. Then motioning to one of his constables, he pointed to the distraught figure of Fynn Vogel, the human who Meryx believed could lead Wesselan to glory and casually remarked, "Bring me the heir-designate".

Nestor watched out of the corner of his eye as the young man pulled himself away from his foster-father to watch the president's body being reverently lifted onto a waiting stretcher, while medics frantically buzzed about. His youthful freckled face with its gentle hazel eyes seemed proof to the hardened rebel that the young man chosen by Meryx was not cut out to lead in a world of intrigue and vice. Then a sly grin came over Nestor's face.

The cub can be easily manipulated to the Cause. Maybe this will work out after all.

Donning a serious and doleful appearance, the Chief of Police reached out to Fynn and with a hand over his heart, bowed courteously. His deep-set eyes glowed with feigned sorrow as he spread his hands apart, like a priest offering benediction.

"Now we see the scope of the treachery," he began and between the palms of his hands was displayed a fabricated message that Diti and he had crafted beforehand.

"What the hell's this?" The fierceness in Fynn's voice shook Nestor from his hope of an easy conquest. But the suave Wessel displayed no dismay at the heir-designate's coarseness.

Lecturing as if a schoolteacher to a plodding student, the Chief of Police spoke slowly. "Here is evidence that the High Commander masterminded the assassination, with the assistance of Francis and Ravenna. And it seems," he said with a flourish to where the homicide detectives had already begun their grisly work, "that your Provost Marshal was aware of the treachery and attempting to foil the plot, was murdered in the process."

Fynn turned an angry eye at the dumbstruck security agents before facing Nestor. The desperation was clear on the pilot's face. "I don't care about that right now. All that matters is Meryx. He'll pull through; there's a fire burning in that man that won't be easily extinguished."

Disbelief caught the Chief of Police at the heir-designate's denial of the reality before him, and for a moment Nestor felt sympathy for the broken man standing in front of him.

"Colonel, he's dead. He was shot by a disrupter. Nothing can patch that up. Nothing." Allowing the truth to sink in, Nestor bided his time like a bird of prey, circling in anticipation of a blood meal. "At the moment, the safety of the entire nation hangs by a thread. Factions loyal to Gomalan must be neutralized and the traitors dealt with expediently and ruthlessly."

The rear door to the air-ambulance began to close and Fynn glared angrily at the Chief of Police. With a glance over his shoulder, Fynn hissed. "For God's sake, let me say my final goodbyes in private! Right now, I'm going with Meryx."

The pilot of the air ambulance was watching Nestor; she could feel his eyes boring into her as she waited impatiently for the moment to slip out of dock. And so with a shrug, the Chief of Police climbed into the front of the vehicle and reaching over, flipped off the intercom to the rear.

"Land us on top of WAF HQ," he ordered, and seeing the surprise on the woman's face, he narrowed his eyes.

But the pilot of the ambulance was no lackey and returned an icy stare. "My mission is to fly the president's remains to the hospital at the Aerospace Wing, where his sister's waiting."

Unused to dissension, Nestor blinked in sudden irritation before he pulled out a trump card. "You want me to clarify that order with General Cavell?"

Shaking her head, the pilot compliantly began to activate the hover fans when to her surprise the Chief of Police grabbed her by the wrist. "I'll be in the rear with the body," he said matter-of-factly while his hand squeezed down hard. He waited for a hint of pain to show on her face before she conceded victory to him with a nod.

"And now, the show begins," Nestor thrilled, as with a whirl of the powerful fans, the ambulance lifted in the air while Fynn bawled like a newborn over the body of his mentor.

***

He could hear his heartbeat, feel it jumping in his chest as he opened the ring.

I have to know, before anything else, he convinced himself and he grabbed the microchip, quickly scanning its contents on his comms device. And there it was: a litany of names that made him draw his breath in, surprise overwhelming him at the scope of the betrayal.

And she recruited them all? By God, that girl's fearless.

Pride filled Pallav at Bafa's accomplishment before he remembered – this was treason. Oath-breaking. Villainous treachery. Yet she had nothing to fear, for he would never betray her secret.

Punching into the aerocar's comms system, Pallav activated a link to Fynn while rehearsing the words that he knew could provide no balm to the pain that would be tearing a new wound in the young man's already broken heart. He could hear the siren in the background as he lifted the aerocar from its dock before Fynn's sombre voice replied.

"I just heard," was all Pallav could muster before a sinister voice broke in.

"Who's that?"

Ignoring the question, Fynn's voice was leaden, almost a whisper. "He's dead Pallav. Some Geiten bitch shot him in the back and he bled to death like a dog on the cobbles."

There it was again, amidst the bells and beeps – that high pitched shrill. "Colonel Vogel, this is not the time. You need to concentrate; there's so much ahead…"

"Go to hell! You useless little bastard; you were supposed to protect him. Now get out of my face."

Pallav swerved onto the skylanes, merging into the stream and aimlessly letting the flow carry him along. "Tara and I are worried about you. After everything that just happened. But listen Fynn, I'd like to take you back to our place. Right now, you need some peace; you need to be with friends, not these people. They don't understand us."

He could hear the hurt in Fynn's voice as he choked back a reply. "Meryx did. He understood. But now he's gone."

It was like Pallav could hear the clock ticking down to another disaster. The siren in the background providing what he thought was a clue, he eased off the skylanes and dropped into the city aeroroute leading to the 1st Styrian Military Hospital. "Listen buddy, you're not alone. You got me and Tara and we're not going to let you go through this by yourself. I'm going to swing by and pick you up. Where are you? Oh and who's that useless little bastard you're with?"

"The Chief of Police. He showed up almost as soon as Meryx was shot."

Pallav could hear the anger building in the pilot once more.

"Proving how incompetent he really is. Right now we're taking Meryx's remains to the hospital at the Aerospace Wing. The Wessel's have some funerary procedures that apparently need to be done before the next sunrise, so that the spirit can find its way," Fynn snorted. "Bloody bullshit! And somehow I've got to preside over his parting ceremony."

That piercing voice again broke in on their conversation. "It's our way…and you're a Wessel now. Your part is crucial."

And then the dam broke. "I told you! Shut the fuck up!"

A thunderous crash resounded over the airwaves, followed by a punishing thud as knuckles struck something fleshy and solid.

Streaming above, Pallav caught sight of a camouflage-coloured air ambulance, sirens wailing as it raced in the opposite direction.

"Fynn, by any chance…you in a military ambulance?"

A weak, low groan was captured in the background. "Yeah, I am. Why?"

Whipping his aerocar about, Pallav engaged the vertical thrusters and ripped through the skylanes, zooming past the Friday afternoon traffic before he managed to slip into the wake of the speeding air ambulance.

"Just making sure," he stalled, perilously cutting in between aerocars as the ambulance made its way to WAF HQ at break neck speeds. "Stay strong. I'll be there soon."

Cutting the link, Pallav stayed tight on the ambulance's tail as he raised Col Hudson Lott.

"Hey Pallav! What a crazy day! What's up?" A hologram of the Commanding Officer of the 2nd Battalion of the 17th Mechanized Infantry Brigade greeted him from his backyard where Hudson was floating on a yellow raft in his pool surrounded by a pack of screaming youngsters.

"You look too comfy there Hudson; you think you can drag your ass out of the pool and throw on your uniform? I'm going to need infantry support, ACOLEVs, RAITs, drones. Can you get in touch with my Dep and get her to rustle up a security battalion…I'm kind of in a bind right now. Whatever you can pull together, get it and cordon off all routes leading to and from Headquarters. And I need you there by yesterday."

Hudson's eyes shot up. "You mind telling me what's going on? I mean, it's my wife's 40th birthday party and you know how that works, right?"

Pallav chuckled and rammed the stick to the right as the ambulance turned off the skylanes. "Indeed I do my friend… but no can do. This isn't a secure line. I'll tell you everything when you arrive at Headquarters. And Hudson, I wouldn't be asking this if it weren't a matter of national security."

Climbing out of the pool, Hudson nodded at the big alien. "Got it. I'll be there in a flash."

Ahead, the ambulance came to a hover as it began to dock atop the Headquarters of the Wesselan Armed Forces and breaking off the chase, Pallav brought his vehicle down in the HQ staff docking pad. Binoculars in hand, he watched as Fynn stepped out on to the roof, followed by Nestor who held a blaster at the heir-designate's head. Two burly police ran from the shadows where they had been waiting, and rounding on Fynn, pushed him forward.

Pallav grimaced as a struggling Fynn was struck across the back then knocked to his knees. From the distance, he could make out Nestor looking about suspiciously as the roar of the ACOLEVs reached his ears.

It's okay buddy, don't worry... Pallav whispered as he lowered his binoculars to the sight of Colonel Hudson Lott sitting astride a dune-rider at the head of his troops. *The cavalry's coming.*

***

"What're we doing here?" Fynn turned to Nestor in surprise as the ramp to the air ambulance swung down and he found himself staring at the rooftop of WAF HQ.

The Chief of Police motioned to an open fire door atop the building where a team of loyal officers garbed in the brown uniform of Styria's police force waited. "Get out," Nestor commanded.

Realizing the peril, Fynn twisted about and slammed Nestor against the stretcher brackets lining the ambulance's side panel and as the raven-haired man collapsed, Fynn tugged furiously at the handle in an attempt to raise the ramp. The flash of shots burst through the air and throwing himself to one side, Fynn rolled behind the gurney on which the body of the late president reposed.

He could hear the groans from Nestor, who unsteadily was pulling himself to his knees. Flames licked through the ambulance, their hot tongues greedily lapping against the gurney behind which he now sought shelter. Through the red flickering madness, he saw Nestor catapulting out of the burning vehicle, the police waiting with weapons at the ready to send him into the darkness of the unknown.

Crawling on all fours, Fynn skirted the stretcher that now began to burn with the intensity of a funeral pyre. With his back against it, he kicked with all his might trying to break down the compartment wall that would lead to the vehicle's cab. Again and again he kicked, sweat pouring down his face as the heat became overpowering. The sweet stench of burning flesh and its clinging smoke stung his eyes and burned his lungs.

This is it, I'm going to die here, he realized with panic, his legs smashing into the steel wall to no effect. Then a cool breeze played across his cheeks, light as a feather. It danced on his lips, lifted a lock of hair and swirled about his nose. And he heard a sound, soft as a whisper, in the breeze.

Go with them, Fynn. You'll be safe. Fynn. Go. Be safe.

He stopped kicking and listened. But the voice was gone; the cool breeze had fled. He knew then, for that voice had been with him, helping him, showing him the way when all else was dark.

And so he followed, crawling on his knees, past the burning flames that were consuming his foster father, through the curtain of fire that raged all about him. From the inferno he appeared, smoke-blackened, soot covered, his hair singed. To have Nestor hold a blaster to his head. To a beast slamming a weapon into the small of his back.

As he fell to his knees, the crash of a fist slamming into his jaw, he could barely make it out, as soft as a summer's breeze carrying him back to Isle Royale on a sunlit day.

Fynn. Don't resist. The time will come. But not yet. Not yet.

It floated on the wind; he could feel its presence, waiting for him while he greedily sucked in deep breaths, gathering strength for a renewed attack.

What'd I have to live for? Everything I loved is gone. There's nothing here for me now.

It reared up and swirled ferociously about him, a maelstrom of fury whipping about him.

I need you to live. For me. For Meryx. For our little girl.

His eyes fluttered in shock as the breeze caressed his face then blew away into the cloudless sky.

I will, he vowed wordlessly. *I'll make you proud, all of you. I'll fight on for you. I promise.*

Shadows of the rebels fell on him as he lay limp on the rooftop, his knees buckled under him, the stench of the acrid flames burning in his nostrils, its heat reaching out with fiery tentacles. A jab in the ribs nudged and probed the extent of his awareness. In reply, Fynn stifled a small gasp and stirred just a little as Nestor's brown leather shoe prodded him again.

"He's out for the count. Grab him and let's go before this thing blows up."

Rough hands dragged him along the hot roof, and through his half-closed lashes he could see the late afternoon sun reflecting off the metal door. The door to the Headquarters of the Wessel Armed Forces. Nestor stood back, watching his beaten captive being manhandled into the building and shielding his eyes, he motioned to the air ambulance's pilot.

He could see the fear in her face, the trembling of her fingers as she approached, unsure of her role in what was surely the kidnapping of

Wesselan's heir-designate. He tried to smile, reassuringly. Because Nestor knew: the success of the rebels was dependent upon the fickleness of the gods. The greedy gods; the hungry gods. Gods that demanded compensation for their fateful interventions.

She would do – the female pilot who stared at him blankly with those ebony eyes, the fear swiftly being replaced with confusion. She would do – a fitting sacrifice to propitiate the gods and accompany Meryx on the trail to the ancestors. She would be his gift to the gods in a cry for their assistance. His white teeth shone in a brilliant smile as with a deft flick of his wrist, the blaster in his hand flashed and the woman, her eyes wide with disbelief, fell in a heap on the burning rooftop.

Wiping his sweaty hands against his trousers, Nestor calmly left the scene of fire and death, secure in the knowledge of the triumph of the Black Hide rebel group.

CHAPTER 28 – SURPRISES

Our dead are never dead to us, until we have forgotten them.

– GEORGE ELIOT

Throughout the nation, people held their breath in disbelief as the newsflash surged like wildfire. Sirens shrilled while children ran unhindered into the streets and their parents stared vacantly at each other in shock. Lieutenant Colonel Summer Filiponi, Commanding Officer of the Targa ACOLEV Regiment, flew at breakneck speed to the Base, skimming in and out of the skylanes. Dirt encrusted under her fingernails, the flowers she'd been dividing with her husband long forgotten. Abruptly, she dropped onto the docking pad and catapulted from her vehicle into the turmoil of the crowd that had gathered. Frightened faces looked up to her, some tear-stained, others contorted with anger, but all needing reassurance. And she knew, as word of the assassination and coup d'état thundered across the Regimental Duty Centre, that there was none to give – for their world had been torn apart.

Across the city, Styria boiled with shocked grief, and incredulous at the news, Magdar and Tara replayed the special bulletin from DNN once more. At the sight of General Diti Cavell, Magdar sneered in disgust. "Lies! Everything they've said…"

"Shhh," Tara reprimanded her friend while the diminutive General Diti Cavell stood beside General Berkan. The WAF Commander of Communications spoke in clipped tones as footage of the assassination played out before their eyes on the holoscreen. It never ceased to grip Tara with wonder at how she felt immersed in the images that seemed to come to life within the room. It was as if she were walking alongside Meryx as he strode with Fynn down the shop-lined Promenade toward the Naraan Tull Market. Crowds rushed past, people on their way home after a long day at work: a man with flowing mustaches carrying a baguette; a mother holding the hand of her child as he clutched his school bag; a tired executive, his back bent with the cares of the day. She jumped out of the way only to have Magdar pull her back down onto the couch and stifle a laugh at her alien friend's irrational reactions. It seemed like a day just like any other; but then, suddenly, it became a moment in history.

Her eyes scanned the crowd, knowing that the unthinkable was about to be played out in three dimensions in Magdar's living room. That was when Tara noticed a clue after the body of a man fell from an open window and crashed against the cobbles. An older woman in a pale yellow scarf pushed a carriage. She raced forward, inserted herself between Meryx and his security detail, then swiveled about in anticipation.

And look who's wearing Luke's hoodie! she marvelled to herself, as a slight figure launched herself at Meryx, while her son sat transfixed with his sisters at his side. *The hoodie I bought him from the Nasaton Commissary! Oh Lord, help us... Pallav's somehow involved in all this!*

The images shocked her almost as much as the words that echoed across the living room from General Berkan:

> *"In Styria today, a tragedy of enormous magnitude has shaken our nation. At Mid+2 hrs, as President Meryx was proceeding along the Promenade, he was struck down by an assassin working for an unholy alliance of senior officers and ministers. Led by the High Commander of the WAF, the small clique of traitors has been apprehended and now await trial for the slaying of President Meryx and the betrayal of our country in a time of war. Police are now searching for the murderer. The heir-designate, Lt Col Fynn Vogel, was with President Meryx at the time of the assassination and is unharmed."*

Berkan took a step back and waited for General Cavell to come to the forefront before continuing in his nasal whine.

> *"In the interim, the functions of leadership for the nation will be exercised by the Vice Commander of the Wesselan Armed Forces, General Diti Cavell, and in keeping with the dying wishes of Meryx, she will offer an overture of peace to the Coalition. Rest assured, citizens of Wesselan, that swift justice will be dispensed. The traitors will pay the ultimate price for their depraved quest for power."*

The images on the holoscreen cast utter terror into Tara's soul. For while General Berkan droned on, she could clearly see the slender figure that had catapulted against Meryx, trying to hold the president down and protect the dying man with their own body. She could barely make out a whisper that caused the president's eyes to flutter in surprise before Fynn flung her off to vent his rage on the lissome shape beneath him. And when the distraught man turned to hold his dying foster father in his arms, Tara's disbelief was whisked away as a fuzzy image of the woman's face appeared momentarily on the holoscreen.

One of Bafa, struggling to her knees, before rolling away unseen into the crowd. Those dimpled cheeks, that dark smooth-skinned face, and there were those eyes - large and golden like honey – she could never forget them. For she had seen how they looked at her husband with a light akin to hero worship – and well Tara knew how that could shift in a heartbeat into a far more dangerous emotion.

Shamelessly, Tara wept for Meryx; she shared her tears with Magdar, she cried for Fynn in his despair, but most of all, Tara wept in fear. But her sorrow did not end there. For before her eyes, Pallav appeared and stood momentarily transfixed on the steps of the Esfara Hotel. She prayed for him to melt into the crowd. But Pallav stood stock still, his glance taking in the grief of his human friend. Then ever so nonchalantly, her husband stuck his hands in his pockets and pushed his way through the throng of onlookers in a bid to catch up with the woman who the entire planet would believe had assassinated the President of Wesselan.

***

Diti needs to know, Nestor realized as he skipped down the narrow staircase from the rooftop, the limp body of the heir-designate unceremoniously being dragged down the steps in front of him. The rhythmic banging of Fynn's heavy boots against the concrete stairs pounded into his head, and instinctively he waited at the next landing until the procession was out of sight and silence once again dominated the deserted stairwell.

Wondering how the Vice Commander was faring without the steadying influence of the now very dead Qislen by her side, Nestor's slender fingers reached into the pocket of his tunic and played with the comms device in his hand.

Has she the nerve without the Black Hide's presence to take on that trio of reprobates who led our country into this unholy war? The laughter of his hand-picked police rose up to greet him and he applauded his choice. All Wessels who had broken faith with their evil government; all officers who wanted nothing more than to live in peace with their Denebian neighbours, but who would not quail at violence, even murder, to achieve the aim. For in the long run, the only thing that counts is the end result.

Hearing the rumble of ACOLEVs in the streets below, Nestor quickly scrambled back up the stairwell and peered out the fire door to watch as the armoured vehicles stormed over the cobbles. In their wake followed a battalion of RAITs accompanied by a swarm of infantry soldiers on dune-riders.

Ah, the good General's on the ball. Soon, those loyal to the old regime will be disposed of and a new era will begin. One in which the Geiten are freed from the shackles of misery and can play their proper role in our society.

Dusting off his hands on his trousers, Nestor hummed a tune as he took the stairs two at a time in his haste to witness the downfall of the High Commander.

***

"Sir, you need to come out here at once." The gruff voice of Sergeant Major Fielen of the Presidential Guards crackled into the Ops Centre where Captain Sartaj toiled. His mood had soured since the encounter between the High Commander and the Vice, and it wasn't lightened by the plethora of message traffic that he was sifting through. Commanders across the country were reacting as expected, filled with doubt and misgivings, and in his CO's absence, it fell upon him to set the record straight.

Grunting his reply, Sartaj charged from the darkened bullpen and angrily shoved open the heavy blast-proof doors to be blinded by the late afternoon sun. That and its reflection off a battalion of ACOLEVs lined up with their turrets pointing at the wide squat HQ building. Rows of RAITs stood stock still beside what looked like an entire regiment of infantry soldiers waiting nervously beside their dune riders. Drones purred above, their steely eyes pivoting in an attempt to capture and exploit any weakness. Amidst the deadly mass of metal and robotics, Sartaj could make out the big chestnut-haired giant flanked by three Wessel officers.

"Figures… Gomalan's pet-alien's involved," he grumbled as the Sergeant-Major motioned over the Platoon Commander.

The old soldier looked about uneasily at the mountain of lethal weaponry ready to bear down on them. "Sir, we're woefully outnumbered and outgunned here. And I'm not sure if you can see…"

"Engaging sensory enhancement."

A film slid across the protective visor of Sartaj's helmet, magnifying ocular and aural capabilities, and suddenly it was as if he stood within the strange clique that had formed in the shade of the big ACOLEVs.

"It can't be!"

The tell-tale bullet shaped head of his Commanding Officer peeked from between the big alien and two Wessel officers. Chewing a droopy moustache with a vigour that suggested he'd missed a week of meals, his haggard-looking CO and the other Wessels were head-bent about a glimmering halo that shone within their treasonous circle.

"It's not good Sir," Fielen commented acidly. "We've been hoodwinked. That is, if we can trust what we're seeing."

Sartaj's eyes widened with surprise as his sensory enhancement device picked up a long list of names that the alien officer was excitedly showing to his colleagues in his strange foreign way of misusing verbs and articles. Yet the meaning was clear enough, and the Guards on the cordon looked at each other in confusion.

Fielen and Sartaj could clearly hear Pallav's calm voice belying his frustration as the alien repeated himself once more to the sceptical CO of the Presidential Guards.

"You understand what this is, don't you Major Visyx?" Pallav's hand waved the strange combination of the black mask and a ring in Visyx's face. "The attack on Farb ASW – how can anyone forget when it was blown off the face of the planet? When the Black Hide rebels hacked into DNN to broadcast their triumph?"

Visyx nodded and Pallav pushed the blood-red ring under the man's bushy moustache. "That woman on the holocast, you recall her? Bragging and boasting about how the rebels could take Wesselan down? This here's the ring she wore in that broadcast as the spokesperson for the Black Hide. And today, I confronted the man in the mask as he was leaning out over the window with a disrupter locked on target. And in case you're wondering, that target was President Meryx. Both the mask and the ring were on Qislen before he jumped to his death rather than being taken in for the traitor he was. Qislen was the Black Hide. Qislen, my superior officer. And the ring…

ah, the ring… inside the big red rock was concealed this list." The big alien pointed at the names floating mid-air and Visyx chomped ever more furiously on the tip of his moustache. "A list containing a complete inventory of every single military member who've been recruited for the Black Hide. From top generals all the way to a couple of recruits."

He held a callused hand out, the gaudy bauble perched in his palm and Pallav offered the ring to Visyx who, stalling for time, examined it as if his first born had just come into the world.

Col Hudson Lott grumbled under his breath as Visyx scratched his head in disbelief, while LTC Summer Filiponi illuminated the gravity of the situation. "C'mon! You got to call off the Guards before Cavell does away with the heir-designate! Otherwise, we're engaging!"

"Enough blood's been spilled," Pallav continued, trying desperately to avoid the need to mow down the stalwart, loyal Guards who in the meantime, had bravely placed themselves between the might of the Wessel forces and Headquarters.

Sartaj could see the narrowed eyes, the pursed lips and recognized indecision in his CO's face and swore. "By the gods! I won't take orders from an alien," he exclaimed and his cheeks puffed out with indignation that Major Visyx had allowed himself to become a hostage in the overthrow of the government. Turning to Sergeant-Major Fielen, he pointed at Pallav. "Take him out," he ordered.

The old soldier's voice rose on the wind, carrying to the confused Guardsmen. "Belay that order," he bellowed, and reaching out he pulled the sidearm from his surprised Platoon Commander's grip and turned it on him. "Sorry Sir, but it's clear in my mind what's happened. And I'm not about to let you trigger a civil war."

Seething with indignation, Sartaj gestured wildly at the armed gathering. "You'd believe this lumbering alien over our own General Cavell?"

"I believe the evidence before my eyes. And so should you." Lowering the weapon, he sighed. "Sometimes it's the outsiders who find the truth when we're blinded by our own preconceived notions. Kóbor's found the connection. And Colonel Vogel's arrival, the shots and fire on the rooftop – what about all that? It all points to the rebels, Sir."

He could see Sartaj ruminating before the young captain nodded resignedly. "I know you're right – but it was easier to trust the word of General Cavell. She's a Wessel, one of us after all."

With a sigh, Fielen handed the young officer his blaster and Sartaj raked his hands through his hair in despair.

"By the Fires of Ru! I killed Air Marshal Francis! And had the High Commander and the Commander of the Army manhandled into cells! I'll be lucky if I end up in prison on kyorn and water for the rest of my very short life."

"Well," the Sergeant-Major replied, a grin on his face, "I guess it's time to redeem ourselves then, isn't it?"

Nodding in agreement, Sartaj holstered his weapon. "Right then," he replied and motioned to the senior Guardsman to call off the cordon. As the relieved Guards stood down to the throaty roar of twenty disrupters charging down, Captain Sartaj and Sergeant-Major Fielen marched together to join the ranks of those standing in the shadows of steely machines of power.

***

"I won't let them take her from us," Fadiya whispered as she and Taso dangled a rubber ring in front of the gurgling cherub. "He has no right whatsoever. That man... what's his name again? Daniel Radu? That Geiten refugee! What kind of upbringing could he give her? A widower with two small boys already. I won't let him have her, Taso. I just won't."

She hadn't even considered that the sickness that laid both her and her husband low for the past month had been transmitted by the little one. She never thought that the illness that slowly began to creep throughout her office might be linked to the little tawny haired baby. That the adopted Tanika who meant the world to both husband and wife could be one of the causes of endless death and pain on Cepheus-9. But for the Samandr's, their suffering had ended with little Tanika's arrival.

For years, the Samandrs had been trying for a baby – the countless medical visits, the tests, the inoculations, and then came the waiting when every nerve was taut only to be frayed time and time again as the results came back negative. Fadiya would watch enviously as her co-workers' bellies grew round and fertile. And worst of all was their return to the office beaming with joy at the new addition to their families – cubicles littered with holograms of drooling infants in cutesy poses. It was disturbing, irritating, and enraging. And while they bitched and moaned about the lack of sleep, the teething issues, dirty diapers and feeding duties, Fadiya listened on in jealous anger, reflecting on their insensitiveness.

Years when the couple should have been watching their family grow were spent researching the latest methods for conception. And they had tried them all – from the painful needles that transformed the once level-headed woman into a roller coaster of emotions, to the unsuccessful recombinant DNA cloning where their genetic material failed to fuse into a viable fetus. Taso shook his head as their finances plummeted while each option was exhausted.

But he knew that what Fadiya wanted, Fadiya would get. Sooner or later, it was inevitable that she would prevail. And so he had agreed, reluctantly at first so as to make her believe that she'd won a victory, to adoption. It was their last hope and in his heart he believed that they had waited too long – babies need young parents – those with energy and youthful vigour. Months passed, seasons blew by like the wind, and then the call came. A baby girl they were told – albeit from an unidentified Denebian woman who had perished in an accident.

"Denebian?" Taso's face crumpled at the word. "Fadiya, we can't accept a Denebian child."

His wife yelled an angry reply. "And why not?" And narrowing her eyes at Taso, she waved a finger in his face. "And don't you give me that old saw about how Denebians cut their teeth on the skulls of their enemies."

Grabbing a jacket, she pulled the recalcitrant Taso by the arm and headed for their space port under full steam. Rifling through the air, her brilliant azure hair streaming behind her like a flag unfurling, Fadiya was a woman possessed. Taso knew that look in her eyes, the one that said 'don't screw with me', but he feared disappointment would once more rear its ugly head and bite his wife on her backside.

Kor! Father to a Denebian, he reflected in anguish, contemplating the horrors of raising a child with war in its blood who originated from that planet of blistering sun and barren deserts. Feeling like a fin-binder out of water, Taso was dragged from the aerocar through the Cepheusian Adoption Agency's hall where glass doors parted to reveal rows of acrylic bubbles in which babies nestled under soft downy blankets and developing fetuses swam freely in an embryonic soup.

A middle-aged woman with an enormous turquoise bun shuffled from under a mountain of files. "Fadiya Samandr?" Taso hovered in the background, feeling invisible as his wife and the counsellor shook hands.

"Why don't you come this way? The child's nesting in 3S." She smiled, her eyes creasing from behind a set of cats-eyeglasses. "Really a lovely little mite, but she does fuss a bit. Quite understandable if you consider her circumstances."

The counsellor's shoes squeaked as she shepherded them along and Taso grew more and more irritated, passing row upon row of tiny Cepheusians who were floating in their crystallite artificial wombs. He felt himself struggling to breath in the overly warm environment and wanted to pull his wife back to the sanctuary of their home.

Our childless home, he reminded himself as the two women halted abruptly beside a bubble in which a tiny pink creature lay sleeping, sooty dark lashes brushing against rosy cheeks. And he was spellbound the minute the little girl-child opened her cornflower blue eyes and blinked at him. At him! It was then and there he fell in love, swearing to himself that no one would ever harm this sweet little angel.

But now their world was being turned upside down. A call from the Adoption Agency, from Madam Turquoise-Bun. "It may be possible," she said hesitatingly, "that the child you were given has a father after all. A Geiten refugee from Deneb, a Dr. Daniel Radu, has been in contact with the authorities asking about a woman who might just fit the description of Tanika's birth mother."

He had heard the scream from the garage over the roar of his aerocar's engines. Downing tools, Taso raced back to find his wife doing battle over the HIVE with the Adoption Agency.

"I want proof," she yelled while baby Tanika stared wide-eyed from a hovering bassinet at the sound of her mother's agitation.

The counsellor shook her head patiently. "Mrs. Samandr, he's not saying he's the father. He's only looking for the woman."

It was then that the tarnish fell from Taso's armour. "Well, you haven't seen anything of that woman, now have you?"

Turquoise-Bun's hologram stared at him, dumbfounded.

"So you say exactly that to this Geiten Radu; you understand?"

And once the link was broken, the squeak of the counsellor's shoes could be heard as she trudged down the polished floors of the Adoption Agency to her office, where the holoimage of a tall, athletic man with cropped blonde hair floated in midair.

"I'm sorry to have to tell you this," Turquoise-Bun started but the handsome alien lifted a hand to stop the words that she did not want to pronounce.

"It was worth a try," he replied understandingly. "I've been everywhere else – hospitals, morgues, heck I've even been to cemeteries; you never know." Daniel stared at the folded hands in his lap before his sandy blonde eyebrows rose in defeat. "I was told to check out the Adoption Agency by the Dopang Precinct Medical Centre – but I knew it was always a long shot."

She nodded, her eyes downcast, and waited for the holoimage to fade. Treachery, like a heavy stone, bowed her head under its shameful weight and she sat motionless at her desk, adrift in a sea of doubt while across the planet on a terrace in his opulent Dopang townhouse, Daniel sighed in defeat. For Erica and her child were truly lost.

CHAPTER 29 – DEATH OF A REBELLION

The only way to escape fear is to trample it with your feet.

– NADIA COMANECI

Click, clop, clop. The sound of footsteps reverberated in his ears as Fynn allowed himself to be dragged along. Cold air, whiffs of mildew. And the crackling of a light needing to be replaced. All clues as to where he was being taken, and imperceptibly Fynn's eyelashes fluttered open ever so slightly to reveal a narrow subterranean corridor illuminated by dim lights that hung by exposed black wires from the low ceiling.

His right hand closed upon the knife that lay concealed at his waist, its cold grip solid and reassuring. The ancient carpet was damp against his fingers as his hand dragged along its filthy surface. He let his hand trail, banging against his steel toed boot while slowly he reached for the dagger snugged up against his ankle.

Two thugs; two knives. But where's Nestor?

The throbbing of his back reminded him of the long-barrelled disrupter that swung over the shoulder of the strapping female rebel who had so brutally assaulted him.

She'll taste the blade first, he decided, pleased that within such close quarters her weapon would be useless.

"We did a good day's work here, Livia. General Cavell will be glad to see that our Chief bagged the human," the short, squat male rebel announced.

The female spat. "Humans! This one went down like a ton of bricks. And I thought we'd have a tough time."

"Nothing that a slam to the kidneys couldn't cure!" The two rebel soldiers chuckled like hyenas while Fynn planned his next move, knowing it would have to come soon.

In the distance, a female voice, sultry as warm honey, flowed down the narrow corridor. Strangely familiar, he racked his brains for its origins while the sound of his assailants' heavy boots pounded through the corridors. Two conspirators, gold brocade adorning their shoulders and red tabs at their throats, glowed with the success of their treason.

"That must be Qislen now," Diti crowed, as the two traitors stepped from the safety of the alcove into the hall to meet their destiny. Disconcerted at the sight of the rebel guards, Diti cursed under her breath.

"You two took your time," the honeyed voice scolded. "I was beginning to believe we had failed. Now what do we have here? Such a pretty boy." Stock still he remained as soft hands took him by the jaw, turning his face into the light before releasing him suddenly. "Throw him in with the rest," she commanded. Fynn's eyes opened ever so slightly and before him stood a fleshy man, his face shadowed in the dim light, holding a blaster as the cell doors creaked open.

"No one in there move a muscle unless you wish to taste death," General Berkan snarled.

Through half-closed eyes, Fynn looked on in horror as Ravenna shielded the High Commander from the rebel general. The tang of fear mingling with sweat permeated the stale air and Fynn knew the time was ripe.

Caught in the dim light, the flash of steel was joined by a red ribbon of blood spurting from a gaping maw in the female rebel's neck. Whipping about on his heel, the dagger dropped like a plummeting falcon to land with talons outstretched, stabbing deep into the squat man's chest. It was over in the blink of an eye, the rebel guards in their death throes on the damp foul carpet while Fynn twisted about to take the surprised General Cavell in his arms. An iron grip seized the diminutive woman by the wrist and her brilliant eyes widened in surprise; a blade, dripping in gore, clasped to her throat as strong arms savagely closed about her.

Mouth agape, Berkan stared in horror as a dagger sped through the air. Eyes wide in bewilderment, he collapsed against the iron bars, the blade protruding from below his collarbone. He clutched frantically at the wound as dark red blood tinged with pinkish froth discoloured the ribbons he wore – recognition in false praise of long and faithful service. Every breath became an enemy, a hiss of pain and shock to Berkan and he was powerless to halt the escape of his captives. A meaty hand slammed down on his chest, covering the wound as the injured man's lips slowly turned purple.

"Stay with us," Gomalan encouraged while one of the staff officers raced from the cells into the alcove for a first aid kit. A search through his one-time adversary's pockets produced his comms device and as the High Commander linked in for medical assistance, Ravenna slowly approached the anguished Fynn whose knife was poised to snuff out the life of the woman whose actions betrayed the entire Wessel nation. Diti's brilliant eyes were clouded by terror as she silently begged the Commander of the Land Forces for assistance.

"Let her go," Ravenna growled to Fynn, her voice low and intimidating. The dark eyes bored into Fynn, hypnotizing and commanding. "Put the blade down, Colonel. You hardly need to soil your hands with the blood of this woman."

He budged not one inch, the knife poised to tear into Diti's soft flesh. "Why should I," Fynn countered angrily. "Why would I let this piece of filth live when because of her treachery Meryx lost his life?"

Warily Ravenna closed the distance as in the background, the sounds of chest compressions were heard above a rising tempo of footprints. "Let her go," she repeated, "she'll be put on trial and sentenced for her crimes. Don't answer Meryx's assassination with cold-blooded murder." Holding out a hand, Ravenna motioned to Fynn. "Give her to me. C'mon Fynn, do the right thing."

A flash of light bounced off the stone wall of the narrow corridor and Fynn turned to face the new danger. From the shadows Nestor appeared, his face contorted in savagery. Pushing Ravenna behind him, he held Diti by the throat, a flesh and blood shield, as Fynn confronted the Chief of Police. His knife flashed like quicksilver under the dim light and as the blade bit into Diti's throat, droplets of berry-red blood sprang from her pale skin.

"Drop your weapon, or she buys the farm."

The pounding of feet resounded across the cold, damp floor while a sinister laugh sent chills down Fynn's spine.

"She's expendable," Nestor snarled and raising his weapon, the Chief of Police fired into the chest of the Vice Commander whose brilliant eyes fluttered in complete surprise before she collapsed into the arms of the shocked space pilot. Shoving the dying woman into the Chief of Police, Fynn lunged for him with his knife poised, while the older man fought to regain his balance.

With reflexes honed from years of street battle, Nestor latched on to the arm raised for the killing strike and repeated smashed it against the stone wall of the dim corridor. Recoiling as jolts of pain surged up his wrist, Fynn lost his grip on the weapon and it fell with a crash onto the damp carpet under foot. In the blink of an eye, Nestor was on top of him, his powerful hands tightening in a noose about Fynn's throat, digging his thumbs into the veins that pulsed in tune with his frantic heartbeat.

Fired by his desire for retribution, Fynn fought to overcome his adversary. Throwing an arm about his assailant's wrist, Fynn's legs twisted about the rebel's torso and bucking his hips he flipped Nestor across him, breaking his arm at the elbow while rolling clear. Screaming in agony Nestor crumpled, and cradling his broken arm to his chest, he waited for the heir-designate to dispatch him along the trail of his ancestors. The trail that would lead to that realm of rot where the evil must trod for the rest of time.

Yet suddenly, a voice called out in that foreign language the humans call English, loud and insistent, demanding his attention, and Fynn halted in his quest for retribution. The taste of revenge evaporated, the lust for murder shattered as Pallav thundered down the corridor, LTC Summer Filiponi fast on his heels.

Nothing existed for Pallav except Lt Col Vogel's face, robbed of the moment where the scales of justice would have been righted. Pallav saw in that face the pain beneath the anger and he locked his eyes on Fynn like a big cat hypnotizing its prey. Nothing else mattered. Not Gomalan frantically performing CPR on General Berkan, not the slender body of General Ravenna on her knees, closing the once brilliant eyes of the Vice Commander. There were only two people in that moment of time. And Pallav was not going to let his friend slip into the shadowy abyss of revenge. And so he took the only action that could salvage the soul of his friend.

It had hung at his side for over 25 years, from the moment his father had hung up his badge, and with pride that Pallav had accepted the legacy. Instinctively, the well-worn grip of his father's Glock 19 9mm was tight in his hand, and as his finger closed on the trigger, Pallav searched the midnight eyes of the man whose life was now forfeit. A deafening roar echoed down the corridor as the weapon fired its lethal charge and Nestor's body jerked with the impact. And then Pallav ran forward, grabbing Fynn by the shoulders and pulling him to his feet.

"You missed," Fynn said matter-of-factly, brushing himself off as Nestor clutched at his thigh with his good arm. Slapping Pallav on the shoulder he reached down for the knife but was surprised when a black boot kicked it from his reach.

"No buddy, I hit right where I aimed," Pallav replied, a beefy hand restraining his friend while Nestor cringed in pain. "This son-of-a-bitch's going to pay for it alright. But we'll let the Wessel Court of Justice decide how to dispatch his filthy carcass."

***

She watched sullenly as a wasp-yellow ambulance put down near the rear loading dock and slowly breaking ranks with the loitering Guardsmen, raised a slender wrist to her lips. A gentle tap, like the first drop of rain against a flower petal, activated the chip embedded under her bronzed skin. And then she waited patiently, as she had to be sure. Her eyes narrowed in confusion as a military police hovervan landed amongst the river stone blanketing the surrounding grounds, kicking up a cloud of dust that swirled in the gentle wind, twisting and turning like the fates of those who had staked their lives in the gamble to bring pride back to the Geiten.

Motionless, she remained on guard, waiting like a statue on the stone ramp that led down from the main entrance to WAF HQ. It was then that the heavy blast proof doors of the docking ramp swung open and she started in surprise to see Nestor in cuffs being pushed along by a giant alien, his face cut and bruised.

"So they've failed," she sighed and then her eyes boggled in astonishment as Guardsmen emerged from the now freed building, shuffling under the weight of lumpy black burdens. And then there he was, the heir-designate, the self-styled ace warbird pilot, Lt Col Fynn Vogel, walking shoulder to shoulder with the High Commander while Ravenna kept pace with the stretcher upon which Berkan lay, a blood-stained shell dressing on his chest. She grunted in disgust until another dark procession filed from the WAF stronghold.

"Livia!"

The rebel Guard stilled the pain in her heart as the cortege of black body bags were lifted into the air ambulance. She wiped tears of anger from her eyes, knowing that within one of those cold heavy duty bags, the body of her friend now lay. Whispering into the embedded chip, her voice an echo of mingled fury and pain, she pronounced the words to them, both safe within the bosom of the rebel stronghold, words that they never thought they'd hear.

"My dears, the Cooling is upon us… we must make haste to leave for warmer climes before we are caught up in the vortex of its bitter grasp."

A sob escaped from Alonz's throat and the young Black Hide terminated the link before turning to Drex'n who took him in his arms. Like a child he cried, but the tears were not of sadness, nor for the failure, as Alonz knew he had played his part well. Rather they fell for his people, the Geiten, who they had failed. Who now lived with the taste of terror on their tongues as they were forced to bow their heads in meek submission under the yoke of their oppressors. Until they could grow strong again, the Black Hide rebels, with stalwart comrades joining their ranks, their fists raised in righteous anger. The Black Hide would surge up once again like the rising flood waters to sweep away the defeat that would paralyze their ranks in the coming days. And the might of the Wessel tormentors would be vanquished at that time.

But both Alonz and Drex'n knew that the time was not now. For now, they needed to survive to perpetuate the rebel cause under the leadership of the chosen one. And so, the burly arms of Drex'n released the young saviour and with a knowing glance, the two men grabbed their gear and strode forth from the room in which the plans for liberty had been born and nurtured and then so cruelly lost. As the door shut behind them, they fled swiftly on foot through the late afternoon crowds, away from their one time sanctuary of hope and dreams to descend into the darkness of despair.

***

She's gone without a trace, he thought. *If I hadn't...*

Stopping himself from another round of pointless blame, Daniel ran his hands nervously through his hair before initiating an interface between HIVE and the Denebian Home Link System. Suddenly he crossed the light years that separated him from Deneb and standing before him was a shadow of his old sparring partner.

"If it's not a good time..." He had to admit that the big man who he had despised for so long looked drained, his green eyes sunken against the broad cheekbones, his tunic smeared with dried streaks of blood.

"Not a good time," Pallav mumbled to himself before staring at his one-time enemy. "Radu, this is about the worst time I could think of."

The evening sun shone through the sliding doors of the balcony onto which he stepped, leaving the noise of the crowd behind. And alone in the presence of Dr. Daniel Radu, whose holoimage had blitzed into his home on the very eve of the worst day in his life.

But perhaps that was the day that Tara kidnapped me and the kids, Pallav reflected sombrely, thinking of how his wife had made the decision to tear their family from everything familiar to zip amongst the stars. *Or was it when I found out that my wife was playing house with the not-so-good Captain of the Space Ark Mayflower?*

Sighing, he threw his tired frame into a deep chair and gestured for Daniel to sit.

Grinning sheepishly, Daniel raised his eyebrows. "I'd offer you a glass," he started, pouring out a couple of fingers of Buffalo Trace into a crystal tumbler back on Cepheus. The big man waved the gesture aside with a shrug and buried his head in his hands as fatigue overtook him.

"Listen, I won't keep you long," Daniel started, "I drew a goose egg. Erica's vanished without a trace."

A sandy eyebrow rose in recognition of the bad news and Pallav shook his head. "Figures. Nothing but bad news today. Why would you bring anything different?"

The squeak of the door reminded Pallav that once again, he'd forgotten to fix it and he knew Tara would be on his case. Again. But the questioning stare on little Jolanta's face made him forget about all that. The tiny girl simply climbed into his lap with the agility of a squirrel and cuddled against his chest, a sweet ball of softness, and unconsciously he stroked the child's silky curls.

Watching the interplay between the gruff man and the little girl, Daniel felt like an intruder. Getting up, he set down his tumbler and made to break the transmission. "I've said my piece, I'll leave you to your family."

"No. Stay."

The shock hit Pallav the moment the words had left his mouth.

"Sit with me Radu. Keep me away from the horror that awaits me behind those doors."

Gently, he plucked Jolanta from her nest on his lap. "Tell your Mommy to pour me a drink. That I'm with a friend outside, okay?" As the little girl scooted away, Pallav stood up and stared out across the waters of the River Panni.

"President Meryx was assassinated today by the Black Hide rebels. Fynn was kidnapped; almost killed. Two generals – dead, and one that may not make it. And the High Commander's asked me to become the next Provost Marshal. Oh yeah, upon promotion."

Turning about, Pallav scanned his crowded home and groaned at the sight of Tara ignoring the diminutive Wessel fosterling. "And I can't even get a drink."

Daniel whispered in sympathy. "Damn... I just want you to know... I combed the entire planet for Erica; I mean, every hospital, birthing clinic... I trudged through the cemeteries; I even went so far as to contact the adoption agencies."

A hand came up and passed through the shimmering image, through the shoulder that it was attempting to clasp. "It's okay Radu. Why do you think I asked you to check into this? It's cause I knew you'd run the search to ground. You're damned persistent, irritatingly so, but an attribute like that can be used for the greater good. I was only hoping... that today... with you showing up... that perhaps there'd be something good we could hand to Fynn... news of Erica that would give him something to live for. Other than the revenge that's burning inside him and consuming him."

A woman's voice startled the two and Daniel winced in embarrassment as Tara handed a glass of something dark and frothy to her husband.

"Daniel," she breathed, her eyes widening in surprise and longing at the sight of her one time lover's holoimage sitting companionably beside her blood-stained husband. Her smile was broad and her voice full of the sunshine that cast a halo of gold about her dark wavy hair. "Should I get Fynn?"

"God no," Pallav sighed. "And add more misery to his day. No. Keep him inside with Magdar and Gomalan. I'll be in shortly."

"I'm sorry," she said softly, a hand skimming her husband's broad back before she turned to Daniel. "You doing okay? How're things on Cepheus-9?"

She repressed a smile watching Daniel's holoimage run tanned hands through the cropped blonde hair, a gesture so familiar to her. "You'd never believe it here, Tara. It's a paradise. We hit the jackpot on Cepheus-9 thanks to you."

Out of the corner of his eye, Daniel noticed the tightening of the big man's jaw muscles.

"But your husband and I, we've got things to discuss. Just between us, you understand. We'll catch up another time."

A muscular arm wrapped around Tara's tiny waist, and Pallav pulled her to him while his pale green eyes stared at his one-time rival. "I think we've pretty much wrapped up here, Dr. Radu. It's time Tara and I return to our family and our guests. Like you said, we'll catch up another time."

The doors slid open and the couple disappeared into the brightly lit home, leaving Daniel alone on the Kóbor's balcony overlooking the Panni. For a moment he stared down at the water running like a river of gold before he glanced back into the dwelling to be confronted with a jumble of plates and papers strewn across the living room table. Childish drawings with jerky lines, their colours mashed together reminded him of times when Max and Lewis were younger.

Smiling with the memory, he turned to take his leave only to be confronted by a portrayal of torment slashed in indigo and black resting on a nearby easel. His analysis of Tara's art was cut short as muffled gunshots echoed in the distance, screams rising like birds of prey with dagger claws drawn, reminding Daniel of the dangers he'd gratefully left behind. Severing the link with a shudder, the *Mayflower*'s Captain fled from the despair of Deneb, and as the glow faded, he believed that chapter of his life was finally closed, for what he thought would be forever.

CHAPTER 30 – GOING HOME

And when the day arrives, I'll become sky and I'll become sea, and the sea will come to kiss me for I am going home.
– TRENT REZNOR

Bent under the weight of the troubles that raged like wildfire through the Wesselan capital, the weathered old warrior sat silently behind the massive desk in his office. The gnarled hand that held the state quill in an unaccustomed grip was poised mid-air, the magnitude of his actions giving him pause to reconsider. For once he set ink to paper, the swirls on the parchment before him would seal the fate of those who he had recently viewed as allies.

Across the desk, Ravenna waited, anxious to be released of the onerous duty that would bring order back to the chaos of the recent days. Yet she wondered if such finality would be the right course of action, for she too had acted rashly in the past and lived to see the traumatic outcome of her impetuousness. The banging of heavy boots on the carpet frayed her nerves and Ravenna glanced outside while Gomalan re-read the documents for what seemed like the hundredth time.

There they stood, or rather, there Kóbor stood – for the heir-designate was pacing back and forth, his agitation at the delay apparent.

If it weren't for the humans... That thought hadn't left Ravenna since Lt Col Vogel's bloodthirsty attack on the rebels in that subterranean hallway had led to her freedom. That and Kóbor's timely arrival. Her midnight eyes followed the young heir-designate in his trek along the corridor until they lit on the big alien standing like a bronze statue across the hall.

It was Kóbor who had taken the shattered body of Diti from its resting place in Ravenna's lap and then pulled her to her feet. Kóbor who placed an arm about her waist and steadied her before she vomited over his polished boot tops. He was the one who shielded her from the vultures of the media who hovered about the perimeter, ready to pounce on the disgrace of the Commander of the Army, the woman who allowed herself to be led by the rebels like an aurox to the slaughter.

Shame blossomed on her scarred cheek and Ravenna stared at her hands. *If it weren't for the humans, we'd be nothing but maggot fodder. And Kóbor... if he knew what I'd done to his family...*

Ravenna sat transfixed while Gomalan chewed his lips with his mind in overdrive and she recognized the harsh duty that he had to perform. Reaching over, she placed a hand on his arm. "We have to do it," she encouraged.

The grizzled head nodded and with a flourish, the stylus bit into the ceremonial parchment, its red ink flowing across the page as Gomalan's signature blossomed on the death warrants that would seal the fate of the traitors.

"It's done," he replied with finality as he savagely threw the stylus down. "Have them taken away and prepared."

The chair shrilled as she pushed away with a grim nod. And then the room swirled about her, and Ravenna gripped the desk with both hands, a bloodless face staring vacantly at the High Commander.

"Ravenna," he started, gently guiding her back to the chair. "It'll be soon behind us. I'll get Kóbor to see to it; he knows what must be done." Pouring the woman a glass of water, Gomalan held it to her pale lips. "The rebels are leaderless – powerless. With Meryx gone, we've got all the room to manoeuvre we need to deal with the Geiten problem."

"I still can't believe Diti was involved in all this," Ravenna replied, rubbing her temples. "And Qislen – the Black Hide!"

"Treason's like a serpent – you're unaware of it until it rears up from behind the rock under which it was hiding to inflict its venom. The trick is," he grinned, "to rid yourself of the poison before it works its lethal effects." And scooping up the death warrants, Gomalan signalled to Pallav who pulled the pacing Fynn into the office with him.

The big alien blanched at the sight of the red ribbon of wet ink dripping on the bleached geiten hide as Gomalan handed the two death warrants to Fynn who eagerly co-signed the documents. Understanding the look of shock on the newly promoted General Kóbor's face, Gomalan felt the need to bolster his friend's courage.

"You face a difficult first act as Provost Marshal – but one that will serve as a lesson to all those who dare rise up against the might of Wesselan."

Pallav steadied himself, for he had never carried out such a grim responsibility and he doubted that the executions would bring about the desired effect. "Then they're to be vaporized?"

The grey haired warrior grunted his concurrence. "And their atoms scattered to the four winds of the Empty Quarter, so that their spirits search for all eternity across the desolate lands in a hopeless quest to reunite with what was once theirs."

"Vaporize! That's quick and easy. Line 'em up on the tarmac and let me send them to their ancestors," Fynn thundered. Glaring into the astonished faces of the others, he snatched the death warrants in his freckled hands and brandished them like a torch in flame. "One burst from my rotary cannons and they'd be nothing but red confetti floating on the breeze."

A glance passed between Gomalan and Pallav, and the big man shook his head. "Buddy, this isn't what Meryx would've wanted. You know yourself…"

"That he'd still be alive if you'd have done your job." Pallav took a step back as Fynn went toe to toe with him. "Weren't you supposed to root out the rebels? And now instead of being busted for incompetence, you're promoted. Promoted!" The strangled sound ended with a sob.

Silently, Pallav shrugged and turned away, saddened by the knowledge that he was impotent to soothe the young man's anguish as Fynn picked up the urn bearing the ashes of his foster-father. His broken voice was a mere echo as he cradled the pale vessel inscribed with the Meryx family crest.

"What Meryx wanted… He talked about peace… forgiveness."

Caressing the cold stone, Fynn gently placed the urn in the sunlight before throwing wide the sliding doors that led onto the long balcony overlooking the capital city. Clouds gathered on the horizon and wind rippled through the trees, their leaves shimmering in the light, silver and green. Placing his hands on the railing, Fynn stared far out into the distance over the land to which he now bore such responsibility and he shivered.

A slender shadow appeared at his side. "He wanted you to lead the country," Ravenna whispered, leaning over the railing beside him. "Take up the challenge – pilot Wesselan to glory."

Perhaps it was the breeze that rustled through his sandy hair, or maybe he could sense something in the High Commander, but when Fynn turned to Ravenna, his mind was clear. Down below, out of sight, he knew the Guards waited in the quadrangle, standing at attention for the arrival of the president-designate. Above the squat building, brilliant red and green pybars circled overhead, their wings tracing graceful arcs in the sky. Fynn knew. It had to be that way.

Inside, Gomalan and Pallav had turned their minds to reviewing the protocols for the executions of Nestor and Berkan when Fynn marched back into the High Commander's office. Inside, where the air was stifling and the bar of lights suspended from the ceiling cast long shadows on the wall. Inside, where they sat like caged creatures. Where no sun kissed their cheeks with its honeyed lips, and the wind was denied its gentle dance through their hair with its loving fingers.

"I belong out there." He pointed to the sky from where the first rains would soon be falling, softly quenching the parched soil to coax life back to their planet. His planet; his home.

The two men looked up from the paperwork over which their backs were bent. Old men, aged by the four walls that entombed them. "Out there in the sky, where my mind is clear and the goals are straightforward."

Pallav removed his hated reading glasses and frowned, knowing that once such a decision is made, it cannot be easily overturned. Yet Gomalan stayed his objections with a casual wave and donned a saccharine smile.

"You wish to denounce the nomination? Do you understand the ramifications of your decision? In time of war, the leadership would be bestowed upon the High Commander."

Swallowing, Fynn thought of Meryx and he stifled a tear and closed his eyes. "I can't follow in Meryx's footsteps – I don't believe in his vision. Forgiveness after everything that's happened? To offer a peace overture? There's no way, no way at all, that I'd ever agree to that. We've got to continue the battle against those loathsome creatures until we teach them to respect life – even if it means that they're annihilated in the process. Revenge from the seat of a Skykiller – yeah – the streets should be running red with Geiten blood. That's what I believe – and the sooner I'm back up in the sky loosing rounds down range, the quicker this conflict'll be mopped up."

Ravenna raised an eyebrow at Gomalan who stifled a smile. "Then I'll prepare the transfer of authority," the High Commander added in haste.

"Do it. Now!"

He faced the tall windows again as Gomalan called for his administrative assistant, but Fynn was lost in a dream. His hazel eyes searched the skies for signs of further treachery, for he could not relax knowing that the very man in charge of the security services, General Qislen, had been unmasked as the Black Hide.

But Pallav… my God, how I've wronged him, he realized in horror as the red fog of fury abated and he turned to see the newly promoted Provost Marshal staring vacantly into space. Looking sheepishly into that bronzed mask of a face, Fynn slapped Pallav on the back. "Listen, I apologize for what I said earlier. I mean, your boss? The leader of the Black Hide? Who knew how deep treason ran within the WAF?"

Pallav shrugged and slipped out from under Fynn's arm. "I deserved it; I fucked up. The thing is, I took Qislen down – but there was a second shooter. Someone's still out there Fynn."

The vision of the beautiful assassin with the golden eyes appeared before him. He could smell her fragrance, feel her body under him as she tried to wrench herself from his grasp. And then the cry from Meryx, and he was left with nothing – no one upon whom to enact revenge, and no one to turn to for encouragement and strength.

"That woman! You know, I'll never forget her – an angel of death in a cloud of Chanel No. 5. Bitch shot Meryx in the back at point blank range. I'll find her one day, and I promise I'll send that demon back to the hell that spawned her."

***

Pallav rose early that day, sitting outside on the balcony high above the city and waiting for the first rays of light to stream above the horizon. Through the early morning mist, the Denebian sun had suddenly erupted in a brilliant fire ball of orange. And he knew it was time. Silently, he padded through the house to Luke's bedroom where Fynn lay asleep on his son's bed. With a hand tucked under his freckled cheek, he looked not much older than the lad and certainly not like the vengeful spirit that now inhabited his body.

He had shaken him awake and saw once more the wide-eyed innocence that Fynn had so neatly packed away behind a mask of savagery.

"It's time," Pallav mumbled and turned away before he could witness the transformation.

Treason, betrayal, oath-breaking – vile words, vile actions – and they required an equally brutal response. That Pallav understood. It would be his duty to see that the reprisals were carried out both swiftly and efficiently and he knew it could not be delayed. They had seen the sunrise – Nestor and Berkan – he had made sure of that. And it would be their last.

A simple command had flown from his lips and it was done: the executioner coming to attention, saluting him before his fingers swiped over a panel releasing the instrument of death. Fynn beside him, bemoaning the lack of viewing windows. In less than a heartbeat, it was over. Greedily Pallav sucked in a deep breath, feeling the freshness of the still cool morning air, his toes wiggling in the black high-top boots, his fingers clenching into fists – he was still alive. He lived.

Yet those behind the thickly shielded passage way had left this world forever. As the heavy leaden doors were thrown open, Pallav blinked, his eyes adjusting to the dimly lit chamber that moments before had shone with the light of thousands of stars as the unleashed energy ripped the traitors apart, atom by atom. The whirr of the fans had grinded to a halt after their grizzly task was completed, yet the stench of flesh having been instantly vaporized clung in the now still air. Or maybe it was his imagination; Pallav didn't know. His mind was as blank as a summer's sky back in his hometown of Custer, South Dakota.

For once Fynn had been mercifully silent as the two men left the execution chamber and together they walked out into the cool morning air where a sleek navy hovercar awaited them. The worst was behind him now Pallav thought as he jumped in to the backseat where Gomalan patiently waited and briskly the driver whisked the trio along the almost vacant skylanes.

Nudging Pallav, Gomalan pointed to the sandy head bobbing on their driver's broad shoulder. "He's dead tired."

Sprawled across the front seat, Fynn was sawing logs with the best of them. Yet all Pallav could see were the faces of Nestor and Berkan, led off to their deaths. An image of haughty pride, the Chief of Police had walked with his head held high. Not a word left his lips as the cloying gravity web surrounded him, while the mortally wounded Berkan had to be carried on a stretcher to the chamber, too weak to protest. Already inside, the corpses of the traitorous General Diti Cavell and the one-time Black Hide were already propped up, awaiting their treacherous kins' arrival and the journey to oblivion. It was a just and fitting punishment Pallav knew, but it would not be enough to staunch the wounds that he had inflicted on Deneb.

Gomalan's gravelly voice slipped past the macabre thoughts that looped like a broken record through Pallav's mind. "You know Kóbor, before you humans came, we Denebians had peace for decades. Sure, we had conflicts. Minor ones. But nothing of this scale … that is… until you came along and brought the sickness."

He could feel his hair standing on end and the pupils of his pale eyes contracted until they were mere dots as he stared open-mouthed at the High Commander.

Chuckling, Gomalan poked Pallav in the ribs. "Don't worry my friend, not many Denebians ever knew about it, and only one of us is alive now."

"We didn't know…" The lie flowed like honey from Pallav's tongue.

Almost merrily, President-Designate Gomalan continued his ribbing. "Didn't know? Or didn't care? You see, Meryx and I had the forensic experts review the med docs on the *Mayflower* and you know what? They were tampered with. Yup, someone intentionally misled us, otherwise we'd have been able to take measures to avoid all the sickness and death."

The old man's lined eyes narrowed and watched as Pallav swallowed and stared out the window into the new day. "And that person was you, Kóbor."

With a heavy sigh, Pallav turned to the High Commander. "It was. It was me."

Raucous laughter erupted from the older man who jabbed Pallav in the ribs again. "Not to worry Kóbor. We milked the antibodies from the blood of our sleepy fighter jock in the front seat and that's how we developed a therapy – so it's all good. Haven't you noticed? It's under control now. And by the way, you actually did us a favour."

Taken aback, Pallav raised an eyebrow questioningly. "How so? Seems to me what I did was destroy a civilization."

Gomalan snorted. "You mean the Geiten – ha – they're not civilized; they're not much more than animals. Scum on two legs. No my friend, your pandemic gave us an excuse to get rid of the pestilence from within our midst and while we're at it, to take over the lands that rightfully should be ours."

Incredulous, Pallav glared at the High Commander. "Meryx's last wishes were to have peace between the nations. That should be honoured, not swept away."

"Our last president had become soft with age – and you can count on it that I won't make the same mistake. No, Meryx failed to recognize the

292

destiny of the Wessel people. For us to rise up amongst the Denebian nations, as the natural leaders of our planet. But you know what? I'm feeling generous today, so I tell you what… Just to ease your guilty conscience my friend, I'll get in touch with Premier Lowena and offer terms to Fyjerlan. Not that they're in much of a position to refuse. Our problem was never with them anyhow."

Gently, the sleek craft docked outside of the High Commander's residence and the driver catapulted from his seat, jolting Fynn from the arms of Morpheus. As the rear door swung open to the brisk salute of Gomalan's driver, a wide grin spread across the old warrior's face.

"You relax my friend – your secret's safe with me. Now my newly promoted general, take my advice – get some rest, take a walk along the river with the wife and kids. Just relax. The hard stuff's behind us now."

The old warrior winked, his face crinkled with delight. "But I tell you Kóbor, we're going to put the pedal to the metal now that I'm in charge. And with you as my new Provost Marshal, the last vestiges of the Black Hide rebels will be rooted out and Wesselan will bring Geitenia to its knees. A few months' time from now, we'll be lord and masters over the lands reaching east to the Tagar Mountains. All thanks to you, Kóbor. You're the catalyst that's making our dreams a reality."

With that, the High Commander threw a cocky salute and the vehicle rose daintily in the air, suspended momentarily while the driver reviewed the hovercar's features with Fynn. Then with a lurch, they were throttling through the air at break-neck speed with Fynn at the controls as they winged onwards to the peak on which Pallav's house was perched. Abruptly, the vehicle lurched to a halt and spiraled earthbound, with Pallav cinching up his harness before the jolt of landing jarred his teeth. Through the window, he could see the flickering of the holoscreen and little Jolanta sitting cross-legged on the floor, mesmerized by her favourite kiddie's show. In his family room, a rainbow-hued bloodwolf danced on two legs next to a shaggy sparkling aurox and his foster daughter clapped her hands in delight while Pallav waited for the driver to open the vehicle's door.

The salute the newly promoted Provost Marshall received was less than crisp, and the driver's eyes burned with loathing for the humans. *How much did he hear*, Pallav wondered, angry at Gomalan for the tactless conversation. But drivers are deaf; they never hear, so they say. So they pretend. Then, they talk – this Pallav knew and glancing down, he took note of the man's name. For if the young driver had not forgotten the conversation between the High Commander and his Provost Marshal, he would soon find himself at an isolated outpost, far in the Empty Quarter, where the sand scorpions would be the only ones to listen to his lunatic rantings and conspiracy theories.

Then Tara marched onto the balcony in her quick and efficient way with Jolanta now trailing at her side. Her eyes took it all in - the pale countenance, the hands clutched into fists, the purple smudges under his eyes that looked through her as if she were made of glass – and she trailed to his side to pry apart an iron fist with her gently probing fingers. Pale lips in a bloodless face mumbled and Tara had to stand on tiptoes to hear the murmur.

"It's done."

"Damn right it is," Fynn interjected, running his hands down his sleep-crumpled uniform before he noticed the frown on Tara's face. "You sure you don't mind me staying here for a while? I mean, I'll be alright on my own."

Swinging Jolanta into the air, Pallav threw the giggling child over his shoulders. *So much has happened over the past few weeks*, he thought while Tara took Fynn by the arm and led him into the house where the delicate fragrance of herbed kyttel stew with dumplings greeted them.

Leaving Fynn to spoon out the food, Pallav padded through the house, past the bedroom where Luke had carelessly left his climbing gear strewn across the floor, past Isabella's room cluttered with holoposters of the crazy Denebian bands whose music Pallav found so irritating. And then he stopped, for he swore he could see Bafa there, braiding Jolanta's wavy, dark hair – but that was a mere shadow, for she had fled, leaving him behind.

Tara's voice rose over the sound of the water pouring from the bathroom faucet, her laughter bubbling and contagious as Fynn regaled her with stories from his failed culinary experiments. And the cool water flowed onto Pallav's hands, splashed over his face, coursed from the glistening silver spigot into the crystal bowl to tumble over the outstretched palms, cleansing and healing.

Big golden eyes stared at him, watching her foster father wash away his sins before little Jolanta tugged on the hem of the big man's tunic, leading him to the dining room.

Where did the hunger come from, Pallav wondered as he spooned the steaming stew into his mouth, *this ravenous emptiness that needs to be filled?*

She should be here, he thought, not knowing if it was Erica or Bafa who he pictured sitting across from Fynn. *And he should be up to his eyeballs in diapers and bottles*, Pallav reflected as Fynn smiled at little Jolanta, who spoke her broken English with child-like charm. Freckled hands hid hazel eyes and fingers parted to make the little girl giggle and clap in delight.

Such simple childlike innocence hidden under all the pain and anger… he never deserved any of this.

Scooping up the empty bowls, for his wife chose to ignore the Wessel labour-sparing household devices, Tara was joined by Fynn who vaulted to his feet to assist in the cleaning-up, leaving Pallav with his youngest daughter. Chubby dimpled hands rose to her golden eyes, and she peeked out behind them, a smile lighting up her face. "Peekaboo, Daddy. Now you can see me!"

Smiling back, he helped the little girl from her chair and taking her by the hand, signaled to Tara of the apron and dish cloth; his astrophysicist wife, now reduced to trading recipes with the other generals' wives.

All because of him. His stubbornness. His thirst for revenge. "We're going for a walk," he announced as the glass doors slid open.

Doubt lingered in Fynn's eyes; he knew, he could tell. A hand went out, and then fell to his side. "He needs time," he whispered to Tara. "You've got a good man there."

"I know." The image of Daniel clouded her mind for a moment before it floated away, a brown leaf falling from an autumn tree. "I'm lucky to have him," Tara replied as she watched her broad-shouldered husband accompanied by the diminutive Jolanta disappear down the clear elevator that plunged thousands of feet into the city below.

Holding the little girl's hand, the two were the very picture of doting father and loving daughter as they traipsed along the city's cobbles, a nod to the historic inner core of the now gleaming capital city. Jolanta skipped alongside Pallav until suddenly her feet seemed anchored to the spot. A narrow sandstone house in a little alleyway, bedecked with brilliant flowers spilling from colourful window boxes stood in front of them. Pulling on his hand, she looked up sadly into her stepfather's confused face.

"Please daddy, I don't want to go back," she lisped in her quickly fading Wesselan accent, her golden eyes moist with fear.

"Never," he replied, swinging her up onto his broad shoulders and he took note of the house where Jolanta's parents had lived. Her hands clasped about his neck and he squeezed her tiny knees, keeping her safe from those who had abandoned his precious little fosterling.

"You're my lucky charm," he kidded as they trotted to the market with his stomach grumbling once again.

Life had begun trickling back to the city's ancient inner core. Stalls were piled high with produce that to Pallav's human eyes appeared both exotic and confusing – conical blue roots with fibrous red veins pulsing along their stalks stood next to purple globes, some sliced in half, their fleshy green interiors on display giving the appearance of a Salvador Dali painting.

"There!" Jolanta pulled back on his head, her knees tightening around Pallav's neck as she pointed to a young woman sitting behind a long table stocked with pink and lemon yellow fruits. "Daddy stop," she commanded. "I want rose cream. Please."

Happily slurping on the delicious fruit cream, the two walked hand in hand through the market as the eyes of the Styrians followed them. He could hear the buzz in his ears, and like an incessant insect whose attentions are unwarranted, it stung.

"General Kóbor... It's him."

"Isn't that the officer who killed the Black Hide and captured the rebels?"

"Yeah, the man who stopped the coup d'état."

"That's him – General Kóbor – the hero of Wesselan."

The smiles were genuine as people stepped out of the way of the doting father who had adopted one of their own.

"An orphan," the voices echoed, "not only a hero, but so caring and compassionate."

It was all made worse for him as Pallav believed that the sentiments were groundless. But with Jolanta joyfully swinging his arm in cadence with their steps, he let the feelings slip away and grinned as she hummed and twittered like a sparrow while they walked down to the river. Ripples swirled on the slow flowing river and a gentle breeze danced on the water's surface while small fat fish darted between the reeds in the shallows.

Pulling Pallav's hand, Jolanta led the big man to the rocky shore where they settled amongst the boulders to watch a crested bird dive from its perch into the murky waters. Pulling off her shoes, the little girl looked up expectantly at her foster father while gesturing wildly at the inviting cool waters of the Panni.

"Go on," he conceded with a laugh as Jolanta splashed her way into the shallows, the water lapping at the hem of her new red dress. He watched her rake little toes along the muddy river bottom, chubby fingers racing through the water in search of the tiny fishes while the crested bird circled overhead ready to pounce if its quarry made an escape.

Just like the second shooter, he thought suddenly with anguish. Streaking from the sky, the bird plummeted down through the river's waves, its talons outstretched. A plume of water erupted into the sky and moments later, white foam broke the surface as the bird emerged only to shake itself off from its fruitless attempt before screaming a raucous call and flying off.

Failure, he mumbled despondently as Jolanta shrieked with joy, sending a shower of water to arc across the sky, droplets falling like quicksilver across his tunic.

"Come Daddy! Come in and play," she shrilled in her accented English. Floating on her back, Jolanta's dark hair spread about her like the river grass while her red dress bobbed in the current. Stripping off, Pallav obediently plodded through the cool waters, watching Jolanta proudly display her newly acquired swimming talents, chubby arms thrashing the surface with ferocity.

A piercing scream cut through the air as the crested bird dove again, plunging deep into the murky river to surface with a large fish in its bright orange beak. The scaly creature writhed fiercely, its tail slapping the water and throwing the bird off balance, it made its escape into the dark recesses of the river.

Pallav could feel the bird's sense of failure as the cool water of the river caressed him, stroking his body with slow silky fingers while Jolanta dog paddled about merrily in the languid waters. Sighing, Pallav allowed himself to float on his back, the sun glistening on his wet skin and he stared into the deep blue of the sky where the clouds of the Cooling had begun to gather like ghostly ships sailing across the windy domains.

Like the Mayflower, he thought and the memory of the gravity nets snaring the valiant Space Ark surged before his eyes. *And Radu! Christ, the look on that bastard's face at the Denebian Assembly when he found out he'd be stuck in Geitenia.* But the memory of how he had manipulated the Wessels into applying the arcane clauses of the Styria Treaty to his crewmates now left a bitter taste in his mouth.

Bubbly laughter reached his ears and pushing away the grim recollection he saw to his horror that Jolanta was being towed downstream by the slow-moving river to where a series of weirs lay. With powerful strokes, he cut through the water while the voice of the rushing torrents cried out to him of the danger.

The water moaned as it was thrown against the hard stones, cascading tortuously over the rocks as it spilled into the depths below. The crashing of the waves pounded against the weir, and in it he could hear the echo of the voices of those rising up from the ashes, condemning him for the suffering that he caused by bringing the human pandemic to Deneb.

Cornflower blue skimmers raced across the water's surface, dipping their long legs into the water while he surged ahead. And in his battle, another evil floated about him, taunting him.

As blue as Erica's eyes... The river mocked him now – how effortlessly his foster daughter floated along, yet for every inch he fought like a tiger.

My God, how many people have perished because of me. Because of my stupid, selfish need for revenge. Please Lord, I beg you, let me reach Jolanta before she is taken, let me save this one life.

His lungs burned with the effort, numbness snaked tingling tendrils along his arms from the frigid waters, yet with every stroke, he closed the gap until he felt his fingers brush against the child's ankle. Scooping up the little girl, waves of relief surged over him as she laughed innocently, unaware of the danger. Pallav relaxed as Jolanta lay secure in his arms, mumbling a pray to the One who protected the innocent while planting a soggy kiss on the child's forehead.

Paddling back to the safety of the shoreline, Jolanta wriggled out of his arms and Pallav took the child's tiny hand in his. Like diamonds, the rays of the sun danced on the water's surface. Beams of brilliant radiance pierced Jolanta's red dress and flowed like fingers of blood downstream and into the future. A future of war and fire that would consume everything in its path. Waist deep in the water, he watched horror-struck as the bright red tendrils cascaded with abandon on their way to the Panni Dam. Winding far into the horizon, he mentally traced the mighty waterway as it ran its course, gurgling through the narrow gorges of the Glodati Mountains and meandering along broad valleys, to disgorge miles away into the vastness of Lake Panni.

From all along its shoreline, the life-giving waters of the River Panni spawned towns and villages where only recently funeral pyres had burned day and night, cleansing them of their dead. Great grey pillars of smoke had risen from the smouldering remains of the unsuspecting innocents who not so long ago had welcomed the *Mayflower* refugees to their world. The memory coursed through his mind – he could feel the heat of the brilliant flames surrounding him, their scorching tongues rising from the fiery embers – and faced with the terror that he had unleashed, he closed his eyes to rid himself of the guilt.

Just when he believed that nothing could dispel the demon that had latched onto his soul thirsting for retribution, there was Jolanta, a radiant smile on her angelic face.

"That was fun, Daddy," she trilled, goosebumps on her arms, dark hair curling on her temples. Holding out her hands, demanding to be carried, Jolanta tilted her head and gave Pallav a solemn look. "But now I wanna go home."

ABOUT THE AUTHOR

Zanne Raby is a military veteran, having served for over three decades across North America, Europe, and the Middle East. Passionate about all things space, as well as our planet's fragile ecosystem, her novels weave fast-paced, team-oriented settings into character-based science fiction. Currently residing in a small town on the shores of Georgian Bay, Ontario, Zanne enjoys hiking, military history, gardening, and Sudoku. And always a good story to pass the time.

Connect with Me:

Friend me on Facebook: https://www.facebook.com/zanne.raby/
Follow me on Instagram: https://www.instagram.com/zanne_raby/
And check out my website: https://www.zanneraby.com/

OTHER BOOKS BY THE AUTHOR

THE FLIGHT OF THE MAYFLOWER
Book One – The Chronicles of Deneb

2080: The world is dying. Fertile land has shrunk due to climate change, followed by drought and famine. Massive waves of refugees seek sanctuary, but Fortress America has shut her doors. The best scientists in the world are building Space Arks to shuttle hundreds of thousands of people to safety on an alien colony. Meanwhile bioterrorists have unleashed a deadly bio-engineered disease that sweeps across the globe. And the lies begin: world leaders insist a vaccine is ready. But the truth is very different, in *The Flight of the Mayflower*, Dr. Daniel Radu, project manager for the Space Ark *Mayflower*, uncovers a conspiracy of global proportions. Joined by a team of global experts, will Daniel and his colleagues succeed in thwarting the devious plot in a desperate attempt at survival?

FIRES OF FURY
Book Three—The Chronicles of Deneb

Now masquerading as citizens of the Collective, the Mayflower crew has a new reason to fear. With the end of the Second Denebian War, Wesselan's General Pallav Kóbor and his astrophysicist wife, Dr. Tara Kóbor, have high hopes that life will return to normal on Deneb-7. Yet nothing can be further from the truth.

In a diabolical plot to erase the scars left by the Second Denebian War, warlord turned Wessel Head of State Gomalan unleashes a fiendish scheme to heal his nation's wounds, while his top soldier, General Ravenna, falls under the spell of a seductive Fyjer agent intent on crushing their ambitions. Dragged into a brutal reality of terror and intrigue, can the Kóbors and warbird ace Fynn Vogel remain unscathed, or will the flames consume them and all that is evil on Deneb-7?

PERIL IN PARADISE
Book Four – The Chronicles of Deneb

Life in paradise can be a killer! Sit under the palm trees, feel the sand under your toes and the sun on your face. Listen to the waves crash against the shore, and watch colourful birds soaring on the tradewinds. You're on the beautiful distant exoplanet Cepheus-9, now home to Dr. Daniel Radu, former captain of the Space Ark Mayflower, and his one-time crewmates. Life should be anything but deadly for the cast of Earth refugees, but when the Interstellar Collective for Peace and Security is rocked by disaster, the gang faces a threatening and uncertain future. Only one man has the courage to confront the dangers: Dr. Daniel Radu, now masquerading as an exobotanist. But what can one lone soul do against the odds?